SILVER IN THE BONE

SILVER IN THE BONE

BOOK 1

Alexandra Bracken

Alfred A. Knopf

New York

THIS IS A BORZOI BOOK PUBLISHED BY ALFRED A. KNOPF

This is a work of fiction. Names, characters, places, and incidents either are
the product of the author's imagination or are used fictitiously. Any resemblance
to actual persons, living or dead, events, or locales is entirely coincidental.

Text copyright © 2023 by Alexandra Bracken
Jacket art copyright © 2023 by Filip Hodas
Map art copyright © 2023 by Virginia Allyn
Interior art used under license from Shutterstock.com

Visit us on the Web! GetUnderlined.com

Educators and librarians, for a variety of teaching tools,
visit us at RHTeachersLibrarians.com

Library of Congress Cataloging-in-Publication Data is available upon request.
ISBN 978-0-593-48165-3 (trade) — ISBN 978-0-593-48166-0 (lib. bdg.) —
ISBN 978-0-593-48167-7 (ebook) — ISBN 978-0-593-65056-1 (intl. pbk.)

The text of this book is set in 11.75-point Adobe Garamond Pro.
Interior design by Jen Valero

Printed in the United States of America
10 9 8 7 6 5 4 3 2 1
First Edition

Or, in the words of the Sistren:

Any thief who dares to steal this book
will find it's not the only thing they took.
A curse shall fall upon their wicked eye,
ensuring that their love of reading die.
May every page appear as blank as snow
as they suffer in eternal woe.

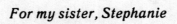

For my sister, Stephanie

ARTHUR'S TOMB

BEDIVERE'S COTTAGE

FAIRY MOUND DWELLINGS

KEEPER OF THE ORCHARDS' COTTAGE

THE BARROW

THE ELDER WOOD

THE MIST WOOD

THE DAUGHTER RIVER

AVALON

SEVEN YEARS AGO
Lancashire, England

The first thing you learned on the job as a Hollower was to never trust your eyes.

Nash, of course, had a different way of saying it: *All sorcery is half illusion.* The other half, unfortunately, was blood-soaked terror.

In that moment, though, I wasn't scared. I was as angry as a spitting cat.

They'd left me behind. Again.

I braced my hands on either side of the garden shed's doorframe, drawing as close as I could to the enchanted passageway without entering. Hollowers called these dark tunnels Veins because they carried you from one location to another in an instant. In this case, to the vault of a long-dead sorceress, containing her most prized possessions.

I checked the time on the cracked screen of Nash's ancient cell phone. It had been forty-eight minutes since I watched them disappear into the Vein. I hadn't been able to run fast enough to catch up, and if they'd heard my shouts, they'd ignored me.

The phone screen blinked to black as the battery finally croaked.

"Hello?" I called, fiddling with the key they'd left in the lock—one of the sorceress's finger bones, dipped into a bit of her blood. "I'm not going back to camp, so you may as well just tell me when it's safe to come in! Do you hear me?"

Only the passage answered, breathing out whorls of snow. Great. The Sorceress Edda had chosen to put her collection of relics somewhere even colder than England in the winter.

The fact that Cabell and Nash weren't answering had my insides squirming. But Nash had never been deterred by the promise of danger, and he was about to discover I wouldn't be deterred by anyone, least of all my rotten bastard of a guardian.

"Cabell?" I said, louder this time. The cold gripped my words, leaving white streaks in the air. A shiver rippled through me. "Is everything all right? I'm coming in whether you want me to or not!"

Of course Nash had taken Cabell with him. Cabell was *useful* to him. But if I wasn't there, there was no one to make sure my brother didn't end up hurt, or worse.

The sun was shy, hiding behind silver clouds. Behind me, an abandoned stone cottage kept watch over the nearby fields. The air was quiet, which always stirred up my nerves. I held my breath, straining my ears to listen. No humming traffic, no drone of passing airplanes, not even a chirp from a bird. It was like everyone else knew better than to come to this cursed place, and Nash was the only idiot too stupid and greedy to risk it.

But a moment later, a fresh wave of snow carried Cabell's voice to me.

"Tamsin?" He sounded excited, at least. "Watch your head as you come in!"

I plunged into the Vein's disorienting darkness. Outside was nothing compared to the barbed cold that wrapped around me now, knifing at my skin until I couldn't draw breath.

In two steps, the round doorway at the other end of the Vein carved itself out of the black air. In three, it became a vivid wall of ghostly light. Blue, almost like—

I glanced down at the broken chunks of ice scattered around the doorway, at the swirling curse sigils carved into them. I turned, searching for Cabell, but a hand caught me, stopping me in my tracks.

"I told you to stay at the camp." With his head lamp on, Nash's face was in shadow, but I could feel the anger radiating from him like the warmth from his skin. "We'll have words about this, Tamsin."

"What are you going to do, ground me?" I asked, riding high on my victory.

"Perhaps I will, you wee fool," he said. "Never do anything without knowing the cost."

The light from his head lamp danced over me, then swung upward. My gaze followed.

Icicles jutted down from the ceiling. Hundreds of them, all capped with razor-sharp steel, poised to fall at any moment. The walls, the ground, the ceiling—all of it was solid ice.

Even in the darkness, Cabell was easy to spot in his tattered yellow windbreaker. Relief poured through me as I made my way to his side, crouching to help him pick up unused crystals. He'd used the stones to absorb the magic of the curses surrounding the doorways. Once the curses were nullified, Nash had taken his axe to their sigils.

All Hollowers could perform a version of what Cabell was doing, but they could only clear curses with tools they'd bought off sorceresses.

Cabell was special, even among the Hollowers with special magic. He was the first Expeller in centuries—someone who could redirect the magic of a curse away from one source and into another, deflecting spells from our path.

The only curse Cabell couldn't seem to break was his own.

"What curse was this, Tamsin?" Nash asked, pointing the steel toe of his boot toward a sigil-marked chunk of ice. At my look, he added, "You said you wanted to learn."

Sigils were symbols used by the sorceresses to shape magic and bind it to a location or object. Nash had come up with stupid names for all the curse marks.

"Wraith Shadow," I said, rolling my eyes. "A spirit would have followed us through the vault, tormenting us and tearing at our skin."

"And this one?" Nash pressed, nudging a chunk of carved stone my way.

"White Eyes," I said. "So, whoever crossed the threshold would be blinded and left to wander the vault until they froze to death."

"They probably would have been impaled before they froze," Cabell said cheerfully, pointing to a different sigil. His pale skin was pink from the cold or excitement, and he didn't seem to notice the flakes of ice in his black hair.

"Fair point, well made," Nash said, and my brother beamed.

The walls exhaled cold air around us. An otherworldly song rippled through the ice, cracking and twanging like an old tree playing puppet to the wind. There was only one way forward—the narrow pathway to our right.

I shivered, rubbing my arms. "Can we just find your stupid dagger and go?"

Cabell reached into his bag, retrieving fresh crystals for the curses that lined the hallway. I kept my eyes on him, tracking his every move, but Nash's gloved hand caught my shoulder when I tried to follow.

Nash tutted. "Aren't you forgetting something?" he asked knowingly.

I blew a strand of blond hair off my face, annoyed. "I don't need it."

"And I don't need attitude from a sprite of a girl, yet here we are," Nash said, rummaging through my bag for a bundle of purple silk. He unwrapped it, holding the Hand of Glory out to me.

I didn't have the One Vision—something Cabell and Nash reminded me of every infernal chance they got. Unlike them, I had no magic of my own. A Hand of Glory could unlock any door, even one protected by a skeleton knob, but its most important purpose, at least to me, was to illuminate magic hidden to the human eye.

I hated it. I hated being different—a problem that Nash had to solve.

"Whew, he's getting a bit crusty, isn't he?" Nash asked, lighting the dark wick of each finger in turn.

4

"It's your turn to give him the bath," I said. The last thing I wanted to do was spend another evening massaging a fresh coat of human lard into the severed left hand of a prolific eighteenth-century murderer who'd been hanged for his crime of annihilating four families.

"Wake up, Ignatius," I ordered. Nash had attached him to an iron candlestick base, but that didn't make holding him any nicer.

I turned the Hand of Glory so the palm faced me. The bright blue eye nestled into its waxy skin blinked open—then narrowed in disappointment.

"Yup," I told it. "I'm still alive."

The eye rolled.

"The feeling's mutual, you impertinent piece of pickled flesh," I muttered, adjusting the stiff, curled fingers until they cracked back into place.

"Good afternoon, handsome," Nash crooned. "You know, Tamsy, a little sugar makes everything nice."

I glowered at him.

"You wanted to come," he said. "Think about the cost next time, eh?"

The smell of burning hair filled my nostrils. I switched Ignatius into my left hand, and my view of the world flickered as his light spread along the surface of the ice, bathing it in an unearthly glow. I sucked in a sharp breath.

The curse sigils were everywhere—on the ground, on the walls, on the ceiling—all swirling in and out of one another.

Cabell knelt at the entrance to the path. Sweat beaded on his forehead as he worked to redirect the curses into the crystals he slowly set out in front of him.

"Cab needs a break," I told Nash.

"He can handle it," Nash said.

Cabell nodded, setting his shoulders back. "I'm fine. I can keep going."

A drip of burning lard scalded my thumb. I hissed at Ignatius, meeting his narrow, spiteful gaze with one of my own.

"No," I told him firmly. I wasn't going to set him down beside Cabell like I knew he wanted. First, because I didn't have to obey the commands of a severed hand—actually, I didn't need another reason beyond that.

Just to torment the impertinent hand, I held Ignatius out toward the wall at my right, pushing the exposed eye closer and closer to its frozen surface. I wasn't a good enough person to feel guilty about the quiver that moved through his stiff joints.

The heat of his flames cut through the heavy coat of frost on the wall, and as each drip of water snaked down it, it revealed a dark shape on the other side.

A gasp tore out of me. The heel of my sneaker caught the ice as I stumbled back, and before I could even register what was happening, I was falling.

Nash shot forward with a startled grunt, catching my arm in an iron grip. The chill of the nearby wall kissed my scalp.

My heart was still hammering, my lungs throbbing to catch their next breath, as Nash eased me upright. Cabell rushed to my side, grabbing my shoulders, checking to make sure I wasn't hurt. I knew the moment he saw what I'd glimpsed through the ice. His already white face turned bloodless. His fingers tightened with terror.

There was a man in the ice, made monstrous by death. The pressure of the ice looked to have broken his jaw, which gaped open unnaturally wide in one last silent scream. A shock of white hair framed his ice-burned cheeks. His spine was bent at tortured angles.

"Ah, Woodrow. I was wondering what he'd gotten up to," Nash said, taking a step forward to study the body. "Poor bastard."

Cabell gripped my wrist, turning Ignatius's light back toward the tunnel ahead. Dark shadows stained the gleaming ice like bruises. A grim gallery of bodies.

I lost count at thirteen.

My brother was trembling, shaking hard enough that his teeth chattered. His dark eyes met my blue ones. "There are . . . there are so many of them . . ."

I wrapped my arms around him. "It's okay . . . it's okay . . ."

But fear had him in its grip; it had ignited his curse. Dark bristles broke out along his neck and spine, and the bones of his face were shifting with sickening cracks, taking on the shape of a terrifying hound.

"Cabell," came Nash's voice, calm and low. "Where was King Arthur's dagger forged?"

"It . . ." Cabell's voice sounded strange rasping through elongating teeth. "It was . . ."

"Where, Cabell?" Nash pressed.

"What are you—?" I began, only for Nash to quiet me with a look. The ice moaned around us. I tightened my grip on Cabell, feeling his spine curl.

"It was forged . . ." Cabell's eyes narrowed with focus as they landed on Nash. "In . . . Avalon."

"That's right. Along with Excalibur." Nash knelt in front of us, and Cabell's body went still. The hair that had burst through his skin receded, leaving rashlike marks. "Do you remember the other name Avalonians use for their isle?"

Cabell's face started to shift back, and he grimaced in pain. But his eyes never left Nash's face. "Ynys . . . Ynys Afallach."

"Got it on the first try, of course," Nash said, rising. He put a hand on each of our shoulders. "You've cleared the bulk of the curses already, my boy. You can wait here with Tamsin until I return."

"No," Cabell said, swiping at his eyes with his sleeves. "I want to come."

And I wasn't going to let him go without me.

Nash nodded and started down the hallway, passing the lantern back to Cabell and aiming his head lamp down the stretch of bodies. "This reminds me of a tale . . ."

"What *doesn't?*" I muttered. Couldn't he see that Cabell was still rattled? He was only pretending to be brave, but pretending had always been enough for Nash.

"In ages past, in a kingdom lost to time, a king named Arthur ruled man and Fair Folk alike," Nash began, carefully making his way around the crystals. He used the tip of his axe to scratch out the curse sigils as he passed by them. "But it is not him I speak of now—rather, the fair isle of Avalon. A place where apples grow that can heal all ailments, and priestesses tend to those who live among its divine groves. For a time, Arthur's own half sister Morgana belonged to their order. She served as a wise and fair counsel to him, despite how many of those Victorian-era shills chose to remember her."

He'd told us this tale before. A hundred times, around a hundred different smoky campfires. As if Arthur and his knights were accompanying us on all our jobs . . . but it was a good kind of familiar.

I focused on the sound of Nash's warm, rumbly voice, not the horrible faces around us. The blood frozen in halos around them.

"The priestesses honor the goddess who created the very land Arthur came to rule—some say she made it from her own heart."

"That's stupid," I whispered, my voice trembling only a little. Cabell reached back, taking my hand tight in his own.

Nash snorted. "Maybe to you, girl, but to them, their stories are as real as you or me. The isle was once part of our world, where Glastonbury Tor now proudly stands, but many centuries ago, when new religions rose and man grew to fear and hate magic, it was splintered away, becoming one of the Otherlands. There, priestesses, druids, and Fair Folk escaped the dangers of the mortal world, and lived in peace . . ."

"Until the sorceresses rebelled," Cabell said, risking a look around. His voice was growing stronger.

"Until the sorceresses rebelled," Nash agreed. "The sorceresses we know today are the descendants of those who were banished from Avalon, after taking to darker magic . . ."

I focused on the feel of Cabell's hand, his fingers squeezing tight as we passed by the last body and moved through a stone archway.

8

Beyond it, the ice-slick path wound its way down. We stopped again when Cabell felt—before he even saw—a curse sigil buried underfoot.

"Why are you so desperate to find this stupid dagger, anyway?" I asked, hugging my arms to my chest to try to keep warm.

Nash had spent the last year searching, blowing off paying work and easier finds. *I'd* found us the lead for this vault . . . not that Nash would ever acknowledge the research I did.

"You don't think finding a legendary relic is reason enough?" he asked, swiping at his red-tipped nose. "When you desire something, you must fight for it tooth and claw, or not at all."

"The path's clear," Cabell said, standing again. "We can keep going."

Nash moved ahead of us. "Remember, my wee imps, that Sorceress Edda was renowned for her love of trickery. All will not be what it first seems."

It only took a few steps to understand what he meant.

It began with a kerosene lantern, casually left beside one of the bodies in the ice, as if the hunter had merely set it down, leaned forward against the freezing surface, and been swallowed whole.

We passed it without a second look.

Next was the ladder, the one that offered safety for the long climb down to a lower level.

We used our ropes.

Then, just as the temperature plunged deeper into a killing freeze, a pristine white fur coat. So soft and warm and just the kind that an absent-minded sorceress might have left behind, tossing it over an equally tempting crate of food jars.

Take me, they whispered. *Use me.*

And pay the price in blood.

Ignatius's light revealed the truth. The razors and rusted nails lining the interior of the coat. The spiders waiting in the jars. All but one rung missing from the ladder. Even the lantern was filled with the Smothering Mother, a vapor that tightened your lungs until breathing became impossible, made from the blood of a mother who'd killed her children. Anyone who opened the glass to light the wick would be dead in an instant.

We passed it all, Cabell redirecting the dark magic of the curses laid between each trap. Finally, after what seemed like hours, we reached the inner chamber of the vault.

The round chamber shone with the same pale, icy light. At its center was an altar, and there, sitting on a velvet pillow, was a dagger with a bone-white hilt.

And Nash, who never struggled for a word, was silent. Not happy, like I would have thought. Not bouncing on his toes with glee as Cabell broke the last of the curses protecting it.

"What's the matter with you?" I demanded. "Don't tell me it's not the right dagger."

"No, it is," Nash said, his voice taking on a strange tone. Cabell stepped back from the altar, allowing Nash to come forward.

"Well," he breathed out, his hand hovering above the hilt for an instant before closing around it. "Hello."

"What now?" Cabell asked, peering down at it.

A better question was probably who he was going to sell it to. Maybe, for once, we could afford a decent place to live and food to eat.

"Now," Nash said quietly, holding the blade up into the gleaming light. "We go to Tintagel and recover the true prize."

We traveled to Cornwall by train, arriving just as a fierce storm blew in over the cliffs and ensnared the dark ruins of Tintagel Castle in its wild, thundering depths. After we battled to set up our tent in the lashing rain and wind, I crashed into sleep. The bodies in the ice were waiting for me in dreams, only now they weren't Hollowers, but King Arthur and his knights.

Nash stood in front of them, his back to me as he watched the surface of the ice rippling like water. I opened my mouth to speak, but no sound came out. Not even a scream as he stepped forward through the ice, as if to join them.

I jolted awake with a gasp, twisting and thrashing to free myself from my sleeping bag. The first bit of sunlight gave the red fabric of our tent a faint glow.

Enough for me to see that I was alone.

They're gone.

Static filled my ears, turning my body to pins and needles. My fingers were too numb to grip the zipper on the tent's flap.

They're gone.

I couldn't breathe. *I knew it. I knew it. I knew it. I knew it.* They'd left me behind again.

With a frustrated scream, I broke the zipper and ripped the flap away, tumbling out into the cold mud.

The rain came down in torrents, battering my hair and bare feet as I scanned my surroundings. A thick mist churned around me, blanketing the hills. Trapping me there, alone.

"Cabell?" I yelled. "Cabell, where are you?"

I ran into the mist, the rocks and heather and thistle biting at my toes. I didn't feel any of it. There was only the scream building in my chest, burning and burning.

"Cabell!" I screamed. "Nash!"

My foot caught on something and I fell, rolling against the ground until I hit another stone and the air blasted out of me. I couldn't draw in another breath. Everything hurt.

And the scream broke open, and became something else.

"Cabell," I sobbed. The tears were hot, even as the rain lashed against my face.

What good will you be to us?

"Please," I begged, curling up. The sea roared back as it battered the rocky shore. "Please . . . I can be good . . . please . . ."

Don't leave me here.

"Tam . . . sin . . . ?"

At first, I thought I had imagined it.

"Tamsin?" His voice was small, almost swallowed by the storm.

I pushed up, fighting against the sucking grass and mud, searching for him.

For a moment, the mists parted at the top of the hill, and there he was, as pale as a ghost, his black hair plastered to his skull, his near-black eyes unfocused.

I slipped and struggled up the hill, clawing at the grass and stones until I reached him. I wrapped my arms around him. "Are you okay? Cab, are you okay? What happened? Where did you go?"

"He's gone." Cabell's voice was as thin as a thread. His skin felt like a block of ice, and I could see a tinge of blue to his lips. "I woke up and he was gone. He left his things . . . I looked for him, but he's . . ."

Gone.

But Cabell was here. I hugged him tighter, feeling him cling back. Feeling his tears become rain on my shoulder. I had never hated Nash more for being everything I always thought he was.

A coward. A thief. A liar.

"H-he'll be back, won't he?" Cabell whispered. "Maybe he just f-f-forgot to say where he was g-going?"

I didn't want to ever lie to Cabell, so I didn't say anything.

"W-we should go b-back and wait—"

We would be waiting forever. I felt the truth of it down to my bones. Nash had finally unloaded his hangers-on. He was never coming back. The only mercy was that he hadn't taken Cabell with him.

"We're okay," I whispered. "We're okay. We're all we need. We're okay . . ."

Nash said that some spells had to be spoken three times to take hold, but I wasn't stupid enough to believe that, either. I wasn't one of the girls from the gilded pages of storybooks. I had no magic.

I only had Cabell.

The dark bristles were spreading across his skin again, and I felt the bones of his spine shifting, threatening to realign. I held him tighter. Fear swirled in the pit of my stomach. Nash had always been the one to pull Cabell back to himself, even when he fully shifted.

Now Cabell only had me.

I swallowed, shielding him from the driving rain and wind. And then I started to speak: "In ages past, in a kingdom lost to time, a king named Arthur ruled man and Fair Folk alike . . ."

PART I

TWO OF SWORDS

1

No matter what they say, or how much they lie to themselves, people don't want the truth.

They want the story already living inside them, buried deep as marrow in the bone. The hope written across their faces in a subtle language few know how to read.

Luckily for me, I did.

The trick, of course, was to make them feel like I hadn't seen anything at all. That I couldn't guess who was heartsick for a lost love or desperate for a windfall of money, or who wanted to break free from an illness they'd never escape. It all came down to a simple desire, as predictable as it was achingly human: to hear their wish spoken by someone outside themselves—as if that somehow had the power to make it all come true.

Magic.

But wishes were nothing more than wasted breath fading into the air, and magic always took more than it gave.

No one wanted to hear the truth, and that was fine by me. The lies paid better; the bald-faced realities, as my boss Myrtle—the Mystic Maven of Mystic Maven Tarot—once pointed out, only got me raging internet reviews.

I rubbed my arms beneath Myrtle's crochet shawl, eyes darting to the digital timer to my right: 0:30 . . . 0:29 . . . 0:28 . . .

"I'm sensing . . . yes, I'm sensing you have another question, Franklin," I said, pressing two fingers against my forehead. "One that's your real reason for coming here."

The glowing essential oil diffuser gurgled contentedly behind me. Its steady stream of patchouli and rosemary was powerless against the smell of deep-fried calamari drifting up through the old floorboards and the rancid stench of the dumpsters out back. The cramped, dark room circled in tighter around me as I breathed through my mouth.

Mystic Maven had occupied its room above Boston's Faneuil Hall Marketplace for decades, bearing witness to the succession of tacky seafood restaurants that cycled in and out of the building's ground level. Including, most recently, the particularly malodorous Lobster Larry's.

"I mean . . . ," my client began, looking around at the peeling strips of floral wallpaper, the small statues of Buddha and Isis, then back down to the spread of cards I'd placed on the table between us. "Well . . ."

"Anything?" I tried again. "How you'll do on your finals? Future career? Hurricane season? If your apartment is haunted?"

My phone came to the end of the playlist of harmonic rain and wind chimes. I reached down to restart it. In the silence that followed, the dusty battery-powered candles flickered on the shelves around us. The darkness gathered between them hid just how dingy the room was.

Come on, I thought, half desperate.

It had been six long hours of listening to chanting-monk tracks and mindlessly rearranging crystals on the nearby shelves between what few customers had come in. Cabell had to have the key by now, and after finishing up with this reading, I'd be able to leave for my real gig.

"I just don't understand what she sees in him—" Franklin began, only to be cut off by the digital wail of my timer.

Before I could react, the door swung open and a girl barreled inside.

"Finally!" she said, parting the cheap beaded curtain with a dramatic sweep of her hands. "My turn!"

Franklin turned to gawk at her, his expression shifting as he assessed her with clear interest—the way she all but vibrated with excited energy made it difficult to look anywhere else. Her dark brown skin was dusted with a faint shimmer, likely from whatever cream she used, which smelled like honey and vanilla. Her braids were twisted back into two high buns on her head, and she'd painted her lips a deep purple.

After giving Franklin a quick once-over in return, she quirked her lips in my direction. In her hand was her ever-present portable CD player and foam-covered earphones, relics of simpler technological yesteryears. As someone incapable of throwing anything away, I was begrudgingly charmed by them.

But the charm quickly faded as she turned her belt around and tucked both into what appeared to be a pink fanny pack. One with fluorescent cats and the words I'M MEOW-GICAL emblazoned across it in glow-in-the-dark green.

"Neve." I tried not to sigh. "I didn't realize we had an appointment today."

Her smile was blinding as she read the painted message on the door. "*Walk-ins Welcome!*"

"I was going to ask when Olivia and I are getting back together—" Franklin protested.

"We have to save something for the next time, don't we?" I said sweetly.

He grabbed his backpack with an uncertain look. "You . . . you're not going to tell anyone I came, are you?"

I gestured to the sign over my right shoulder, ALL READINGS ARE CONFIDENTIAL, then to the one directly below it, WE ARE NOT LIABLE FOR ANY DECISIONS YOU MAKE BASED ON THESE READINGS, which had been added three minor lawsuits too late.

"See you next time," I said with a little wave that I hoped didn't look half as threatening as it felt.

Neve swept into his seat, propping her elbows on the table. She rested her chin on her palm with an expectant look.

"So," she said. "How's it going, girl? Any interesting jobs lately? Any nefaaaarious curses you've untangled?"

I shot a horrified look at the door, but Franklin was already out of earshot.

"What question would you like answered by the cards today?" I asked pointedly.

I'd accidentally left my work gloves—made from a distinctly reptilian hide called dragonscale—hanging out of my bag two weeks ago, and Neve had recognized them and made the unfortunate connection about my real job. Her knowledge of Hollowers and magic meant she was likely one of the Cunningfolk, a catchall term for people with a magic gift. Although I'd never seen her around the usual haunts.

She reached into the pocket of her shaggy black fur coat and pressed a rumpled twenty-dollar bill onto the table between us. Enough for fifteen minutes.

I could do fifteen more minutes.

"Your life is so exciting," Neve said with a happy sigh, as if imagining herself in my place. "I was just reading about the Sorceress Hilde the other day—did she really sharpen her teeth like a cat's? That seems painful. How do you eat without constantly biting the inside of your mouth?"

I tried not to bristle as I leaned back against my chair and set the timer. Fifteen minutes. Just fifteen.

"Your question?" I pressed, wrapping Myrtle's crochet shawl tighter around my shoulders.

In truth, being a Hollower was 98 percent boring research, 2 percent deadly misadventures trying to open sorceresses' vaults. Reducing it to light, glorified gossip prickled every nerve in my being.

Neve tugged at her black shirt, distorting the image of the pink rib cage that covered it. Her jeans were ripped in places, the tears revealing the shock of purple tights beneath. "Not very talkative, are you, Tamsin Lark? Okay, fine. I have the same question I always have: Am I going to find what I'm looking for?"

I glared at the cards as I shuffled, focusing on the feeling of them fluttering between my fingers, and not the intensity of her stare. For all the bounce in her step and the cheeriness of her words, her eyes were dark pools, always threatening to draw you in deeper with their ribbons of gold. They reminded me of my brother's tiger's-eye crystals, and made me wonder if they were connected to her magic gift—not that I'd ever cared enough to ask.

After seven shuffles, I started to draw the first card, only for her hand to catch mine.

"Can I pick today?" she asked.

"I mean . . . if you want to," I said, fanning them out facedown on the table. "Choose three."

She took her time in selecting them, humming a soft song I didn't recognize. "What do you think people would do if they found out about sorceresses?"

"What they always do when they suspect witches," I said dryly.

"Here's the thing." Neve hovered her fingers over each card in turn. "I think they would try to *use* their power for their own ends. Sorceresses have spells that predict the future more accurately than tarot, right? And find things . . ."

And curses that kill things, I thought to myself, glancing at the timer. The part of me stirred that suspected all these visits might be a ruse to size me up for a potential recovery job. Most of the work Cabell and I did as Hollowers was for-hire; we went into vaults looking for lost or stolen family heirlooms and the like.

Neve laid two rows of three cards out on the table, then sat back with a satisfied nod.

"I only need one row," I protested, then stopped. It didn't matter. Anything to kill these last ten minutes. I gathered the remaining cards into a neat pile. "Go ahead and flip them."

Neve turned over the bottom row. Wheel of Fortune reversed, Five of Wands, Three of Swords. Her face scrunched up in annoyance.

"I read the three positions as situation, action, and outcome," I explained, though I suspected she knew all this. "Here, the Wheel of Fortune reversed is saying you've been drawn into a situation that is beyond your control, and you'll have to work harder to see your search through. Five of Wands advises you to wait out the situation and not jump into things if you don't have to. And the outcome, with Three of Swords, is usually a disappointment, so I'm going with, you won't find whatever it is you're looking for, through no fault of your own."

I turned over the pile of cards in my hand. "Bottom of the deck—the root of the situation—is Page of Wands reversed."

I almost laughed. It was the card that always came up in her readings, signaling impatience and naïveté. If I actually believed in this tripe, it'd be pretty clear the universe was trying to send her a message.

"Well, that's just the cards' opinion," Neve said. "Doesn't mean it's true. And besides, life wouldn't be half as fun if we couldn't prove people wrong."

"Sure," I agreed. The question was on the tip of my tongue. *What exactly are you looking for?*

"Now let's do you," Neve said, turning over the second row of cards. "And see the answer to whatever's been on *your* mind."

"No," I protested, "really, that's—"

She was already laying cards out: the Fool, the Tower, and the Seven of Swords.

"Oooh," she said, all drama as she took my hands in hers. "An unforeseen event will liberate you to explore a new path, but you must watch out for a person who seeks to betray you! What question has been on *your* mind, hmm?"

"No question," I said, extracting myself from her grip. "Except what I'm having for dinner."

Neve laughed, pushing her chair back. I looked down at the timer.

"You still have another five minutes," I told her.

"That's all right, I got what I needed." She freed her CD player from her atrocious fanny pack, hooking the earphones around her neck. "Hey, what are you doing tomorrow night?"

Money was money. Resigned, I reached for the leather-bound book beside me. "I'll put you down for an appointment. What time?"

"No, I mean to hang out." Seeing my blank look, Neve added, "*To hang out*, a phrase commonly used to suggest that people grab a meal together, or see a movie, or literally do anything that involves enjoyment."

I froze. Maybe I'd read this situation completely wrong. My words were as awkward as they were stilted when I finally managed to get them out. "Oh . . . I'm sorry . . . I'm not into girls."

Neve's laugh was like chiming bells. "Tragic for you, but you're not my type. I meant as friends."

My hands curled under the velvet tablecloth. "I'm not allowed to be friends with clients."

Her smile faded for a moment, and I knew she'd recognized the lie for what it was. "Okay, no problem."

She lifted her old foam headphones over her ears as she turned to go. They did nothing to stop the reverberating bass and distorted whine of melancholic guitars from leaking out. A woman's cosmic wailing flooded into the room, backed by a shuddering drumbeat that made me feel anxious just hearing it.

"What in thundering hell are you listening to?" I asked before I could stop myself.

"Cocteau Twins," Neve said, pushing up her headphones. Her eyes glittered with excitement. "Have you heard of them? They're *amazing*—every song is like a dream."

"They can't be that amazing if I've never heard of them," I said. "You should turn it down before you lose your hearing."

She ignored me.

"Their songs are like different worlds." Neve wound the headphone cord around the bulky device. "I know it seems silly, but when I listen to them, it pushes everything else away. Nothing else matters. You don't have to feel anything but the music. Sorry, you probably don't care."

I didn't, but guilt welled in me all the same. Neve made her way to the door just as Cabell opened it. He blinked at the sight of her before she brushed past.

"Bye!" Neve called, hurrying down the stairs. "Until we meet again, Oracle!"

"Another satisfied customer?" My brother lingered in the doorway, brows raised as he ran a hand through his shoulder-length black hair.

"But of course," I said, throwing Myrtle's shawl down. After scraping my tangled hair back into a ponytail, I gathered up the cards, neatening them into a pile. I reached for the small velvet bag I used to store them, only to stop when I saw what was at the top of the deck.

I had never liked the Moon card. It wasn't anything I could explain, and that only made me hate it more. Every time I looked at it, it was like trying to tow a sinking memory back to the front of my mind, which had never forgotten anything before.

I drew the card closer, studying the image. It was impossible to tell if the moon's luminous face was sleeping or merely contemplating the long path below. In the distance, misty blue hills waited, guarded by two stone towers, silent sentinels to whatever truth lay beyond the horizon.

A wolf and a hound, brothers in fear, one wild, the other tame, howled up at the glowing orb in the sky. Near their feet, a crayfish crawled from the edge of a pool.

My gaze drifted to the dark hound again, my stomach tightening.

"How did it go today?" Cabell asked, drawing my attention back to him.

After taking my cut of the day's earnings and locking the rest in the safe, I held up two hundred-dollar bills.

"Hey, hey. Look who's buying dinner tonight," he said. "I await the fabled Lobster Larry's Unlimited Seafood Tower."

My brother was all lanky height and had little meat on his bones, but he looked perfectly comfortable in what I'd come to think of as the tried-and-true uniform of Hollowers: loose brown slacks and a belt laden with the tools of the trade, including a hand axe, crystals, and vials of fast-acting poison and antivenom.

All of which were needed if you wanted to empty the sorceress's vault of the treasures she'd hoarded over the centuries and keep both life and limb.

"Why not just eat garbage from the dumpster out back instead?" I said. "You'll get the same dining experience."

"I take that to mean you want to stop by the library and try to drop in on some potential clients before we order pizza for the tenth night in a row," he said.

"What happened with the key for the Sorceress Gaia's job?" I asked, reaching for my bag. "Was there a match in the library's collection, or did you have to go to the Bonecutter after all?"

To open a sealed Vein, one of the magic pathways the sorceresses created for themselves, we needed bone and blood from the one who created it, or her kin. The Bonecutter sourced and procured them.

"Had to ask the Bonecutter," he said, passing the key to me to examine. It looked like two finger bones welded with a seam of gold. "We're all set to open the tomb this weekend."

"God's teeth," I muttered. "What did the key cost us?"

"Just the usual," he said, shrugging a shoulder. "A favor."

"We can't keep handing out favors," I said tightly, making quick work of switching off the music and the battery-powered candles.

"Why not?" He leaned a hip against the doorframe.

The small movement—that careless tone of voice—brought me up short. He'd never reminded me more of Nash, the crook of a man who had reluctantly raised us and drawn us into his profession, only to abandon us to it before either of us had passed our first decade of life.

Cabell cast a quick look around my Mystic Maven setup. "You'll have to ditch this bullshit gig if you want to be able to pay the Bonecutter with actual coin next time."

25

Somehow we'd arrived at my least-favorite conversation yet again. "This 'bullshit gig' buys us groceries and pays for the roof over our heads. *You* could ask for more shifts at the tattoo parlor."

"You know that's not what I mean." Cabell let out an irritating hum. "If we just went after a legendary relic—"

"If we just found a unicorn," I interrupted. "If we just uncovered a lost trove of pirates' treasure. If we just caught a falling star and put it in our pockets . . ."

"All right," Cabell said, his smile falling. "Enough. You've made your point."

We weren't like the other Hollowers and Nash, who chased mist and dreams. Sure, selling a legendary object on the black market could make you thousands, if not millions, but the cost was years of searching for an ever-dwindling number of relics. The magic users of other parts of the world had secured their treasures, leaving only Europe's up for grabs. And, besides, we'd never had the right resources for a big get.

"Real money comes from real jobs," I reminded him. And whether I liked it or not, Mystic Maven was a real job, one with flexible hours and fair wages graciously paid under the table. We needed it to supplement the for-hire work we took from the guild library's job board, especially as the number of those postings thinned and clients cheaped out on the finder's fees.

Mystic Maven may have been a tourist trap built on incense and fish-stick-scented woo-woo nonsense, but it had given us the one thing we'd never had before. Stability.

Nash had never enrolled us in school. He had never forged identity paperwork for either of us, the two orphans he'd collected from different sides of the world like two more of his stupid trinkets. What we had was this world of Hollowers and sorceresses, unknown and unseen by nearly everyone else. We'd been raised at the knee of jealousy, fed by the hand of envy, and sheltered under the roof of greed.

The truth was, Nash hadn't just forced both of us into this world—he had trapped us in it.

I liked the life we had carved out for ourselves, and the small measure of stability we'd scrounged now that we were older and could fend for ourselves.

Unfortunately, Cabell wanted what Nash had: the potential, the glory, the high of a find.

His lips compressed as he scratched at his wrist. "Nash always said—"

"Do not," I warned, "quote Nash at me."

Cabell flinched, and for once, I didn't care.

"Why do you always do that?" he asked. "Shut down any mention of him—"

"Because he doesn't deserve the breath it takes to say his name," I snapped.

Draping my leather satchel over my shoulder, I forced a tight smile onto my face. "Come on, we'll check the library's job board and then stop by the Sorceress Madrigal's to give her the brooch."

Cabell shuddered at the mention of the sorceress's name. I patted his shoulder. In all fairness, she'd fixated on him at the consultation with an intensity that had alarmed both of us, even before she decided to lick a drop of sweat from his cheek.

I locked up and followed Cabell down the creaking staircase and out into the boisterous night. Tourists milled around us, merry and pink-cheeked from the crisp early-autumn air.

I narrowly avoided colliding with several of them as they craned their heads to gawk at the Quincy Market building. The sight of them leaning in for photos in front of restaurants, eating apple cider donuts, pushing strollers with sleepy kids up the cobblestones toward their hotels.

It was a vision of a life I'd never known, and never would.

2

Echoing laughter greeted us as we entered the atrium of our guild's library, turning my skin as cold as the marble walls.

Nothing good ever came out of a Hollower fete, especially this close to midnight, when curses thrived and people's judgment turned soggy with drink.

Now I wished we had stopped for dinner instead of walking over to Beacon Hill, where the library occupied an inconspicuous town house.

"Ugh," I said. "Perfect timing."

"You do have a knack for always running into the people you least want to see," Cabell said. "It's almost like the library is trying to tell you something."

"That I need to find a way to steal their keys so they can't get back in?"

Cabell shook his head. "When are you going to realize that pushing people away only ends one way—with you alone?"

"You mean my happily-ever-after?" I shot back, making sure I'd shut the door firmly behind me.

The All Ways door had been removed from a powerful sorceress's vault over a century ago, when our Hollower guild was founded. Unlike the sorceresses' skeleton knobs, which were used to anchor one fixed end of a particular Vein to the other, the All Ways door could open an infinite number of temporary passageways—it could take you anywhere you could picture clearly in your mind, so long as you'd been given a copy of the door's brass key.

Cabell and I had inherited our membership key from Nash, who had received it upon the reluctant acceptance of his application to the guild. His required donation—the shield of Aeneas—had been a notable enough relic that the other guild members were willing to overlook his rather scruffy reputation.

The problem with the All Ways door was that the library became a required stop no matter where you were going. While we could walk to the library and wait for Librarian to notice us and open its hidden door, the easier method for entry—and the one most guild members used—was the All Ways door. All you had to do was stick your membership key into any old nearby lock, open the door, and you'd be there in seconds. We used the one on the linen closet in our North End apartment more often than not. Once at the library, we could use the key again on the knob of the All Ways door to continue to wherever we were headed next.

We'd be passing through again on the return trip, and my stomach turned, imagining multiple doses of this gathering.

The tension in Cabell's face eased a bit as he leaned back, looking down the long, polished hall to the central chamber of the library. The warm glow of candles was an invitation and made the white flecks in the stone floor glow like a trail of stars.

"It's not Friday, is it?" I asked. Friday-night show-and-tells were dedicated to the Hollowers drinking and preening about various relics they'd found and vaults they'd survived. Any hope I'd had of quickly saying hello to Librarian before heading out crumbled like clumps of sand in a fist.

"Tuesday. Looks like Endymion Dye and his crew are back from whatever expedition they were on, though," Cabell noted.

Hating myself for my self-sabotaging curiosity, I stole a quick look down the hall. Sure enough, Endymion Dye stood at one of the worktables, surrounded by guild members, all of whom were chirping and fluttering around him, trying to get a word of worshipful praise in. His shock of pure-white hair still came as a surprise, no matter how many times I saw him. It had been the parting gift of a sorceress's curse three years ago.

My jaw tightened. There was something unsettling about him beyond his obscene wealth, beyond the fact that his family had founded this guild and he got to set the rules, beyond even the piercing gray eyes that seemed to cut straight through you. He had an elusive air, as if none of us deserved the privilege of knowing his true feelings or intentions.

Even Nash, the man who grinned his way through chaos, had given Endymion a wide berth. *The guy's into some hinky shit, Tamsy,* he'd said one day as we'd passed him on the way to the sole guild meeting Nash had decided to grace with his presence. *You steer clear of him, hear me?*

The rare instances when I'd seen Endymion, he'd always been so perfectly composed that it was almost unreal to see him now, speckled with dust and grime from a recent expedition.

Still, he wasn't half as annoying as his son, Emrys. The younger Dye, when not blowing through the inheritance no seventeen-year-old deserved, or bragging about whatever relic he and his father had found, seemed to exist solely to test the limits of my sanity.

"You don't see Trust Fund around, do you?" I asked.

Cabell leaned into the hallway again. "No. Huh."

"*Huh,* what?" I said.

"Weird his father wouldn't take him," Cabell said. "But I haven't seen him around the library in weeks. Maybe he started at some new bougie boarding school?"

"I can only hope." There was no chance in any hell Emrys would give up hunting for relics, even temporarily.

Endymion ignored the chatter of the Hollowers, his gaze concealed by the firelight reflecting off his thin-framed glasses.

Cabell put a comforting hand on my head and said, "Wait here. I'll pull the job notices so you don't have to deal with them."

I reached for the supply bag Cabell had draped over his shoulder, relief threading through my whole body. "Thank you. I've run out of witty retorts for the day."

I leaned against the cold stone wall, listening as the other Hollowers exuberantly greeted Cabell like a prodigal son. After they'd gotten over his edgy tattooed loner exterior, they'd embraced Cabell. His deep laugh and the trick of rapturous storytelling he'd learned from Nash *almost* outweighed his unfortunate association with the Lark family.

But every time he shuffled off for a show-and-tell or to meet one of them for drinks, I had to bite my tongue to keep from reminding him that they all still called us *the Larcenies* behind our backs.

Which might have offended me if it had actually been clever.

They didn't respect him, and they sure as hell didn't care whether he lived or died, either. They never had. When the two of us had needed their help as children, the guild's so-called unity was nowhere to be found.

That was the first lesson Nash taught me—in life, people only looked out for themselves, and to survive, you had to do the same. At least the sorceresses were honest about it and didn't go through the motions of pretending to care about anyone else.

Cabell hurried back toward me, holding up three job notices, all written in Librarian's emerald-green ink. "A couple of good ones, I think."

I took all three, studying the names of those requesting recovery work. Most seemed to be Cunningfolk. Good. We needed a break from sorceresses.

A fresh wave of gleeful hooting made me glance down the hall again.

Endymion was removing the protective wrappings of his find with agonizing slowness. Then, with the kind of dramatic flourish these people couldn't resist, even when it meant manhandling priceless artifacts, he dropped the relic back onto the table. The thunder of the impact rolled through the library.

The massive book was leather-bound, its cover cracked with age and heat. The thick stack of pages, edged with silver, looked as if they'd spent the last few centuries attempting to escape. Only a heavy metal lock bearing the tree symbol of Avalon held it all together.

A pang of envy, one I resented the hell out of, sliced through me.

"The Immortality of Callwen . . . ," I said. A collection of the sorceress's memories written in blood upon her death. While it was common practice for sorceresses to create them now, this was rumored to be the oldest of its kind.

The library cats, hidden in the upper shelves, hissed at the presence of the curses woven around the tome. The sound was like rain sizzling against a hot roof.

The other Hollowers pounded the tables with their fists. My pulse outran the raucous beat as I faced the All Ways door.

"All right," I said, sliding our key into its knob. "Where to first?"

After hours of crisscrossing between Boston, Savannah, Salem, and St. Augustine, we'd struck out on all three jobs. Two had been completed by another Hollower from a different guild, and for the third, the client had been hoping to pay us with her extensive button collection.

The only thing left now was to close out the job we'd done for the Sorceress Madrigal.

"All I'm saying is that those pearl buttons were rather fetching," Cabell continued, dodging the after-dinner crowds in New Orleans's French Quarter.

"They were shaped like stars," I said, my face scrunching.

"You're right, I take back what I said," Cabell answered. "They weren't fetching, they were *enchanting*. I think they would look lovely on you—"

I knocked my shoulder into his, rolling my eyes. "Now I know what to get you for Christmas."

"Uh-huh," Cabell said, taking in the sight of the iron balconies above us. A thin moon illuminated New Orleans in all its colorful glory and seemed to hang lower than usual.

"Why don't we live here?" He sighed happily.

I could have named a dozen reasons, but only one mattered: Boston was our home. It was the only one we'd ever had.

We both instinctively slowed as we approached an unremarkable side street. An ivy-covered black mansion waited at the dead end of the alleyway, just beyond the last amber-colored pool of lamplight.

Rook House's black gate creaked open at our presence, unbidden. Hawthorn berries littered the ground along the crooked walkway to the front porch. I held my breath, but their rotten stench found me anyway, slithering into my nostrils and lingering there.

The way my heart thumped painfully against my ribs stirred up the memory of waiting outside other mansions like this one, clutching Cabell's small hand, praying that Nash wouldn't get himself killed bartering with the sorceress inside.

"You're sure you have the brooch?" he asked, even though he knew I did.

"I'll be fine," I told him.

"I can come with you, really," he said, casting an uncharacteristically anxious look up at the house.

I pulled a black leather journal out of my workbag and pressed its worn cover against his chest. "Try a couple of potential key words while you wait."

Nash's journal, one of the few possessions he'd left behind, was a chaotic mess of stories and notes about relics, legends, and the magic users he'd crossed paths with over the years. Likely knowing his nosy young wards might read it, he'd written some of the entries in a key-word cipher. While we'd managed to figure out the key word to decipher most of the entries, the final one, written just before he'd vanished, had eluded us for years.

Cabell took the journal, but his uneasiness remained.

"It's my turn," I said. When it came to delivering goods to sor-ceresses, one of us always stayed outside, just in case the other was trapped inside with a client who refused to pay. I gave his arm a re-assuring squeeze. "I'll be fast, I promise. Love you."

"Don't die," he responded, leaning against the fence with one last sigh.

The Sorceress Madrigal's home seemed to shiver with its own cold. The windowpanes chattered like teeth in their frames, and the bones of cracked marble and ironwork groaned in the breeze.

My gaze drifted up over the mansion's age-worn face as I ap-proached the sinking porch.

"All right," I whispered to myself, rolling my shoulders back. "Just a delivery. Get the payment, get out."

I always made it a point to research our clients before meeting with them, thereby significantly increasing our chances of securing the job and making it out of the meeting alive. But there'd been next to noth-ing about Madrigal in our guild's library, and even Nash's journal had only been semihelpful.

> *Madrigal—crone, master of all elemental affinities. No known relations. Never accept a dinner invitation.*

Her work notice had remained untouched on our guild's job board for months before I summoned the courage to take it.

My fist tightened around the brooch in its velvet pouch. Negotiat-ing this job had come close to shattering my nerves, and they felt brittle again as my mind worked through all the contingencies if things went sideways. The wretched truth was, there was precious little we *could* do if Madrigal refused to honor our contract and pay us. That was the nature of doing business with a more powerful being; their whims were as changeable as fire, and you always had to be ready for the next burn.

The door opened before I could raise a hand to ring the bell.

"Good evening, miss."

The sorceress's companion all but filled the massive doorway, with his impossible height and shoulders as broad as the street was wide. Dearie, she called him, and whether that was his name or an endearment, I thought the safer thing was not to ask.

He bowed as I came closer, his features just as indistinguishable as the first time I'd come. A leather mask clung to the top half of his face like a falcon's hood, shading his eyes, and he had poured his massive body into a fine, old-fashioned butler's uniform.

"If you would be so good as to follow me, miss." The man's accent was strange, melodic in a way that didn't sound entirely human, and likely wasn't. Though they were rare in our world now, the sorceresses often bound creatures of magic into service for their long lifetimes.

The companion stepped back into the waiting shadows behind him. The smell of warm wax and candle smoke flooded my nose as I passed by him. The gold pin on his lapel, a chess piece with a horned moon over it—the mark of the Sorceress Madrigal—winked in the light of a nearby candelabra.

A wailing sax dueled with the sparkling notes of a piano from somewhere deep inside the house, slowly working themselves into a frenzy.

Finish the job, I thought, feeling the edges of the brooch dig into my palm.

"Is your mistress home?" I asked.

"Oh yes, miss," the companion said. "She's entertaining."

My stomach hollowed. "Should I come back?"

"No, miss," he said. "That would displease her."

And like any good sorceress's companion, he knew better than to risk doing that.

"All right," I managed to say, hanging back a step to allow him to lead. I'd been so nervous on my first visit that Rook House had only registered as a blur of velvet and incense. Now I could take it in.

Like week-old cut flowers, the fine furnishings, artwork, and gilded trinkets had browned with age. The waste of it all was as breathtaking as the damp, stained rugs and the overwhelming reek of mildew and rot.

Wilting red silk covered the walls. A table inlaid with bone leaned against the wall, bearing a vase in the shape of grasping hands, a pair of opera glasses, and a half-drunk goblet of what might have been red wine but could have just as easily been blood.

Lording it over the hallway, glowing in the candlelight, was a portrait of a wary-looking young man in an old-fashioned uniform. A bright red lipstick kiss was pressed to his painted cheek, and a knife had been driven through the canvas, right where his heart would have been.

Creeping dread gathered on my skin, crawling like a nest of centipedes. We followed the music until the carpets gave way to black-and-white-checked tiles. Candles flickered to life as we passed, but their light wasn't enough to ease the feeling of inexorable gloom.

The entry fed into the round atrium at the center of the house. A stained-glass dome arched over the grand staircase, depicting a lush garden full of trees and climbing flowers, beneath a luminous crescent moon. It turned the red carpets and marble of the grand staircase a putrid shade.

Rather than go up the stairs, we turned toward two crimson doors, both carved with the sorceress's mark. The music eased, just enough for me to catch the murmur of voices inside. I closed my eyes as the companion raised his hand to knock.

The doors opened, and music spilled from the room like blood from a cut throat.

I straightened the best I could, lifting my chin as I followed Madrigal's companion through the doorway. There, a girl stared back at me. Round face, too-big eyes, hair that was neither brown nor blond, and pale as bone.

Me.

The room was covered in mirrors, each running from floor to ceiling. The furniture looked as if it had been carved right from the glossy black stone floors, then stretched and twisted into strange shapes. Candles lined the floors and sideboards. Hundreds of flames became thousands as their reflections multiplied in the silvered glass around us.

At the very center of the room, catching the splatters of crimson wax dripping from the chandelier above, stood a banquet table.

My stomach cramped at the sight of the platters piled high with carved meat and pies. Chocolate ravens tracked me with their gumdrop eyes from their vantage points on towering trays of sweets and cakes.

A woman sat at the head of the table, her body wrapped in a thundercloud of black tulle. Harsh lines of blush contoured her face. A stream of fiery hair ran down her back, but the sorceress (or some poor servant) had twisted two sections into loops above her ears. The length of black pearls and diamonds strung between them jangled as she looked over to us.

She looked the way countless legends had tried to portray the infamous Morgan le Fay. Seductively sinister.

"Miss Lark. How . . . punctual." She blotted her lips with a black lace napkin and held out a hand.

My heart surged up into my throat as I took the first step toward her, my boots suddenly too loud and my clothes too disheveled to be here, drowning in the room's seething iridescence. I stopped again when I saw she wasn't alone at the table. Several unmoving . . . men? Life-sized dolls? They were dressed in tuxedos, each one's chest held upright by a black velvet ribbon knotted to their chair. Each had a different taxidermied animal head covering their own like a hood—a bear, a lion, a stag, and a boar.

"Come now, I assure you my guests are well behaved," Madrigal said. "I trained them myself."

None of them seemed to be moving, until the guest seated to her left leaned around the massive candelabra that had blocked him from my sight.

Emrys Dye.

3

Unlike the others, he wore no animal head. It meant I could watch as the blood drained from his face and his lips parted with obvious surprise.

Before that moment, I had prided myself on how rarely I was caught off guard. I'd spent years methodically dosing myself with suspicion the way others might suffer drops of poison to build up a tolerance. When you always expect the worst, nothing can cut deep enough to shock you.

But whatever I had expected, it wasn't . . . *this.*

As always, Emrys's features were prep-school perfect—his looks carefully cultivated through generations of arranged marriages between beautiful, wealthy people, all with that indescribable *something* Cunningfolk seemed to possess that set them ever so slightly apart from the rest of us mortals. It made you want to stare a second too long.

That allure was hard to resist—even with Emrys, until you discovered the repulsive personality beneath the mask.

He wore a silky black tuxedo, the bow tie hanging open around his neck. His chestnut hair was its usual rakish mess. He ran a careless hand back through it as he surveyed me with his different-colored eyes. One eye like pewter, the other as glittering green as the emerald on the brooch I'd brought with me.

My feet no longer remembered how to work. Unfortunately, the same couldn't be said for my mouth.

"What are you doing here?" I blurted out.

"What an absolute pleasure to see you, too, Tamsin," Emrys said, reaching out to clutch the neck of a nearby bottle of champagne. His earlier shock had evaporated, leaving only his usual smooth tone. "Back from another thrilling adventure to recover lost junk? I imagine whatever Mistress Madrigal had you find was a lovely break from your usual dreck."

"Back from another quest to bolster your fragile male pride?" I returned sweetly. No wonder he hadn't been at the library.

Emrys laughed as he filled his champagne glass to the brim. "Well, you've got me there, Bird."

I wanted to snarl. If anyone was a bird, it was him. The way he fluttered around, making a nuisance of himself and leaving a mess for someone else to pick up.

"You seem to be laboring under the delusion that your predictability is charming and not, in fact, supremely boring," I told him.

"Boring?" His grin widened. "Not sure I've ever been called that before."

"Ah-hem." A sharp noise from the sorceress's throat brought me crashing back to the present.

Madrigal reached over to a platter of food at the table's center and speared cuts of meat and cheese onto her long nails. Her fingers moved like knives, scraping against one another to drop the food onto her plate. I cast a quick look, searching for rings that bore sigils.

"He, Miss Lark," Madrigal said, "is my guest."

And I, my mind hissed in reminder, *am not.*

"I would ask you to stay, but there's barely enough food for the two of us, as you can see," the sorceress continued, a note of false contrition in her voice as she stroked the roasted pig's nose.

"Of course—" I jerked my head in some approximation of a bow.

"Of course, Mistress Crone. I've completed your request and have come to deliver the brooch to you."

I fought to keep still as I waited, but the sorceress said nothing. I risked a look up through my lashes. The sorceress merely returned to the food in front of her, spearing several pieces of fruit from a nearby platter. For several agonizing moments, the only sound between us was the scrape of her fingernails and the gnashing of teeth.

Emrys absently bit his lower lip as he looked to the sorceress. His other hand curled against the glossy table.

I forced myself to look away.

"I didn't realize the two of you were acquainted," I heard myself say. *God's teeth,* I thought, *shut up, Tamsin!*

"And I did not realize you kept a tally of my acquaintances, Miss Lark," Madrigal said. "Dearie?"

The air whirled blisteringly hot at my back. Dearie's enormous body began to twist around itself. Pressure built like a looming storm, electrifying even the air in my lungs until I couldn't breathe at all. Light twined around him as his massive body shifted into a new form.

Pooka, my mind supplied through my slow-dawning awe. The shapeshifters of the Fair Folk, able to take whatever form they desired for their tricks and travels. I didn't possess the One Vision. I could only see him because he willed it.

The hawk flew forward, perching on the high back of the sorceress's obsidian chair, watching me with unnerving stillness. Madrigal reached up, feeding her companion a strip of rare meat from her plate.

"Where's Cabell?" Emrys asked, startling me from my thoughts.

"What do you care?" I asked, tugging my jacket sleeve down.

"I didn't realize I was forbidden to give a damn about a member of my guild."

"*Your* guild?" I said. "Try *our* guild—"

"Children," the sorceress interrupted. "What, in the entirety of our short acquaintance, has made you believe I'd countenance a petty fight I cannot even participate in?" She turned toward me. I bit the inside of my lip until I tasted blood to keep from reacting. "I don't recall you being so surly at our last meeting, nor that you were uncivilized."

The air seethed with unspent magic, forceful enough for a mere mortal like me to register it stinging my skin. I chewed my lip.

Her power felt different than the other sorceresses I'd dealt with—heavy and edged with lightning. Ancient. It had to be because she was a crone, the highest status a sorceress could attain. Her mastery of magic spoke to a vast knowledge of spell and curse sigils. So vast, I thought grimly, that I might not even recognize the one she'd use to kill me.

"I'm afraid she has a natural predisposition toward surliness," Emrys said, his tone suddenly as warm and smooth as bourbon, "but it's all part of her unique charm. And, really, what's the point of being civilized when you could be interesting instead?"

Madrigal let out a thoughtful hum, considering this. The pressure gathering around us released, as if it had been exhaled.

"I wasn't raised to be a lady, if that's what you're asking," I managed to say. "Not like you. There's no one in the world like you. Not for beauty, not for power."

"I've never enjoyed an overegged pudding, beastie," Madrigal said, a mild tone of warning in her voice. "But speaking of tasty morsels, where *is* that delightful young man who accompanied you on your last visit? I barely got a glimpse of him and was hoping for a better introduction."

"He . . ." I grasped for an explanation that wouldn't insult or infuriate her. "He had another commitment tonight."

"Another commitment more important than me?" Madrigal asked.

My body was strung tighter than catgut. "My apologies."

"How terribly annoying." Madrigal glowered into her goblet of wine. "Tell me, Miss Lark, for I do not often understand the mysteries of the mortal mind: What keeps you from clawing out your brother's heart when he annoys you?"

"Willpower, mostly," I said before I could stop myself. "And weak nails."

Emrys let out a shocked laugh. The Sorceress Madrigal was silent for a moment, then her head fell back in a howl. The sound was more animal than human.

I took another step forward, then another, until I was close enough to slide the brooch from its protective cover and place it on the table beside her.

"I suppose I must pay you now," Madrigal said with a pout. She held out her hand, and a blood-red sachet appeared in her palm out of thin air. I hesitated for a moment, then took it, then risked a look inside to make sure the sorceress hadn't filled it with stones or pennies.

To my surprise, Madrigal let out another sharp peal of laughter. "I see you have much experience working with my sistren, Miss Lark, but both of you may rest assured that I always pay for work well done."

Work. So Emrys was here for work—not a favor, which I might have been quicker to believe. I'd known that the Dyes had direct dealings with sorceresses from time to time, to trade for information or sell their findings, but it was nothing like the uneasy contracts Cabell and I made with them. Most of our guild found it pitiful we had to take the jobs to stay alive.

I whirled to face Emrys. "You're here for a job?"

"What if I am?" he challenged, his eyes flashing.

"Did Daddy cut off your allowance, Trust Fund?" I asked. "Or did he just tighten the leash?"

Emrys's expression darkened. "I don't see how it's any of your business."

No. *No.* He wasn't about to take good work from me. I needed it in a way he'd never understand.

"Mistress Crone," I said, fighting to keep the desperation out of my voice, "if you're pleased with my recovery work, it would be my pleasure to take on another assignment from you."

"Are you so desperate that you have to poach work?" Emrys shot back with a new, unfamiliar edge. "Not that I doubt your wisdom, Mistress Crone, but Tamsin—Miss Lark—doesn't have the most basic requirement. She's not one of the Cunningfolk and doesn't possess the One Vision."

It was the truth, but something about the plain way he'd said it, the acknowledgment that it was something to be ashamed of, felt utterly humiliating.

"Unlike you and your best friend nepotism, I don't need the One Vision to do my work," I retorted.

"She makes a fair point, beastie. You cannot deny that Miss Lark has been successful, even with her impediment," Madrigal said, picking up the brooch and holding it toward the candlelight. Her smile grew slowly. "Perhaps a little competition is in order, then. I'd be quite curious to see which one of you is able to deliver the Servant's Prize first."

The Servant's Prize. The words rattled harshly in my memory, familiar but impossible to pin down. I knew that name . . .

Emrys's lips compressed as he sat back. A bead of sweat worked its way down the side of his face, following the path of some sort of welt or scar. I leaned into the table, momentarily distracted by the sight of the jagged line of raised skin. It stretched down, disappearing beneath his jacket, but as he turned toward the candlelight, it disappeared altogether, as if I'd imagined it.

"She can't handle the work, Mistress," he said finally. "And we've already come to our agreement."

"Don't listen to him," I said quickly. "I'm nothing like him or any of the other hacks. I do a better job with half the resources and for half the price. And as you know, I recover specific items for clients—I don't sell relics to any creep who can pay."

Madrigal ignored us, still studying the way the brooch glowed in the candlelight. With a flick of her fingers, she broke the silver orna-ment in two, letting the emerald spill into her palm. Without a word, without so much as drawing another breath, she popped it into her mouth like a piece of hard candy and swallowed it whole.

My mouth opened. Closed. "I . . ."

Didn't want to know.

"I will concede that Miss Lark's lack of the One Vision would be a problem for this particular search," the sorceress said, placing a hand over Emrys's. Heat burned in my chest. Her nails stroked his skin as if he were a pomegranate to be split open and devoured.

Good. They deserve one another, a voice hissed in my ear. *Let her eat him alive.*

But the movement drew my attention to something else I'd missed before, equally curious. For the first time since the day I'd met him, Emrys Dye wasn't wearing his family's ruby signet ring.

". . . And yet, I cannot resist a game, especially with such worthy opponents," the sorceress continued. "Miss Lark, if you bring me the Servant's Prize first, I will pay you a hundred times what you have received tonight."

My heart lurched with embarrassing longing. "Then I'll be the one to bring it to you."

Whatever *it* was. No sense in revealing that bit of ignorance, espe-cially when the name had already stirred something in my memory.

One of the other guests, the one wearing the bear's head, shifted in his seat with a small, pleading moan. My stomach turned.

"Wonderful, Miss Lark," Madrigal said. "I shall enjoy this compe-tition more than you know. But the time has come for you to depart. Dearie, please escort her to the door—"

Emrys's chair screeched back. His right hand clasped his left as if to fiddle with the ring no longer on his left pinky.

"Mistress," he said, his smile practically fluorescent with charm, "please do me the honor of allowing me to escort Miss Lark out."

"Well . . . fine. I am always in favor of good manners," Madrigal said, flicking her fingers at us. "Especially as they will lead you back to my table."

Another spike of heat punctured my center.

"Thank you," I said through gritted teeth, "for the opportunity to serve you—"

Emrys gripped my arm, keeping his gaze straight ahead and his expression cold as he hurried me out of the dining room and back through the atrium. It was only when we reached the foyer that he slowed enough for me to yank myself free.

"Touch me like that again and you'll wake up one morning without hands," I hissed.

I tried to grip the freezing door handle, but Emrys was there first. Using his height to his advantage, he reached over my shoulder to hold the door shut. I turned to punch him in the chest, but he caught my wrist with his other hand. This time, he released it the moment I tugged at it.

"Listen to me, Bird," he said, voice low, "this is *my* job. You don't want any part of it."

The house's biting cold only made his breath warmer as it fanned across my cheek. Emrys leaned down, bringing his stormy gaze level with mine until the sharp words evaporated from my tongue.

I had seen every shade of Emrys Dye over the years—the little princeling drunk on wine, the boisterous storyteller in the library's firelight, the careless flirt, the reader absorbed in his quiet work, the dutiful and adoring son. But I had never seen him like this, his expression as bleak as frozen glass. If I had shoved him away just then, I wasn't sure he wouldn't shatter.

"I think you mean *my* job," I said coldly. "Are we done here?"

"We're not," he said. "I saw your face when she offered. You have no idea what she's talking about, let alone what you're in for."

I drew closer, but he still didn't pull back. "If you don't like what you see, stop watching me."

"Tamsin," he began, his voice softer now. "Please—"

A loud, metallic clatter drowned out his words. We both jumped at the noise, and as Emrys turned, I slipped out from under his arm and opened the door.

At the other end of the entryway, a small, hunched woman in a black maid's uniform slowly dropped to her knees, moaning at the silver tray and broken glass at her feet.

I was forgotten in an instant. Emrys rushed toward her, his tone low and soothing. "It's all right. It's all right, I promise."

The woman shook her head, incoherent with dismay. Emrys lifted her from the floor with infinite care, drawing her over to a nearby chair. My breath caught. Not even the stringy gray hair covering much of her face could disguise the deep-set lines of her sagging skin, the bulging veins, or the white of her one visible eye, where the iris and pupil should have been.

The maid's hand strayed to hover over his wrist, his arm, just for a moment. Her eye welled with unshed tears, and the pain in her face was unbearable enough that I almost looked away. The cut of Emrys's jaw became more pronounced as he clenched it, struggling to master whatever storm was building in him.

The muggy night air and stench of hawthorn berries beckoned, drawing me outside. But something made me look back just once more, to see Emrys on his hands and knees frantically picking up the shards of glass in the instant before the door shut.

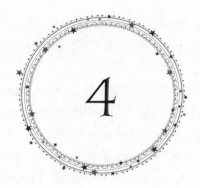

4

My feet carried me swiftly down the path, seeking the safety of lights and milling crowds on Bourbon Street. Cabell looked up at the sound of my steps, alarmed. The gate swung open in front of me and I rushed through, hooking him by the arm and dragging him back up the alleyway.

"What's wrong?" he asked.

I tugged on my right earlobe, our signal for *Not now, someone could be listening.*

I didn't stop until we were surrounded by hundreds of people out carousing in the streets, stumbling in and out of bars. Rainbow lights strobed around us as we snaked our way through the crowds, heading back in the direction of the Vein we'd opened with the All Ways door.

Music pulsed until I was sure I could feel the bass line thrumming in my blood. Finally, I couldn't wait any longer and pulled him into a shop of junky tourist gifts and fake voodoo candles.

Cabell gripped my shoulders, searching my face, then the rest of me. "Are you okay? Are you hurt?"

"I'm fine!" I said, raising my voice over the music. "Listen, Dye was there—"

"What?" he shouted, gesturing to his ears. "Dye?"

"He's working a job for her, but she offered it to us, too," I said. "If we can get it first, pay is a hundred times this job!"

He waved me off. "I thought you just said a hundred times—"

"I did!" I glanced at a swaying couple as they entered the store. "It's for something called the Servant's Prize? I think we should go to the library tonight and—"

This time, I knew he had heard me. His expression shuttered and he swung back to the street, stalking toward the waiting Vein.

"Hey!" I said. "This is an incredible opportunity."

"No, it's not," he said, his face harder than I'd ever seen it. His skin glistened with sweat, and it was beginning to soak through his shirt. He pushed up his sleeves, revealing the bands of black tattoos. Each tattoo represented one of the curse sigils he'd broken over the years, trophies on his skin. "We aren't taking this gig, Tams."

Realization stole over me. "Do you know what the Servant's Prize is? It sounds familiar, but I can't place it."

His breathing grew more and more erratic. "I don't know. I have no idea what the hell it is, but we aren't getting mixed up with that sorceress again. There's no way we can beat Dye to the prize with all the resources he has, it's not a good idea, we can't—we can't—"

He turned his back to me, reaching out an arm to stop me from coming closer.

"What's happening?" I asked him. "Are you okay?"

Cabell panted, his ribs expanding with each harsh breath as if trying to tear through his skin. Sweat dripped from his chin to the ground as his body vibrated with unspoken pain.

The seconds stretched out like years. A hum grew in my ears as I watched the tension seep through Cabell's body, stiffening his shoulders. He fell forward, supporting himself against the rough stone wall.

Finally, he shook his head.

"You're all right," I told him, my voice calmer than I felt. "Just take a breath. Listen to the words I'm saying." I swallowed against the lump in my throat. "In ages past, in a kingdom lost to time, a king named Arthur ruled man and the Fair Folk alike . . ."

"Tams—" he choked out. Panic trilled in me. Distracting him

with a story was usually enough to avoid a shift, even when he was furious or upset. "Back . . . up . . ."

He was silenced by a loud *crack* as his bones shifted beneath his skin.

The movements were so forceful, they pulled and pushed at his shirt, tearing the fabric along his shoulders and rigid spine. He staggered, reaching blindly for me, for a wall, anything to support him.

A single, sharp thought tore through my shock. *Not here.*

This couldn't happen here, with all these people around, singing and snapping selfies, blissfully unaware of the danger they were in.

I exploded into action, gripping his wrist and all but dragging him the last few blocks to the opening of the Vein in a closed-up convenience store. Moaning in pain, Cabell stumbled as his feet slid from his boots. I slowed, wrapping his arm around my shoulder and mine around his waist, then kicked the front door open, and we lurched into the waiting passage.

Darkness encircled us and the room blurred. Breath roared in my ears as his ribs contracted beneath my grip and shrank. The All Ways door crashed open against the wall, spitting us out onto the cold marble. The sound of clattering tools rippled through the atrium, drowning out even the sound of the voices from the library's inner chamber.

"Was that the door?" I heard someone ask.

Cabell curled into a ball, his hands pressed to his changing face. Desperate, panting, I crawled back toward the All Ways door and shut it, my hands shaking so badly I almost couldn't get the key back into the lock, let alone visualize our apartment.

The Vein opened with a sigh, and I stopped only long enough to remove the key.

Cabell was dead weight in my arms, muttering and senseless with pain, as we tumbled into the endless black of the passage and the door slammed shut behind us.

It was the apartment's smell, sweetened by a neighbor's laundry, that told me we'd arrived. Then we burst through the linen closet door, tumbling onto the threadbare rug. The whole building seemed to groan at the impact.

I scrambled onto my hands and knees, crawling back toward the closet and slamming its door shut once more so no one could follow.

"Cabell," I said, my voice sounding distant to my ears. "What's happening?"

"I don't . . . ," he said, fisting a hand in his hair. "Tams, I think—"

His face went terrifyingly slack, and I knew. I knew exactly what was coming the instant before his shoulders hunched, before the dark hair rippled out over his arms, before his bones began the work of re-shaping themselves into something that wasn't human.

"Take a deep breath," I said. "Just focus—focus on my voice. You don't have to go. You don't. You control it, it doesn't control you—"

His shoulder shrank from my desperate grip as he fell to his knees.

"I'm gonna—" I spun toward the nearby loft space we used as an office and fumbled for an idea, any idea about what to do. "I'm going to go get more crystals—I'm going to get—"

A low, thunderous growl rose behind me.

I turned.

The hound was massive, almost more wolf than dog. Its shaggy black coat shimmered like spilt gasoline, rippling with each step forward. Cabell's clothing hung off it in tatters.

The sound of claws clicking against the battered floorboards stirred a primal terror, one as old as life itself. Strings of saliva dripped between its long white teeth. Adrenaline surged in me, bitter on my tongue, pounding through my blood.

There was nothing human left in those dark eyes.

The shift had been coming on more often over the last year, but I'd always been able to pull him back. To return him to himself. He hadn't had a completely uncontrolled transformation since we were kids, when he was just a pup.

"Cabell?" I whispered.

The hound stopped, cocking its head to the side.

"Listen," I said, trying to keep the tremor out of my voice. My mind was moving too quickly, flipping through the extensive archive of references and Immortalities in my memory. I never forgot a thing I saw or read, but this—there had never been any need to find something to shift him back to his human form. He had always been able to do it himself.

"Listen to me," I said, holding out a hand. "That's good. That's good, Cab. Focus on what I'm saying . . . In ages past, in a kingdom lost to time, a king named Arthur ruled man and the Fair Folk alike . . ."

The hound let out a whine, but stayed, giving itself a vigorous shake. The vise around my stomach eased as I took another step forward. "This is a story about his beloved friend and knight Lancelot . . ."

There wasn't time to run. There wasn't time to draw in a breath.

Not before it lunged at my throat.

Instinct alone saved me.

I threw up an arm as the hound tackled me. A scream tore out of me as its fangs ripped into the flesh of my forearm, piercing skin and muscle to scrape the bone.

Pain blistered me, but it was the sight of my own blood painting the hound's teeth crimson that made me scream again.

Saliva foamed and sprayed against my face as the hound snapped and bit at the air to get to my face. My mind had emptied, but my body wanted to survive. Needed to. Somehow I drew my knees up enough to kick the dog away. It whined again as it struck the floor and rolled onto its feet.

I dragged myself back, and back, with that one arm, trying to build distance between us, trying to get to my feet, trying to get to the office alcove, where there were tonics and crystals and—

The hound's limbs went rigid as it released an earsplitting, unearthly howl.

52

"Cabell!" I choked out. "Please—snap out of it!"

The hound stalked forward, its hackles raised along the ridge of its spine like needles. It was too fast—its jaws locked around my foot, forcing me to kick its snout and skull and whatever part of it I could reach to free myself.

I'm going to die. The thought seared my mind, agonizing. *He's going to kill me.*

Unless I killed him first.

The hound lunged again, but so did I, grasping for the letter opener just beside the mountain of research books on my desk. I spun around, slashing wildly through the air to ward it off. Instead of backing away, the hound let itself be cut as it came for me. My body was gripped with a single, desperate drive for survival.

I can't.

The letter opener fell from my hand, spinning against the floor. I took a step away, then another, as the hound briefly turned its attention to licking a deep cut on one of its legs.

I can't.

He was still Cabell. Inside, somewhere, this hound was my brother.

And he was going to kill me.

The dog prowled forward between our two desks. My back bumped into the bookshelf near the window, and just like that, I had nowhere left to go.

I reached back, throwing book after book at the hound, unleashing all of the anger and desperation throbbing inside me. The hound snapped at them, yelping and whimpering when a few managed to hit it.

I sucked in a ragged breath as it backed away, turning its snout up toward the ceiling. Its howl reverberated through our small apartment as if trying to summon others to the hunt.

The hunt.

The idea pierced the fog of pain in my mind. I risked a glance to my left, toward our pack, the one we only used when we needed to camp out before entering a vault. It leaned against the buckling leg of Cabell's desk, just out of reach.

"Listen to me, Cabell," I said, moving slowly toward it. The hound turned back, flattening its ears against its skull as it growled.

I kicked the bag over, letting its contents clatter out onto the floor. The silver box of tranquilizer darts, the ones meant for bears and other predators, magic or mundane, slid out among the mess of notebooks and tools.

There would only be a second . . .

Less.

The hound leapt. So did I.

My body slammed against the floor with the full weight of the snarling creature on my back. My hair caught between the hound's teeth and was ripped out of my scalp. I threw one elbow back, unable to get the silver box open with my shaking hands, slick with blood. I bashed it against the floor and it sprang open just as the hound plunged its teeth into my shoulder.

I twisted around with a feral sound of my own and jammed the dart into the bulging muscle of its neck.

The dog yelped, bucking against me. I held its face away with one hand, keeping my grip on the dart until the animal shuddered and, finally, lay still.

"It's all right," I told it, wrapping an arm around its back. "It's okay now."

It collapsed on top of me with one last snort and a low, mournful whine.

My neighbor pounded on the wall between us. "Everything okay?"

"We're fine!" I called back, hearing the tremor in my voice. "Sorry!"

We were on the ground floor. It was amazing no one had seen what had happened through the window.

I held the hound tighter, until the fur fell away. I held him until his bones began to break and reshape as he moaned in pain, deliriously clawing at the floor. My breath ached in my throat, and I squeezed my eyes shut, refusing to release the burn of tears.

Because every curse could be broken.

Even his.

5

I was being watched.

The guild library was quiet, save for the crackle of the fire in the old stone hearth and the whisper of the books tucking themselves back into place on the shelves. I'd been annoyed to find Phineas Primm, an old Hollower with more scars on his face than fingers left on his hands, reading in one of the overstuffed leather armchairs. His gaze had narrowed as he'd followed my path to my usual worktable.

It wasn't until an hour later, when I looked up from yet another reference book that had no record of the Servant's Prize, that I realized two more Hollowers had quietly arrived. One, Hector Leer, watched me through the shelves of old map scrolls. Septimus Yarrow leaned against a shelf a few rows away, pretending to read an Immortality. I recognized the silvery snakeskin of the Sorceress Ardith's Immortality, volume one.

I'd read the complete set of that Immortality at least three times now, combing through all six hundred years of her memory for any sign of what Cabell's curse might be, and could confirm that the most interesting thing the Sorceress Ardith ever did was die.

In her early years, the entries were readable but dry. The later volumes, especially in the last decades as her sister began the slow, methodical work of dosing Ardith with poison to steal her collection of venom, became more of a misty stream of consciousness.

There was nothing in it to engross the reader for more than a few minutes. And while I was used to being eyed with suspicion, this was something completely different. Because they weren't just looking at me—they seemed to be tracking what I was reading, too. Phineas appeared to be jotting down actual notes.

Finally, I couldn't take it anymore. "Something I can help you with, gentlemen?"

Hector and Phineas both startled and turned away, but Septimus was as serene as the frost gathering on the windows. No wonder he and Endymion Dye were such pals. Both had that smooth, refined way about their speech and appearance, smiles brittle with contempt.

"No, kitten," Septimus said, coming toward me. "Just wondering what a little girl like you is doing in the library so very late, and alone."

"Not staring at teenage girls like an absolute creep," I said.

He gave me a cold smile as he sat on the edge of my table, purposefully crowding my space. He craned his head to see what I was reading, and his low black ponytail slipped over his shoulder. "The High Kings of Ireland? Any reason you've decided to explore the stories of the mystical Emerald Isle this fine evening?"

His brown tweed suit was the least conspicuous part of him. He'd traveled the world over and turned up several legendary relics, including Herakles's club. He carried himself like a warrior king, his sharp, dark eyes always searching for the next battle.

"I'm almost done with it, if you'd like to read up on Balor of the Evil Eye. He's your ancestor, right?"

A smile slithered across his face. "You're just like your father, you know. Always with the smart mouth and sly fingers."

"He's not my father," I said coldly. My gaze drifted down to the pin on Septimus's lapel. It was identical to the one his bestie, Endymion, always wore: a hand holding a silver branch. How cute. The rich asshole version of a friendship bracelet.

Septimus looked confused for a moment. "Well, then, your *guardian*. He stole my hand axe—"

"I'm not sure what you want me to do about it," I said, keeping my voice low. "You know as well as I do that if he took it, he took it to the grave."

"You sure about that?" Septimus asked, bracing a hand on the long worktable to lean in closer to my face. I fought not to squirm under the scrutiny. "Where was it that he left you and your brother again?"

My instincts prickled. It was time to end this charade.

"Librarian!" I called sweetly. "Mr. Yarrow is bored and needs your help finding something interesting to read!"

Librarian let out a chirp of acknowledgment, dropping the stack of new books he'd been sorting, always ready and willing to be ruthlessly helpful, even if it meant spending hours recommending different titles.

Septimus gave a humorless laugh as he rose from the table and called out, "Never mind, Librarian." With one last glance at me, he added, "That looks like quite the nasty wound on your arm. Take care, kitten. I'd hate to see you end up with one much worse."

The bite on my forearm throbbed beneath its bandage as I gave him a dismissive flick of my fingers. I'd cleaned it as well as I could and glued the worst tears in my skin, hoping for the best. Most of the shallow cuts and bruises were covered by my sweater, but every time I shifted in my seat, they made themselves known.

I reached for an Immortality in my stack of books.

It was an old favorite. Unlike some of her sistren, who were about as interesting as an empty paper bag, the Sorceress Hesperia was a diamond. Devastatingly sharp and glittering in turn, she'd had personality in spades.

Cyrus of Rome is sculpted by the hand of a generous god. His piercing blue eyes watch my every move from across the darkened bedchamber . . .

I took a long drag of my instant coffee.

No one knew exactly how the Immortalities were made. I used

to imagine the words draining from some sorceress's mind, her blood like ink as it dripped from her ears to pool on the floor. A river of it gliding its way to the nearest paper it could find, whether it was tissue or newspaper or sheaves of parchment. And once it found what it needed, the thoughts would begin to stain the pages, one letter at a time, until the letters became words, and the words formed a memory.

One after another, until her whole life was recounted as her last breath left her body.

But an hour later, I closed that heavy tome too, grimacing at the feeling of the furred cover. Downy white tufts drifted up into the silent air like dandelion seeds, making me sneeze.

Frustration turned into a battering ram against my ribs as I sat back, wrapping my woolly blue cardigan around me. Over the last four hours, I'd gone through at least two dozen compendiums, archived Hollower journals, appendices, Immortalities, and other ancient references. And turned up precisely nothing.

The sorceresses had their powers, the Cunningfolk their Talents, but I had always had my memory. Once I saw something, or read something, I never forgot it. I had read nearly every tome in the guild's library at least once, and once was all I usually needed to commit a book to memory.

Usually. I had seen that phrase—*the Servant's Prize*—somewhere, and it was both startling and infuriating to have to search for it again. Even Librarian couldn't locate it within his vast stores of obscure knowledge.

I flipped my phone over to glance at the screen. No messages. No response at all to any of the hundred calls or texts I'd sent to Cabell to check on him.

The Servant's Prize . . . The Servant's Prize . . .

A "prize" could be anything—something won, or merely an object granted as a token or reward. A weapon, a garment, a piece of jewelry, an object of power, even a lock of hair.

"Botheration," I muttered.

I rubbed at my dry eyes and drew in a long, steadying breath. The sweet, musky smell of old books and leather filled my lungs, smoothing the sharper edges of my frustration. The stained-glass window behind me exhaled in turn, letting cold tendrils of autumn air slip around me to toy with the candles on the long, ink-stained worktable.

I liked our guild's library better than anywhere else in the world. The consistency of it, the thousands of escapes each book provided, the unfailing presence of Librarian clomping through his day's work. It was a star that was visible in every season, undimmed by clouds and distance, and the one promise in my life that had been kept.

A library was a home to those who dreamt of better places, and this one was no exception.

I rolled my thermos of instant coffee against the table, letting my thoughts drift.

At the sound, a few of the library cats poked their heads out from the gaps between the books. Others napped in puddles of candlelight, tails swishing as they dreamed. More hunted along the baseboards for hidden curses and tasty little mice.

The working cats were as much a part of the library as the books. The building, once a sorceress's vault, had been riddled with hidden curses even before the guild members started bringing in sealed Immortalities and spellbound relics. Generations of cats had roamed its halls in the years since, and their preternatural ability to suss out the presence of subtle magic had frequently been the last line of defense between Hollowers and certain, hideous death.

At a faint *squeak-squeak,* I glanced over to the bookshelves near the fireplace, only to find one of the cats, Pumpkin, batting at the rolling ladder, moving it out of the way to rub herself against a familiar ridge of leather book spines.

While the upper shelves, tucked just beneath the ceiling, were a graveyard of damaged or outdated books, the bottom ones were reserved for the works that formed the foundation of what Hollowers did: the collections of folklore, fairy tales, and myths.

Even Nash, that paragon of neglectful guardianship, had made it a point to teach Cabell and me about them—how to categorize the tales and, more importantly, how to use them to gauge if a relic might be real.

Maybe I'd been thinking about this all wrong. I'd assumed there might be another, more common name for the prize, but I hadn't even thought to wonder about the "Servant" it belonged to.

I glanced at the stack of encyclopedias, journals, and Immortalities beside me, then back at the shelf.

I made my way over to the shelf, aware of the eyes tracking me.

I pulled out a random selection of tales—German, Russian, Norwegian—in addition to the ones I knew I'd really need, then returned to my table. Almost immediately, Pumpkin leapt up onto the stack, meowing in irritation at being ignored.

"Shoo, you adorable menace," I said, pushing her off the books to thumb through the collection of German tales. The Grimm Brothers never let me down.

With a cry born from the depths of hell, Pumpkin streaked across the table, pouncing on the books with enough force to send them shooting across the table and onto the floor.

"You incorrigible beast," I whispered. "And after all the treats I've snuck you!"

Pumpkin only curled up on a book of Japanese legends, licking her paw in satisfaction. I glared at her, then leaned over my chair to retrieve the scattered volumes. Most were fine, but the back cover of *Legends of the Moors* now bore a fresh scar courtesy of an unhinged cat, and *Tales of Camelot* had landed facedown.

I winced as I picked it up. The pages, delicate as dried bones, were bent at tortured angles or partially ripped at their edges.

I smoothed the deep wrinkles in the pages, my fingers easing over a wood-block print of a woman in an elegant gown, her long hair flowing around her shoulders like streams of sunlight. A knight crouched before her, one hand extended. Beneath it, in minuscule font, was the caption:

The Lady of the Lake, known as La Dame du Lac in French manuscripts, bestows the favor of a magical ring upon Lancelot in Avalon.

Someone, with a dark stroke of ink, had added an apostrophe between the *L* and *a* of *Lancelot. L'ancelot.* One small mark that revealed the origin of the name and whispered its meaning.

I knew so little French, but it was just enough for a hunch. I pulled out my phone, schooling my expression to stay as even as possible, and searched to confirm my suspicion.

Ancelot. *Servant.* L'ancelot. *The servant.*

My lips compressed with the effort it took not to react. This was a story I knew. It had been one of the last Nash had told us before he left in the night and never returned.

The High Priestess of that age had fostered Lancelot as a child and raised him in Avalon. When he was old enough to face the dangers of King Arthur's court, she had given him a ring on behalf of her goddess, known as the Ring of Dispel, or the Dispelling Ring.

It was a relic capable of breaking any curse or enchantment, but the catch—and there was always a catch—was that to wield the ring, you had to claim it by deadly force.

In other words, kill the current owner, and spend the rest of your life anticipating the same fate.

Damn him, I thought, pinching the bridge of my nose.

I'd brought up the Ring of Dispel as a potential cure for Cabell's curse years ago, but Nash, treasure-obsessed Nash, had insisted that it had been destroyed before Avalon was separated from our world.

But if Emrys Dye was searching for Lancelot's ring on behalf of Madrigal, not only had it not been destroyed, Madrigal believed it could be found.

Which meant *I* had a chance—a real chance—to break Cabell's curse and end this.

There were numerous references to the ring in the Immortalities of the sorceresses who had come from the Otherland, but only one within the last hundred years. The Sorceress Rowenna's Immortality.

I forced myself to pretend to finish the German fairy tales, then flip through the Russian lore. All the while, my mind was working, combing through my memories of Rowenna's Immortality until I could bring a picture of the relevant page to mind.

> *How I wish I had not lost the Ring of Dispel to that horrid*
> *cow Myfanwy. Now I've nothing left of Avalon . . .*

The library, unfortunately, didn't have Myfanwy's Immortality, but there was a chance—one as good as any—that the Dyes had it in the private collection they kept in the library's basement.

But first, I needed to confirm something else.

I opened to a random page in *Legends of the Moors* and counted down from a hundred before flipping wildly to another page and letting out a false gasp of surprise. Then, collecting my things in a hurry, I left the books on the table and rushed toward the atrium, calling out "Good night, Librarian!" before pretending to open and shut the All Ways door.

There was another door, this one hidden, in the paneling just to the right of it. I pushed on an inconspicuous piece of molding, and it opened, revealing the stairs to the loft. I climbed slowly, avoiding the steps that I knew creaked. The dusty attic space, crammed with various crates of supplies, greeted me. I didn't bother turning on the light or glancing at our old sleeping bags rolled up in the corner. I lay down on the floor and peered through the crack in the floorboards, my heart hammering.

Septimus and his cronies were just out of my line of sight, but I could hear them clearly as they made their way over to my worktable to pick up *Legends of the Moors*.

"—how do we even know for certain that she's searching for it?" Hector asked in a hushed tone.

I drew in a sharp breath, trying to hear over the sudden rush of blood in my ears.

"They take work from even the weakest of the sorceress scum, and if the Council wants it, so do the rest of them," Septimus hissed back. "The reward would be too great for them to pass up."

Rat scat, I thought.

None of this could be a coincidence. They had to be talking about the Ring of Dispel.

It was bad enough that Emrys wasn't the only other Hollower searching for the ring; now it sounded like the entire Council of Sistren was involved—and they had a head start. The thought left a bitter taste on my tongue.

"Maybe we should have just grabbed her and been done with it," Phineas said. "I don't want to be trudging over all the moors of England looking for his rotting corpse. What if one of them finds it before us? We'll never get it out of the Council's claws, and then it'll be Endymion's wrath we have to worry about—"

"Be quiet, you old fool," Septimus snapped, closing the heavy book and storming toward the All Ways door. "Enough of this. We can't lose another hour."

My pulse rose to match the quick clip of his steps. Horror was slow to come, but no less poisonous, as his last words echoed over the polished stone floors beneath me.

I rolled onto my back, my thoughts whipping up into a furious storm of worry and fear. As I lay there in the dark silence, Septimus's earlier words pierced through the chaos in my mind.

Where was it that he left you and your brother again?

I pushed myself up off the floor, feeling as though I were moving through cold, dark water as I made my way back downstairs. I passed beneath the library's marble archway, and the message carved into it:

THOSE WHO STEAL THE TREASURES WITHIN
WILL DIE FORGOTTEN BY PEN, FRIEND, AND KIN

The founding members of the guild had traded services with a sorceress to cast the curse, and its sigils, carved into the wall, were behind a pane of glass above Librarian's desk to keep the cats from trying to maul it. They still gathered in front of it every day, hissing. Waiting for one of us stupid humans to remove the long-festering dark magic.

But no one ever would. It was the only insurance policy the guild had that the donated relics and books wouldn't be taken from the building, even by the Hollowers who had originally brought them in. Bad enough to have your library key rescinded and lose access to its temple of information. Being cursed into obscurity, stripped of all bragging rights, had proven a bridge too far for most Hollowers, who lived and died by their reputations.

"Librarian?" I called.

Heavy steps pounded across the floor as Librarian emerged from the back office, random bits of paper and packing tape stuck to his metal frame. I warmed at the sight of him and the familiar soft whirring of his inner mechanics.

The automaton moved as if he had been crafted yesterday, not thousands of years ago in the workshop of Daedalus—or Hephaestus himself, depending on which legend you wanted to believe. To most, he must have looked like a strange android, or a bronze statue that had suddenly come to life and stepped off its pedestal.

The strange, ancient quicksilver that gave life to him flowed through the gaps in his metallic joints and around his eyes. His metal, unmoving expression used to unnerve me as a kid, but now I found its dependability comforting.

"Yes, young Lark?" he chirped in ancient Greek.

In his past life, when the library had still been a sorceress's vault, the automaton had guarded the treasure inside, though he was the most prized relic of her collection. The guild had successfully managed to retrain him to serve as both the caretaker of the library and the impartial enforcer of its rules. But while you could show an automaton how to vacuum, you apparently couldn't teach him a modern language.

Cabell, ever the wonder, had picked up the three ancient languages we used most often in our line of work almost instantly when we were twelve, which had been beyond frustrating. Even with a photographic memory, it had taken me months to memorize ancient Greek, Latin, and Old Welsh, and I was still bad at speaking them.

"Do you know if the Dyes have the Sorceress Myfanwy's Immortality?" I heard myself ask. "Downstairs, maybe?"

"No," Librarian said. "They do not."

I started to turn back toward my worktable, only for Librarian's strange voice to bring me up short. "They do not, for it was ruined a day past. Young Dye asked me to dispose of it."

"Ruined," I repeated through gritted teeth.

"Yes, by a leak," Librarian said, clearly repeating the lie Emrys had told him. "A tragedy."

Librarian had no idea how true his words were. Emrys had taken the sorceress's memories about the Ring of Dispel for himself and ensured the rest of us would never see them.

But that only proved to me that the Servant's Prize and the Ring of Dispel were one and the same. There was something else to this. A suspicion that buzzed in my skull like a hornet.

I sat down at my table again. My skin was icy as the windows behind me as I pulled out Nash's journal and flipped to the last entry.

The coded message was surrounded by dozens of the words Cabell and I had tried to unlock its secrets. Taking a piece of scrap paper, I added another to that list. *Lancelot.* And another. *Dispel.* And another. *Ring.*

I drew in a deep breath and tried one last word. *Myfanwy.*

The name of an obscure sorceress we'd never had business with, who had done almost nothing remarkable with her magic, who had been destined to become little more than a footnote in someone else's story.

Using *Myfanwy* as the key, I rearranged the letters of the alphabet and started substituting them for the ones he had written. A word emerged. Then a sentence. Until, finally, the answer to the shadowy question that had haunted us for nearly seven years took sudden shape. A ghost of the past materialized in front of my eyes.

It wasn't a message, or a memory, but a note to himself.

Must go alone and remove weapons before approaching— sorceress wants proof it's Arthur's dagger before trade— how? Tintagel, quarter till midnight. Use phrase I have your gift to identify self.

A strange calm washed over me.

Tintagel.

The place where we'd camped after weeks of searching for Arthur's dagger Carnwennan.

The place where Cabell and I had gone to sleep inside our tent, only to wake to find our guardian gone.

The place where Nash had met a sorceress under the dark cloak of night to trade the dagger for the Ring of Dispel.

6

After bandaging his wounds the best I could, I had left Cabell to rest in his bedroom before heading to the library. As I came barreling out of the linen closet, riding high on my discovery, I was brought up short by the sight of his open bedroom door and empty bed.

"Cab?" I called. He'd cleaned up the wreckage of our fight. The sharp, lemony scent of stain remover rose around me, the chemicals hard at work soaking up blood from the rugs.

"Here" was the quiet response.

I moved down the short hall into the dark living room, then turned toward the kitchenette, only to realize the shadow on the couch was my brother. I switched on the overhead lights, my lungs tightening as I wondered how long he'd been sitting there alone.

Cabell winced against the sudden flood of brightness. An open bottle of beer sat in front of him on the coffee table, still full. He looked down at his crossed arms, eyes unfocused on the curse sigils tattooed there. Aside from some cuts and bruises, he looked whole. Just not completely himself.

I sat down on the floor on the other side of the coffee table. Without thinking, I pushed the sleeves of my shirt up as I leaned against it.

"Did I do that?"

Cabell still wasn't looking at me. The words were as hoarse as if he'd had to scrape them out of his throat.

I didn't like lying to my brother, so, instead, I asked, "What do you remember?"

There was no light in his eyes—there was nothing at all. His shoulders slouched. "Enough."

"Can I get some elaboration on that?" I asked, keeping the words light.

"All of it. Every last second. Is that what you want to hear?" His nails were darker and longer than they usually were, and there was still a thick patch of hair on the back of his hand. I stared, blood surging in my ears.

Impossible, I thought. The lingering effects of the curse had never held on to him this long.

"Sorry," he said after a moment. "I'm angry at myself, not you."

Something dark was brewing in his expression, like storm clouds gathering. The air seemed to shift around us, churning with the force of his thoughts. I was afraid to move, to breathe, and unleash that first lash of rain.

"It wasn't your fault," I said. "You have to know that."

"Why couldn't I stop it this time?" he asked. "What happens if there's a next time, and I can't shift back at all? What if next time—" The words caught in his throat. "What if next time, I kill you? Do you think I could live with myself after that?"

"There doesn't have to be a next time," I told him. "That's what I want to talk to you about."

Cabell made a noise at the back of his throat but said nothing.

"There may be a way to find the Ring of Dispel after all," I whispered.

"So?"

For a moment, I couldn't even speak.

"*So?*" I repeated. "Did you hear what I just said?"

"Sure did," he said coolly.

"It's not just that," I said. "Madrigal hired Trust Fund to find it, and I found out tonight that other sorceresses are looking for it, too. And so are Septimus Yarrow and his goons. I finally cracked the last journal entry, Cab. Nash was trading Arthur's dagger for it the night he disappeared. That's why he brought us to Tintagel."

A cold drip moved down my spine at his unwavering expression. The lack of surprise. The lack of anything at all. A darkness so bleak, no light could escape it.

"Yeah," he said. "I know."

The apartment receded around me. The din from the street outside was swallowed by the thunderous beat in my chest, the pulse pounding inside my skull.

Then, all at once, the moment crashed down over me in a wave of pressure and horror that was as suffocating as it was painful.

"You knew?" I demanded. "All this time?"

"He told me that night after you fell asleep," Cabell said.

My lips parted, but no sound emerged.

"He made me promise not to tell you," Cabell continued, lifting one shoulder in a shrug.

I knew Nash had been telling Cabell things—teaching him, in a way he'd never teach mortal me—but that had been *Nash,* not Cabell. We'd been left twice: by our birth families and then by Nash. We'd only ever had each other, and to survive on our own, there couldn't be secrets between us. I'd understood that, and I thought Cabell had, too.

"He was meeting a sorceress," I explained. "She survived the encounter and went on to die and create an Immortality that Trust Fund destroyed. But I think if we go back to Tintagel, we might find something we missed before. Nash might have hidden something there for us to find."

"Stop," Cabell said sharply. "Just . . . stop. Do you even hear yourself? *Think* about it, Tamsin. It's obvious what happened. The sorceress

70

took the dagger, and then she killed him. That's why he didn't come back. The only question left is what she did with his body. I didn't tell you because I didn't want you to have to live with knowing we could have saved him—like I have all these years."

He was right. That was the most obvious and logical conclusion to draw. But I wasn't about to let logic beat me in a fight.

"That's not a reason to not tell me," I said. "And that's not the only explanation. Nash could have been cursed to lose his memory or be trapped somewhere. If there's even a chance he's alive, we have to find him and the ring first, or someone else will finish him off to get it."

"He's dead," Cabell said. "Let me say that again: He. Is. Dead."

The words smothered that tiny flame of hope I'd kept burning.

"So he's dead. It doesn't mean the Ring of Dispel isn't out there. We can try to retrace his steps, figure out who killed the sorceress." Cabell was shaking his head, and the sight made my throat tighten and my voice rise with desperation. "We could find the ring and barter with Madrigal to have her use it on you."

"Barter with a sorceress?" Cabell scoffed. "Grow up, Tamsin. This isn't a fairy tale. There are no joyful family reunions, magical saviors, or happily-ever-afters. There's just *this*."

He gestured to the thatch of hair on the back of his hand. I stared at him, and as the moments passed in silence, the pit of my stomach began to hollow and twist.

Eventually, he let out a humorless laugh. "You don't get it. I don't even have the choice to give up. It's obvious where this is going. It's been obvious for years, but you've been too stubborn to accept it."

"It's not obvious!" I said. "I know it's hard to believe in the possibility, but this is the best lead we've had."

"You don't know a damn thing," Cabell spat. "Tell me, what's so great about this life that I have to fight to stay in it, Tamsin?"

I drew in a sharp breath, struggling to keep my blood from heating to a boil.

"If you've known about the ring all this time . . . if you've felt this way for years . . . why let me research ways to break the curse?" I demanded. "Why let me test out theory after theory on you?"

"I never understood why you kept rereading all those books when your memory is perfect." He shrugged, and it was the most heartless thing I'd ever seen my brother do. "But it kept you busy, and it seemed to make you feel better."

"Me?" I said, drawing back.

"You know what your problem is?" Cabell said, seeming to relish my discomfort as he took a long sip of his beer. "You think you can control everything and that'll keep bad things from happening, but the world doesn't work that way, Tamsin. You're just as powerless as the rest of us. Actually, you're even more powerless, which makes it even sadder."

"So just to clarify, you don't care if I go after Nash and the ring?" I said. "You don't care that Hollowers and sorceresses are going to be looking for us in order to find him? You want no part of it, and it doesn't matter to you at all?"

"It doesn't," Cabell said, pushing up to his feet and moving toward the front door, "because I doubt you'll make it far, given that you don't have the One Vision. But go ahead and try. See how far you get with Ignatius. You live your life however the hell you want to, and it's high time I start doing the same."

"Stop it," I said, barely getting the words out. "You sound just like—"

"Like who?" Cabell snapped, sliding on his boots. "Like *Nash*?"

I flinched.

"At least he went out doing what he wanted," Cabell said, reaching for the leather jacket he'd inherited from our guardian. "And if I haven't got much time left until the curse takes me, that's exactly what I'm going to do, too. I'm done wasting time and I'm done pretending any of it matters just because you're scared to death of being alone."

I bit my tongue until I tasted blood.

"You really are just like him," I said, standing. If he was going to hurt me, I could hurt him right back. "You throw up your hands the second it gets hard."

"And yet you're the one chasing after him," Cabell shot back. "Pretending like you're doing it for me. For the *ring*."

I froze.

"Of course this has *nothing* to do with you wanting to find him," Cabell continued. "It has *nothing* to do with us staying in Boston, even though he claimed that's where they left you. What were you expecting? That one of your deadbeat parents would see you out on the street? Recognize you? Regret ever dumping you off like—"

A searing heat sliced through my chest.

"Do not," I warned him, "finish that sentence."

Cabell gripped the doorknob but didn't move.

"*You* are my only family," I told him. "I'm going after the ring as soon as the Sorceress Grinda sends someone to pick up the locket we recovered for her. She said it would be tonight."

Cabell didn't even acknowledge that I'd spoken.

"There are too many people after the ring to wait—and too many people who suspect Nash was the last to have it," I said. "If you won't help me, at least pack a bag and try to disappear until this is all over."

"I'll do you one better and not come back at all." He opened the door and stepped out. Either his voice was a whisper, or I imagined his last words as he brushed past: "Love you."

"Don't die," I told him anyway.

The door slammed shut.

My knees felt like they were made of sand. I sat heavily on the edge of the wooden coffee table and finished off the last of his beer.

I knew he was in pain; I saw the flickers of it every day like light catching a prism. He'd been a touch more reckless than usual, but I'd assumed it was fueled by his frustration and his impatience to find a solution.

It never occurred to me he'd try to destroy himself before the curse ever could.

I should have stopped him from going out. Made him stay and talk it through with me. It was never a good idea to wander the streets this time of night, even with a small knife on your keychain and salt in your pockets.

Grow up, Tamsin. This isn't a fairy tale.

Fairy tales—the original stories, as opposed to the rosy retellings—were all thorns and misery, and a truer mirror to humanity than anyone wanted to believe. But for Cabell to act like I was a child caught up in daydreams was almost more than I could take.

The problem with siblings, I decided, was that they spent years gathering up all these little daggers of observation and learning exactly where to slip them between your bones.

And anyway, Cabell was the one who had wanted to search for Nash long after it became clear that Nash had discarded us like the last sip of cold coffee. *He* was the one who had clung to the idea that Nash was still out there, trying to make his way back to us. *He* was the one who had cried about it every night those first few months, when we were sick with hunger and exhaustion and were sleeping rough in the winter woods.

At Tintagel, there'd been no evidence of a fight, no evidence of any curses being cast, not even tracks that might have indicated Nash had drunkenly staggered over the edge of the cliff bordering the ruins of the castle. The cold sea never returned his body to the rocky shores. The only footsteps we found in the mud and snow had led to the castle, and there weren't any leading away.

But if he was alive, why hadn't he come back? Why hadn't he used the ring to break Cabell's curse?

I shut my eyes, giving my head a hard shake. It didn't matter whether Nash was alive without the ring or dead and buried with it. I just needed his last known whereabouts to pick up the ring's trail before the others did.

But to do that, I was going to need a few things. Including, I thought with a scowl, the One Vision, as Cabell had oh-so-gently pointed out.

And there was only one way to get what I needed . . .

A calm settled over me as I mentally sketched out the beginnings of a plan. As each step came into focus, my body began to feel solid again, and the world seemed to steady around me.

Stooping, I gathered up the explosion of mail on the floor I'd previously ignored.

I unrolled the newspaper, glancing at the front-page headlines. Surging gas prices. The upcoming World Series. A freak ice storm in Britain.

The last one caught my eye enough to make me skim the first few paragraphs:

> Overnight, roads across Great Britain iced over despite a lack of snow and a week of record-breaking high temperatures . . .

I brought everything into the kitchen—and dropped it all onto the counter with a horrified gasp.

"Florence, no!"

I scooped up my little potted succulent from her place on the windowsill. At the movement, she dramatically dropped her sickly brown leaves, leaving only a bare stem.

"What happened?" I asked. "You were fine the other day—was it too much water? The heat? Winston is hanging in there, so what happened to you?"

Winston was the aloe plant that had been left for dead in my neighbor's trash can along with Florence.

A slight movement caught my eye. I glanced up through the window in front of me, only to be met with the sight of an enormous toad staring right back.

I startled. "God's teeth—"

The toad didn't blink. Instead, it let out a loud, irritated croak. And then, when I didn't move, another.

I leaned over the sink and opened the window. The toad had nestled down into the window box I used to grow herbs, including a bit of rosemary to keep any wandering spirits with bad intent from slipping in.

"You're crushing my mint," I complained.

The toad jumped up onto the windowsill, revealing the small bit of black ribbon attached to its leg. The mark of the Sorceress Grinda—crossed keys—was embossed in silver.

Finally, I thought.

We'd finished her job weeks ago, but she hadn't wanted me to deliver it to her home somewhere in Italy, as she was away "dealing with grave matters related to the Council of Sistren."

I'd assumed she simply didn't want a mortal, let alone a Hollower, to know the location of her main residence. Most sorceresses didn't. Though others, like Madrigal, were simply too powerful to fear anyone.

"I have it," I told the creature. "Give me a second."

I dashed into the office alcove, slowing as I approached the card table I used as a desk.

Where my half of the alcove was a chaotic storm of papers, bolts of fabric, magazines, books, and various broken tools I couldn't bring myself to get rid of, Cabell's was as neat as a pin. Most of his crystals were carefully organized in clear acrylic containers, with others left on the nearby windowsill to charge in the light of the next full moon.

I retrieved the ruby-encrusted locket from the safe beneath the desk, unwrapping the silk to ensure all was present and accounted for. Its stones glowed in greeting, and I quickly covered it again before it could inflict whatever infernal curse it no doubt possessed.

"Got it," I told the toad, only to hesitate, unsure of where to put the locket.

It dutifully opened its mouth, but I held the locket just out of reach above its warty head.

"Payment is due upon receipt," I said, "and we can only accept cash or the equivalent in gold or gemstones—"

The toad croaked and made a retching noise. One, two, three chips of sapphires dropped into the planter's dirt, coated with a thick layer of mucus. The toad's mouth stayed open, the bubbled membrane of its vocal sac extended as it let out an impatient croak.

I leaned over the sink, carefully, gently, placing the locket inside its waiting mouth. "Don't choke on it."

The companion turned and leapt back into the night.

"Yeah, a pleasure doing business with you, too," I muttered, digging out the sapphire chips and washing them under the faucet's sputtering stream. I didn't shut the window, needing the cool air.

The quiet of the house wrapped around me again, interrupted only by the sudden blare of a neighbor's TV bleeding through the wall.

I poured myself a glass of water, futilely tipping some of it into Florence's pot. The sight of the plant tore at me in a way I hated. It looked . . . finished.

My brother's words drifted through my mind, slipping into the quiet of the kitchen with the chilled autumn breeze.

What's so great about this life that I have to fight to stay in it?

I pressed the edge of the glass to my lips, my gaze sliding back over to the door. If that was what Cabell wanted, to let go, then . . . did I have any right to interfere?

"Yes," I whispered.

Before I realized what I was doing, I dug my tarot deck out of my bag and slid the cards free of their velvet pouch. I didn't shuffle them, I only set them down beside Florence and turned the top card over.

On it, a woman in a white dress sat blindfolded, holding two crossed swords in front of her. Behind her, a rocky sea. Above her, a crescent moon. A portrait of balance. Careful deliberation. Advice. Two of Swords.

Weigh the options. Take your time. Listen to your intuition.

"What the hell am I doing?" I dropped the card.

There was a rattle in the bushes outside the window—a blur of movement and color that shook the leaves as it streaked by. I pushed up onto the counter, leaning partly out of the window to see what—or who—it had been. There was nothing but a few footprints that could have come from anyone, at any time. It had probably been nothing more than a feral cat.

Still, I shut the window firmly and locked it.

My gaze fell back to the tarot card.

If I couldn't force my brother to fight this . . . to *want* to live . . . I could at least give him a real choice.

I gathered what I thought I'd need for traveling, putting the sapphires in an envelope for Cabell and leaving them on his desk, then sent him one last text: *Leave the city as soon as you can.*

I switched the cell phone off. No one was going to use it to track me. And with a final look at the apartment, I inserted my library key into the closet door just as the sky lightened with a dawn I wouldn't be there to see.

7

"—and here Richard, the Earl of Cornwall, one of the wealthiest men in all the land, built his dream of a great hall, with a goal to surpass even the legends of what Tintagel had once been. Centuries before, the settlement had seen trade from all over the Mediterranean, and hosted ancient kings, perhaps even serving as the site of their coronation—"

I'd already heard the tour guide give her talk three times now, exuding the same amount of passion earlier, when the skies had been clear, as she did now, when thunderheads loomed on the horizon and bitter winds whipped the sea into a frenzy, warning of worse to come.

A true Cornishwoman, undaunted by the sight of the roiling storm making its slow march to shore, she'd merely planted her feet more firmly upon the ground and started shouting. In the last few minutes, it had grown more and more difficult to hear her above the howling air and the churning crash of the restless sea below.

Wrapping the oversized flannel coat tighter around my body, I turned my gaze back out toward the dark, rough sea one last time, then retreated farther into the craggy ruins of what had once been Tintagel Castle.

A light rain began to patter the slate stones. The steely sky brought an eerie glow to the slick lichen and moss clinging to the crumbling walls. Mist rose from the ground like disturbed spirits, swirling into unknowable patterns around us. A shiver ran along my entire body as it unfurled itself around me, pulling me into its hazy depths.

"You can see how the walls of the great hall had to be reconstructed after earlier iterations fell to the sea—"

Another guide, wearing a yellow slicker, hurried over to the small group, calling out, "Terribly sorry, but that'll be all for today. If the winds pick up even a little more, you'll all be carried off the island."

That garnered a few nervous chuckles and looks from the tourists. It was a typical understatement. Within seconds, the billowing gales were whipping at the foolish lot of us from all sides, and nearly sent an elderly woman soaring into the sea.

"Follow me," the guide shouted, "back to the bridge!"

I had come up to the ruins hours ago, refamiliarizing myself with the place after nearly a decade away. Walking it, breathing in the damp brine of the air, noting the sounds of the waves and birds.

Remembering.

We had come once or twice before that fateful night when Nash left, largely because the man couldn't resist a windswept landscape of legend any more than he could an Arthurian relic.

Convinced that Excalibur had been returned to Avalon before the pathways to the Otherlands were sealed, he'd set his sights on the lesser goal of Arthur's dagger. He'd searched the ruins here before we'd continued to other parts of England.

Finding the dagger had brought me so close to death that I'd learned there was a smell to its presence—a sharpness, like the sky before snow.

Now, being back here . . . there was the strangest sense of unraveling in me, as if something had come unknotted without me realizing it. My stomach had been clenched so tight for the last few hours, I hadn't been able to eat anything.

I fell in line at the rear of the tourist pack as we walked to the modern bridge that stretched between the two sections of the ruins. The narrow land bridge that had made the castle nearly unconquerable to enemies in earlier centuries had long since eroded, meaning you had to take one of two footbridges—the modern, upper one, built with steel and wood and slate, or an ancient wooden one below, where the narrow strip of land had washed away.

I gripped the handrail of the modern bridge and fought across it, keeping my eyes on the woman in the bright yellow slicker to guide the way. The wind hurried me along, pushing at my back until I returned to mercifully solid, if incredibly slippery, ground.

I followed the others down the winding old steps carved into the fiercely rocky ground. The stone's natural color amid the wild grass made the trails look like silver serpents gliding over the rise and fall of the land.

It was as beautiful a place as any for a legend to be born.

According to Geoffrey of Monmouth's *Historia Regum Britanniae*—which Nash referred to as "the racy garbage cult hit of the Middle Ages"—King Arthur had been conceived within the old castle's walls. His father, Uther Pendragon, had lusted after Igraine, a woman married to Gorlois, Duke of Cornwall. In a twist that would have made the equally questionable Zeus weep with pride, Uther had Merlin, the great druid and later great adviser to King Arthur, transform his appearance so he looked like Gorlois, allowing him to enter the castle and lie with another man's wife. And poor Gorlois was left to conveniently die in battle days later.

Geoffrey of Monmouth hadn't written the truth, he'd assembled a mosaic of oral folk stories and shameless fiction, but there *was* a kernel of truth to what he had created, even if that truth was sensationalized almost beyond recognition.

Still, it was easy to see why Tintagel and the nearby village had captured the popular imagination. They were dramatic and untamed, the sort of place you'd meet a sorceress for a trade.

I looked back over my shoulder as the rain picked up with brutal force. The ruins of the castle were silhouetted against the rolling mounds of furious clouds.

Drifting back from the tourists, slowly creating distance as they made their way toward the village, I darted off the main trail and onto the soggy grass, cringing as freezing rainwater soaked through my socks and jeans.

"Where are you . . . ?" I muttered, shielding my eyes. If the knot had come undone—

I found the bedraggled yellow ribbon straining against the thick patch of heather I'd tied it to. My shoulders slumped in relief. I put out a hand, feeling for the string of wood tablets that ringed the camp.

The spell sigils woven into the garland manipulated the air and light to conceal what lay within from mortal eyes.

Unfortunately, that included my eyes.

Not for long, I thought, my heart giving a hard lurch inside my ribs.

The area designated for visitor camping was to the north of where I'd set up my own site. If I was here to figure out where Nash had gone, then I needed to retrace our steps. Nash had liked this little flat piece of earth. It wasn't very sheltered but had a clear view of the ruins.

With an outstretched hand, I shuffled forward until my boots hit the rocks I'd left to mark the entrance. Unsurprisingly, Cabell was usually the one who dealt with this, always guiding us back—

Something sharp twisted in my gut as I turned my back to the onslaught of rain. My face was raw with cold, but I couldn't feel my fingers or toes at all, and I wasn't sure which sensation was worse.

Before I could untie the garland's knot, a different garland unknotted, and a different tent flashed into view.

The thing was a blue monster of nylon and polyester, state-of-the-art and meant for an entire family, not the lone smug teenage boy standing at its entrance.

"Evening, neighbor!" Emrys called over the rain. "Find anything interesting down at the ruins?"

"No," I told him. "This is *my* spot. I was here first."

He cocked his head to the side, giving me a look of false pity. "And how would you propose to prove that? I could have been here the whole time behind my wards and you never would have known. It's a shame you don't have the One Vision."

I snarled, feeling the wind lift the back of my jacket as I tore my tent's stakes out of the ground, gripping the flapping red fabric to keep it from flying away.

"Aw, don't be like that, Bird!" he called after me.

Picking up my unrolled sleeping bag, backpack of supplies, and workbag, I half slipped, half marched farther down the hill. I settled on a new spot behind an outcrop of large boulders that would at least hide me from his view until I could find a better place after the storm.

My boots fought the mud and dead wild grass, struggling for purchase as I labored to get the stakes back into solid ground. Once the tent was up, I threw my drenched belongings inside and tried to scoop out the water pooling in the bottom of the ancient tent with my hands.

I reached back to zip up the door flap, only to stop. A scream built at the base of my throat.

Emrys's tent was right next to mine again, as if he'd somehow folded it up, put it in his pocket, and then taken it back out. This time, he sat in a collapsible chair, a battery- or magic-powered heater at his feet, a steaming bowl of something in his hand.

"Soup?" he offered.

"Go. Away," I growled.

"Not a chance," Emrys said. "You really think I'm going to let you out of my sight? You coming here proves my theory that it was Nash who traded for the ring. He was the one who went after Arthur's dagger—"

I zipped up the tent, shutting out his words.

My tent shook helplessly against the driving wind and rain. Its water-resistant material had long since given up the fight, with peeling patches over its many holes, but it hardly mattered now that everything I owned was waterlogged.

I should have used Madrigal's coins to book a room in the nearby village. I could be comfy and toasty next to a fire, listening to the rain patter against the windows. But I'd left the money for Cabell, in case he needed to rent a room somewhere else until the search was done.

I reached over, putting my cooking pan beneath the worst of the leaks and my tin cup under another.

"Perfect . . ." That would last about five minutes.

I sighed as I pulled off my boots and wet socks and then the sopping flannel jacket. I rubbed my hands over my arms briskly, trying to get my blood moving.

It was no quieter inside the tent than outside, with the baying storm battering the canvas, threatening to pry the stakes from the ground. But something about the smell of wet earth, the drip of water, the clean air . . . familiarity curled around me like a cat, warming me in a way I hadn't expected it to. Still, between Emrys and the memories Tintagel brought back, I was on edge. Nothing seemed to settle the feeling that I had something crawling beneath my skin.

I switched my LED lantern on and unzipped the sleeping bag in an attempt to dry it. I forced myself to gnaw on a few pieces of jerky and stale dried fruit I'd found at the bottom of my traveling backpack.

Chewing, staring up at the peak of the tent, I felt my mind starting to wander. Wondering what Cabell was doing. If he had listened to me and left town.

He didn't want to come, I reminded myself. *You don't need him.*

I set the rest of the jerky aside, my stomach too tight to eat another bite. Rain lashed at the tent, making the fabric jump and shiver. I knew I should find a way to brush my teeth and wash my face, but now that my heavy body was finally still, I couldn't make it move.

Instead, I closed my eyes and drew up a memory I'd fought to bury for years.

That night had been like countless others. I'd smothered the small fire and we'd gone in to eat a bit of soup. I could see Nash as clearly as if he were sitting beside me now: the hardened echo of a face that might have once been handsome, reddened from too much drink and sun; the blond hair and stubble glinting with silver; the misshapen bridge of his nose, which had been broken one too many times. He'd had the eyes of a child, sky blue and sparkling as he wove one tale after another.

Hit the hay, Tamsy, he'd said, looking up from where he was scribbling notes into his journal. *Get some sleep while you can. We're leaving at first light.*

We're leaving. The worst promise he ever broke.

I'd replayed the memory hundreds of times, straining to find some small detail I might have missed.

I opened my eyes, bringing my hands to rest on my stomach, feeling the rise and fall with each breath. Even with the wind outside, the silence coming from within the tent was stifling. I drummed my fingers against each other, trying to ease the sensation of swarming flies beneath my skin.

Loneliness coiled around me. It was the only way to explain what possessed me to reach into my workbag for a familiar lump.

"Oh, all right," I muttered. "This is deeply pathetic of you, Lark."

Ignatius's bleary eye blinked open as I set him beside my sleeping bag and lit his wicks. The air around us shimmered as magic spread with the heat of the tiny flames. The eye rolled between me and the roof of the dripping tent, the skin around it wrinkling with disdain. Knuckles cracking, Ignatius tried to curl his wretched fingers down, either to extinguish the flames or scuttle away like a crab.

"If you even think about escaping," I warned him, "just remember that you only need three fingers to work, and if I catch you, I'll take the middle one first."

Ignatius straightened his fingers but dripped a petulant glob of wax onto the sleeping bag, just to have his say. As it turned out, a staring contest with the hand and eyeball of a psychotic murderer did not, in fact, lessen the hollow feeling in the pit of my stomach, or do anything, really, except make me suddenly afraid he might try to light my hair on fire.

There'd been a second—many seconds, actually—when I'd almost left him behind. Taking him on a stroll around the grounds of Tintagel to look for magic in full view of tourists had been out of the question, and, well, I hadn't wanted to believe I might need him. Not with the arrangements I'd made with the Bonecutter.

It's a shame you don't have the One Vision.

The fact that Emrys could have been there the whole time, watching me, *laughing* at how pathetic my supplies were . . . A fresh wave of anger rushed through me, incinerating that last bit of resistance and fear.

If he wanted a challenge, he was about to get one.

At the bottom of my satchel was the small brown-paper parcel that had been delivered to the library. I'd woken up in the attic and come down to find that Librarian had left it for me at the base of the stairs. The Bonecutter had only needed four hours to track down what I'd asked for.

Inside the rumpled paper was a wooden box, no bigger than a pack of cigarettes. The inner compartment slid out with the slightest urging from my thumb, revealing the vial inside. I unwound the long scrap of parchment wrapped around it, set that aside for a moment, and lifted the bottle. It was made of clear glass, twined with decorative silver whorls like vines. The glass dropper barely touched the thin layer of crimson liquid inside, which shimmered maliciously like an oil slick in Ignatius's revealing light.

Basilisk venom.

I breathed in deeply through my nose, my hands trembling from cold or nerves or both. I'd read about the venom's ability to grant a mortal the One Vision years ago, when I was envious of Cabell's magic. But with the serpents now extinct, their venom was perishingly hard to come by.

More importantly, the venom, like every other so-called solution I'd researched, was worse than the problem itself.

I picked up the handwritten note again, squinting at the elegant swirl of violet ink letters.

Dear Miss Lark,

How splendid to finally have a request that's not for a Vein key. I have procured the venom as requested and feel I must remind you of its dangers. Should you survive the toxin entering your body, the hours that follow will likely be the most unpleasant of your life. I have heard of agonizing pain, fever, and hallucinations from those bitten by a basilisk and therefore must imagine the same will be true for you, as is the possibility of permanent, rather than temporary, blindness. For your purposes as I understand them, place one large drop in each eye.

Proceeding means you recognize I am not liable for your death, altered mind, or any permanent loss of functions, et cetera. As per usual, payment in the form of a favor will be collected at a later date of my choosing. I shall save a special one for you.

As always,
Your humble procurer

More debt, but worth the weight on my soul if it meant saving Cabell.

And as for the venom . . . the pain, fever, hallucinations, and blindness I'd known about, and I wasn't afraid of any of them. Of course, all of that was only if the venom didn't kill me. Not even Nash had been willing to tempt those odds.

There's nothing wrong with the way you are, Tamsy, he'd said when I'd suggested the venom. *If you aren't born with the sight, that's the way of it.*

Clearly there *was* something wrong with me, otherwise he wouldn't have left me behind, time and time again.

"You've never been a coward before," I said, curling my fingers around the vial. "And you're not about to start now."

I picked up Ignatius by his candlestick holder and blew out his wicks, then wrapped him in his length of silk. "Time for bed."

With him safely secured in the bag, its straps double-knotted, I lay back on the sleeping bag again. Just unscrewing the dropper was enough to release a truly evil smell into the air.

Thinking twice, I reached for my traveling pack's thick leather strap. I bit down on it as I brought the dropper above my right eye.

A single bead of crimson liquid clung to the end of it, shivering as my hand shook.

Then it fell.

I groaned around the strap, my free hand clawing at my sleeping bag as my body twisted and curled, absorbing the agonizing burn of the venom.

I couldn't do a drop in the other eye—I couldn't do it—

You have to, you have to, you have to, my mind chanted. *For Cabell.*

I lifted the vial again, pulling the last bead of venom into the dropper. Willpower and courage weren't enough. I had to hold my left eye open to keep my body from instinctively blinking the poison away.

My legs kicked up and my teeth tore down into the strap, breaking it. The poison worked through my mind, darkening the roots of my thoughts before setting it all on fire.

The air went black around me. I clawed at my face, biting the inside of my mouth to keep from moaning.

Can't see, I thought desperately, even as a voice, calm and low, whispered, *It's a side effect. It'll pass.*

Did I say that out loud? Was someone in my tent?

My blood rose to a boil in my veins, drawing up things I didn't want to see but couldn't forget. Other fires. Places near and far and nowhere now. Faces long gone.

Faces of the dead.

Nash's voice rolled through my mind, unbidden.

Come on now, Tamsy, it's not so bad.

There was something there in memory, surfacing. Golden light. Sand. Then it was gone, chased by the shadowy monsters gathering outside my tent. I tried to drag myself away as the entrance to the tent fluttered, unzipping slowly. Eyes flashed gold in the dark, burning with hunger, only to burst in showers of sparks.

My breath came as quick as my thundering heartbeat, and I couldn't get enough oxygen, couldn't cool the fire in my chest. Sweat poured down my face, stinging my dry lips. Once I started vomiting, I couldn't stop, even as my stomach knotted with agony. I clawed at my eyelids, desperate to remove the burning glass shards slicing into my eyes and hollow the sockets. Heat billowed within me, until I was sure my skin would blister from the inside.

There was no sleep, there was no waking, there was only this. Hours passed in seconds, seconds like hours. The visions came in a dark prism, each making less sense than the last. Vaults. Curse sigils. A sword cutting through bone. A hound running across the sky. A hooded figure walking into unknowable depths of black water.

But they slowed, the torrent of images merging into one. I saw myself at the ocean's edge, two swords crossed against my shoulders, a growing stain of crimson at the hem of my white gown as the tide tore at it again and again.

"*Bird?*"

I turned my head toward the shadow at the entrance to my tent. Its shape quivered as it moved into the pool of a single lantern's light. Something heavy and freezing cold pressed against my forehead, and I squirmed away.

"What in hellfire did you take?" There was a sound like rummaging, and he swore again.

Thief, I thought. He was a thief. No—not real. A hallucination like the rest of them. A memory of something that would never happen.

The heat inside me was suffocating, moving through my muscles like a razor. I twisted, trying to release it.

"Stop—*stop*—"

The shadow disappeared again, ushering in cold air, only to appear once more. I struggled against the feeling of hands on my shoulders, of being held in place.

"No," I begged. "Please . . ."

"It's all right, you're okay—"

A lie. A lie . . . the darkness came again, pure and all-consuming. The next thing I knew, I was flat on my back, stretched out over something soft and cushioned. The air had taken on a sweet, green smell, and my skin felt cooler than it had in hours. A light, damp pressure covered my eyes.

Nothing hurt; my head felt heavy as I breathed in the faint smell of mint, but my body only relaxed against the ground, like a seed trying to find a way to slip down into the darkness beneath the surface.

Emrys?

I must have said his name aloud, because he responded. "Here."

Darkness swam in my vision again, and I couldn't tell if my eyes were open or closed. The only thing I knew for certain was that voice.

"I'm here."

8

When I woke again, I was facedown on my sleeping bag, my body as heavy as stone.

I drew in a sharp breath. My head pounded, feeling like it might spin up and off my neck. I propped myself up onto my elbows, closing my eyes until the wave of nausea passed.

Alive, I thought.

Mint, beeswax, and another scent I couldn't identify—incense?—drifted around me. I rubbed grit from my eyes, only to jolt when my mind caught up and I realized I could see again.

Did it work? The thought was searing.

I held my hands in front of my face, turning them over and back again. There was a smear of something on the back of my left hand—an ointment, speckled with flecks of fragrant green leaves. It was on my chest and face, too, cool to the touch and soothing with its mint scent. The bites on my arm were slathered in a different ointment and had been rebandaged. I lifted the coarse fabric to find the wounds nearly healed.

I reached for the canteen beside the sleeping pad, desperate to clear the disgusting taste from my mouth. Empty.

Finally, I remembered.

I rose, first to my knees, and then my feet, and when the world stopped spinning, I stumbled out of the tent into the lavender sky of early morning. I caught a hint of coffee somewhere nearby, but it was the cold bite of the clean, damp air that cleared my mind.

Emrys sat with his back to me, nurturing a small campfire within the ring of our combined ward garlands, combining our two camps into one. He lifted a kettle from the flames and stirred its contents once more before pouring the dark liquid into two tin mugs.

He turned, holding one out to me. "Helped myself to the coffee packets in your bag. Thought you wouldn't mind."

My entire body felt exhausted, as if I'd been awake for weeks, but that didn't dull my outrage. "Well, I do mind. I didn't bring that many!"

He still held the mug out, waiting. "All the more reason to drink this so it doesn't go to waste."

I trudged forward, sitting on the damp ground with a noise of irritation. After passing the mug to me, Emrys picked up his own. He blew on the steam rising from it, then took a deep sip.

"Holy *gods*," he said, coughing and pounding on his chest. "Did you harvest this from the pits of hell?"

"If you hate it so much, give it back." I tried to pull the mug out of his hand, but he held it up and away.

"It's like Lucifer himself shit in the cup," he said, giving said cup an accusatory look.

"Hilarious," I said, reaching for it again, "but I won't let you waste it."

"No, no," he said with a martyred expression. "I can suffer a bit of poison in the name of caffeine."

He took another big gulp and gagged.

"Feel better now?" I asked.

"Better? No. Radioactive? Yes." Emrys gave me a look of deep disbelief. "Do you . . . actually *enjoy* drinking that?"

"Yes," I said. "Though I take it black, without a spoonful of whining."

"It's not whining," he said. "I'm genuinely wondering how you still have internal organs at this point."

I rolled my eyes as he took another sip and shuddered.

"Sorry it isn't up to your usual standards," I groused. "Not all of us have a personal barista at our beck and call."

"Not all of us would be stupid enough to try basilisk venom to induce the One Vision," he shot back. "So you at least have me there."

My jaw set. "I'm alive, aren't I?"

"Barely," he said. "You're welcome, by the way. I used all of my cooling salve, and I don't have the herbs to make more."

My mouth dropped open.

After *years* of tormenting me with innuendos and clues and forcing me to chase rumors . . . he had revealed his ability, the one granted to him through a long line of Cunningfolk ancestors.

Emrys was a Greenworker.

"Ah, she finally figures it out," Emrys said.

I let out a sardonic laugh. "Your dear papa must have been *so* disappointed his only son turned out to be a flower whisperer. No wonder you both kept it secret from the guild."

Having the ability to commune with and nurture plants wasn't exactly useful in our line of work, at least when compared to some of the other magic gifts out there.

His expression hardened. "That's one ability more than you have."

If I'd had anything other than instant coffee in my mug, I would have thrown it at him. "Oooh, someone has some petal-soft feelings about it, huh? Noted."

"You have a funny way of showing gratitude, Bird," Emrys said. "Drink this before you pass out, please. You're extremely dehydrated."

I took the water bottle as resentfully as I could.

"I'm not going to say thank you," I told him between sips. "I didn't need your help, and I didn't give you permission to come in my tent."

"Forgive me for being concerned when I heard you screaming," Emrys said. "You had a hundred-and-seven-degree fever. Your brain was on the verge of boiling itself and would have without my help. It's called empathy—you should try it sometime."

I bit the inside of my mouth to keep from snarling at him again when he was only trying to get a rise out of me. Instead, I studied him out of the corner of my eye, my bitterness gaining a new edge when I saw his top-of-the-line gear, including a collapsible axe.

Emrys wore an expensive-looking navy turtleneck sweater, loose slacks, a baseball cap, and polished leather hiking boots. Maybe because of the chill, he'd already pulled on his thick Hollower gloves—made of the finest dragonscale and passed down through generations, no doubt. They were meant for repelling light curses, not hiking.

"I was fine," I said after a while, stupidly self-conscious of how bad I must look—still wet, and now covered in dirt and ointment.

"Did it even work?" he asked, exasperated. At my uncertain expression, he added, "There aren't little greenlings or other Fair Folk around to test it on. Step outside the curse wards. You should be able to see everything inside them now."

Botheration. I should have thought of that.

I rose stiffly, clutching my mug of instant coffee for moral support.

"Turn around," I told Emrys.

"What? No."

"Turn around," I ordered. "Or shut your eyes."

"Gods, you are so annoying," he muttered, but did cover his eyes with one hand. "There. Happy? Or are you incapable of feeling any emotion besides spite?"

"Spite *and* irritation," I corrected him.

It felt wrong to do it in front of him—something this important, something that could prove to be nothing at all. I didn't want him to be a witness.

I didn't want him to see the way my hands shook around the coffee mug, just a little, as I stepped over our joined protective wards. With one last steadying breath, I turned back to the camp.

I inhaled sharply. Two tents, one blue, one red, were there. The campfire. Emrys with his hand over his eyes, his posture growing tenser by the moment. I could see all of it, and more.

Faint, iridescent threads of magic were braided over the garlands, pulsing and shimmering. It was such a small display of magic, but the sight of it electrified me. Exhilaration stole those last traces of anger and filled me with something I hadn't felt in a long time.

Joy.

It fluttered in my chest, a softly feathered wing, and for once, I didn't release it. I didn't chase it away before it could escape. I reached a finger out toward the threads and one reached back, humming as it curled around my finger. Tugging, as if to pull me back inside the protective circle.

I'd thought I understood so much about the hidden world of magic and had forced myself to be satisfied with only catching a pathetic glimmer of it now and then. The truth was, I'd been even more of an outsider than I'd ever realized, let alone accepted. I hadn't known anything at all.

I swallowed hard, stepping back over the wards. It felt like sparks were shooting through my blood, and not even my unwelcome companion could dampen the rush. Nothing but death could take the gift of the One Vision away from me now.

"Well?" Emrys prompted.

"It worked," I said, trying, and failing, to sound nonchalant.

"Great," he said. "You'll actually be able to repay my favor, then."

My jaw dropped. "What happened to 'empathy'?"

The code we agreed to upon joining our guild had only three big rules: The first person who lays hands on a relic claims it. No one shall ever intentionally maim or kill another guild member. A favor given must be returned on the giver's terms.

Emrys finished the last of the coffee and rinsed his mug out with some of the water from his bottle. He reached for my mug, forcing me to polish off the rest in a single chug, and cleaned it the same way.

"I should have known you'd reject the code," he said. "It's not like Nash ever honored it."

And just like that, those final traces of my excitement were snuffed out. "I'm not Nash. What is it that you want?"

"When you were feverish, you were talking about needing to check the ruins," he said. "I want to come with you when you look for whatever it is you think might be there."

"How do you know I won't try to pull a fast one on you?" I asked, letting ice creep into my tone.

He only smiled. "Don't worry, Bird. As fast as you are, I've always been faster."

"You're an odious little reptile, you know that?" I told him, seizing his water bottle for myself.

Emrys smirked. "Do whatever it is you need to do to stop looking like a walking corpse. We have to be down at the ruins before they open for the day."

I waited until I was back inside my tent before blowing out a guttering sigh. I changed into the other, slightly dryer undergarments and pants I'd brought with me, wincing at the cold. Emrys was whistling as he smothered the fire, as if to remind me he was still there, waiting.

The fever *had* unlocked something in me. A memory of the ill-fated Egypt job. No amount of walking around yesterday had shaken it loose because there was no obvious reason to connect the two places. But my subconscious had pushed me toward Nash's trick of hiding things in doorways.

The castle's silent ruins had kept his secret for seven long years. Something was buried there; I could feel it down to the marrow of my bones. All I had to do was find it.

We waited until the sun had climbed above the horizon before packing up our camps and venturing to the ruins. So far, I hadn't seen a tour bus pull up in the village, but I knew it was only a matter of time.

We'd have maybe an hour and change before the tour guides arrived to open the site.

I drew in a breath of cold air as we trudged along the path, our boots crunching. It was early October, but the gorse and heath were still in bloom, tempting us to stop and admire them, even with their hidden thorns. The wild grass and ferns had renewed themselves, erasing any trace of the many travelers who had passed over and through them. Here and there, the land seemed to shimmer and wink, hinting at vestiges of ancient magic hidden among the stones and bramble.

After the battering storm the night before, I was rewarded with one of those achingly beautiful golden mornings, the kind that seem to promise the day will carve itself into memory as one of the best.

But I knew how fast things could take a turn, and I was already bracing myself for disappointment.

"What are we looking for?" Emrys asked.

"I remembered something last night," I said. "A memory I hadn't thought about in years."

The Egypt job.

Emrys said nothing, waiting for me to continue.

"Every now and then," I began, "Nash would bury things in doorways for safekeeping. Under tiles and floorboards. They were always random locations. I don't know how he kept them all straight in his head."

The memory of Nash's explanation filtered through my mind. *People search outside, and they search in, but never the between. That's where the truth is hidden, where no one thinks to look.*

"You think he left something in one of the doorways at Tintagel?" Emrys gave me a look that confirmed how flea-brained my plan was. "People are going to have a serious problem with us going around digging hundreds of holes in the ruins. Can you narrow it down at all?"

Not for you, I thought. It was so unfair that he was here for this, but pride wouldn't let me go back on my word. "Maybe."

"I'll take that as a no," Emrys said. "You don't think he would have tried to bury anything down in Merlin's Cave, do you? That's where Merlin supposedly carried the infant Arthur out to safety, right?"

I shook my head, surveying the dramatic sweep of the land. The waves hissed against the shore below us. "No, he'd be rightly worried about the tide uncovering anything he buried there and dragging it out to sea. I think he would have used a spot or structure that would have been in use during Arthur's time. The Dark Ages."

Emrys put his gloved hands on his hips. "And knowing his flair for the dramatic, I'm guessing he would have found a spot on the inner ward."

The inner ward was the "island" of the ruins, separated from the mainland by a chasm. It was where we had spent the most time during our past visits with Nash.

Realization dawned like sunlight breaking through the clouds.

"You know where it is," Emrys said. "Don't bother lying—it's written all over your face."

I twisted my expression, turning it sour. "I think so."

If Nash had left anything behind, it would likely be in the same place I'd been drawn to the day before. I'd lingered in that spot for hours, looking out across the sea like a sailor's widow. I'd felt a pull to go there, one I couldn't blame on the venom or any hallucination.

Avoiding the security cameras, we jumped the gates guarding the ruins. Rather than take the more visible—and safer—modern bridge, we took the older, more dangerous, one, then climbed the spiraling stairways to the inner ward. The smell of the wind was pure salt and greens, but its dampness crept through my flannel coat, through my skin and muscle, right down to the bone.

The north gate of the inner ward was a slate curtain wall, anchored by an arched doorway that now only served to frame a view of the sea. It was a striking image, certainly, but it was the ruins of the great hall itself that stole the breath from my lungs.

The thrill of it started as a tingling in my toes, quickly spreading up my spine to engulf my heart. For the first time, Tintagel lifted the dreary mask of decay and revealed a hint of its ancient, secret face to me.

With the One Vision, the few remaining walls of the structure were suddenly lit with iridescent colors. The longer I looked, the clearer the enchanted murals became. Though the intensity of the design had faded like paint in the sun, I could still make out shimmering scenes of dragons, nameless gods, and lush forests.

Just to the right of the doorway, a silvered path stretched out over the cliff's edge toward the sea; it was impossible to tell where it ended, or if one could cross it to reach the distant horizon.

My amazement was in stark contrast to Emrys's nonchalance. He'd seen it all, and likely far more impressive displays, before. I tried not to stew in that resentful envy as he circled the ruins.

We made our way toward the arched doorway in the curtain wall. I crouched down, studying the slate pavers they'd installed.

"Knife, please," I said, holding out a hand behind me.

He passed it over, nodding to a stone paver on the left-hand side of the arch, raised slightly above the others. "That one looks a bit off-kilter, right?"

"It's probably just from the storms," I said, setting my bags down.

"You *can* hope, you know," he said. "It won't kill you."

Kill me, no. But like all good torturers, hope drew out your suffering, taking its time to lift your spirits so the inevitable crash of disappointment would come twice as hard and painful.

"Keep an eye on the bridge and the other side of the ruins. The guides will be here soon to open the place up," I said. "Watch for the one with the short, wavy blond hair—she's quick as a fox and mean as a wasp."

He raised a brow. "Any relation?"

I glared at him, then returned to the task at hand, sawing at the crusted earth between the stones.

"This is a really idiotic idea, isn't it?" I muttered.

"What ideas aren't idiotic until proven right?"

The retort died on my tongue. The stone came away from the dirt and cement with ease.

I wasn't the first one to have cut into it.

"God's teeth," I breathed out. My pulse stopped, only to jump again.

Nestled inside an unnatural hole in the hard earth was a small leather bundle, wrapped in a child-sized plaid raincoat for protection from the elements.

My old raincoat.

Emrys dropped to his knees beside me, his eyes going wide as I shook the contents of the leather pouch loose onto the ground between us, letting them fall onto the wet stones.

A slip of paper, and a silver coin that was nearly black with tarnish—no, dried blood. My heartbeat thrummed in my ears, and my whole body seemed to clench. I turned the coin over, rubbing my thumb across it.

There was an inscription on the back. The words wound around the edge, and the letters were almost like sigils. I couldn't tell if I was hallucinating again, or if it was the One Vision, because those very same marks began to shiver and shift. Rearranging their strange lines into letters, then words, that I recognized.

"*I am the dream of the dead,*" I whispered.

"What in hellfire does that mean?" Emrys demanded.

I turned toward the scrap of parchment that had fallen from the pouch, peeling it off the ground. Considering the conditions of the hole it had been hidden in for seven years, and Nash's spidery penmanship, the short note was devastating in both its clarity and its brevity.

The ring will win the favor of her heart. Do not follow.
I will come when it is finished. If I do not return, bury this
coin as it is with ash and bone.

The writing was so formal for Nash that it took me a moment to process what he had written.

"Her heart?" Emrys rolled his eyes. "Don't tell me your guardian went to all this trouble to win over a lady friend."

"You say that because you never saw him get slapped by a woman in every Hollower joint we went to."

I picked up the coin again, studying it.

"*Do not follow,*" I repeated. "Wow . . . between his disappearance and the annoyingly clever hiding spot I saw him use exactly once, Nash really overestimated my ability to put two and two together."

It was so typical of him, too—Nash operated on an entirely different plane of existence than the rest of us at times. He was always constructing some great hunt, some great mystery, some great tale around himself, orchestrating every aspect to his satisfaction. If destiny wouldn't give him a big enough role, he would rewrite the script for himself.

Do not follow. A surge of anger heated my blood. My eyes stung, but it was only because of the cold wind needling at me. Only that.

The bastard had expected me to find this note quickly enough to catch up with him. Tracking *had* been one of the few genuine skills he'd taught us, and he'd obviously assumed my memory would be the only clue we needed. But he'd made this into too much of a game. Why not just leave the leather pouch inside the tent with us? Why put so much faith in a ten-year-old girl whose first concern had to be keeping her brother alive?

Somehow, even with the amount of time and distance between us, I was still discovering new ways I'd disappointed him.

And all of this for some nameless woman. *Win the favor of her heart?* What was he, a poet now? *Her heart*—as if he—

All of my thoughts fell away, save for one.

Her heart. Not just anyone's heart—*her* heart. The Goddess's.

"You just figured something out," Emrys said. "Don't lie, because your expression sure didn't."

A sudden wind tore the note away and cast it high up into the air. I gasped, trying to grab it, but it was already flying out to sea, soaring like a pale bird toward the waves.

I shifted the paver back into place and pressed both fists down on it until the mud sucked at it again.

"That's for me to know," I shot back, sliding the coin into a secure pocket in my workbag. I looped the strap across my body and reached for my backpack. "Your favor's been repaid, so scram."

Emrys gripped my arm as I stood. "What did the note mean?"

I wrenched myself free. "Wouldn't you like to know?"

He took a step toward me, his expression hardening.

Behind him, a small figure peered around the edge of a crumbling wall. She wore an oversized black velvet blazer covered in pins and a rainbow crochet scarf wrapped around the lower part of her face. But I recognized her all the same—the dark brown skin, the braids twisted into two buns on top of her head, those massive sunglasses—even if I couldn't believe it.

"Hey!" I shouted, pushing past Emrys.

The girl from the tarot shop bolted as I ran toward her, but by the time I reached the spot where I'd seen her, she had vanished. There was no one on either bridge. It was as if she'd jumped into the sea or slipped into some unseen crevice in the cliff. I made a wide circle, searching, but only found a few small footprints.

"What was that about?" Emrys asked.

"I thought I saw . . ." My feet slid to a stop as I came to face the bridges again.

Even at that distance, I knew him. It was the all-too-confident walk and that head of long black hair. Septimus was now leading a handful of other men across the modern bridge. Other Hollowers, I assumed, some from our own guild.

"Seriously?" I grumbled, backing up. "See you later, Trust Fund."

I'd have to take one of the winding trails out of the ruins and hope I didn't bump into any of Septimus's other henchmen along the way.

I started to go, only to stop again as Septimus waved to someone back on the mainland, motioning in the direction of the village.

More Hollowers appeared near the official entrance to the ruins. A tall, dark figure struggled to break free from the grip two of the bulkier men had on him. One waved back in acknowledgment of Septimus's apparent order.

Cabell. My chest constricted painfully. I pivoted back away from the bridge, starting toward the path that would wind down to the wooden bridge below. If I could make it across without anyone seeing me and get to the village . . .

The rattling of another pack trailed after me.

"Where are you going?" Emrys demanded.

"To help Cabell," I snapped.

"There's too many of them," he protested. "You'll never get him away."

"Watch me."

He lengthened his stride to catch up to me, keeping pace at my side.

"What are *you* doing?" I asked.

"You think I'm going to let you out of my sight when you hold all the answers?" he said, shaking his head. "Not a chance, Bird."

9

The village was just waking up to the first of a fleet of tourist buses when Septimus and the others turned off the main street and made their way to an old barn at the town's edge.

I followed close behind, ignoring Emrys the best I could as we approached the rickety building and crouched beneath one of its cracked windows.

The glass was clouded with dust, but I could still make out a few things: crates of cider and beer marked for the Excalibur Pub, excess traffic cones and road signage, and what appeared to be several sets of armor and the back half of a horse costume. The earthy smell of hay and the animals that had once occupied the stalls permeated the walls, a fading reminder of a past life in which Nash, Cabell, and I had slept in whatever shelter we'd been able to find.

I couldn't make out what they were saying as Septimus pushed Cabell into one of the stalls and a Hollower I didn't recognize bound his hands with a zip tie.

I rolled my eyes and a moment later saw Cabell do the same. *As if* Nash hadn't taught us how to break a zip tie and pick the lock on handcuffs, given his vast experience with both.

For several minutes, neither of us moved or spoke. I ignored the knowing hum that came from beside me.

"What now?" Emrys whispered. "Don't tell me you've already run out of ideas for this daring rescue."

"Shut up or go away," I told him. "I'm waiting for a few more of them to leave before going in."

"Uh-huh," he said. "Well, if we're going to be here awhile . . ."

He turned his back to the barn's wall and pulled out a small knife and a chunk of wood from the side pocket of his trousers.

The movement of his hands was almost mesmerizing as he worked. Soon a spiral shaving dropped to the ground, then another, until he had carved away the grit of the bark and rounded the wood's harsh edges.

I would have pegged him as having a more upper-crust hobby than whittling—something like foxhunting or collecting Fabergé eggs or summering on a superyacht.

Not that I spent much time pondering what Emrys got up to in his personal time.

"Was Cabell late in meeting you here?" Emrys asked. "Or did the others bring him along?"

I gave him a narrow look. "Why don't you tell me? Isn't that Daddy's pal in there?"

The knife stopped midstroke.

What had Phineas said at the library? *We'll never get it out of the Council's claws, and then it'll be Endymion's wrath we have to worry about . . .*

"If he's looking for the ring for your old man, why are you working for Madrigal?" I pressed. "Why aren't you in there with Septimus and the others?"

"That's none of your business," he muttered, his gaze fixed on the piece of wood in his hand.

"You've now made it my business," I hissed back. "Don't tell me—"

Emrys's head suddenly snapped up, and before I could even think to react, he'd snagged my wrist in his hand and pulled us both away from the wall. *"Look!"*

Around the corner, a girl emerged from behind a nearby building. Her braids were twisted into buns on her head, and she was still wearing the furry coat she always did—and that hideous fanny pack, of course.

I pressed a hand to my face and groaned. I really hadn't imagined her earlier.

Neve. From the tarot shop.

"Uh . . . ," Emrys began. "What is she doing?"

She ran straight for the barn, her face set with determination. She slid to a stop a few feet from the side of the structure and threw an empty aluminum can at the wall. There was something dark on it, almost like . . .

She'd drawn a spell sigil on it.

"Huh," Emrys said.

Neve reached into her fanny pack and pulled out a long, thin piece of wood. One end of its narrow body was capped with an obsidian blade, an athame of sorts, used to carve sigils. The other was edged with silver to conduct the flow of magic.

My stomach felt like it was about to fall out of my body.

"Wand," I said, rising.

"Sorceress," Emrys finished, clutching his whittling knife in his fist.

"Give me that," I said, reaching for the blade.

He pulled it away. "And give you the opportunity to stab me with it? I think not."

I turned back just in time to see Neve grin as she pointed the silver end of the wand toward the can.

"Neve!" I called out. "Don't!"

The words were lost to the thundering blast of pressure that radiated out from the can, throwing Emrys and me back several feet. I covered my head as the spell shredded the barn's wall and sent slivers no bigger than matchsticks raining down over us.

Only, they never struck. A grunt came from above me, and a moment later, my mind registered the weight and heat at my back. My face burned as I shoved up against where Emrys was covering me. "Get off!"

A section of the roof buckled without its supports, crashing down with enough force to make the ground shudder. The sorceress leapt back, her mouth forming a small O of surprise.

The men inside yelped and shouted as a violent tremor ran through what remained of the building, threatening to level it.

Cabell, I thought, clawing my way back onto my feet. My ears rang as I stumbled forward—just as Cabell broke his zip tie and used his shoulder to ram his way through the brittle wooden wall behind him.

But by the time I'd rounded the corner to intercept him, he was gone, dodging and weaving his way into the village. I tried to follow the path I thought he might take, pushing through curious townsfolk and tourists who'd come to see what the commotion was, but when I glanced back at the barn, it was Septimus who met my gaze.

"There!" he called, throwing an arm out.

Hide, hide, hide, my mind chanted. Cabell would find somewhere safe to wait them out, and I needed to do the same. All I could see, though, were homes and shops. Until, ahead, a boarded-up pub, clearly undergoing some sort of renovations, called to me like a beacon.

I ran around to the back of it but found the walls stripped down to studs, leaving no place to hide.

The garden was littered with construction materials, but there were no workers around. There was, however, a rickety garden shed. I pulled a bobby pin out of my hair and started to pick the lock, only to find it was already open.

I ducked inside, my lungs burning, my side cramping, and threw the door shut behind me. I locked it, but still searched for something to brace the handle with.

There was nothing inside the shed besides a few broken lawn chairs, storage boxes, and Emrys Dye.

He scrambled to his feet from behind a stack of crates. "*No.* Absolutely not. Get out."

"Are you serious?" I said.

"I was here first!" he protested. "Find a different hiding place!"

The shed creaked, trying to settle its weary old bones. Our boots kicked up the smell of dirt and dead grass.

"*You* find a different hiding place!" I shot back. "You're the one who insisted on following me here!"

Cold air and sunlight flooded the shed as the door swung open. I launched myself forward to shove my way past whoever had found us. At the feel of hands clamping around my arms, I yanked back, trying to free myself.

"Tams! It's me—it's me!"

The warm leather smell of Cabell's jacket wrapped around me as his arms did. I gripped him back, my throat aching with the depth of my relief.

"Are you all right?" I asked him.

"I'm fine," he said.

My relief was short-lived. Behind him, Neve stepped into view, her wand still clutched in her fist.

"*You!*" I seethed.

"Me!" she confirmed cheerfully. "See, we get to hang out after all!"

I was vaguely aware of Emrys nearby, his hand hovering over the axe in his travel pack. I don't know what my expression must have looked like for Cabell to put a steadying hand on my shoulder.

"Tamsin, this is the Sorceress Neve," he said. "And she's got an offer you're going to want to hear."

10

"*Sorceress,*" I repeated, letting venom ooze into the word. "That was quite the act you put on for me, pretending you were one of the Cunningfolk."

"You know each other?" Emrys asked, finally relaxing his stance.

"Yup, we go way back," Neve said.

"Yeah, all the way back to last month," I deadpanned.

"Longer than that." Neve smiled. "And by the way, I never told you I was one of the Cunningfolk. That was your assumption, and you know what they say about assumptions."

My gaze narrowed. "Explain."

"They make an ass out of you—" Neve began.

Cabell held up a hand, gently interrupting her. "What my sister wants to know is how you tracked her down in the first place."

"I was getting to that," Neve said, crossing her arms over her chest. "So, here's the thing. My auntie *is* one of the Cunningfolk, and her magic gift allows her to find lost things."

Absently, she touched something hidden beneath her shirt, just at the breastbone. A necklace of some kind—a locket or a crystal, maybe.

"Nashbury Lark sought her out seven years ago to see if she might be able to locate Carnwennan, the dagger of King Arthur," Neve continued. "Auntie couldn't find it through her scrying or even through vision walking, which frustrated her greatly, as I'm sure you can understand."

"We are intimately acquainted with dead ends in our line of work, yes," I said. A feeling winnowed through me, sharp and quick. The memory followed in its wake. "The shop in Charleston?"

Neve's hands clapped together. "You do remember! I was supposed to be in bed, but I listened at the top of the stairs."

Tucked behind King Street and open only after midnight, the shop resembled an apartment more than a business. I remembered the way the moonlight had woven itself through the many scrolls of maps tied together in neat bundles. Mountains of them, like stacks of hollow bones, waiting for their turn.

Neve's aunt, Linden Goode, was easy to recall, with her warm voice, her apron smelling of sweet mint and lemon as she bid us welcome and ushered us inside. Cabell and I had been sent off to a corner with a bowl of stew to wait for her and Nash to conduct their business. We'd only just been able to see her instinctively reaching for maps. Her selenite dowsing crystal had looked like a star amid the candlelight of the dark room.

She had sung low and deep, and the crystal had begun to spin and spin, fruitlessly searching for the dagger Nash so desperately wanted. In the end, I'd been the one to find it through plain old-fashioned research and good guesses.

"We'd chased down every other lead at that point," I said faintly.

"Normally she won't help Hollowers find treasures they'll only sell, but he said he needed it for one of his children, so she agreed," Neve explained. "Nashbury gave his address as your guild library, so I kept an eye out for you there and you actually showed up, allowing our destinies to collide once more."

"So what was all that stuff in the tarot shop about?" I asked. "Just to toy with me?"

"I was trying to feel you out," Neve said, as if it were the most obvious thing in the world. "Which I did. And now we're here, hiding in this shed. You, confused. Me, with an offer."

"Yeah, about that," I began. "Could you at least put the wand away first?"

"Oh—yeah, of course." She glanced down at it as if surprised she was still gripping it, then unzipped her fanny pack, somehow managing to slip the wand inside. It had to be spelled to hold more than it was meant to.

"Okay, seriously, what's the deal with the bag?" I asked when I couldn't stand another second of staring at its terrifying cats.

"Isn't it so cute?" she said brightly. "It even came with a hat that I think would look *really* good on you if you want to borrow it for a disguise."

Neve retrieved a dark bundle from the depths of the fanny pack and shook it out, a black baseball cap with two green-lined cat ears attached to the top of it and the words FELINE SPOOKY! embroidered between them.

"She *absolutely* wants to borrow that," Emrys said, delighted.

"Your proposal . . . ?" Cabell prompted. I felt his hand shift from my shoulder to grip the back of my jacket, clearly afraid I might launch myself at our smirking rival.

"Yes, proposal. Right," Neve said. "Here's the thing—I think we should work together." She glanced at Emrys. "Not you. I don't know you."

"Emrys Dye, at your service," he offered wryly.

She sniffed a bit at that, and I warmed to her, just a little, for having no reaction to his family name.

"I can use my magic to help locate your father—Nash—and you can use the ring on whatever curse you may need broken," Neve said. "Then I can claim it for the Council of Sistren."

The name of the governing body of sorceresses always made the hair on my arms prickle.

"Do you know what they want it for?" I asked.

"I have no idea why they want it." Neve shrugged. "I only know they do, and *I'm* going to be the one who brings it to them. It's the only way I'll be assigned a tutor and progress with my training."

"You don't have a tutor?" I asked. That tracked with her being raised by one of the Cunningfolk, not her mother or another sorceress relation. "Then how are you able to cast?"

"Um, hello," she said, clearly annoyed. "I taught myself."

I exchanged a look with Cabell, who only raised his brows in reply. I'd never heard of a sorceress who hadn't been taught by another sorceress—usually one of her own blood relations.

"Ah, so they won't accept you into their ranks because you don't have formal training," Emrys said. "But the only way for you to get formal training is to be accepted into their ranks. That's utterly maddening."

"I'm beginning to like you," Neve told him. "You can stay. For now."

"Good," Emrys said, "because I have an offer of my own."

"Can't wait to hear *this*," Cabell muttered.

"We all want the same thing, and we all have a piece of the puzzle that will help us get it," he said. "Neve has her power, of course. Tamsin knows where Nash has gone. And I think I know how he got there."

"What?" I asked.

"*What?*" Cabell echoed. "Tams, you know where he went?"

"Oooh," Neve said, looking from one to the other of us. "This sounds promising."

I glanced at my brother, flashing him a meaningful look. "Can I talk to you outside for a second?"

He obliged, following me out and shutting the door behind us. We walked a few paces away.

"What exactly are we doing?" I whispered.

"Prague-ing," he answered simply.

The Prague job had been Nash's first and only time voluntarily working with a sorceress, long before he found Cabell and me. The sorceress had been a novice, new to her craft, and had hired Nash to retrieve a rumored vial of ichor—the divine blood of gods—from the tomb of her ancestor. Ultimately, he'd used her inexperience against her. The tomb had a rebounding curse so that whoever broke the curse at the entrance could not enter without falling dead. There'd been no ichor inside, and he never had to worry about her coming after him.

I blew out a harsh breath through my nose. "That's not going to work. She may come off inexperienced, but she's way too smart and way too knowledgeable about magic to not figure it out eventually. And as you know, withholding information only works for so long."

Cabell winced at my tone, running a hand through his shaggy dark hair. He looked to me again, his expression twisting with regret. "What I said at home—"

"It doesn't matter," I said.

"It does," he pressed on, leaning back against the rock beside me. "I shouldn't have kept the information about the ring and Nash from you, but I promised him."

"Cab, I do get it," I said. "For my part, I'm sorry I didn't see how much you were struggling with everything."

He was silent for a long time, working his jaw as if fighting the words he wanted to say. There was a hardness to his face that had never been there before, a new piece of armor to hide his feelings behind.

"I shouldn't have walked away," he began hoarsely. "I should never have let you leave to do this on your own. I really had my head up my ass about the whole thing. It's just . . . hard to hope."

"The only thing that really matters to me is that you're here," I said. "Took your damn time with it, though."

He let out a rueful laugh. "And my punishment was getting caught by some of the stupidest Hollowers in our guild."

I tried to summon a smile, but it wouldn't come. After a moment, Cabell looked down, hugging his arms to his chest. Up close, he looked terrible. His pale skin emphasized the dark, heavy circles beneath his eyes. He'd lost some weight in recent weeks, and it had left a hollowness in his cheeks I hadn't seen since we were children.

I swallowed against the lump in my throat. This was what we always did after we argued: kept things light so we could float above the dust settling between us. When you only had each other in life, no fight was worth the risk of shattering that bond. It should have been enough that he'd changed his mind and come; that was its own apology.

But it wasn't. Something ugly had been revealed the last time we'd been together, like overturning undisturbed soil to find worms and bones hidden below. And now, having seen the truth of it, I didn't know how to go back—that was what scared me the most.

"You're with me on this, right?" I asked, feeling myself choke up. Feeling that searing desperation again. It had to be fine. We had to be fine.

"All the way," he said. "I want to find the ring, and I want to know what happened to Nash, and I really don't want you to get yourself killed stumbling around without the One Vision."

"About that . . . ," I began.

Cabell's face fell. He leaned in closer, studying my eyes until I turned away. "You didn't. Tell me you didn't."

Of course he'd figured it out—I'd spent the better part of a year begging Nash to find the venom for me.

"I did, and I have no regrets because it worked."

Cabell swore under his breath. "Where did you even get the basilisk venom?"

"Where do you think?"

"What was that about not taking on any more favors?" Cabell shook his head. "I swear to every god in the sky that if you ever do something this stupid again, I'm going to kill you myself."

"Noted," I said, quickly turning us back to the matter at hand. "You're sure about working with a sorceress?"

"She doesn't know the ring has to be claimed through deadly

force," he said, his voice low. "I grilled her on it while we were looking for you."

"She could have been lying," I pointed out. "Playing us."

"Like she played you back in Boston?" He arched a brow at my scowl. "Oh, come on. It happens to the best of us. As Nash used to say—"

He stopped himself, his gaze drifting to the ground.

"Mistakes are like wasps," I finished quietly. "They'll keep stinging if you let them."

Cabell let out a soft sigh.

"Look," he began, "you may be right and Neve will put all the pieces together on her own. But I know we can get to Nash and the ring first. I *know* we can. Keeping her and Dye close is the best way to stay one step ahead of them."

"Fine," I said, relenting. "We'll Prague it and deal with the fallout later."

He put a comforting hand on my head, drawing me closer for a brief hug. "Man . . . after all this time . . . I can't believe Nash might be in Avalon. Maybe he got trapped there. That would explain why he never came home."

The mention of Nash's name reminded me of what else we'd found hidden with his note.

Taking Cabell's arm, I led him back to the shed and fished out the tarnished coin to show both him and Neve.

"Do either of you recognize this or know what the engraving means?"

Cabell smoothed a thumb against the words. "*I am the dream of the dead,*" he read. "I've never seen anything like this, but there is magic attached to it. It feels cold. Neve?"

She shook her head. "No clue."

Emrys had been so quiet and still, leaning against the wall of the shed, that I'd nearly forgotten he was there until he spoke. "There's no need for it to remain a mystery, folks. The note said to bury it with ash and bone if he didn't return."

Cabell blinked. "Does anyone just happen to have some bone on them?"

I shook my head.

Neve let out a happy hum. "You are all in luck . . ."

The sorceress went to work pulling out an array of small bones and skulls from her pack, setting them on the ground. When she finished, she waved her hands over them, as if presenting her very own dead-animal petting zoo.

"Doesn't it creep you out to collect bones like this?" I asked.

"Why would it creep me out?" Neve asked. "Death is beautiful, and people only fear it because they see it as an end, not the beginning it is. Also, I think the little ones are kind of cute. I mean, look—"

She selected a tiny bird skull with a jagged beak and, pitching her voice higher, said, "Hellooo, Tamsin. Pick me for your oh-so-mysterious coin and I will be your grim companion on this dark journey of discovery."

Cabell laughed. I didn't.

Neve put the skull back down and picked up the bone beside it. It was in a glass case edged with gold and shaped like a foot, complete with empty sockets on the toenails, where jewels had likely been.

"This may be an even better option," Neve said. "It's part of the foot of Saint Henwg."

"Who?" I asked.

"Well, exactly," Neve said. "It's not like the bones of well-known people are easy to come by. I borrowed it from Auntie." She sighed. "Okay, no, I stole it."

The sorceresses loved few things more than revenge, even if that revenge waited centuries. From what I'd read, they took considerable pleasure in using the bones of those whose burgeoning religion had violently destroyed the ancient pagan faiths.

"And then *here* we have—"

"Let's just use the saint's bone," I said, cutting her off. I dug a small hole in the dirt floor with my collapsible axe and gave the coin one last look before tossing it in. Neve opened a flap on the bottom of the foot, and a miserable, yellowed bone the length of a finger dropped beside the coin. All four of us leaned in, staring at it.

"Huh," I said.

Emrys lit a small branch with his lighter, then passed it to me. As it burned down, ash and embers drifted into the hole.

"Do you think that's enough?" Cabell asked.

"It better be," I said, kicking the loose soil back into the hole. I crouched down, patting it firmly in place just to be sure.

We waited and watched. And still nothing happened.

I shook my head, making a noise of disgust at the back of my throat. Anger burned in the pit of my stomach. Typical Nash, playing stupid games like this just to seem mysterious.

"Maybe it takes a minute?" Neve suggested. Her eyes were soft in a way I instantly hated.

"You can wait a thousand years and I promise that nothing will ever come out of that dirt," I said, sitting beside my bags and wrapping my jacket tighter around me.

"It was worth a shot," Cabell said. Disappointment was etched into his face and seemed to weigh heavy on his shoulders.

"So," Emrys said into the silence that followed. "Now that we have that out of the way, are we good to work together, or do we need to stand here and argue about it for another ten minutes?"

I rolled my eyes. "What do you bring to this again? Other than preening and striking dramatic poses, of course."

"Hilarious, Bird."

"That's not her name," Cabell snapped.

"Tamsin thinks she knows where Nash went based on his note," Emrys said. "And if my hunch is correct, it's not in this world."

For the first time, Neve's excitement dulled. "Not in this world? You think he went to one of the Otherlands?"

Cabell turned to me with an encouraging look. "Go on, Tams."

"Not until we get some kind of assurance from Dye that this isn't a trick," I said.

Emrys groaned. "You are so damn stubborn. Fine . . . here."

He took his pack off his shoulder and retrieved a palm-sized bottle, setting it on the ground between us when I didn't immediately take it. "Madrigal gave this to me."

"Madrigal?" Neve said, perking up. "Is it true she turned her last lover into a chandelier?"

"No," Emrys said. "But thank you for that horrifying mental image. She thought there was a chance the ring had crossed into an Otherland and gave this to me to summon the Hag of the Mist. She's the only creature outside the Wild Hunt capable of manipulating the mists that separate our world from the Otherlands. We can completely bypass the original sealed pathways."

Neve frowned. "Are you sure we should be summoning primordial creatures? Don't they always want something in return for their service?"

"Hence the offering," Emrys said, gesturing to the bottle. "To summon her."

I bent to retrieve it, holding it up in one of the shafts of light sneaking in through the walls around us. Leaves I didn't recognize, several quartz crystals, and three glowing fangs were suspended in thick, dark blood. The clear glass bore the sorceress's mark—a chess piece with a reverse crescent over it.

"We just have to find a liminal place to call her," Emrys said. "Like a crossroads."

"What about a cave?" Cabell suggested.

"That would work," Emrys said. "Merlin's Cave, between land and sea."

I leveled a look at him. "If you're so sure he went to an Otherland, why do you need us?"

"Well, for one thing, it seems useful to have a sorceress around," Emrys said. "And for another, I think Nash went to one of two

Otherlands tied to Arthur and his knights. I'm not sure which, and I only have one offering to make to the hag."

"What are your guesses?" Cabell asked.

"Either Avalon, where the ring was created," Emrys said, "or Lyonesse, where it's said the darkest and deadliest treasures known to man were hidden before it was splintered from our world."

I schooled my expression, revealing nothing. The kingdom of Lyonesse, a contemporary of Camelot, was believed by mortal men to have been drowned by a monstrous storm, slipping into the sea and largely out of memory.

"The treasure hoard is only rumor," Cabell said, shaking his head. "And if it's true, then the part about the terrifying monster protecting it is also true."

"Precisely why I am desperately hoping Tamsin is about to tell us it's Avalon," Emrys said.

The darkness crept in so slowly, I didn't notice that the others were fading from sight until they were nearly gone. What little sunlight had managed to reach us through the cracks in the old wood faded to complete darkness.

"What in blistering hellfire . . ." Cabell bumped into me as he felt for the shed's door.

"Open it," I told him. "It's right behind you."

Cabell's voice was strangled. "It *is* open."

Neve gasped as she felt her way forward, trying to follow the sound of our voices out. "What's happening?"

The world around us had been submerged in impenetrable darkness. As my eyes adjusted, I could just make out the shapes of the buildings around me.

"Is it an eclipse?" I asked.

"An unforecast one?" Emrys scoffed. But after a beat, he added, "You don't think it's the coin, do you?"

"No way," I said. It couldn't be. Something that small couldn't contain enough magic to do *this*.

Other voices joined ours from the nearby buildings, shouting questions and calling out for their loved ones.

But as quickly as the darkness had come, its stain began to lift, lightening to a funereal gray before the blue of the sky peeked through.

"Whatever just happened can't be good," Cabell said. "I say we get a move on."

"It would help to know where he was going," Emrys pointed out, turning to look at me. I bit my lip, swallowing the last of my misgivings.

The ring will win the favor of her heart.

With one last look at my brother, I said, "Avalon. I think Nash went to Avalon."

A sharp laugh split the air. My chest hollowed at the sound of it, even before the others joined in.

One by one, Hollowers stepped out from behind the surrounding fences and buildings, circling in tight around us. Neve started to reach for her fanny pack, but I gripped her hand, stilling it just as Septimus appeared, leaning against the pub's exposed frame.

"Hear that, boys?" he called to the others. "We're going to the fair isle."

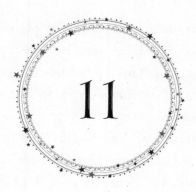

11

The shock that seized us by the throats only lasted an instant. In the space between one heartbeat and the next, Cabell dove for the shed, where all our things waited, only to be brought up short by one of the men who'd taken him prisoner.

"We meet again," the Hollower gloated. "Thought you'd slipped the noose, did you?"

Cabell spat in his face. I didn't see the punch flying toward the side of my head until it had already landed, cracking my world in two and sending me to the wet ground.

"Hey!" Cabell tried to lunge for whoever had hit me. I sat there, momentarily dazed. Neve wrapped an arm around me and helped me to my feet. I couldn't see Emrys's face, only that he had looked my way. Everything around me was a blur.

"What are you doing here?" There was an edge of shock to Septimus's voice, and something else. If I hadn't just suffered a head wound, I would have said it was fear. "How . . . is it possible?"

As the dark spots faded from my vision, I finally saw what had caught his attention. Or rather, who.

"I came to find the ring," Emrys told him. "Thank the gods you're here, though. They caught me searching the ruins of Tintagel and I've been trying to get away ever since."

Neve gasped in outrage. I might have taken a swing at Emrys, but he grabbed me first, holding me firmly in place by the back of my neck. The more I struggled, the more Hollowers gathered around us to help him. I forced myself to stop before someone worse took over.

"But your father—" Septimus began, still struggling to piece together a whole thought.

"I want to surprise him," Emrys said. "And return with the ring. Haven't you ever tried to impress your old man, Yarrow?"

"You need to go home," Septimus said. "One of my men will take you. Your father must be worried sick."

"That's where you're wrong," Emrys said, releasing my neck with one last warning squeeze before he strode out in front of us. His voice was light and his smile winning. "You need me to tell you how to get to Avalon, and we need them to track down Lark for us."

"Emrys . . . ," the other man said, shaking his head.

"I'm coming with you." Emrys's smile was strained. "Please. It's my last chance to do something like this."

Septimus sighed. "All right. Stay close to me through this, hear me? I'd rather not be murdered by your father."

"Of course," Emrys said.

His last chance to do something like this? Why? Were they on the verge of foisting him onto some fancy ivy-laden college? Maybe he took the job from Madrigal to prove he didn't need a degree, but even that didn't make sense.

"How will we travel to Avalon?" Septimus asked.

"Don't you dare," I warned Emrys. This was what we got for trusting him—I knew better, and still, I'd led him here. I'd given him our only clue to find Nash.

And he didn't even have the decency to look at me as he said, "The Hag of the Mist."

Neve hissed. "You'll pay for this. I hope you enjoy the taste of eels, because they're going to be pouring out of every orifice you have."

Septimus swung toward her, as if just noticing her for the first time. Neve was taller than I was, but his size meant he could loom over us both, blocking out the sun like a second eclipse. "And who is this?"

I gritted my teeth, my pulse rising with fear. Some Hollowers saw sorceresses as a means to a treasure-laden end, believing they were like black widow spiders—only deadly when provoked. But many I'd encountered hated sorceresses with a startling vehemence, usually because a family member or mentor had been killed on the job by a well-placed curse.

If any of these Hollowers fell into the latter category, Neve might have to defend herself against their darkest fantasies of revenge.

As if in answer to my thoughts, Neve straightened, throwing her shoulders back as one hand crept toward her fanny pack. "I'm—"

"She's from one of the small West Coast Hollower guilds," Emrys said smoothly, not looking at either of us. "Neve. She has a way of tracking Nash once we get to Avalon."

His lie put me on the back foot. The tension in my face eased as a question took shape out of my growing suspicion. *What are you up to, Trust Fund?*

Cabell fought against the hold the Hollowers had on him, and his struggle only intensified when he saw that Septimus's men had taken our bags from the shed and added them to their collection of supplies.

"We should wait until the castle ruins close for the day," Emrys said, briefly catching my gaze as he turned to face Septimus.

This time, his eyes held a message. *Trust me.*

I shook my head. *Never.*

Emrys Dye was playing a dangerous game—the only question was with whom.

Merlin's Cave was smaller than I remembered it being; then again, the last time I'd stood here, I'd been smaller myself.

The cave itself was really a tunnel, one carved by ancient waves or some great beast burrowing into the mountainous dark rocks. To access it, you had to take a winding path down from the ruins above and enter through a small, rocky beach.

The sea held back its foamy fingers as we trudged across the sand and pebbles. The nearby waterfall was loud enough to drown out the sound of my heartbeat in my ears.

I stopped at the entrance of the cave, only for Septimus to shove me forward again. The damp air was heavy with the scent of brine and decay. Condensation turned everything slick, making it difficult to continue when the sandy beach turned to a field of jagged scree. The walls were sharp and forbidding around us, each its own warning that this was not a place for mortals.

Several Hollowers turned on their flashlights, guiding the way in when the new moon failed to.

Nash used to say that humans were nothing more than sparks falling into the fire of time, but I was no spark, and there was no heat here. Just a whispering chill, its cold lips moving against my skin, speaking unknowable secrets.

"Here," Septimus said once we reached the midpoint between the two ends of the cave. "This will do."

I caught Neve's gaze briefly, and it was enough to see what she wanted to do. Fight. Run. The idiots hadn't taken her fanny pack, likely thinking it was too small to hold anything useful or dangerous. Even with her hands bound, she'd still be able to get to her wand.

I shook my head in reply. We were outnumbered. We'd have to find a way to escape once we were in Avalon.

Neve was clearly unhappy, but she seemed to accept it. She glared at Septimus as he passed by. "You really should be extra careful when we go inside—I've heard hags prefer the taste of pompous numpties to even that of the common idiot. Something about mushier brains."

He raised his arm as if to backhand her. Both Cabell and I lunged, trying to block his hand, but it was Emrys who stopped him.

"Mr. Yarrow," he said, all pleasantness as he held up the bottle containing the offering. "We should continue."

Septimus sneered. "Fine."

Cabell tried to edge closer to me, only to be blocked by a Hollower.

Emrys walked out to the front of the group, pulling the heavy cork from the bottle and setting it down on a dark stone.

"Hag of the Mist," he said, his voice rough. *"Mistress of mists, born of the land of ancient shadow. Servant of none, taker of all, heed these children, answer our call."*

The Hollowers gasped as, all at once, their flashlights and LED lanterns went out like smothered flames, leaving the cave in boundless shadow.

A rattling hiss of laughter rose behind us.

My head had hollowed out again, of thought, of feeling, of anything other than the knowledge of the presence looming behind us like a gathering storm.

"Do you . . . do you accept this offering?" Emrys asked.

"I accept," the hag hissed, her voice like snakes sliding against one another. *"What is it you desire?"*

There was a sound like the flutter of leathery wings, and the air shifted behind me.

"We . . . ," Emrys started, then cleared his throat. "We seek passage. To and from Avalon."

"Ahhhhh . . . ," the hag breathed out, *"so you seek that which is denied to you. The sword of legend, the sleeping king, the tower fair . . ."*

Emrys's voice echoed against the stones. "What would you ask in return?"

"What do you mean?" Septimus interjected. "You gave her the offering—"

The creature reeked of infernal decay and rancid bile. My stomach turned violently as my back burned with awareness of her. Out of the corner of my eye, I saw a pale, withered hand reaching out as if to cup my face.

My body vibrated with terror as something—a finger, a claw—drew down through my hair and along the ridge of my spine, cutting through the tangles and knots, like a mother combing a child's hair.

"For a sole journey into Avalon for your party, and one passage in return," the hag continued, *"I ask only for a lock of this hair."*

Her hand, her claws, returned to stroking my scalp, lifting a few strands here and there until I thought I would vomit or scream.

"What do you want it for?" Emrys asked sharply.

"What does it matter?" Septimus growled back.

"It is of no concern to you," the hag replied. Something oozed onto my cheek and shoulder. *"Perhaps it is only because it is so very pretty . . . like the sunlight lost to me."*

My heart thundered, threatening to burst from my chest. I don't know how I got the word out. "Fine."

There was the faintest movement as her claw curled, and she cut an untold number of hairs at the nape of my neck. Her skin felt like a dead fish against mine.

She leaned in close to my ear again. *"For you, I offer this: a secret that is yours to share. They, too, delight in blood and burn in light."*

I tilted my head, trying to parse her words. I shut my eyes until the oppressiveness of her presence lifted.

"What an interesting child you are," the hag murmured, her voice fading in my ears.

The flashlights and lanterns flickered on once more, and it was only then that I knew the Hag of the Mist was gone.

Breath burst out of me as I doubled over, still shaking.

"Tamsin?" Cabell called out. "Are you all right?"

I couldn't speak. Not just yet.

Cold, damp air billowed past my face, and when I forced my eyes open, I found a swirling vortex of mist hovering before us, its center darkening to pure black.

"What is that? A Vein?" one of the Hollowers asked.

"There's one way to find out," Septimus said.

He gripped the collar of my jacket and yanked me forward. The mist circling the opening began to spin in a frenzied ring. Threads of black escaped the darkness at its center, winnowing through the air, darker than even the shadows around me.

It was the last thing I saw before Septimus pushed me into its icy grasp.

12

It was nothing like a Vein.

I hurtled forward through the infinite dark, riding a powerful wind. I opened my mouth to gasp for breath, but there was no air to take in. Then, almost as quickly as it had begun, it was over.

I exploded out of the passage, landing on my knees on the soggy ground. I had only a second to roll away before Neve and Cabell followed, stumbling out after me.

Septimus was next, then a paler-than-usual Emrys, holding our workbags. The other men spilled out behind them, fading into shadows as a velvety mist gathered around us.

"Make them carry their own things," Septimus said to Emrys. He pointed his hand axe at us. "Try anything, get even a step ahead of where I want you, and you'll find this in the back of your skull."

Emrys uncharacteristically kept his eyes down as he gave me my workbag. When he moved back toward Septimus and the others, Cabell took the opportunity to come to my side.

"Are you all right?" he asked urgently.

"Let's . . ." I shook my head. "Let's just focus on this Prague job."

He took my meaning. Our only objective now was to find a way to escape.

Neve wrapped her furry coat tighter around her middle. "Wh-why is it so cold?"

Behind us, several of the Hollowers, including Emrys, had pulled on their head lamps and switched them on. Their beams tracked against the thick wall of mist ensconcing us, only to converge on two dark shadows in the near distance.

We stood at the edge of a body of water—if it could even be called water. It was a vile ooze, thick with clumps of black, tarry mud. My pulse throbbed at my temples.

"Is this Avalon?" Cabell asked hoarsely.

A muscle feathered in Emrys's tight jaw as he came forward and studied the water. His eyes slid toward mine and I knew, without him having to say the words, that his thoughts were perfectly aligned with mine.

Something isn't right.

The dark shapes in the mist took final form as two flat barges parted the white fog and floated toward us. The lanterns hanging from the hooks on their far ends were unlit and creaked with the faint swaying of the vessels.

For a moment, no one dared to move. A rivulet of icy sweat trickled down my spine.

"Ladies first," Septimus said, sweeping his hand toward the nearer barge.

My stomach was a knot as I stepped over the low rail of the barge and into the sludge of soggy leaves that had collected on the flat deck.

Neve followed with her head held high, careful not to slip as we moved toward the far end. Emrys had his own axe in his hand as he gestured for Cabell to fall in line beside us. The relief I felt at not being separated from my brother on different barges was short-lived; Emrys seemed intent on standing directly behind me, close enough for me to feel the heat coming off his body.

The other Hollowers, all dozen of them, hesitated to follow, looking very much like they were rethinking this job.

"Get a move on," Septimus barked. "Or there'll be no pay!"

In sharp contrast to the others, Septimus looked invigorated—

triumphant, even splattered in dark mud, with his ratty hair whipping loose of its tie. He kicked the other barge off the bank and then jumped onto ours. The barge rocked as his weight was added, and it needed no help to dislodge itself from that strange shore. I turned one last time, frantically trying to commit the location of the portal, and our way back, to memory.

There was no current in the stagnant water that I could see, but the barges moved forward all the same, floating inexorably toward some unknown destination.

An odd *bump-bump-bump* rose up around us, and it seemed to have no source until Neve suddenly pulled back from the edge of the barge with a strangled sound. I leaned forward, cursing my own damned curiosity.

Rather than clumps of moss or earthy decay, the water was littered with the bodies of birds and the pallid bellies of rotten fish. Bile burned up my throat.

Threads of sickly yellow mist wove themselves through the white, and within seconds, the air had turned dark and bitter. The putrid color deepened and became a foul haze that reeked of brackish hell.

Neve coughed violently; I could barely see her through the mist and tears that streamed down from my burning eyes. Several of the Hollowers began retching.

"Where has the hag taken us?" Septimus demanded.

No one had an answer for him.

Noxious vapors stewed around us, roiling, parting enough to torment us with glimpses of the Otherland. A black sky. Shards of giant boulders, jutting up from beneath the water like teeth. The dismembered pieces of what had once likely been a colossal statue of a woman.

An upturned stone hand, collecting dank water and filth, was nearly the size of the barge. But it was the sight of the woman's head, half submerged in the water, that left me trembling. A mud-crusted snake slid through a crack in the statue's eye, disappearing into the rancid water.

Neve pressed a hand to her throat, looking as though someone had reached inside her chest and ripped out her lungs.

"Goddess," she whispered, and nothing more.

The beams from the Hollowers' head lamps scored the mist, piercing it in places. The men were communicating with each other using the kind of sly, quick looks and deep frowns that promised mutiny.

I was startled out of my thoughts by a soft touch on my arm. Emrys pressed something hard and cold into my hand—a pocketknife. I bit my lip as he leaned his long body around mine and reached for a crooked post jutting out of the water.

His expression was almost pained as the post crumbled to sooty dust at the first brush of his gloved fingers.

It wasn't until I saw the enormous roots rising above the water like serpents, strangling one another, that I realized what they were.

Trees.

None of us were aware of how close we were to the waiting shore, not until the barge slammed up against something, nearly throwing us into the ooze.

This time, Septimus was the first to step down, his face screwing up in disgust as his boots stuck in the thick mud. The mist thinned with our movement as we followed, trudging forward.

There had to have been thousands of trees here, once titans in height and breadth. Their remnants had either hardened and hollowed or turned gray as ash. Emrys couldn't stop staring at them, his forehead creased.

"What is this?" he asked quietly. "What could possibly rot them this way?"

The few leaves that remained were withered. The mulch of decayed growth littered the forest floor, in some places several feet high. A dry streambed had become nothing more than a final resting place for an unspeakable number of dead creatures.

The group spread out as we made our way through the trees.

Neve was at my back, her wand clutched in her hand. Cabell fell in place beside me, retrieving my axe from where it had been tied to my traveling pack.

I felt hyperaware of each step I took, not just because of the grasping mud but also the faint jangle of my belongings.

"There should be villages scattered around the isle," Neve whispered.

"Are there any other landmarks we can look for?" I asked as quietly as I could.

"There's a tower at the center of Avalon," Neve said. "That's where its order of priestesses is said to reside. The nine sisters."

Right. Right, I'd seen that mentioned in a handful of the Immortalities. Though as the years had gone on and the generations of sorceresses had grown more distant from their ancestral home, the details around the priestesses had become just as inaccurate as most fairy tales.

"I'm starting to think we're the only ones here," Cabell muttered, moving ahead of me. "At least the only ones still breathing."

My stomach cramped with the fetid smell of the mist, but there was nothing in it to throw up. I didn't see Cabell through the wall of pale air until I'd nearly collided with his back.

He was shaking.

"Tamsin," Cabell breathed out, his lips barely moving. "Don't move."

My eyes slid left, following his line of sight, until, finally, I saw it too. A shifting shadow among the trees.

There was no moonlight to illuminate its form, but my sight had adjusted to the darkness, and even our distance couldn't disguise the cold savagery of the creature tearing at the carcass of what had once been a horse.

The creature had the near shape of a man, but stretched and bent, its joints all harsh, unforgiving angles. The hairless limbs were overly long and spindly, the way a spider's might be. For one terrible moment, I couldn't tell if it was filthy rags or tattered flesh hanging from them.

What the hell is that?

Emrys and Neve came up behind us, their footsteps soft as they moved over the diseased lichen and unsteady ground. I held out both my arms, stopping them. Emrys sent me a questioning look, but I only pointed to his head lamp.

I knew the moment he saw the creature too. His body turned rigid. Holding his breath, he reached up slowly and clicked the light off.

The creature's head shot up, blood and stringy muscle dripping from its mouth. Disgust and terror flooded my body, and any instincts I had to run, to fight, to do anything other than stand there, vanished like breath in the air.

The creature's face was sunken with decay, leaving a void of flesh and color, save for the white of its glowing eyes, and its bloodstained teeth. Teeth it had used to rip the flesh and muscle and innards of the horse away, reducing it to clean-picked bones in a pool of the animal's own blood.

The creature rose, dropping the leg from its mouth. Its limbs unfolded like an insect's, awakening some deep, primal fear in me. The mist rolled between us, but when it thinned again, the creature was gone.

"Where did it go?" Cabell whispered, breathing heavily.

"What the hell is that?" one of the Hollowers shouted. "What is it doing—?"

A piercing bark answered, not half as terrible as the ones that answered back from the darkness that surrounded us on all sides.

There was a soul-curdling scream. The Hollower's head lamp beam vanished. Then another.

And another.

"Get back to the boats!" Septimus bellowed. "Now!"

Cabell and Neve rushed forward first, their feet slapping through puddles of water and sludge. Emrys stood stock-still, staring at the spot where the creature had been, rooted so firmly in place I had to grab his arm and yank with all my might to get him moving again.

Another head lamp gone. Another.

The mist swirled around us in chaotic patterns as the party rushed in every direction. I slammed into Neve, who had turned back at the water's edge. I craned my neck around, following her terrified gaze.

A head, hairless and slick with sludge, rose from the putrid depths. Its eyes gleamed silver as they caught the light of a head lamp.

And then it wasn't one, but many. The filmy water bubbled as they emerged from the dark depths and floated toward us.

Cabell grabbed my shoulder, drawing me closer to his side as he held out my axe. "What the hell do we do?"

I shook my head, choking on words that wouldn't come. There was no way back to the barges. No way forward.

There was only the slick crackle of flesh rent from bone and the helpless screams as one by one the lights vanished and the mist devoured us whole.

13

A long, icy hand clamped around my ankle and I screamed.

Emrys lunged forward with a cry, severing its gray arm with one axe blow. The creature howled and screeched, sinking back into a hole in the ground.

I kicked the hand free from my leg, shuddering. And then we were running, all of us, running harder than I thought my body could ever manage, even lit by fear.

The forest blurred around us, the hollowed trees toppling as the creatures leapt from one to the next, keeping pace. Out of the corner of my eye, I saw Septimus weaving through the stalks of dead grass and bramble. Blood, so dark it was nearly black, sprayed through the air as he battered the creatures with his axe. The two Hollowers who flanked him vanished, tackled to the ground and torn to bloody ribbons of flesh that turned the mist a revolting pink.

"What are they?" Cabell gasped out.

"Revenants?" Emrys suggested.

Gods, I hoped not. The living dead couldn't be killed by mortal weapons, and would only continue to rise again, no matter how many parts we cut off.

My memory tore through all the thousands of books it had consumed, but nothing matched the description of these creatures—no etchings, no brief passages in compendiums and bestiaries, nothing.

Without knowing what they were, we wouldn't know how to kill them. Wounding them with blades was only slowing them down.

"We need to drop the bags!" Cabell shouted.

"No!" The creatures' claws kept snagging the leather, but I would be dead and damned before I lost the last of our supplies.

Pulling out the small pocketknife, I slashed blindly through the air as creatures leapt down from the trees, trying to trap one of us beneath the cage of their bodies.

"Tamsin, duck!" Emrys shouted. As I did, he swung his axe over my head, lodging it in the side of one of their soft skulls. Cabell led us through the diseased trees, deeper into the heart of the isle.

It was a moment more before I realized the screaming from the other Hollowers had stopped.

They're all dead, my mind taunted.

All that was left now was us. The creatures, strings of saliva seeping between their teeth, turned toward us in unison, realizing the same.

I glanced at the sorceress, and the plea must have been etched into my expression.

"I can't cast while running," Neve said between gasping breaths. "I need to carve the sigils—"

One creature dove for her, grasping with two front claws, and I ripped her away. Emrys followed up with his axe, bringing it down and severing one of the limbs.

The other clawed his arm, tearing through the layers of fabric and into his flesh. He stumbled with a curse, nearly dropping the axe. I lunged and jammed my knife into one of the creature's lidless eyes.

"Come on!" I told Emrys, taking his arm.

"My hero," he managed to get out.

"I don't have time to think of an annoyed comeback!" I panted. "Just—"

As they had before with Neve, the creatures swung their hungering faces toward Emrys—toward the wound weeping blood on his arm.

The hag's words came back to me like a nightmare. *They, too, delight in blood and burn in light.*

The old, fetid, rotting hag. She knew exactly what awaited us in Avalon.

God's teeth, I thought. It didn't matter how far we ran or if we managed to find a place to hide. They'd be able to track us.

"The tower!" Neve shouted to me. She didn't need to finish the thought for me to understand what she meant.

"We won't make it!" I told her. The creatures would overrun us long before we found it in the disorienting maze of the dead forest.

We broke into a clearing, one littered with the same jagged boulders we'd seen in the water. The dead grass was waist-high, snapping underfoot and catching on my flannel coat as I pushed through it.

Ahead of me, Cabell tried to navigate us through the rocks, but there were too many of the creatures now. I fell back as they swarmed like ants, crawling up the trees and over the stones. Within the span of a gasp, I was cut off from the rest of the group.

Emrys spun around, searching for something—me. The moment his eyes met mine through the chaos, raw panic seized his expression. *"Tamsin!"*

He tried to run forward, but the spidery creatures slid into the gap between us.

"They hate light!" I shouted to the others.

Neve scooped up a stone from the mud and set to work trying to carve a sigil into it. Cabell stood in front of her, warding off the creatures to buy her more time.

The creatures snarled, turning toward the entrance to the clearing where Septimus and two of the Hollowers were stumbling out of the forest, their backs to us.

Septimus was drenched in the creatures' dark blood, screaming back at them as he smashed his axe into any limb that reached for him. One of the Hollowers with him was overrun and tackled to the ground. The creatures descended on him with claws and teeth, tearing out his throat, giving the others the opportunity to advance deeper into the clearing.

Where do I go? The thought twisted my stomach. I slashed at the creatures that leapt toward me, but each strike only seemed to renew their bloodlust.

"Tamsin!" Emrys called again. I pivoted, using his voice to reorient myself toward the others. When a path opened in that direction, I seized the chance and ran. Rancid clouds of breath bloomed with each step. Crackling bones and joints, chittering teeth—I didn't need to look to know that the creatures were right behind me.

Something caught the collar of my coat and wrenched me back. I screamed until my throat turned raw. The scent of death was inescapable as I thrashed, fighting to free myself. My foot slipped, and then I was falling, but not into the gaping maws of the monsters.

"Where do you think you're scampering off to, kitten?" The voice was right beside my ear.

Septimus.

He banded an arm around my chest and held me up in front of him. And somehow, the fact that it was him, and not one of the monsters, was even more terrifying.

He swung me to the right, one last flesh-and-blood shield to save himself. A blistering fury overtook me, and I heard the fire of it echoed in Cabell's and Emrys's pleas.

"Don't! Septimus!"

"Let her go!"

I tried to slip my coat off, to slash back at him with my knife, but Septimus pinned the hand with the knife to my side and used his other hand to grip the back of my neck. A creature chittered with excitement as I was presented to it as its latest dinner course.

"Nothing personal," Septimus sneered from behind me. "But it's time for you to actually be useful—"

The stench of blood was smothering, but a sudden calm came over my mind, like the moment you surrender to a powerful current and use its force to carry you toward whatever fate awaits.

I wasn't going to die for him, and I wasn't going to save him, either.

My palm was slick with sweat, forcing me to grip my knife tighter as I adjusted the angle of its blade. His grip had slackened just long enough to do what I had to.

"Purr, kitten," I snarled, then slammed the knife into his leg, just above the knee.

Septimus screamed, the sound wrenching from his chest. It was pure animal. He knew—he knew as he fell to the ground, unable to run, as he lost his grip on me, what would happen next.

The axe fell from his hand as one of the monsters slammed into him, claws tearing into his chest.

I grabbed for the blood-soaked weapon, my mind barely registering that its handle was still warm from his skin as I hacked at the monsters around me. I turned, crashing into Emrys. His eyes were wild as he gripped my arms, his face stricken.

"Are you okay?" he asked, his voice breaking. "Are you all right?"

The only thing I could gasp out in response was *"Run!"*

We did. A creature impaled itself on my blade; another bit at my hair, as if to drag me to the edge of the trees, where more of them waited.

Neve's scream exploded through the clearing. I whirled around, my heart rioting in my chest, searching for her and Cabell in the darkness. I took a running step forward, only to stop as the clouds parted overhead like curtains and a pillar of blue-white light poured down over the sorceress.

The creatures screeched in protest, falling back—but not far enough to be saved as the light fractured, slicing through the air like shards of glass. The air whistled and I ducked down, covering my head as the creatures were torn to shreds of viscera. The light's heat burned them from within, creating a ring of smoldering fires.

"Tamsin!"

I looked up to find Cabell rushing toward me, his face stricken with terror as he slid the last bit of distance between us.

"I'm okay, I'm okay!" I told him.

He hauled us both up and dragged me toward the others. The pillar of light expanded to reach us before we reached it, incinerating the creatures but passing over my skin like a warm stream. I felt a tug at my core, as if it were pulling me into its protective depths.

Wiping the mud from my face, I shielded my eyes.

Neve stood behind a shocked Cabell, her arms outstretched in front of them. Magic blazed around her like a wild flame, nearly blinding in its intensity. Her braids had fallen out of their buns as we'd fled, and now lifted at her shoulders, rising with the incandescent swell of power. The intensity of her expression, her face glittering with sweat, was as breathtaking as the way her power electrified the air and turned the clearing into the heart of a star.

Neve's eyes flicked to us, her face set with the kind of determination that made you ache to see it. The raw potential of her power was stunning. I looked around, trying to find the sigil she had used. A large stone was at her feet, but the sigil for a protective spell was only half finished. But that was impossible—this power had to be drawn and channeled through the marking.

"Neve . . . ," I began.

"I can't hold this much longer," she warned, her voice crackling with magic. "It's too much—"

"How are you doing this?" I asked her.

She shook her head, clenching her fists. "I don't know—I thought we would die and it just—it just happened—"

The magic flared brighter, hotter. The monsters retreated into the shadows of the trees.

"I don't suppose anyone has a half-decent idea for how we could survive this," Emrys said faintly, a hand pressed to the wound on his arm.

"I'll take a bad idea at this point," Cabell said, his expression dark. He was still panting, but it was the hair growing thicker and darker on the back of his hands that had me terrified.

"Are you all right?" I asked him.

Cabell, for once, didn't lie about it. "Need a second. Need to slow my heart."

Emrys's eyes shifted off where Cabell crouched, face pressed to his filthy hands, breathing deeply. I gave a small shake of the head at his questioning look.

"What are the chances they'll get bored of being obliterated and go away?" I asked.

The barrier flickered. Briefly, I wondered if I had pissed off a god of luck in a past life.

"Guys," Neve said, her voice cracking. "I'm sorry, there's nothing left—"

I moved close to her side, holding the axe out in front of me. Emrys's back was pressed to my side as he faced the other way, burning hot in the freezing air. Cabell staggered to his feet again, his face flickering with shadows as he fought to keep his grip on his mind and body.

We are going to die. That strange, deep calm returned, cold and accepting. *We're going to die.*

"We'll try to get to the tower Neve thinks is at the isle's center," I said. "If we can find some sort of shelter—"

A blazing light tore through the air in front of us, soaring past the devastated trees to slam into the nearest creature's shriveled skin. I jumped as it went up like a match, screeching until I thought my eardrums would burst. Spinning, I searched for the source, but there was no need.

A volley of flaming arrows flashed through the dark, streaking over our heads. Neve's magic was a shield against the heat of the burning world around us, and I knew the second she released it, we would be consumed, too.

"Is that . . . ?" Cabell began, spinning around.

The horses and their riders charged at a full gallop, sending the remaining monsters scattering like rats back the way they'd come, seeking the cold relief of the dank water.

The flames illuminated the knights' silver armor as they circled the barrier, bows at the ready. Their horses stomped and pawed at the ground, shuddering with the unspent exertion. Five in total.

"Release your magic, sorceress!" one of them shouted.

Neve startled at the vehemence of the words and didn't do as she was told. If anything, her magic burned brighter than it had before.

The same knight sheathed his sword with a sound of quiet fury. The others waited, slashing and shooting at any mindless creature that dared to approach us again. When Neve still didn't drop the shield, the first knight reached up, ripping his helmet off.

A long silver braid, shining bright as the sword in her hand, spilled from beneath it. The face that stared down at us from her black horse was pale and freckled and young—not the grizzled, scarred man I'd been expecting.

"I said," the young woman ground out, "release your magic, sorceress."

Emrys was the first to shake off his shock. "Not to be an ungrateful wretch, but won't that roast us alive?"

"Our fire will not harm you," said another, removing her own helmet. She was dark-haired and dark-eyed, her tight curls fluttering around her head with the foul breeze. Her skin was a rich brown, save for the place where a raised pink scar ran down one cheek, and her expression was coolly reassuring.

The others followed. All young.

All women, it seemed.

"Unless you want to die here with the rest of the travelers, I suggest that you come with us now," she continued. "We will take you to safety."

"Not the sorceress," the silver-haired one snapped. "They can devour her."

"Cait," another admonished.

"Who are you?" I managed to get out.

"I'm Caitriona of the Nine," the girl with the strange silver hair said. "These are my sisters. I do not know how you've come here, but I can tell you that this is no place to die."

"And where is this place, exactly?" Emrys asked politely.

Some part of me—some small, hated corner of my heart—had held on to a dying ember of belief that Neve might have made a terrible mistake. That she had somehow brought us to another realm, another place far from the one where Nash was trapped with the ring.

That same ember was crushed beneath the heel of the girl staring down at us, suspicion creasing her brow. Neve's magic faded like a hurricane easing to a gentle fall of rain.

"Do you not know it by sight?" she asked sardonically, pulling her helmet back on. "You have found the blessed isle of Avalon."

PART II

THE
WASTELAND

14

We rode across the misty isle in a ferocious storm of galloping hooves and clattering armor. No one had said a word since leaving the clearing, and none of the others had bothered to give us their name. I could practically feel their eyes shifting to Neve again and again, the outright hatred that radiated from them like our breath fogging the air white.

We had all accepted having our hands bound yet again as the condition for riding with them—*accepted* being the only option aside from being left there to be eaten.

Neve had been placed behind Caitriona of the Nine. All the priestesses rode stiff-backed because of their metal cuirass—a chest plate that extended around their backs—but with Caitriona, the armor seemed to conform to her body instead of the other way around.

We passed through a maze of dark wilderness and mist. My inner thighs were soaked through with the horse's foaming sweat and from the strain of having to squeeze them tight to keep from being bucked off.

"You can hold on to me," my knight said quietly. "I'd rather not have to stop and pick you up if you fall and crack your skull, if it's all the same to you?"

I snorted. "Fine by me."

My hands were only loosely bound, which made it easier to grip the bottom edge of the armor around her back.

"Do you have a name, or are you just of the Nine?" I asked.

Now it was her turn to snort. "Betrys. Of the Nine."

"All right, Betrys," I said, some of my frustration falling away. "Thanks, by the way."

"No thanks are needed," she said, her voice quiet and dignified. "It is our responsibility to protect the isle and those living within it."

"That"—I tried to think of a delicate way to put it—"seems complicated. Is all of Avalon like this?"

Betrys fell back into that tightly held silence, gently kicking the horse to drive it faster.

I glanced over to where Cabell—naturally—seemed perfectly at ease riding behind another of the knights, a girl with pale skin and close-cropped hair the color of bark. They spoke quietly. He caught my eye and gave me a smile that was too grim to be reassuring.

The Nine. The order of priestesses who conducted the rituals of Avalon and directed the worship of the creator Goddess they believed in.

Apparently, they'd undergone a bit of rebranding in the last several hundred years, because I had no memories of reading about them barreling through the shadows of the isle on horseback to battle monsters. And Nash, a loyal servant to hyperbole and lover of exaggeration, wouldn't have left such a dramatic detail out of his campfire tales.

The name slid through my heart like a blade. *Nash.*

Until now, I'd been so consumed with survival that I hadn't been able to think of anything else, including the reason we'd come in the first place.

I cast my gaze around the shadowed land, wondering how Nash could possibly have survived this place. The rotting trees, the barren streambed that had become a trail for the horses, swarms of insects stripping the rotting flesh from the bones of one of the monsters, stone cottages with no lights inside . . . What *could* survive here beyond scavengers and creatures who lived only to sate their hunger?

The mist was inescapable, hovering above the land like a chilling manifestation of resentment—of lost love, of lost beauty, of whatever this place had once been. Its damp fingers traced icy patterns into my skin.

The tower Neve had described took its time in revealing itself, as if needing to watch us from a distance to decide whether to allow us to approach. As we came closer, my eyes couldn't devour the sight of it quickly enough. The sheer size of the tower and the imposing walls that surrounded it left me light-headed.

And that was before I realized it had been built into the trunk of a colossal tree.

Stark branches fanned out over the walls, sheltering the courtyard below from the black, starless sky. It was unlike anything I had ever seen. The tree primitive and ancient, the tower medieval, speaking to the last contact this Otherland had with our mortal world.

The Immortalities I'd read were created long after the last sorceresses had been exiled from Avalon. None had seen this very sight with their own eyes.

"What's that tree?" I asked Betrys.

"We call it the Mother," she said. "It was the first life on the isle. The first gift of the Goddess."

The deep moat around the structure held only a few feet of murky water and far more sickly weeds, but it was still impossible to cross without a bridge. I was relieved to see torches burning along the wall, and the shapes of men and women high above us.

"Open the gates!" the silver-haired knight called. Her horse danced on the stones of the path, as anxious as the rest of us to get inside.

The old wooden drawbridge lumbered down slowly, groaning with its own weight. Its edge had barely touched the ground in front of her when she charged across it. A metal portcullis lifted from within the walls, revealing the shadowed courtyard beyond it.

Betrys and I brought up the rear of the group, and no sooner had we passed through it than the portcullis lowered and the bridge rose.

Several men wearing chest plates, some armed with crude-looking swords, others with simple bows, rushed up to us.

"Blessed Mother," one said as the silver-haired knight swung down from her horse. "Were they . . ."

"The source of the light?" Betrys finished. "Yes. Can you take the horses?"

"But—" another man began, staring at us with something akin to shock and fascination. "Who are they?"

Betrys slid down from her saddle and reached up to help me. I hadn't appreciated how tall—or strong—she was until she all but lifted me off the horse like a snot-nosed kid.

"Do what Caitriona says," she whispered to me. "Do not fight whatever she has planned. We shall have this sorted soon, but she has a protocol she prefers to follow."

She led us around the impressive tower, through gaps between rough-hewn buildings and hastily built wooden structures, and past a small dirt arena, complete with archery targets, blade-battered posts, and straw-stuffed dummies.

Caitriona marched us on, guiding Neve by the shoulder, to a narrow, winding staircase nestled inside the far right corner of the wall. Rather than up to the ramparts, we went down.

And down.

And down.

I slowed, but Betrys nudged me on. The stench of straw, rat droppings, and mildew met us at the threshold, a dire warning of what we would find inside the chamber.

As Caitriona stepped inside and removed a heavy ring of keys from a hook on the wall, the candles lining the narrow walkway flickered with sudden fire. They burned away the thin layer of mist trapped in that darkness, and in their struggling glow I made out six distinct iron-barred cells.

Caitriona opened the nearest one, guiding a clearly exhausted Neve inside. The sorceress eyed the way Caitriona gripped her wand, looking like she wanted to say something. They'd taken our weapons before we'd mounted the horses, but now they removed our restraints to separate us from our bags. My heart dropped like a stone when I felt Betrys pull at my workbag.

"I'll cut the strap if I have to," she warned. "You'll get them back, I swear it."

I glowered but handed it to her, using the moment to duck into the same cell as Neve. It would be easier to make some sort of escape if we weren't all separated.

The door slammed heavily behind us and locked with a sound that seemed to reverberate to the back of my teeth. Emrys and Cabell were forced to share a cell directly across the walkway from us.

With no promise of when they might return, Caitriona and the others left, their heavy footsteps battering the stairs before fading altogether.

"Really?" I called after them, banging my hands on the bars. "A dungeon? *Seriously?*"

"Tams," Cabell said, sounding spent. "Please. Screaming at them didn't work in Giza or Athens, and it's not going to work here, either."

"Exactly how many dungeons have the two of you been in?" Emrys asked.

The memory of those two jobs with Nash was enough to turn my mood even uglier. I blew out a hard breath through my nose, crossing my arms over my chest and leaning a shoulder against the cold metal.

Neve leaned back against the side of our cell with a weary sigh.

"Are you okay?" I asked her.

"Define *okay*," Neve said, giving me a look of exasperation.

"I meant are you hurt?" I asked. "What was that spell you cast?"

"Don't know," Neve said, the words heavy with fatigue. "I panicked and it just happened."

Cabell and I shared a silent look of understanding. If his curse could be triggered by extreme stress or emotion, it stood to reason that a sorceress's power worked the same.

Something at the back of the cell caught Neve's eye. She stumbled toward it, kneeling where a root, coiled into the shape of a fist, had breached the stone wall.

"No way," she breathed out. "Scarlet elf cap *and* turkeytails? Oh, Neve, it's your lucky day."

"Really? Turkeytail?" Emrys asked, straightening.

"Calm down, soil sniffer," I said, "it's fungi, not buried treasure."

By the time I came to stand beside her, Neve had already carefully extracted several small mushrooms from the root.

"Are either of those types edible?" Cabell asked. "Because I could really use a bite of something."

"How can you eat after what we just saw?" Emrys asked, aghast.

"His stomach is the most powerful motivator he possesses," I said.

"You say that like *your* motivator isn't esophagus-melting instant coffee," Cabell said.

"That's what *I* said!" Emrys crowed. "And no, not edible. At least not without cooking them first. Turkeytail is usually consumed in powder form—"

"No one cares, Dye," I said. "Well, except for Neve, I guess."

"Fungi *are* amazing," Neve said, her voice breathless with a stunning amount of excitement, given her obvious exhaustion. "Amazing."

"Because . . . you can use them to poison people?" I ventured, struggling to follow.

"No, of course not." Neve gave me another look. "Because they're harbingers of death."

"Obviously," I said, my voice faint.

"Neve," Cabell said. "Has anyone told you that you're kind of goth?"

"She means they're rotters. They decompose dead organic material and return its nutrients to the soil," Emrys said, staring at the wall opposite him. "So something else can be born from that death. The fact that they're there isn't a good sign for the health of the tree."

"Wonderful," I muttered.

Neve looked up at me. "Don't be afraid of fungi. There's so much beauty in that decay."

"If you say so."

"Tamsin used to love mushrooms," Cabell piped up.

I gripped the bars of my cell, glaring at him. "Don't you dare."

Cabell smiled. "She used to think the tiny greenling Fair Folk liked to use them as little houses and umbrellas."

"I'm sure they do!" Neve said, her face bright. "The mushroom is the fruit of the fungi, see, but the most important part of it is underground, the mycelium pathways that connect entire forests. Trees even use them to communicate with each other. I bet the Mother tree is connected to those in the sacred apple grove—maybe even all of the isle's trees."

"It is. Every bit of wildlife is connected to that tree," Emrys said. "Why else do you think the whole island is dying at once?"

I looked back at the roots; the cold, damp air curled around my face, as if studying me in turn.

It was a long time before I spoke again—or maybe not long at all. Time seemed to have no form or meaning in the dim light. I started to do laps of the cell, just to stay awake. Seeing a faint scratching on the wall, I wiped the grime away from it. The strange letters there shifted and twisted, becoming ones I recognized.

I blinked, rubbing at my eyes. "Did I just imagine it or did the words on this wall decide to become English?"

"The One Vision is more than sight," Cabell said from the cell across the walkway. He had stretched out on his back, using his leather jacket as a cushion. "It'll translate languages you see or hear to the one you speak, and translate the words you're speaking for the listener."

"Excuse me?" I sputtered. "Are you telling me that I'm the only one in the guild who actually had to learn to speak ancient Greek and Latin?"

"Hellfire, Bird, you actually learned those languages?" Emrys said, eyes wide.

Cabell gave me a consoling look. "What does the writing on the wall say?"

"Hang on," I said, my irritation growing, "can we just go back to the part where no one bothered to mention the language thing?"

"I didn't want to make you feel any worse about it than you already did," Cabell said. "And honestly, after a certain point, I thought you would have figured it out."

"Why wasn't it mentioned in any of the books?" I asked. "Or Immortalities?"

"Because it was common knowledge for people who actually had the One Vision?" Cabell offered. "You know how many historical details have been lost that way. I assume that's why none of the Immortalities referred to the Mother tree either."

I sent him a withering look. "Any other long-held secrets you want to mention now?"

"No, but I'm still wondering what the wall says," he answered.

I turned back, reading it aloud for them. "*He is the way.*" There was another line scratched into the stone to the right of it. "*You shall know our pain.*"

"Creepy," Emrys said, "but intriguing."

"Wake me up if things get more intriguing," Cabell said with a wave of his hand.

Eventually, I sat down myself, leaning against the wall opposite Neve, who had curled up and gone to sleep. Emrys was a mirror of me across the way.

I squinted through the dim candlelight as he reached inside his boot and pulled out a small knife, then took a small chunk of wood from his jacket pocket.

"How the hell did you get that by them?" I demanded. They'd searched us thoroughly.

"You think I'm going to reveal my secrets to the only real competition?" he asked with an infuriating wink. "Though if you're up for a game of Two Truths and a Lie—"

"I think I'll pass," I interrupted, rolling my eyes. He had helped us earlier—through his usual brand of charm and lies, of course, but helped us nonetheless. Still, it didn't mean I had to warm to him and his inane quirks.

"Suit yourself." He resumed his whittling, focusing on it with surprising intensity.

"What's that going to be, anyway?" I heard myself ask.

He looked up, and it was only then that I noticed the pallor of his face and the dark stain on the sleeve of his sweater—he hadn't wrapped his wound.

"Dunno," he said. "It hasn't revealed itself quite yet."

My jeans were torn at the knee, a neat split from one of the creature's claws. It made tearing a strip of the fabric away easier. Emrys looked over at the sound.

"Here." I bundled it into a ball and threw it across the walkway between us.

It landed just beyond the bars of his cell. He stared at it.

"I know it's not clean, but you have to bind your arm," I told him. "If you bleed to death, I'm not dragging your corpse back up all those steps. Given the size of your ego, your head alone must weigh fifty pounds."

He reached through the bars carefully, stretching as far as he could until the fabric hooked onto his fingers. "Even with this, you still owe me one."

"You and your favors," I muttered. "As far as I'm concerned, we're square."

"I got us here, didn't I?" he said. "Both with the offering and by convincing Septimus that you all had to come."

I rolled my eyes so hard they actually ached with the force of it. "Here I thought you tricked your father's henchmen out of common human decency. And the bottle came from Madrigal, so that hardly counts."

"Fine. We're even, then." He knotted the fabric over his arm. "But thanks. Are *you* okay?"

My heart gave an unwelcome little murmur at the way he was studying me in the flickering candlelight.

"I'm fine," I told him.

But the memory was there when I closed my eyes. The rush of their spidery limbs over me. The stench of death on their hot breath. Septimus's look of pure rage.

"I'm fine."

"You said that already." Emrys stretched a hand out through the bars again, as if needing to test the distance between us.

The sickening crunch of bone and cartilage. The wet spill of blood on the ground as they ripped Septimus apart. The way his last breath had been a scream.

The creatures had torn him apart, but I had killed him.

I drew my knees in close, trying to gather some warmth at my cold center. It was strange how that realization had been so slow to catch up with me, but now that it was here, it was like a third prisoner in the cell, chained to my conscience.

"He deserved it," I said hoarsely. "Didn't he?"

"Yes," Emrys said, the word searing. He turned more fully toward me, gripping the bars with his other hand. "Look at me."

I don't know why, but I did.

"Yes," he repeated. "Anytime you doubt it, anytime you start to worry you did the wrong thing, I'll tell you that. And even if we're old and gray and I can barely remember my own name, I'll remember *this* and I'll still tell you the same."

I released a soft breath, letting my head fall back against the damp stones. It would have been so easy to reach my own arm out between the bars and see how close our fingers were. It would have been so easy to thank him.

The way he was looking at me . . . His words had wound something up in my core, the tension spreading through me until my whole body felt unbearably tight. Like any word, any movement, might twist it a tiny bit more, until it snapped and I unraveled. I didn't know what would happen then. I didn't want to know.

So I cut the thread myself.

"That was a very moving speech, Trust Fund," I said. He flinched at the name. "But I'd prefer you tell me why you took this job, and why you're so worried about Daddy Dearest finding out about it?"

Emrys drew in a sharp breath, saying nothing. He slid his arm back through the gaps in the metal, letting it fall across his lap. Any small bit of guilt I'd felt at shutting him down evaporated with his silence. He kept saying those words—*trust me, believe me*—but with him, they were little better than smoke and shadows. Much like his performance with Septimus and the others.

"I'm getting that ring, Tamsin," Emrys said.

"No," I promised. "You're not."

Cabell pushed up suddenly from the ground, twisting toward the stairwell.

"What?" I asked.

He held out his hand, quieting me.

"—there are *rules*. An order to these things." The words echoed down the stones. I recognized the crisp alto of Caitriona's voice, not to mention the imperiousness that shot through each word like a steel-tipped arrow.

"You did the right thing. It is never wrong to be cautious, especially in times like these." I scrambled up onto my feet at his unfamiliar male voice.

"There's a difference between caution and cruelty," came another voice, this one also young and female, with a bit of rasp. "Why not come fetch me to dress their wounds—or were you too preoccupied with not bothering to ask why they've come?"

The young woman appeared a moment later, hurrying down the

remaining steps, Caitriona close behind. She wore a simple blue dress tied at the waist, but the color had long since faded as the fabric turned threadbare. Her hair naturally curled like rippling water, and as she moved into the light of her lantern, I saw it was inky blue in color. Her amber-toned skin was flushed with emotion. She had bold, thick brows, a strong nose, and a quirk to her lips, but her brown eyes, the pupils ringed with an unusual luminescent blue, were gentle pools of emotion.

"It's as I thought," she said, placing her hands on her hips. "Miserable, the whole lot of you."

"*Miserable* about sums it up," Emrys said, hauling himself up with his good arm. Unable to resist a touch of flirting with the new arrival—typical.

She let out a *tsk* of irritation at the sight of the makeshift bandage I'd given him.

The others arrived on the girl's heels. Caitriona had removed her armor, leaving only a loose linen tunic tightly belted at the waist and dark brown breeches tucked into leather boots. She lifted her chin, surveying us with that same look of suspicion she'd had in the forest.

"Nice of you to remember we're still alive down here," I muttered. "Who's Sir Grump-a-lot?"

"How dare you speak of him with such disrespect," Caitriona said, one hand landing on the dagger strapped to her thigh.

The man held up both of his hands. "Easy, Cait. It's all right."

He was average height, his silvery hair holding only hints of its past blond. He had a full beard, neatly trimmed, and a rather magnificent scar that cut across the bridge of his nose and ran down his right cheek. One hand was covered by an armored gauntlet, and it took me several long moments of studying him to realize there wasn't a hand beneath it.

He surveyed me in return with hard gray-blue eyes and a frown.

Caitriona fell back toward the stairwell at his words, glowering.

She kept her eyes on him and stayed close, as if waiting for another command.

"Always one for delicacy, our Cait is," the other young woman said. She held out her hand toward Cait, wagging her fingers expectantly. Cait shot her a look of deep annoyance before handing over the heavy ring of keys on her belt.

"I'm Olwen," the girl continued, unlocking Emrys and Cabell's cell first. "That is Sir Bedivere, protector of the tower and all of us who survive within its walls."

The knight stooped his head in a small bow at the acknowledgment. "As much as these old bones can protect anyone, at least."

Cabell caught my gaze as we stepped out of our cells. I knew exactly what he was thinking, because Nash, with all of his many stories, had ensured there'd be just one thought in both of our minds: *the* Bedivere—of Arthur's knights?

I eyed the man, trying to take quick stock of him. What I remembered from Nash's effusive stories was that Bedivere had been King Arthur's marshal and one of his closest companions, sacrificing a hand in battle to protect his king.

He'd survived Arthur's final battle and been sent to return the famed sword Excalibur to Avalon's High Priestess. He had done it with great reluctance—so much so that the dying king had to chastise him into completing the task. Then he'd retired to a hermitage and passed out of legend.

Or so it was told.

If this was truly the original Bedivere, and if there was any truth to the wider web of stories that branched out around him, he might have accompanied Arthur's body here to Avalon, to his resting place. The sleeping king was kept alive through magic, until the day he was needed again.

But that would make Bedivere hundreds of years old—over a thousand, I corrected myself. I knew the Otherlands had been removed from the mortal realm through a spell that shifted them out of time's natural flow. I'd assumed that they existed in a state of suspension, almost like a held breath, but some semblance of time had to pass here, even if it was off from our own, otherwise how would anyone grow or age?

Though . . . the sorceresses were incredibly long-lived. Who was to say the same magic that extended their lives didn't grant a kind of immortality here?

"And do any of you have names?" Olwen prompted.

"Oh—right, sorry," Cabell said, and did the honors introducing us.

Olwen circled Neve, who still wore her exhaustion plainly, all but swaying on her feet. "You must be the sorceress? Yes you are. My—you hear the stories, but they simply cannot compare. You're from the mortal world, yes? Your manner of dress is fascinating." She turned to Emrys, lightly touching the denim knotted around his arm. "What sort of fabric is this?"

"Olwen," Caitriona said sharply. "If you must heal them, *heal* them quickly so we may discover their purpose in coming here."

The other priestess rocked back on her heels. "I'll need to bring them to the infirmary, of course."

"Of course," Caitriona repeated, the portrait of exasperation.

"All of my tools and tonics are there," Olwen continued. She gestured dramatically to Emrys's arm. "Would you allow this poor, weary traveler to be afflicted with skin-rot? Must I sharpen my blades and resign myself to cutting it from his body once it festers?"

Emrys startled, pulling back. "Excuse me?"

"All right," Bedivere said good-naturedly. "You've made your point, my dear." He turned to us, inclining his head toward the stairs. "This way."

15

Olwen's infirmary was in the sprawling courtyard around the tower, perhaps not so coincidentally located beside the small fighting arena I'd noticed before. The stone structure had been there for a long time, judging by the tilt of the foundation and the worn grooves leading to its doorstep.

Earthy greens mingled with the animal scent of the tallow candles scattered around the room. At the far edge were two cots, but most of the space was taken up by a worktable cluttered with pots and bowls of ground herbs. It was an apothecary as much as a place of healing.

The back wall was lined with shelves to the low-slung roof, brimming with various baskets and glass containers. The latter's floral shape and faint iridescence made me wonder if they were the work of the Fair Folk.

The space was hardly bigger than the dungeon, but in an odd way, its diminutive size was reassuring. There was no space for anyone or any*thing*, really, to hide.

Which was why I was so surprised when I nearly tripped on a small figure crouched behind the worktable, fishing around in the baskets on the lower shelves.

"Flea!" Olwen cried, shooing her away. "You've already eaten the last of my dried berries—out with you!"

"There was more, I saw 'em!" the girl protested. She couldn't have been more than ten by the look of her, all gangly limbs and sparrow-like bones.

"Those are elderberries, you little jobbernowl," Olwen said, leaning down to meet her at eye level, "and if you eat but one of them, they'll turn your stomach inside out and, mark my words, you will not like how your supper tastes the second time it crosses your tongue."

The girl scowled, her milk-white face smudged with dirt and soot. "You're a right grump. Don't ye need to go down to the pools or something? Take a wee bath?"

Olwen narrowed her eyes, and the bright blue rings around her pupils seemed to flare in warning. I looked between her and the girl, confused.

"This is Fayne, better known to us as Flea," Caitriona said, holding out a hand to the girl. Flea shot to her side, but not before giving us all a rather glorious stink eye.

"Who's they?" she asked suspiciously.

"Who *are* they?" Caitriona corrected with surprising gentleness. She extracted the girl's hand from her mouth just as Flea began to bite at her nails. "That is precisely my question."

"First, though," Olwen cut in, "who appears to be bleeding the most?" When no one immediately responded, Olwen turned to Emrys. "It's you, I'm afraid. Sit on the cot and remove your tunic, if you please."

Emrys hesitated, his gloved hands twisting. "I'd rather not, if it's all the same to you."

Olwen pulled back, confused. "I assure you, there's no need to spare my modesty."

"Oh no, I was talking about my own delicate sensibilities," Emrys said as he lowered himself onto the stiff spine of the cot. Untying the bandage, he shrugged off his mud-caked jacket and pulled at the torn sleeve of his sweater and undershirt. "Could you just cut it?"

"You lose a bet and get an embarrassing tattoo or something?"

Cabell asked, leaning back against a wall. Covered in grime and blood, Emrys no longer looked the part of a princeling.

"You know I love a bet, but, alas, no. Not all of us can be as stoic or manly a specimen as you, Lark," Emrys said.

He was smiling, but there was a sharpness there I hadn't expected. One I immediately wanted to press against, just to see what would happen.

"Will you at least take the gloves off?" I asked.

Neve swayed on her feet, falling against my shoulder. I caught her before she could drop to the floor.

"Neve? Are you all right?" I asked. Cabell came to her other side and helped me lower her into the room's lone chair.

"'S fine," Neve said, her head bobbing. She tried to wave away our concerns. "Just . . . tired."

Olwen was there in a heartbeat. "Got a touch of the swoons from using all that magic, do you? Flea, will you put those hands to use and start a fire? Do you remember the mixture for the hot tonic?"

"One part cinnamon," the girl said sullenly, "one part toad tongue—"

"What?" Neve asked, eyes going wide.

"The girl is having a laugh," Bedivere clarified.

"That was unkind," Olwen told Flea. "And you need to prove to me you've been studying."

Flea huffed out a sigh but got to work kindling a fire and setting a small cauldron above it. She used a nearby jug to fill it with water and recited, in a petulant voice that made me instantly like her, "One part cinnamon, three parts apple—boiled fifteen minutes."

"We've barely any of the apples left," Caitriona protested. "The blessings of the sacred grove are not for the likes of sorceresses."

"It's really fine," Neve said weakly. "I just need to rest."

"Without a good cup of tonic, you'll need to sleep for a fortnight to regain your strength," Olwen told her. "We saw your light from here. That was no small magic."

Caitriona scoffed and looked on the verge of saying something snippy to that, but Bedivere placed a calming hand on her shoulder.

"Let's begin with how they found their way to the isle, shall we?" he suggested. "The pathways have been sealed for an age."

"They're looking for their father," Neve said sleepily.

I turned to her, horror streaking through me. My mind struggled for words, any sort of lie to undo what the sorceress had just done. "No, we—we were—"

In a single statement, Neve had exposed our plan and blown any possible cover.

"Is that true?" Bedivere asked. To my surprise, he and the others looked intrigued.

"Yes," I said finally. I could admit, however begrudgingly, that the best lies often bore a piece of the truth. "We think he became . . . disoriented in the mists. He may have been searching for a way here."

Flea stood from the small hearth, her face alight with more than the fire's glow as she looked to Caitriona. "Oh! There's the—"

"Hush," Caitriona told her sharply. "Don't you have chores, Flea?"

"I finished 'em," the girl shot back.

"What were you going to say?" I pressed. Flea's words had made my heart skip with possibility, but now she only glared at me, retreating to stand in front of Caitriona.

The crackle of the firewood was the only sound between us for several moments.

"I don't mean to be a bother, but . . . ," Emrys said weakly, "I wouldn't have taken the bandage off if I'd known you wanted to have an in-depth discussion first."

"Oh dear, yes," Olwen said.

She retrieved a pair of shears from the worktable and set about cutting his sleeve and removing pieces of it from the open wounds. Emrys hissed as she dabbed at it with something that smelled vaguely sweet and not at all like alcohol.

"I assume, having traveled here with a sorceress," Bedivere said, "you are all aware of the true nature of magic and the Otherlands. Yet, even without knowing what's become of Avalon, why would he search for the isle?"

"That's our question too," I said. "He was one of the Cunningfolk, so he knew the stories of the isle."

"Cunningfolk?" Olwen repeated. "That's not a term I'm familiar with."

"People born in our world with a magical gift of some kind," Cabell clarified.

"I see," she said. "Is it because they're descended from different beings? For example, my mother was a naiad, a water nymph. And our sister Mari is an elfin. We were born with abilities that our sisters do not possess."

"No one's really sure," Cabell said. "Possibly."

I hadn't realized the priestesses of Avalon could be anything other than human, but this at least explained Olwen's unusual hair and eyes.

"What sorts of magic gifts?" Flea demanded.

"Well, for example," Emrys said, looking up at the rack of herbs drying over his head, "I can tell you that's horehound, most commonly used to ease coughs, yes?"

Flea looked distinctly unimpressed, but Olwen was delighted. "Aren't you clever. How did you know?"

"It told me as much," Emrys said with a shrug. "I can also tell you that you planted it in largely barren soil, that it knew what it was as it sprouted from your seeds and fought to break through the ground, only to never see the sun. That it knows its purpose, and your face, but very little life lingers in it now after being cut from its roots. It fades more each day as the bundles dry out, but it's not painful."

Olwen reached for the nearby shelf, retrieving a small silver compact. As she opened it, a honey-sweet scent was released into the air. Scooping a generous heaping of yellow ointment out onto her fingers, she applied a thick coat over Emrys's jagged wounds. The bleeding stopped completely as it dried and hardened into a shell-like finish.

"It must be magic, otherwise you gave yourself a good crack on the head coming in," Olwen said faintly. "Speaking with plants . . . we can feel the life in them, of course, the soul granted by the Goddess, but they have thoughts and feelings?"

"Of course they do," Emrys said. "Memory, too."

"As I was saying," I interrupted. "Our, uh, father . . ." The word pained me to say. "He loved the stories of the isle. He may have found a way in—some sort of tear in the boundaries between our world and yours—or he may have accidentally fallen through."

"I'm far more concerned that the sorceress was able to open the path," Caitriona said. "The ancient protective wards still stand. What trickery have you used? Is it not enough that your kind has poisoned our land through your curses?"

"Wait—" I began. "You think the sorceresses cursed Avalon when they were exiled? How long has the isle been like this?"

Caitriona's lip curled. "It was a long-festering curse. Slowly altering the land over centuries in the shadows until two years ago, when it fully bloomed."

"That's impossible," Neve said sharply. "The sorceresses saved Avalon. They had no reason to destroy it."

She might as well have taken Olwen's shears and stabbed Caitriona in the heart.

The priestess's face burned with renewed color as her temper boiled over. "Saved Avalon? Your kind betrayed the Goddess, relinquished your faith, and now serve only yourselves!"

"Sorceresses still believe that the Goddess exists and that she created us, we just don't think she has much to do with us anymore, so we have to decide our own fates," Neve managed to get out.

"Then you know nothing of the comfort of believing an all-loving Mother cares about you and watches over you," Caitriona said. "What a sad, dark existence."

"You don't know anything about our existence," Neve said with an impressive amount of heat, given that she looked ready to keel over.

"Here's the thing—without *my kind,* as you so rudely put it, *your* kind would have ceased to exist because you refused to do what had to be done. So, you're welcome."

Caitriona drew back like a snake about to strike.

"What are you talking about?" I asked, looking between them.

"I'm also confused," Cabell said.

"Thirded," came Emrys's voice behind us.

"Mother's mercy," Olwen muttered. "Must we speak of it?"

"We must," Caitriona said, still staring at Neve. "Tell them your blood-soaked tale, and tell it true."

"You bet I will," Neve said coldly. "Sorceresses call it the story unspoken. The betrayal so painful, the memory of it was cursed to never be recorded, even in Immortalities. It can't be read, only heard. My auntie told it to me."

The story unspoken. I'd seen that phrase thousands of times; the sorceresses used it to refer to their exile, but their memories never captured the story itself.

"What is it?" I asked. "What was the betrayal?"

"It's known as the Severing—" Neve began.

"The Forsaking," Caitriona interrupted. "It is known to us as the Forsaking."

"Fine, whatever. The Forsaking. It's the story that matters, not the name." Neve sniffed, her fingers curling against the table. "And the story begins with the druids. What they did."

I leaned forward, listening. It was well known to Hollowers that at least one order of druids had survived the Roman invasion of Celtic lands, and that they'd sought refuge in Avalon before the Otherland was severed from our own.

Beyond that, we had only the barest facts about their practices. The druids had been leaders, seers, and storytellers. While there had been a few female druids in far ancient times, they were rare exceptions to what ultimately became all-male orders. Several Immortalities mocked their robes and headdresses and their strange methods of scrying with dripping spoons. There was a saying the sorceresses seemed to love, too—*as dour as a druid.*

"Soon after they arrived in Avalon, the druids, resenting their loss of status, pursued a dark ambition. They sought out Lord Death, the master of Annwn, the realm of the wicked dead," Neve said. "He gave them dark magic so they could overcome the High Priestess's control and rule the isle for themselves. They would have turned it into a place of worship for their vicious god—and they tried."

"Tried how?" Cabell asked.

"There used to be many priestesses," Olwen explained, giving Neve a chance to rest. "Avalon is—was—a peaceful place; they had no reason to fear the druids, whom they worked alongside. Because of this, the druids were able to kill all but a handful of priestesses, even those merely in training, while they slept. Then they . . ."

Olwen paused, taking a moment to clear her throat and compose herself. "The druids killed every young girl on the isle, as a warning to those who might fight their rule, and they did it using Lord Death's power so their souls could not go on to the Goddess."

"Holy hellfire." I glanced at Cabell, whose face looked as bloodless as mine felt.

"The surviving priestesses, including the High Priestess, took shelter in the forests, but they were divided about what to do next," Neve said. "Here's the thing. Because of the restrictive rules of the Goddess's faith—"

"How dare you," Caitriona snapped.

"Allow her to finish," Olwen said, holding up a placating hand.

"As I was saying," Neve began again, "there are . . . certain beliefs you must hold and follow to keep the favor of the Goddess, including that you cannot use magic for selfish gains or to seek revenge."

"Ah," Emrys said. "Okay, I'm following again. Priestesses and sorceresses draw from the same universal magic, and only differ in how they use it."

"Precisely," Caitriona said. "We use our magic for healing, to cultivate our isle, and to protect those around us."

"Which is exactly why nine priestesses, led by High Priestess Viviane, were willing to surrender the isle to the druids to stop the killing," Neve said pointedly. "But seven, led by Morgan, King Arthur's half sister, as you might recall, *justifiably*"—she paused to emphasize the word—"fought back, killed the druids, and those sisters who lived to tell the tale were exiled to the mortal world because of it."

"It's the reason only nine priestesses remain in service of the Goddess," Olwen added. "As one dies, another is called. It has taken an age for all nine of us to be called."

Neve turned to face Caitriona again, fighting the drugging pull of exhaustion as she said, her voice firm, "Morgan and the others loved Avalon. They would never have cursed it."

"How could *any* curse be powerful enough to turn this place into a wasteland?" I asked.

I looked to Cabell, watching his expression for any hint of his thoughts. If it was a curse, he'd have felt it. He didn't turn to glance my way, though the way he shifted then, shuttering his expression, was acknowledgment enough. He placed two fingers against his opposite palm, our signal for *Later*.

Caitriona spun toward me. "You question my honor?"

"No one has said such a thing," Bedivere said, his gruff voice soothing. "Do not forget that the code also states that all those we encounter deserve truth, kindness, and good faith."

When Caitriona spoke again, she was more composed. "Before they were cast out, the sorceresses planted the seeds of dark magic they called a curse. One of sickness and pain, and it lingers still, rotting the isle."

"If that's true," I said, "then what are those creatures? Where did they come from?"

"They," Caitriona answered, her eyes cold, "are our dead."

16

The silence seemed to splinter with unspoken emotions. Neve, with her obvious devastation. Caitriona, still blazing with anger. Olwen disapproving. Bedivere's discomfort. Flea's wide-eyed wonder as she stared at her very first sorceress.

The neglected cauldron on the fire boiled over, its contents hissing and spitting like a living thing. The noise made Olwen jump to her feet, and that small movement was enough to break the suffocating hold Caitriona's words had cast over the room.

The sweet scent of apples and cinnamon curled around us as Olwen busied herself with ladling the hot liquid into a cup for Neve.

Neve blew on the steaming drink for a moment before taking a tentative sip. Her expression transformed in an instant, softening with wonder as she glanced down into the cup. Already, her color looked better and her expression more alert.

"Your dead . . . ," Neve began. "You mean, the curse transformed them?"

"Yes," Caitriona said sharply. "Again, I ask, *how* did you call the mist and bend it to your will? How did you pass through the wards that should have repelled you, Sorceress?"

"My name is Neve, not Sorceress," she said, pressing a hand against that small lump hidden beneath her shirt. "And I'll answer only to the High Priestess of Avalon."

"How unfortunate for you, then, that she's been dead for over a year," Caitriona said, a muscle in her jaw feathering. "The Nine is eight."

The young girl, Flea, turned scarlet, gulping down a huge breath. It was enough to make my own stomach clench in sympathy. I knew what it was like to have those big feelings and not be able to let them out—not ever.

Flea shoved past Caitriona and Bedivere, running into the night.

Olwen rose from tending the cauldron, and her hands went to her hips. "Well, now you've done it."

Caitriona's head fell back with a groan. Just before she stepped out into the courtyard, she turned back one last time, drawing in a breath.

"Don't trouble yourself, Cait," Bedivere said before she could speak. "I'll stay with Olwen and see that they're brought to their chambers with no trouble."

Caitriona turned, stiff-backed, toward the door.

"Wait," Neve said, her voice firm. She held out a hand. "My wand, please."

Caitriona tightened her fist around it. "You'll have it back when I decide you can be trusted."

"I don't need a wand to work magic," Neve said, her voice deceptively light. "And you can toss that shiny silver hair all you want, but I neither want nor need your trust, let alone your approval."

Caitriona stormed out into the waiting dark. The door slammed shut behind her, rattling every bottle on the nearby shelves.

"She's pleasant," I noted, hugging my arms to my middle. With the flames fighting to stay alive after their dousing, the infirmary had chilled.

As she passed the hearth, Olwen raised a hand, whispering something like a chant beneath her breath, stoking the embers back into a blaze, damp wood and all. Neve drank the sight down as if she were dying of thirst.

"You must understand," Olwen said, returning her attention to wrapping Emrys's arm in a clean bandage. "Cait's only aim is to protect the survivors. I'll not hear a word against her."

In truth, I didn't care about Caitriona or any of them. We'd come here for a reason, and that was the only thing that *could* matter.

"Do you agree with Caitriona's story of how the curse on the land came to be?" Emrys asked, easing some of the tension and changing the subject from how we'd gotten here.

"I believe it is a curse, yes, though I'm less sure of its source." Olwen rested her cheek in her palm, thinking. "Avalon was once a place where there was no true sickness. No hunger. No suffering. But I've read about the pestilences of the mortal world and cannot help but see the similarities now in how the darkness has spread."

Some sort of magical disease or virus? It was a terrifying idea, and not one I'd seen referenced in any book or Immortality.

"Does your magic work with all plants?" Neve asked Emrys. When he nodded, she had more questions for him: "What did you feel being out in the woods? Did the trees tell you anything?"

"Nothing," Emrys said with a small shudder. "Absolutely nothing. It was terrible."

"It began two years ago." Olwen nodded, breathing in deeply. "The curse came for the others first. The smallest of the fae, no bigger than flowers, then those who tended the sacred grove, the animals, even the trees and their dryads. My naiad kin."

She looked down at her hands again, collecting herself before continuing. "Any creatures who did not seek the shelter of the tower perished—which is to say, nearly all. The dark magic sickened and killed them, but it had a different effect on our dead. It caused them to . . . rise again. Transformed and corrupted of mind. Now they care only for their hunger."

"Mother of all," Neve whispered.

"We call them the Children of the Night, because they hunt in the dark hours," Olwen said. "They are living, and yet I feel nothing of the Goddess in them anymore. They can't seem to bear any light, and only fire can stop them. And fortunately for them, our skies have been overtaken by shadow. We have only a few sunlit hours each morning before the darkness returns."

"That must make it nearly impossible to grow anything," Emrys said.

"We have spells to mimic sun, but as the darkness spread, we lost our groves and fields to blight," Olwen said. "As you might imagine, Avalon now knows something of hunger."

"We are managing well enough, thanks to the Nine," Bedivere said gently. "Our food stock will carry us through another few months yet."

Olwen mustered a small smile at his praise.

"And you really have no idea what caused it?" Cabell pressed.

"Caitriona has her theory, as you've now heard vigorously told," Olwen said. "Some of my sisters agree, while others think the land sickened because the Goddess turned her back on us after the bloodshed."

"What about the druids?" I asked. "You said they worshiped Lord Death and used magic he gave to them—that they massacred *children*. Why aren't they higher on the list of suspects?"

"They might well be the source of our woes," Olwen said. "But we were raised with the belief that the sorceresses' choice was the worse of the two betrayals, because it came from those our elders loved and trusted most."

"That's ridiculous," I scoffed.

"Perhaps, but pain wears many faces—anger, suspicion, fear," Olwen said quietly. "When my sisters and I were called by the Goddess, we had to leave our families and homes behind to come to the tower for our training. High Priestess Viviane became like a second mother to us all. She taught us everything we know about the Goddess, magic, and ritual. But her grief from the Forsaking was also part of that inheritance, and it is difficult to dismiss that when it feels like a dismissal of her as well."

"Hang on," Cabell said. "Viviane? Was there more than one High Priestess with that name?"

"Only the one," Olwen confirmed with a sad smile. "And to answer what I suspect is your next question, yes, she was hundreds of years old at her death. Likely almost a thousand, if we were to measure her life by the more rapid passage of time in your world."

"Even factoring in the different timelines," I said, glad to at least have that confirmed, "not even sorceresses live that long. How did she manage it?"

"The magic of the vow she took to the Goddess—the one we all take as priestesses—kept her alive until nine new priestesses were finally born," Olwen continued. "The Forsaking was a scar on Viviane's heart, and she never forgave those who caused it. Some of my sisters have inherited her sentiments, though not nearly to the same degree."

"And you?" Neve asked.

"I understand why the sorceresses did what they did, though I can't condone it," Olwen said. "I know Sir Bedivere feels the same."

"Indeed." The old knight leaned against the doorframe, looking contemplative. "Such was the greed of the druids that I believe they would wish ill upon Avalon if they themselves could not rule it."

"Is there any proof either way?" Cabell asked. "Wouldn't death magic feel different than the power we draw from?"

"I couldn't say," Olwen said. "We have but one other clue to the cause of the sickness."

Olwen moved toward the shelves, her fingers skimming leather spines and scrolls until she found a small volume, the thick parchment pages roughly bound with knotted string. The One Vision bled and swirled the symbols on the first sheet into words I understood: *Wisdom of the Mother.*

"Here it is . . ." She cleared her throat, flipping her magnifying glass down in front of her eye. *"Three magics to be feared: curses born of the wrath of gods, poisons that turn soil to ash, and that which leaves one dark of heart and silver in the bone."*

Olwen set the volume down. "There's no record of such an affliction—*silver in the bone*—anywhere else. I feel certain the tower's

174

healer would have noted it in their own records, having examined some of the sorceresses and druids killed in the struggle. And yet . . ."

Olwen shifted back to her worktable, retrieving what appeared to be a long-necked forceps from a leather roll of tools. Then, her hand skimming over some of the covered jars and baskets, she retrieved what looked to be a weighty jar from the shelf and placed it on the worktable.

With a flick of the wrist, Olwen pulled the fabric away, and I found myself staring at a shriveled human head.

"Ooooh!" Neve gasped, captivated.

"Augh!" I gagged.

Olwen removed the lid from the jar, sending a foul odor into the air. It was the reek of death, made fouler by the green ooze the head had been suspended in.

Using the forceps, she fished the head out and set it down on the table, oblivious to the repulsed looks around the room. Even Bedivere, the battle-hardened knight, grimaced.

"Gather around, please," she said.

When only Neve did, Olwen looked up, confused.

"Not all possess your fascination with such things, dear one," Bedivere reminded her. "Perhaps a warning might not go amiss in the future."

The old knight spoke in such a fatherly manner, gentle with his advice and calming in a storm of emotions. Both Caitriona and Olwen adored him like a father—it was clear in the way they looked to him and responded to his words.

"I will work quickly to spare your stomachs," Olwen said.

Using a different metal tool, she opened a sickly flap of skin on the back of the skull. Beneath the wrinkles of the shriveled layer of flesh was the gleam of pure silver, as if the entire skull had been dipped into a molten vat of it.

"Hellfire," Cabell said in amazement, stooping to get a better look. "This happens to all of them?"

"All of them, and all of their bones," Olwen said. She looked to Neve, who was peering at the skull with obvious fascination. "Neve, perhaps you might be able to help me in my research. My knowledge of cursework is admittedly quite thin, and we do not possess many such accounts."

"Of course," Neve said, her eyes widening. "I'm sure we can figure this out."

My brows rose. That was quite the optimistic take.

"It's strange, isn't it?" Olwen said to Neve. "How we are born of the same isle and to the same Goddess, but now use our magic in such different ways. But I am glad to have met you, Neve, and though they may be frightened now, I know my sisters will come to share my gratitude."

"I can think of at least one who wouldn't agree," Neve said.

"She only needs time," Olwen promised. "If I am absolutely certain of anything, it is this: the Goddess led you here to us. All of you."

As Olwen spoke, I watched Bedivere's reaction. The old knight had seen his share of death and darkness, and his stony expression gave his thoughts away. He recognized the futility of the situation, just like I did.

"And I'm glad of it," Olwen said, "for there have been many days when it has felt as if the Goddess has turned her heart from us. Yet here you are. The path opened for you."

There was a faint knock on the door, and Betrys stepped inside, hugging a bundle to her chest. "You missed supper again."

"Well, I was rather preoccupied," Olwen said defensively.

"When are you not?" Betrys said in gentle admonishment.

Betrys set the bundle down on the table and opened the fabric to reveal a small chunk of bread and what looked like cold gray stew. My mouth watered.

"Thank you, sister," Olwen said.

"I don't need thanks," Betrys said. "I need to know that you're taking care of yourself. You'll go to the pools tonight, won't you? Any of us will be glad to accompany you."

"Yes, yes," Olwen said dismissively.

Betrys glanced over her shoulder at the rest of us. "I've orders to bring you to the springs to wash. You'll be given a change of clothes the others will find less alarming and be brought to private chambers to rest."

"What about our stuff?" I asked.

"You'll be reunited with your belongings there," Betrys confirmed. "However, there have been questions raised about this—"

She reached into a bag at her side and pulled out a familiar bundle of purple silk. Cabell coughed, sending me a look of *Do something*.

Emrys stood from the cot and came forward, intrigued. I watched the slow rise of his eyebrows as Betrys unwrapped Ignatius and held him up into the candlelight. His crusty eye remained mercifully closed.

Botheration. I'd completely forgotten about Ignatius. How had Septimus not stolen him—how had he not fallen out in all the chaos of the last two days?

I clasped my hands behind my back, and it took just about everything in me not to react in the silence that followed. Over the years, I'd learned that a speedy defense only made you look guiltier.

"Oh—I have one too!" Olwen said, delighted. She went back to her shelves, lifted the fabric from one of the covered jars, and proudly displayed a wretched-looking hand suspended in that same green gunk.

Olwen beamed. Betrys shuddered.

"You do it on purpose, don't you?" Betrys asked weakly.

"Never," Olwen said innocently. She covered the container again.

That fleeting moment had given me enough time to work out a strategy: play the victim, not the suspect.

"You had no right to go through our things," I said.

"Didn't we?" Betrys asked. "Strangers show up in our lands and we have *no right* to ensure they aren't bringing weapons or more dark magic with them?"

Bedivere stood behind her, silently backing the words. He took the Hand of Glory from her, careful to touch only its metal holder. His top lip curled in disgust. "What is the magic attached to this . . . thing? I can feel its presence, but it does not reveal itself."

The hand remained stiff and the eye shut. It was a true reflection of how grim our situation was, and my heart swelled a bit at Ignatius's loyalty.

"Is that . . . ?" Neve breathed out, daring to come a bit closer.

"I always wondered how you managed—" Emrys began.

"To find such—ah, a uniquely carved torch?" I finished. "Very lifelike, isn't it?"

"Very," Betrys said, eyes narrowing. "And its magic?"

"To brighten its glow," I answered.

"My sister is drawn to strange and dreadful things," Cabell offered fondly.

"Love 'em," I said, not missing a beat. "Bring me the macabre, all things forbidding and ghastly—as long as they're not possessed by angry spirits."

Emrys snorted in amusement.

"Why do you think I spend so much time with this hideous wretch?" I said, jerking a thumb in his direction.

"Ha," he said. "And here I thought it was for my repulsive personality."

If I'd been in Betrys's place, I would have made me light the wicks and prove my ridiculous torch story. Instead, she simply took my word for it and passed it back to me.

"Flea has a similar fascination," she warned, "and the habit of collecting odd things, so I'd keep an eye on it if I were you."

I felt Ignatius's own eye roll beneath its lid as I rewrapped him and took a stab at changing the subject. "You said something about bathing?"

"Yes," Betrys said. "I did. If you'll follow me?"

"Actually . . . ," Emrys said. "I'm exhausted. Is it possible to be shown to wherever you're going to have us sleep?"

"I'll accompany you," Bedivere told him.

"Wait, if you wouldn't mind," Olwen said, catching Emrys's arm. "That is, if you aren't *too* tired, would you take a look at my garden and see if there's anything I may not be hearing from the herbs about what they need to thrive?"

My eyes narrowed on the place her fingers still curled around the crook of his elbow. Really? It couldn't wait until morning?

Something clenched in my chest as he nodded. I forced myself to look at the floor. He'd never been able to resist the opportunity to charm before, so this was hardly a surprise.

It was just that we had come here together—the four of us. It seemed important to stay together until we had a better grip on what was going on.

But Cabell had his hand on my shoulder and was guiding me out through the door before I could say anything at all. The door shut behind us on Emrys's soft laugh, snuffing out the faint but soothing glow that had briefly sheltered us from the cold and dark of this Otherland.

And if we had dared to forget them, even for a moment, the restless Children of the Night had not forgotten us. They shrieked from the other side of the old stone walls, piercing the peace of the courtyard. Relishing their starless night.

17

Betrys led us across the courtyard, toward a door in the fortress's wall. A man in armor leaned over the rampart above us, curious. Behind him, a fire pot licked at the sky, doing little to brighten it.

At Neve's sharp gasp I looked back, only to do a double take. A massive figure, nearly ten feet tall, slowly lumbered around the tower's stone face, heading toward the tree that served as the tower's foundation and spine.

Its body was like a rough sketch of a human, cobbled together from twisted branches and roots, with hollows near the joints. They groaned and creaked as the creature walked. Atop its head was a spiked crown of twigs and leaves. As it moved, the seams of its body exhaled a mist that glowed green in the night.

As it turned to observe us, the mist illuminated its eye sockets, but its face seemed to have no mouth, no expression.

"Cripes," Cabell breathed out.

"That's Deri," Betrys said when she realized we were no longer following her. "The hamadryad bound to the Mother tree. All of the trees of Avalon once had their own hamadryad caretaker, and there were other unbound dryads to assist them, but . . . well, you've seen what's become of the land."

I gave a dazed nod, acknowledging her words. The hamadryad

stooped, scraping dark muck from the tree's bark in slow, thorough strokes.

"Come on, then." Betrys tilted her head toward the waiting door, and we followed. Beyond it was another spiraling staircase, and, yet again, we descended.

After a while, the stairs widened. A distant rush of water echoed on the stone walls, and the air gained an almost mineral taste, not unlike the smell of dust just before the rain. The deeper we traveled, the brighter it seemed to become. Soon the faces around me, my skin, my hair, my clothes—everything was awash in strange cerulean light.

We made one final turn around the stairs, and the springs unfurled below. I slowed. Cabell tried to nudge me forward, but I couldn't bring myself to move just yet.

The cavern was vast, its arched ceiling decorated with carvings of young women—the Goddess and priestesses, I presumed. The structure was supported by the shoulders of three massive statues. One, a young woman wearing a crown of flowers and a flowing gown. The second, a peaceful motherly woman in an apron, a basket and loom carved around her feet. The third was an elderly figure, stooped and wearing a cloak that swirled around her and depicted the stars and phases of the moon. These were the three aspects of the Goddess: maiden, mother, crone.

At their feet, a river of glowing water ran down the center of the chamber, seeping out from a split in an enormous root of the Mother tree, as if it were sap. Narrow tributaries branched out from it, filling smaller round pools. Mist or steam rose from the surface of each, promising much-needed relief for my stiff and sore muscles.

Bitterness warred with awe in me. How many breathtaking places, how many wondrous sights, had I missed before I'd had the One Vision? Nothing in my imagination could compare to what I'd seen here, either for beauty or for monstrosity. To the Tamsin of even a week ago, it would have appeared to be nothing at all.

Tidy bundles of clothing with surprisingly modern-looking undergarments had been placed beside three of the individual baths. I toed the top layer, a thin towel for drying off, revealing a simple tunic and dark brown breeches below.

"This is incredible," Cabell said, turning to look around. "What makes the water glow like that?"

Otherworldly light shimmered from the depths of each pool, creating a soothing ambiance in what might otherwise have been a creepy, cavernous space. I set the wrapped Ignatius down on the bottom step, well away from the pools.

"The water is said to be tears of the Goddess," Betrys said. "Flowing from her heart, which resides at the center of the Mother tree."

I cringed. "I think I liked it better before you brought up bodily fluids."

To my surprise, Betrys laughed. "It's restorative—healing in a different way than what Olwen can do."

Neve breathed in deeply, as if relishing the rain scent. Her wide eyes glimmered with wonder.

"I need to take my hour on the watch," Betrys explained. "I trust you don't mind waiting until I return to show you to your rooms?"

"Honestly," Cabell said, "you'll probably have to drag us out of the water."

She turned her back to us. "I'll take your clothing to be laundered if you'll leave it there beside the baths."

We undressed awkwardly, careful not to look at one another. Covering myself with my arms, my face burning from being so exposed, I stepped down into the water and tentatively stretched a foot out.

I shivered with pleasure at its warmth. The longer I stared into the swirling mist gathering on its surface, the more intolerable the chilled air around us felt. I descended farther into the pool, then plunged, immediately finding its smooth bottom with my toes.

There was a weight to the water I hadn't expected, as if it were thick with salt. A ledge had been carved into it at the perfect height to sit with my head and shoulders above the surface.

Days of dirt and blood lifted away from my skin. My whole body softened, and my mind was quick to follow. I breathed in deeply, then dunked my head beneath the water, scrubbing at my hair and face with my hands.

I surfaced again with a gasp, wiping the hair from my face. Cabell sighed as he settled fully into his pool. He turned to face me, bracing his arms on the rocky edge. "This beats the Roman baths in Algeria, eh?"

"And we didn't even have to break in to use them," I said. "A novel concept for us."

I hadn't realized Betrys was still standing there until she breathed out two words: "Those symbols . . ."

I followed her gaze down to Cabell's tattooed arms and shoulders.

"Why would you cover your body with curse sigils?" Neve asked, pulling herself up to look over the side of her bath. She had carefully twisted her braids up and away from the water.

To show off all the curses he's broken, I thought. *To seem cool and mysterious to girls who have no idea what they mean.*

"To remind myself curses are only dark because of how they're used," Cabell said.

Betrys looked as if she might say something else, but she only turned, hurrying up the steps with our things.

"You have to stop doing that," I whispered to Neve, coming to the edge of my own bath.

"Doing what?"

"Telling them everything before we figure out how they'll react," I said. "The whole leap-before-you-look thing with you is getting old. We need them on our side if we're going to be able to look for Nash."

"You really don't trust anyone, do you?" Neve said, shaking her head.

"I trust people will always lash out when they're afraid," I said. "And that they'll do anything when they're desperate enough."

Neve sank back down into the water with a grateful sigh. Guilt, my least-favorite emotion, bit at me.

"Are you all right?" I asked her. "You've had a rough few hours."

That was putting it far too kindly. In truth, I'd seen a lot of the world and expected the worst of it, but I'd been shocked by the malice toward her.

"Yes," she said with her usual resolve. "But I'll be better once I have my wand back and we find Nash and the ring."

I nodded.

The thing was, you spend so long being afraid of sorceresses and all the ways they can hurt you that you don't necessarily think about the way the world hurts them back. The way it punishes them for that same power.

I'd brought her here, to a place where sorceresses were reviled. Where she was outnumbered and just as much at a loss about what was happening as Cabell and I were. A place of monsters.

I sank down, letting the water rise above my chapped lips. The stinging there eased within a heartbeat, but the regret lingered.

"Avalon is a place of beauty," Neve said softly. She stared straight into the mist gathered in front of her and recited from memory. *"The most beautiful of all of the Otherlands, for it was born of the Goddess's heart, as dear as a child. The groves are ripe with ancient secrets and a bounty of golden apples . . ."*

"Not the noxious stench of impending death?" The joke was grating, even to me.

"After everything I'd read," Neve started again, keeping her back to us, "I had this vision of it in my mind for years. It was as sacred to me as the stories my auntie told me about my mother. They were both distant and beautiful."

I leaned my head against the edge of the pool, my hair dripping over my face, curling around my cheek like a tender hand. "Does it really feel like a curse to either of you?"

Before the One Vision, I'd been able to sense magic the way you

184

could feel a shift in the air's pressure. It had been amorphous and ever-changing. Sometimes, with the older curses, you could even feel the fury or spite radiating from the sigils. Gaining the second sight had ripened those senses, making them fuller, and it was still expanding in ways I couldn't completely comprehend.

"It does," Cabell said, "and then it doesn't. I'm not sure how to explain it."

Neve finally turned to face us, drawing herself up. I did the same, watching their faces in the cerulean light.

"It feels similar—icy and harsh—but somehow more concentrated?" Neve groaned. "I'm not making any sense."

"I agree," Cabell said. "I think it was the druids and whatever magic they gained from Lord Death. It doesn't feel like the magic we draw from the universal source."

It felt good to fall into our usual back-and-forth pattern of theories. He had always been the more valuable player in our work partnership, but I'd made it a point to retain as much knowledge as possible.

"I don't know much about Lord Death," Neve said, brow furrowed.

"There are a number of different legends about him," I said. "The one Nash told us was this—he was a powerful enchanter in the time of King Arthur and at one point even traveled with Arthur and his knights. But he broke an oath and was placed in charge of Annwn as punishment, as much a king as a jailor for the souls too dark to be reborn."

"What was the oath?" Neve asked.

"Nash never said, so I'm not sure he knew," Cabell said. "I've never read that account anywhere, either, so he could have invented it. Most know Lord Death as the leader of the Wild Hunt, roaming between worlds to collect wicked souls for Annwn. His power allows him and his retinue to pass through the mists separating the Otherlands."

"Creepy," Neve said with just a little too much appreciation. "Now I'm even more convinced the sorceresses were the ones in the right. Lord Death and the druids would have done unspeakable things if they gained control of Avalon."

"Well, if we're right, they managed to do unspeakable things anyway," I said. "Case in point, we almost got eaten by the undead."

The three of us sank back into a heavy silence at the mention of our crossing. When I closed my eyes, the dark violence of the night crept up behind me, wrapping its bony fingers around my throat.

And Septimus's face . . .

As if sensing my thoughts, Cabell reached across the small distance between us and put a heavy, reassuring hand on my head. "We'll be all right. We're going to find Nash and the ring, and we're going to find safe passage back to the portal."

I knew how hard it was for him to say that—to be willing to leave behind the man he'd idolized for years. The least I could do was force a smile. "Right."

I twisted back around, keeping my back to them, breathing in the damp air. My wet hair clung to my face, but I let it hang there.

"I feel like I could fall asleep here," Neve said, her own eyes closing. "All I need is a warm mug of chamomile tea, a hypoallergenic pillow, and a good book."

"Is that all?" I said, amused.

"I have no books, but I *do* have stories," Cabell said, his expression brightening. There was color in his cheeks again, and his pale skin was no longer the sickly hue of bone. Even the hollows beneath his eyes had faded.

Maybe Betrys was right, and the pools healed more than the body. They also touched the spirit. The soul.

"No," I begged. "No stories."

"Speak for yourself," Neve said eagerly. "Tell me one of your favorites."

"I'll do you one better," Cabell said, sending a splash of water over to me, "and tell you one of Tamsin's favorites."

I knew exactly which one he meant. "That's not my favorite."

He frowned. "Yes, it is. You used to beg Nash for it over and—"

"Okay, fine," I muttered. "Just tell it, then."

Cabell straightened, running his hands over the water's surface. He cleared his throat. "In ages past, in a kingdom lost to time, a king named Arthur ruled man and the Fair Folk alike, but this is a story that came before that, when he was a mere boy."

Something in me clenched. The cadence, the rhythm of his words—it was so much like Nash.

"He had been smuggled out of Tintagel Castle shortly after his birth by none other than the wise druid Merlin, who knew Arthur's life would be in danger as the various lords warred over the right to rule, including Arthur's own father, Uther Pendragon. Arthur was brought to a noble family and raised as their own. One day, a great stone appeared in the land, with a mighty sword thrust through it. The stone bore a strange message: WHOEVER PULLS THE SWORD FROM THIS STONE IS THE TRUE-BORN KING OF BRITAIN."

"Who put the stone there?" Neve asked. "Merlin?"

"Yes," Cabell said, impatient with the interruption. "So, a tournament was called, and all the great lords and their sons entered, including Arthur's foster brother, the knight Sir Kay. Realizing he didn't have his sword, Kay sent his squire, Arthur, to find one for him. And Arthur, seeing that the nearest one was the very sword embedded in that strange stone, went to it. He gripped its cold hilt and pulled it free with ease, much to the shock of everyone around him. And that is how Arthur's true identity, and his fate, were revealed."

I sank back down in the water, letting the warmth ease the unwelcome burn from my eyes. It was a stupid story, with an even more unrealistic ending.

"Is any of that true?" Neve asked.

Cabell shrugged. "Does it have to be?"

Bright indigo lights rose in the pools around us, sending playful splashes of water between them. Their energy and erratic motions spoke of pure, unbridled mischief. The lights suddenly clustered over one bath, drawing its water up into the shape of a bird. It soared over our heads, dripping like rain, only to transform midair into a cat. It flicked its translucent tail against Neve's cheek and she laughed.

"Nixies," Cabell said, watching them.

Their lights reminded me of a question, one I'd been forced to push aside for more pressing ones.

"Neve," I began. "Why did Olwen hum her spell for the fire instead of drawing sigils?"

Sorceresses had a carefully curated and precise way of calling magic; they drew power from the universal source of it, yes, but their collection of sigils instructed the magic to perform a task.

"I don't know," Neve said. "There are many ways of using magic—just look at the Cunningfolk. They don't use sigils, either. Maybe spellwork is just more . . . instinctive for priestesses."

"That could be why you were able to cast that incredible spell, Neve," Cabell pointed out.

"I'll ask Olwen," Neve said. "I think we can learn a lot from each other."

I nodded, letting the quiet dripping of water and splashing of nixies ease the tension between us.

My gaze drifted up over the nearest statue—the maiden. Her expression was knowing as her stone eyes watched over us, and it made me think of what Caitriona had said earlier about the security of knowing that a greater being was there to care for you in your life's journey.

But I couldn't imagine what god remained in this land darkened by death.

18

A half hour later, Betrys's voice carried down the steps. "All finished?"

I stood from the water, wrapping myself in the towel and moving behind the maiden statue's feet to dress. My wet hair dripped onto my shoulders, allowing the chill to cut deeper—and that was before I put on my sludge-soaked boots.

I hadn't realized Neve had followed me over to change until I heard her gasp.

It took me a moment to understand what had startled her. I reached for my tunic, but she gripped my arm, turning me more fully toward her.

I tried to curl in on myself like a leaf, blood rushing to my face. For the first time since it happened, I'd managed to forget about the blue-black stain on the skin over my heart. It was shaped like a hideous, sinister star.

"Tamsin . . . ," Neve whispered, her eyes huge as she backed away. "That's a death mark."

I pulled my tunic over my head, my pulse fluttering with a strange panic. "No, it's not."

"You were touched by a spirit," she said. "How did you survive?"

"It's *not*," I insisted, gripping my jacket and throwing it over my shoulders. A blisteringly white field of snow flashed in my mind, the incorporeal hand stretched toward me, the pain like a knife to the heart—

"What kind was it? A poltergeist? A wraith?" Neve pressed, trailing after me as I made my way back toward the stairs, where Cabell and Betrys waited.

I whirled on her, my face aching, my body as tight as a drum. "It's *not a death mark.* That's an old wives' tale."

Neve held up her hands. "All right. It's not a death mark. Great Mother, relax, will you? I didn't mean anything by it. Death marks are nothing to be ashamed of. Most people don't even survive the touch."

The silence between us was painfully awkward as we made our way back up the stairs. Cabell shot me a questioning look. I ignored it, letting exhaustion claim my thoughts. Let it empty my head of anything other than imagining the small stretch of floor I'd be able to lie down on for a few hours.

Betrys gave us each a looking-over in that silent way of hers, the scar on her right cheek somehow more pronounced with her frown. Rather than take us to one of the outer buildings or into the walls again, she led us to the tower itself.

In the shadowed light, it was hard to make out the details of the first level; it seemed to be a great hall, in which countless tables had been assembled in two long rows.

The aisle between them led to yet another ornate statue, this one of the Goddess herself, dignified in face and posture, colored bone white. Small bowls of unseen treasures, dried bundles of wheat, and dying flowers were arranged around her in offering. A candle flickered from a chamber carved into the center of her chest, turning the natural cracks in her stone surface to glowing veins.

The walls were painted as though the artist had wished to bring the forest inside. Something about the way the candles shivered and guttered along the tables and walls made it seem like the trees and flowering undergrowth were alive. As if we had been offered a glimpse into the isle's past.

Neve came to stand beside me, and I followed her reverential gaze up to the chandeliers and the garlands of dried greens and flowers strung between them.

My heart gave an involuntary kick against my ribs. Why would they heap offerings upon the idol of the Goddess and lovingly decorate the hall when all it could ever be was a reminder of what they'd lost and would never get back?

"This way," Betrys said gently.

To the far left was a large winding stone staircase, its walls carved into the body of the tree. As we climbed, there was a dull thudding in my ears, and I couldn't tell if it came from my own heart or somewhere inside the tree.

The upper levels were a breathtaking meeting of tree and stone, seamlessly entangled like smoke and steam. On the second floor, I slowed, peering into an enormous open chamber. Dozens of sleeping people were spread across blankets and straw-stuffed mats. I scanned them quickly, searching without luck for Nash's ugly mug.

Betrys brought us to the third floor, to a hallway lined with grim-faced doors. She opened the closest one, motioning to Neve and me. "I hope you won't mind sharing . . . ?"

Inside was a handsome four-poster bed that looked large enough to sleep an entire family. A simple tapestry of deer and birds hung along one wall, and there was already a fire in the hearth.

"The people sleeping downstairs . . . ," Neve said, hesitating. "How can we accept this when they're on the floor?"

Speak for yourself, I thought. I could accept this gladly.

"They choose to sleep together for comfort and protection," Betrys reassured her. "These chambers are normally used by the priestesses of Avalon, but my sisters and I prefer to sleep among the others in case a need to defend the tower arises in the night."

Well. I put my hands on my hips, tilting my head back. Annoyingly, I now felt a little bad too.

"Many of our elders are resting in the other chambers, so I ask that you keep as quiet as possible," Betrys continued, giving me a particular look. "And do not wander the halls."

"Will we be able to meet the other Avalonians?" I asked. If he was here, Nash would have to be among them.

Betrys merely opened a door for Cabell and left without another word.

"Come on," Neve said, giving my arm a gentle tug. "It'll be better to look for Nash after a few hours' sleep anyway."

I sighed, shooting Cabell an uncertain look.

He nodded, that hopeful smile still on his face. "Better to be sharp, right?"

"Right," I echoed.

Neve picked up the candle on the small bedside table, carrying it over to the tapestry for a better look before turning to the wardrobe. A painted fox and hare were caught in a circular chase across its doors. Opening it, she found our bags stowed inside and two long coats made of a patchwork of different fabrics.

"Wand?" I asked, already knowing the answer by her expression.

She moved to sit down on one side of the bed. I sat on the other, my back to her. The room didn't have any sort of window or opening in the wall, allowing the heat of the fire to linger with us. It took me a moment to realize that I wasn't smelling smoke—instead, four stones with carved spirals had been pressed together in the hearth, flames flickering lightly upward.

"Salamander stones," Neve said quietly. "I've read about them. Never thought I'd actually see them."

"An ongoing theme of this misadventure for all of us," I noted, moving outside the fire's glow. I ran my hands along the walls, keeping to the edges of the room to ensure there were no hidden entrances or spellwork. As impressive as the large stones were, their cheerful glow did nothing to offset the constant baying of the creatures in the ravaged forest below.

"How are we ever going to sleep?" Neve asked.

I blew a wispy strand of hair out of my face. As tired as I'd been on the way here, I was wide-awake now. Neither my mind nor my body seemed willing to wind itself down, so I went to retrieve my bag from the wardrobe.

"I think I have some pills or a tonic," I said, rummaging through it. "Let's just make sure they didn't help themselves to anything—"

I swore.

"What?" Neve asked, twisting around.

"I left Ignatius at the springs," I said, hanging my head.

"Who's Ignatius?" Neve asked.

"The Hand of Glory," I said.

"I *knew* that's what it was!" she said, glowing with excitement. "Where did you find one? Did a sorceress make it for you? Does it really open locked doors?"

"That, and more," I said, then, resigned, added, "I have to go get him."

Stupid, stupid, stupid. Of all the idiotic moves I'd made in recent days, this was the most boneheaded. Ignatius had behaved himself so far, but if one of the priestesses or Avalonians found him and he decided to open his eye and take a look around . . .

I didn't want to know what they would make of something as sinister as a Hand of Glory.

"Do you want me to come with you?" Neve asked. "It's a long walk through the dark."

I hesitated, surprised by how hard it was to turn her down. "I can manage on my own."

"At least take this." Neve offered up the candle and its iron chamberstick.

"There's plenty of light on the way," I protested.

"Please," she said more forcefully. "It would make *me* feel better."

"All right." I sighed through my nose. "But only to end this conversation."

"Uh-huh." Neve let out a knowing hum. Knowing what, I had no idea, but I didn't like it, or the smile that came after. Retrieving her CD player and earphones from her fanny pack, she slipped the latter over her ears.

"Go to sleep," I told her.

"I'll see you when you get back," she said, still with that same tone. She leaned against the thin pillow and headboard, stretching her legs out over the blanket. Her music followed me into the hallway.

I was still replaying the moment as I made my way down through the tower, creeping past the hall of sleepers ensconced in whatever they dreamt of in this nightmare realm.

Shielding the struggling candle flame with my hand, I crossed the courtyard quickly, glancing up to make sure no one was watching from the walkway along the high defensive walls. By the time I'd made it down the stairs to the springs, I was out of breath.

I forced myself around the last curve of the stairs, chest burning, legs like bags of sand. Breath wheezed out of me as I scooped up Ignatius, still wrapped in his purple silk. I turned back toward the stairs like a prisoner facing the gallows.

"Botheration," I muttered, and went to sit on the maiden statue's enormous foot instead. Looking up at her from below, I added, "Sorry, girl."

I knew it was a mistake the moment I leaned back against her cold stone ankle. My body went heavy as the last bit of momentum left it.

I might have stayed there, sprawled out with only a candle and a demonic sentient hand for company, if I hadn't heard the quick strike of feet on the stone steps.

I slid down off the side of the foot, blowing out the candle as I landed in an ungraceful crouch. It had to be Olwen, but on the off chance it wasn't . . .

My pulse thrummed in my ears as I waited, risking a quick lean around the statue. Then another when I saw who it was.

Emrys stood at the edge of one of the pools, staring down into its glowing depths. His face was so devoid of emotion, it was as if his spirit had been ripped from his body. The sight of it sent an un-expected pang through me.

And then he removed his gloves. One, two, dropping to the stone. I leaned forward, trying to see, but between the dozens of feet that separated us and that incessant cerulean light, nothing seemed un-usual.

Not until he reached for the hem of his sweater and undershirt. The muscles of his back tightened as he pulled both over his head.

The iron chamberstick slipped out of my fingers and clattered to the ground. Emrys whirled back, eyes wide with surprise or fear or something worse, but it was too late. I'd seen them.

"What the hell did that?" I rasped.

I *hadn't* imagined the scar on his face at Rook House. It continued down along his neck, across his breastbone. That single, ragged scar fed into dozens of others, their brutal seams raised red and angry. My eyes couldn't follow them all as they stretched over the taut muscles of his chest, his arms, his back, down below the sharp, low V of his ab-dominals.

He looked like a glass figurine that had been knocked from its shelf. Shattered, and hastily put back together.

Emrys's face was rigid as he reached for his sweater and pulled it over his head, as if that could erase what I had seen. I stood there, un-able to move.

"Are you following me now?" he asked angrily, picking up his gloves and turning to storm back up the steps.

"What did that to you?" I whispered. The heavy layers of clothing, the refusal to take his gloves off—no glamour would have hidden this from anyone with the One Vision, so he hadn't bothered.

"Leave it, Tamsin," he said, his voice like ice.

Somehow, I'd crossed the distance between us. Somehow, I was taking his hand, turning it over to see where the scars continued over the tendons and muscles of his forearm.

"What the hell is going on? Did those things—" No, it couldn't have been the Children of the Night. I would have seen it happen. "Did Madrigal do that to you?"

He ripped his hand free, but he hadn't turned fast enough to hide the agonized shame that spilled over his features.

"Emrys!" He stopped a few steps above me but didn't turn. "What happened?"

His hands curled at his side. "Do you care?"

I couldn't tell which of us was more surprised when I shouted, "Yes!"

We stood there staring at one another, breathing hard. The walk had winded me, but it was nothing compared to the heaviness that welled in my chest at how pale his face had gone.

"What happened?" I whispered.

His throat worked hard as he swallowed. "I made a mistake. There—are you happy? It turns out I'm as big an idiot as you've always thought."

"This happened on a job?" I asked. "It wasn't Madrigal?"

"It had nothing to do with her," he said. "And it has even less to do with you."

He left me standing at the bottom of the steps, his footfalls creating a thundering echo in my skull. It wasn't the exhaustion that kept me there, staring at the place he'd been, but the shock that still had me by the throat.

There were any number of curses that could shred a mortal to pieces, flay the skin from their muscle and bone. All agonizing.

None survivable.

A new question seemed to arise with every step I climbed. How long had he had these scars?

I half expected to see him in the courtyard, and again at the entrance to the tower, but the only person waiting for me there was a stone-faced Caitriona.

I froze.

"Look, I just forgot this—" I began, for once not having to think of an excuse.

"I've spoken to my sisters," she interrupted me. Even in the light of the torch she held, her face was inscrutable. "And it's been agreed that I'll take you to see your father tomorrow."

I stared at her, heart thrumming wildly in my chest. "Really?"

He's alive. The words seemed to take flight in my chest. Somehow, impossibly, Nash, like the most tenacious of rats, had survived sorceresses, debtors, and a growling wilderness of monsters.

"Indeed," Caitriona said, turning sharply on her heel to head back into the tower. "Rest while you can. We leave at daybreak."

19

"*This* is daylight?"

Cabell's smile was grim as he leaned against the simple fence that bordered the courtyard's training space. "Sure it is. It's gone from pitch black to bleak gray."

"So glad you can still find an ounce of humor to squeeze out of this," I grumbled.

He pulled away, feigning fear. "Oh no. Don't tell me you used the last of your coffee packets at Tintagel?"

The mere mention of instant coffee was enough to darken my mood. I had a cracking headache from going so long without my sludgy elixir of life.

"Good thing you have the best brother in all the many lands," he said, reaching into his satchel for a small thermos.

My eyes widened as I snatched it from him and unscrewed the top. The smell of bitter, chemical coffee rose with a wisp of steam, greeting me like an old friend. I looked at him again.

"I actually think I might cry," I said, hugging the container to me.

"I made nice with the elfin cook, Dilwyn, and got some hot water," Cabell said. "It turns out not even the Fair Folk can resist one of my winning smiles."

"Are you sure she didn't just give it to you so you'd go away?" I asked, taking a sip of the sweet, sweet sludge.

"You're welcome," he said.

Feeling unusually sentimental, I added, "You are the best brother, you know."

"Nah, I'm just trying to free my sister from whatever demon possesses her precoffee," he said. "And anyway, it's not like you had much of a choice on the brother front."

"Fate did right by us," I said. "Just that once."

Cabell hummed in thought. "Fate, or Nash?"

"Did you sleep at all last night?" I asked, changing the subject. "I think I managed an hour at most."

"Lucky," he said. "I got maybe ten minutes, thanks to the sweet lullaby of screeching."

I was used to sleeping in strange places, drifting off as soon as my head touched a soft surface, whether it was my hands, a pillow, or a bundled-up shirt. Yet every time I'd closed my eyes last night, my memory had turned traitor. It flashed between the monsters in the woods, the life draining from Septimus's face, Emrys's scars, and Caitriona's words. *I'll take you to see your father.*

I hugged my arms around my middle, trapping some warmth beneath my flannel jacket. I drew in a deep breath of the foul air, made worse by the pungent smell of excrement and animal sweat wafting from the stables a stone's throw to our left.

A short distance away, Deri had scaled the Mother tree, packing what looked to be woody abscesses with straw and moss. The hamadryad was joined by dozens of tiny green figures, who were cleaning rot from the tree's body and stripping dried pieces of bark off to eat. The sprites were no bigger than my hand and had bodies like twigs and heads like pale green rosebuds. Their wings were translucent and glimmering, almost like a dragonfly's.

Behind us, Betrys and one of the other Nine, Arianwen, were moving through sword drills under the watchful eye of Bedivere. The clatter of their wooden practice weapons punctuated the quiet of the morning, chased by a grunt or *"Ha!"* of effort.

"That's it," Bedivere said, "lean into it—yes, Ari, that's it."

Arianwen had cropped her brown hair close to her scalp, which only served to emphasize the loveliness of her face. She moved with a fluidity I envied, her full figure unimpeded by the leather practice armor as she swung her arm up and down, arcing the blade slowly, then quick-quick, *tap-tap*.

Betrys met her every blow with practiced ease. It hardly seemed like a fair match; Betrys had a solid five inches on the other girl, which meant she had the longer reach with the blade and Arianwen had to move faster, strike with more power, to even out that advantage.

Then again, I supposed, real fights were only ever fair by chance.

"She *did* say daylight, didn't she?" Cabell asked, peering up at the sky. He was all but bouncing on his heels, as impatient as I was to get going.

"She did indeed," I groused.

"And *cease*," Bedivere said from behind us.

Both girls fell back, returning their wooden swords to a nearby rack. Betrys used the sleeve of her tunic to swipe the sweat from her brow, then wrapped an arm around the other priestess's shoulder, giving it a squeeze. "I told you you'd have it in no time."

Arianwen beamed, leaning into her. It was hard to tell if her face was sunburned or merely flushed from the training. "Are you off to the kitchen?"

"Cook awaits my skilled knife," Betrys confirmed. "You?"

"Mari needs help with the laundering," Arianwen said. "Are the two of you waiting for Cait?"

With my brain thick with fog, it took me a moment to realize she was talking to us.

"Yeah," I said, a bit more harshly than I meant. "Unless we have different concepts of *daybreak,* she should have been here a while ago."

Arianwen's brows rose. "It's not like her to be late—you don't think she'll need someone to go with her, do you?"

"I'll be joining them," Bedivere told her with a small, knowing smile.

"Yes," Arianwen continued, "but are you absolutely *certain*—"

"It's the laundry, Ari, not the gallows," Betrys said, shaking her head.

"Easy for you to say—you won't be smelling like lye for a fortnight," Arianwen said.

"Yes, but you get to use the wash bats," Betrys said, guiding her away. "I know how much you enjoy beating the dirt out of linens."

Arianwen sniffed, her voice trailing off with her steps. "It *is* invigorating."

"I'll see if I can't find Caitriona," Bedivere told us, scratching at his white-tipped beard. "I'm certain she's only making her morning rounds."

"And here I was hoping she'd fallen into a well, never to be heard from again," I muttered.

"We're not going anywhere," Cabell promised, elbowing me hard in the ribs.

I leaned back against the fence, too annoyed to respond. My eyes drifted around us, moving aimlessly over the stones and the blurs of people passing by.

While the cover of night had given the tower an air of hallowed mystery, the bleak light had burned that lie away.

Now its structures wore their raggedness as plainly as starved bodies. Sections of stones had been chiseled away, revealing desperate patch-up jobs, and more than a few walls slumped so badly they had to be braced. Mildew, rust, and soot smeared themselves over every surface, somehow giving the impression that everything was slowly sinking into a boggy abyss.

The banners depicting the Goddess's symbol, a three-hearted knot at the center of an oak tree, hung listless in the still air.

Worse, patches of the Mother tree had turned a sickly gray, spotted

201

with mushrooms. I didn't need Neve to tell me that these fungi were likely eating the decay inside it. Even Deri looked weaker—the wooden parts of his body brittle. It didn't escape my notice that several Avalonians were either studying the rot on the tree or working to help Deri try to cut it from the trunk.

I sighed, eyes skimming the courtyard again. Neve was still cheerfully greeting the horses that had been tethered outside of the stables, which stood on the other side of the training ring. They, along with the infirmary, were located behind the tower. According to Cabell, one of the stone buildings at the front of the tower was the kitchen, a cramped, boilingly hot space ruled by its cook, Dilwyn. She was an elfin, no bigger than a child, but she more than made up for her diminutive size with her no-nonsense personality.

Laundry, I presumed, could only be done in the springs, unless they wanted their clothing and sheets to come back with more bloodstains and fewer washers.

Waiting had also given us our first real opportunity to see and be seen by the survivors of Avalon. Most of them gave us a wide berth as they took their places on the wall or carried up water from the springs. Some watched with obvious curiosity, others with outright suspicion. Some even regarded us with terror, dropping their pails and tools to retreat into the tower.

The worst, though, were the faces that revealed nothing at all, as if the horror of what they'd confronted had hollowed them of spirit. They moved from task to task without lifting their eyes, like restless spirits imprisoned in a mindless loop, operating on pure muscle memory.

These people, though—they knew they were trapped. They'd utterly surrendered to it.

Cabell followed my gaze, his voice hardly a whisper. "How can this be Avalon?"

"Stories are always more beautiful than the truth," I said. "That's why Nash couldn't bring himself to live in the real world."

But perhaps he'd found himself trapped in this one. Caitriona's words to me last night—*I'll take you to see your father*—had implied that he wasn't here, within the walls of the fortress, but some part of me had still expected to see his face among the others this morning. I wanted to enjoy his shocked reaction, dine on his disbelief.

I'd overheard Betrys and Bedivere discussing some sort of watch outpost in the forest as they'd set up for the session with Arianwen, and that seemed like our probable destination.

Cabell sighed. "It's so strange to think he's alive after all this time, and we're going to see him. I'm not even sure what I'll say."

"I'm not going to say a word." The hope I felt was tinged with bitterness, like the bite of a sour berry. "I'm going to punch him in the throat."

He laughed. "Come on. You really think he'd willingly stay here if he had a way of getting back? Time works differently here. He could think only a few months have passed."

Given how much we had changed in the last seven years, it was strange to think that Nash might look exactly as he had when he'd vanished. Even his old jacket—the one Cabell wore now—bore the marks of our travels and travails over the years, remolding itself to fit its new owner.

Most of the Avalonians wore some version of what Neve, Cabell, and I had been given—a homespun tunic and pants that clung close to the leg. Some of the women chose to wear a simple head covering; others, almost in defiance of the rotting world around them, adorned their foreheads with thin silver strands strung with colored stones.

Dresses that might once have been rich in color, like jewels, had been humbled by hastily repaired tears and stains. Others had been split down their centers and transformed into the coats or short jackets and vests worn by all. None of the armor, steel or leather, seemed to fit its wearer, or else it had been obviously hammered into a different shape.

"Sorceress," someone hissed. By the time I'd turned, it was impossible to tell which of the passing men it had come from.

Neve, mercifully, was too far away to have heard, but I knew by the nervous shift of her weight that she felt every one of those gazes on her.

Aled, the stable manager, matched the descriptions I'd read of the elfin almost exactly—silky dark hair, pale green flesh, a stocky build, and an affinity for animals. Neve continued to sneak looks at him as he stood on a stool and showed her how to saddle the horses. Now and then he shifted his weight between his left leg and the piece of wood that comprised the lower part of his right.

"What's got yer face so sour?"

Flea appeared behind us, weaving her small body through the fence to sit atop it. She'd tucked her straggly white-blond hair up into a heavy knit cap, and her face was smudged with even more dirt than the night before.

"Where'd you come from?" I asked, amused.

"My mam said the Goddess 'erself sent me in a basket down the ol' river," Flea said, shrugging a shoulder. "Like all babes. 'Cept the two of you. Looks like yer mam was a goat."

"You're a horrible child," I informed her.

She pushed off the fence and dropped into the perfect mockery of a curtsey. "I thank ye."

Caitriona and Bedivere rounded the side of the tower, both dressed in a light shell of armor, having forgone the stiff-jointed greaves and helms.

There was a slight press against the workbag slung at my hip. My hand lashed down, catching Flea's wrist as she tried to stealthily retreat with something in her fist.

"A curse on ye!" Flea growled, struggling to extract herself from my grip. I turned her hand over, revealing a small selenite crystal. Cabell whistled.

"Not bad," I told her. "Clever to wait for the distraction, but next time don't go for the obvious." I held up the thin bracelet of braided silver I'd slipped off her other wrist to make my point. "Look for the opportunity to fetch a real prize."

Her eyes bulged as she grabbed at her bracelet. "That's mine, thief!"

"What's this?" came Caitriona's husky voice. "Are you stealing from a child?"

I gave the girl a look as I released her. "You can keep that crystal."

"You sure you should have told her that?" Cabell murmured as the others approached.

"Just doing my part to raise the next generation of disreputable girls," I said, then added, more loudly, "Merely showing young Flea a little trick."

The girl scowled and made a gesture that was rude, regardless of the century and world.

"What are you doing here, Flea?" Caitriona gave her a stern look. "Rhona has been searching for you all morning. You cannot keep hiding from your lessons."

As Caitriona came toward us, Emrys suddenly appeared behind her. He hung back several steps, his hands in his pockets. Though he'd changed out of his filthy slacks and sweater, he'd still managed to completely mask his body beneath long breeches, a long tunic, and a scarlet vest that buttoned up to his throat.

"I'll take Flea to the library," Olwen said, hurrying up behind them. "Perhaps you'd like to join us, Neve? I can show you our collection."

I couldn't tell who seemed more shocked by the suggestion, Neve or Caitriona.

"But the library—" the silver-haired girl protested.

"—is an invaluable resource to all," Olwen finished, taking a grumbling Flea by the hand. "Shall we?"

Neve looked between her and us, uncertain. "I'd planned to go with them . . ."

"Stay," I told her. "Really, it's fine."

I didn't like the idea of separating, but I did—begrudgingly—trust Olwen to look out for her. And, well, questioning Nash about the Ring of Dispel would be a simpler thing without Neve there.

Neve nodded, and some of the tension around her eyes eased.

"Let us be off before the light is gone." Bedivere glanced at Emrys. "Are you coming?"

"I am indeed," Emrys said, sounding like his usual self, even as he refused to look at me. "It's a lovely morning for a ride, don't you think?"

"I'm afraid there's only four horses who've the strength for the journey." Aled's green skin went ashen. "I hadn't realized—"

"I'm sure Tamsin won't mind if I ride with her," Emrys cut in, coming to stand beside me.

"What are you doing?" I whispered.

"Going with you to see your father, obviously," he said, never once glancing my way.

I rolled my eyes. Of course he'd never let us go without him—not when the Ring of Dispel was possibly at stake. I hadn't yet told Cabell what I'd seen in the sacred springs, but Emrys's little maneuver made me want to do it then and there.

Aled leaned against the fencing with a grimace, taking the weight off his right leg.

"Are you well, Aled?" Caitriona asked.

"Fine, fine," he said, massaging the place where his knee met the wood.

The carved limb clung to his skin through a series of braided roots that shifted, alive, to accommodate his massaging hand. Emrys looked on in awe.

"'Tis only the damp making trouble again," Aled said. "It leaves a sore where the skin rubs, is it not so?"

It took Bedivere several moments to realize that the question had been directed at him. He gripped his gauntlet with his hand. "Oh—yes. Always on days such as this."

Bedivere's face tightened with what might have been a hint of annoyance—there and gone. He turned to Caitriona. "Shall we?"

"Yes, of course." She cast a quick, assessing look our way. "Have any of you trained with a blade?"

Emrys's hand went up. Both Cabell and I turned to stare at him.

"Put your hand down, man," Cabell told him, crossing his arms over his chest. "I saw you almost knock yourself out messing around with Librarian's mop two weeks ago."

"Well, that's hardly his fault," I said. "That was probably the first time he'd ever seen one."

"I've taken fencing lessons since I was seven," Emrys said, ignoring us both. "That does use a thinner blade, though."

I rolled my eyes. Of course he had.

"It'll be a different weight and balance than you're accustomed to," Bedivere warned.

"I'll manage," Emrys said.

The old knight went to retrieve a long sword from the rack, passing it to Emrys by the scabbard. Caitriona looped it over his shoulder so it rested against his back. I'd somehow forgotten he was left-handed until he reached back to test the distance to the sword's hilt.

"I have some limited experience stabbing and bludgeoning things," Cabell offered, and was given a mace.

I took a small dagger and removed my jacket so Caitriona could place a thin mail shirt over my tunic. The others did the same.

I eyed my white horse and her impressive saddle, trying to steady my heart before it could start its own gallop.

Emrys leaned close to my ear. "Need a boost up?"

I knew he was needling me. All I needed to say was that I'd ride with Cabell—in fact, Cabell was looking at me, as if waiting for it, one brow arching higher with each moment I kept my mouth shut.

I wasn't going to let Emrys find the ring, and I wasn't about to let him win this little battle, either.

With a noise of disgust, I swung myself up into the saddle on one stirrup. Emrys climbed up behind me with annoying ease. I drove my elbows back as I took the reins, trying to wedge some space between us.

Instantly, I regretted my decision. He was inescapable—the press of his hard chest against my back, how his thighs braced against mine. His breath was soft as it fanned my hair, and despite the heat of him and the animal beneath us, a shiver danced down my spine, sparking against all those places where his bigger body fit itself to mine.

"Want to make bets on how long it'll take for me to fall off the back of this beauty?" he whispered.

"No, because I'll just push you off myself," I told him.

His chest rumbled against my back with a laugh. A tentative hand ghosted along my hip, silently asking.

"Fine," I heard myself say. "But don't get any ideas."

The muscles of my stomach jumped and tightened beneath the layers of cloth and cold chain mail as his long fingers flattened against it. I looked down, taking in the raised edge of the scar that ran over his wrist to the back of his hand.

Emrys leaned forward until I could feel his heart pounding against my back—somehow faster than even my own. The smell of him enveloped me, driving out the decaying world around us for a single moment. Pine and the breath of the sea filled my lungs.

"Wouldn't dream of it," he murmured close to my ear.

We rode in silence, following Caitriona along a well-trodden path through the blistered bodies of the trees.

The carpet of decay—blackened leaves, animal carcasses, withered moss—dampened the clip-clopping of the horses. I kept my eyes on the trees and jagged rocks. There were far too many places for the Children to hide, folding their spidery bodies into crevices or retreating into the impenetrable darkness of caves created by the rise and fall of the rugged land.

I looked up, trying to see the sky through the gnarled branches of the dead trees. I could almost imagine it—how Avalon might resemble Tintagel if it were alive with the glow of green life.

Emrys's body was rigid behind mine, his fingers unconsciously curling against my stomach as he surveyed the ravaged wilderness.

Less than an hour had passed since we'd left the tower when we entered a different stretch of forest. The trees here were in orderly lines, and the mist draped itself from their naked branches. The sweet rot of fruit assaulted my senses.

"The sacred grove?" I guessed.

I felt, rather than saw, Emrys nod. "Must be."

A flicker of light caught my attention, and I turned the horse toward it. A fire burned a short distance away, at the head of a narrow watchtower that jutted up from the ground like a crooked finger. In the darkened air, its flames became the only beacon to guide the way.

My heart pounded against my ribs as Caitriona slowed her horse and dismounted, casting a thorough look around before tying it to a post. One by one, we did the same.

Caitriona lifted the heavy latch on the tower's door. I pushed inside, Cabell close behind.

Dust swirled around us as thick as the mist beyond the stone walls. The grayed light bled in through a small opening in the wall, falling eerily on the still scene within.

A tattered sleeping bag. An unlit lantern. A rumpled candy wrapper.

The skeletal remains of a man sinking into the grasping earth.

20

The others blurred at the edge of my vision, becoming shadows. Unspent breath burned in my lungs. I couldn't release it. I didn't dare move and disturb the dust swirling around us. To shatter the strange dream that had me in its snare.

"We call him the Stranger," came Caitriona's voice from behind us. "For he never had a name or face to us. We did not bury him, in the hope his kin would come."

Something heavy thumped to the ground. Cabell's dark form moved slowly, so slowly, to kneel beside the remains.

Look, I told myself, fighting the need to turn away. *You have to look.*

"—this your idea of a cruel joke?" Emrys was saying. His harsh voice grated in the stillness of the watchtower. "You couldn't have given them any kind of warning? It might not even be him—how can you be sure this isn't someone born of Avalon?"

Bedivere bent, his armor creaking as he retrieved the silver wrapper from the ground. Baby Ruth.

Nash's favorite.

"He had already succumbed to death when we lit the beacon of this watchtower last year," Caitriona said. "Had he arrived after, he would have been able to use the shelter as it was intended—a safe place to hide from the Children of the Night."

Her voice drifted away as I focused on Cabell's hand reaching toward the remains.

The bones were browned beneath the remaining shreds of clothing, likely picked clean by insects or the Children. Ribbons of a once-white shirt clung to the exposed rib cage, swaying with the shifting air. The pants seemed modern, but it was difficult to tell after so long.

Cabell started there, feeling along what remained of the pockets. Turning the boots over. Even his practiced, delicate touch made the leather break and crumble.

"It might not even be him," Emrys repeated.

Though he wasn't on the sleeping bag, it was a peaceful pose, as if he'd merely taken off his boots and lain down to sleep and death had pulled the spirit from his body. Both hands were visible. No rings. No jewelry of any kind.

"What are you doing?" Caitriona asked, moving to stop Cabell as he knelt beside the head. "We searched through his clothing and found nothing—"

He shrugged off her hand, gently lifting the back of the skull from the ground. There, protected between the bone and the cold earth, was the well-preserved collar of the shirt. He turned the delicate fabric out toward me.

Inside, stitched by the hand of a little girl, were five letters in yellow thread.

N. LARK.

"I knew it," he breathed out. "I knew that if he was alive and had the ring, he would have used it to help Avalon . . ."

"The ring?" Caitriona asked, her voice sharp.

Cabell released the fabric and the skull, falling back from where he'd been crouched. He draped his arms over his knees and bent his head. His shoulders shook as he cried, the tears dripping silently to the black tattoos on his forearms, to the ground.

At the sight of him, as raw as a newly opened scar, that thin tether, the one that had barely kept my mind from shattering, finally snapped.

Rage and pain bellowed up in me, unbearable with their white-hot blades. My view of the remains blurred. A driving pressure threatened to crack open my skull and reveal the roiling memories and feelings I'd fought so hard to lock away.

I hated him. *I hated him.*

I was reaching for the mace before I knew what I was doing, lifting its impossible weight over my head as I staggered toward the skeleton. Caitriona lunged to stop me, but it was a different pair of arms that locked around my waist, pulling me back from the body.

"You can't." Emrys's voice was calm, even as I tried to pull myself free, even as the scream tore out of my throat. "I know, Tamsin, but you can't—"

Can't. The word shuddered in my mind. *Can't.*

The mace dropped from my numb fingers as I sagged back against his chest. Emrys held on, keeping me upright as the rage burned through and left my body hollow.

I wanted to destroy whatever was left of Nash—destroy him like he'd tried to destroy us.

Once you've heard the crack of a bone resetting itself and taking new shape, it embeds itself in your mind like a barbed root. I heard it then, accompanied by a sharp inhale. Cabell doubled over beside the skeleton, his back arching up at an unnatural angle.

The pain—the tide of grief that had violently swept over him—it was too much.

"Are you well, lad?" Bedivere asked from his side.

"No," I gasped out. "Cabell, it's all right—take a breath—"

Bones shifted beneath the thick layer of Cabell's leather jacket, slithering like serpents under a cover of leaves. They bulged up as they broke and reknit themselves into different, monstrous shapes. His vertebrae arced up one by one as his body curled into itself like an old scroll.

"What in the hell . . . ?" Emrys breathed out.

Caitriona reached behind her, gripping the hilt of her sword and taking an instinctive step in front of Emrys and me. She focused her gaze on Cabell's writhing form. Ready to kill.

"Cab, listen to me!" I pulled myself forward, but Emrys hauled me back. "Listen to the words I'm saying, focus on them . . . In ages past, in a kingdom lost to time—"

The familiar phrase died on my lips as Cabell went rigid. His hands tore at the loose strands of his black hair until I was sure he would pull it away in bloodied clumps. Bedivere either hadn't heard me or hadn't cared to. His grip on Cabell's shoulder tightened as he knelt beside him. He held up a hand, stopping Caitriona's path forward.

"Lad," he said softly. "Cabell, isn't it? Look at me. Look me in the eye."

I twisted and tried to drop, but Emrys's arms were a steel band across my center. His heart was pounding in time with mine. His breath hitched as Cabell lifted his head.

Though his back was to us, the elongating shape of his skull and the emergence of canine ears were obvious. I looked away, squeezing my eyes shut against the image.

Not now, I thought desperately. *They'll think he's one of the Children—they'll kill him—*

"That's it," Bedivere said, his gruff voice low and soothing. "Look at me and only me. Are you the master or the servant?"

Cabell reached for him with clawed hands—not to attack, but to grip the man's arm as if it were the only thing keeping him from being carried away by the dark river roaring through him.

"Are you the master or the servant?" Bedivere asked again.

"M-master," Cabell managed to say. His body began to shift again, cracking and twisting horrifically as it resumed its human shape.

"How . . . ?" I breathed out.

Emrys's grip loosened as he leaned close to my ear. "Coaxer?"

"Tell me your name," Bedivere said.

There was a clear command in his tone, one that reverberated around us like a soft echo. As he spoke, I saw a faint shimmer in the air where his hand rested on my brother's hunched shoulder.

Emrys was right. Bedivere had magic that apparently worked similarly to a Cunningfolk Coaxer. Able to soothe and commune with beasts.

"Tell me your name," Bedivere said once more.

"Cabell." My brother's voice was clear, his form human.

Emrys released me then, and I darted toward Cabell, dropping to my knees beside him. He sagged into my arms, clutching me like he needed to remind himself of what was real. He looked up at Bedivere with amazement. I gripped his arm, helping him to stand.

"Is it a curse, then?" the older man asked.

Cabell nodded. "I've had it my whole life."

Someone hissed behind us, though I couldn't be sure if it was Emrys or Caitriona.

The question would remain unanswered. Outside the tower, our horses began to whinny, stomping and pawing at the dirt. Caitriona moved toward the door, looking out, her hand already on her sword's hilt.

"We're losing the light," she said. "It's past time to leave."

"That's it?" Emrys asked.

"Our days are short," the girl said, "but I assure you, my patience for this sort of foolish delay is shorter."

"We can't leave his body like this," Cabell said. "We need to bury it—"

"No, we don't," I said. "Leave it. We're not dying for him."

The horses were so thoroughly spooked that not even our presence settled them. The speed with which the light was departing, drawing back over the sky like a riptide, turned my blood to ice.

I climbed back into the saddle, allowing Emrys to settle behind me. My gaze never left Cabell as he staggered out of the watchtower. The hair was still receding on his arms as he hauled himself up onto his dapple-gray horse. When Bedivere nodded to him, he gave a curt nod back.

"I'm not going to ask if you're okay," Emrys told me quietly.

"Good."

"I wouldn't dream of saying I'm sorry about Nash, either," he added.

"I'm glad," I said, clenching the reins. "Because I know you wouldn't mean it—all you care about is the fact that he didn't have the ring."

I'd barely spoken above a whisper, but somehow Caitriona had heard it.

"Yes, *the ring*," she said, circling her horse around ours. "I look forward to hearing your explanation once we're back at the tower."

I clenched my jaw, keeping my eyes straight ahead on the dead moss dripping from the branches above the waiting path.

"And this time," Caitriona said, clicking her tongue to get her horse moving, "perhaps you'll be so good as to tell us the true reason you came to Avalon."

21

We rode back to the tower at a grueling pace that left me feeling breathless and bruised by the time the gate was shut behind us.

"Come with me," Caitriona told us. An order, not a request.

We fell into line behind her as we made our way up into the tower. Up past the storage and sleeping halls. She only stopped when we reached the third floor of bedrooms. Glancing back over her shoulder, she met Bedivere's gaze and nodded.

"This way, lad," Bedivere said, guiding Cabell off the stairs and down the dark hall. Cabell said nothing, his black hair a curtain in front of his lowered face. My pulse leapt, clearing the haze from my thoughts.

"Wait," I rasped out, hurrying past Emrys down the stairs. "Don't take him—"

Bedivere held out a hand, stopping me before I could follow. The look he gave me was almost unbearably kind. "Don't trouble yourself. I'll watch over him."

Panic trilled in my body. They couldn't separate us. Anything could happen to him. "Come with me, Tamsin," Caitriona said.

Emrys's hand closed gently over my arm, urging me back up the stairs.

"It'll be all right, lass," Bedivere told me. "This once, give his care to another."

No. That wasn't right. Cabell was mine to protect. He had been for as long as I could remember.

"Now, Tamsin," Caitriona ordered.

"I'll be okay," Cabell whispered. "It's all right, Tams."

"Please don't hurt him," I begged. Cabell stopped outside his door, his hand resting on the latch. He didn't turn around. "He can't control it."

"Why would I hurt him?" Bedivere asked, his blue-gray eyes soft. "He's a good lad."

"Come on," Emrys urged, his fingers lightly squeezing my elbow. "He'll be all right."

Cabell opened the door to the chamber he shared with Emrys and disappeared into it. Finally, I relented, shaking off Emrys's grip and climbing the last section of stairs.

Caitriona led us to the uppermost floor of the castle. The smell of old parchment, ink, and leather greeted us on the top step as if to say *You're here, you've found me, you're safe at last.*

The library.

The space was awash in warm, gentle candlelight. Each flame was cleverly amplified by a glass orb around it, providing illumination to the tables that radiated out from the center of the room. Ornate tapestries were draped over each of the walls.

But most breathtaking of all were the rows of bookshelves, carved to resemble a grove of trees. Their branches were made of silver, and their leaves of mirrors, to carry the light and spread it evenly around us.

Neve sat at one of the tables beside the fire, a large text open in front of her. Olwen wandered the shelves behind her, seeming to search for something. Both looked over at our unceremonious entrance.

"What happened?" Neve rose from her chair, a hand pressed to her chest. I hated the soft, pitying look on her face, but hated my traitorous heart more for squeezing at the acknowledgment.

Olwen pulled out two seats for Emrys and me. Emrys went willingly to his, collapsing heavily into it and letting his legs sprawl out in front of him. I had too much adrenaline still whispering beneath my skin to sit down.

I paced beside the bookshelves, glancing now and then at their gilt spines and the titles there—*Remedies for All Ailments, Beasts of Other Realms, Lord Death*—before moving to touch the brittle edges of stacked scrolls.

As I turned the corner to the next row, an elfin—the sister Olwen had told us about—appeared in my path, startling like a fawn.

Like Aled and Dilwyn, she was slight, with greenish skin like an unripe fruit, but her long, dark hair was shot through with a thick streak of white. Compared to the others, she seemed . . . not fragile, exactly. It wasn't her size, either. It was more that, looking at her, I had the strangest sense that she was there with us in her body, but not her mind.

The elfin turned to Caitriona. "You took them to see the Stranger? Was it the man they're searching for?"

"Yes, Mari, it was," Caitriona said.

"Tricked us into thinking he was still alive, only to introduce us to a corpse, is probably a more accurate description," Emrys said coldly.

Neve looked at Caitriona, outraged. "How could you do something like that?"

"This is not about my deception," Caitriona said, "but your own."

"Cait," Olwen chided.

The other girl sighed, bowing her head. "I apologize for deceiving you, but I cannot, and will not, apologize for doing whatever I must to protect this isle."

"Good," I said. "Because I'm not going to apologize for doing whatever *I* must to help my brother."

She gazed down at me, imperious and unyielding. But I saw a flicker of something in her expression—a murmur of understanding in a vow of no surrender.

"Why didn't you warn them he was dead?" Olwen asked, aghast. "I've never known you to be dishonest."

"I wasn't *dishonest*!" Caitriona said, the words bursting out of her. She crossed her arms over her chest, turning her face away. "I was being careful. I did not believe their story to be truthful. I needed to see their unguarded response to the Stranger."

"Well, congratulations, you proved yourself wrong," Emrys said. "By the way, withholding information is still dishonesty."

Caitriona's freckled face flushed. She opened her mouth, only to close it. When she finally spoke, she'd regained her composure. "Regardless, you left out several essential pieces of *your* story."

"Explain, please," Olwen said, eyeing them both.

It was strange to hear the story recounted by Caitriona, with all the remoteness of someone who hadn't been forced to close an old, unfinished book.

"Your brother is cursed to shift into a hound?" Olwen asked, her brows raised. "Truly?"

"Yes." My stomach churned, hating that I had to share this with near strangers. It didn't feel right to talk about it when Cabell wasn't here. "He used to be able to push back against the shift, but it's happening more often. Any intense emotion triggers it."

Emrys made a small noise at the back of his throat. "How long has he been like this?"

"Actually, I think the better question is how Cabell was cursed," Olwen countered, resting a cheek against her palm in thought. "Was he born with it, or was it cast upon him?"

"We don't know," I said, then hesitated. "Our guardian found him as a boy. He was wandering alone on the moorland of our mortal world, with no memory of anything but his own name. We have tried . . . everything . . . *everything* to break its hold on him. Tonics, the Cunningfolk healers, even sorceresses. Without knowing who cast the curse or why, there's no way to know how to break it."

Neve stared down at her hands, lost in thought. No one seemed sure what to say, but better silence than hopeful platitudes that would never amount to anything but wasted breath.

"I wish you comfort in the loss of your guardian," Mari told me. "May his memory remain even as the Goddess grants his soul new life."

"Please ask your Goddess not to bother," I said bitterly. "There are better uses for her time."

Both Caitriona's and Olwen's eyebrows rose sharply. Mari merely tilted her head, studying me in a way that was unnerving.

"If I may," Olwen said. "My confusion lies in the fact that, in spite of this, you have journeyed into Avalon to search for him . . . ?"

"They weren't looking for him," Caitriona said, crossing her arms over her chest. "They were after some sort of ring they believed he had. A ring that breaks curses."

"Oh," Mari said, eyes sharpening with sudden, startling focus. "The Ring of Dispel?"

Olwen ran a hand over her ink-blue hair. "Goddess bless you for reading every book in this tower, Mari. Is that the one made by High Priestess Viviane?"

"Yes, for Sir Lancelot, who was raised here by her before joining Arthur at his court," Mari said. "After I read of it in her writings, I spoke to Sir Bedivere. He witnessed its power on more than one occasion."

I slumped into the seat beside Neve, unsure of how to feel now that my theory of Bedivere was confirmed.

"So you search on behalf of Cabell for this ring," Caitriona said. "Which may once have been in your father's possession."

"Why not tell us that from the start?" Olwen asked. "No one would fault you for wanting to help your brother. We would have been glad to offer any assistance we could."

"Because of the nature of the ring," Mari said in that dreamy, far-away voice of hers. "And what it requires to wield it."

God's teeth, I thought.

"That's not—" I began, panic making the words stick in my throat. I grasped at the thinnest of straws to change the subject. "I just didn't know if I could trust any of you to help us. Was I supposed to tell you

220

this after you threw us in the dungeon—which, by the way, if this is supposed to be such a peaceful and beautiful place, why do you have a dungeon?"

"That's actually where we used to lock up the wine and mead," Olwen supplied helpfully. "Some of the small fae developed a taste for it, and around Beltane—"

She stopped when Caitriona placed a hand on her arm.

"What's required to use the ring?" Neve asked.

"It's not—it—" I turned to her, my jaw working, but it was too late.

"The ring was created for Sir Lancelot by a priestess who was unusually skilled at silver craft—blessing jewelry and other objects with the Goddess's power," Mari said. "Giving them purpose. But rather than destroy the curses and enchantments cast upon its wearer, the ring began to drink them in. It learned the taste of blood, and liked it."

My pulse spiked.

"That's not—" I tried to interrupt.

"Let her speak," Caitriona snapped. "Another word from you and you'll be back down in 'storage.' Go on, Mari."

And so Mari did, and the last bit of control I had over our situation finally slipped away.

"The Ring of Dispel will only obey the master who proves their worth by killing its last one. It can only be claimed through death."

22

I felt Neve's gaze on me like a brand, blistering with silent accusation.

You don't owe her rat piss, a voice whispered in my mind. *If she didn't do her research on the ring before setting off to find it, that's her fault.*

It didn't stem the burn of bile that rose in my throat.

"If this ring can break curses and we think there's a chance it's been returned to Avalon, why aren't we out searching for it?" Olwen asked. "Isn't this the blessing we've been praying for?"

"And risk countless lives searching outside the tower's walls?" Caitriona shook her head and looked at me. "As it stands, your father is dead, and the ring is seemingly lost. What is it you intend to do now?"

"The same thing you should all do," I told her. "Leave this festering slice of hell and return to the mortal realm."

The most surprising thing wasn't the way Caitriona recoiled at the suggestion, but the way Olwen and Mari averted their attention toward the mirrored leaves of the shelves, as if hit with the guilt of suddenly hearing their own thoughts echoed back to them.

"The isle is our home," Caitriona said. "It was the pride of our ancestors, and the gift of our Goddess. You may have no faith in the greater tapestry of fate, but we do. I know there must be a way to restore the land and the Children to that which they once were, and I will continue to fight every day to find it."

"Fight how?" I said. "It's been two years and you're no closer to stopping this. You've already lost. The only question is how many more lives you're willing to sacrifice."

Caitriona's face flushed with barely suppressed anger. None of the other sisters said a word. Seeing my earlier suspicion validated was the worst kind of victory—hollow and bitter to its core.

"Whatever happened here was fatal," I continued. "You have the power to open the path back to the mortal realm, don't you? This isle is dead, and the people here are next. How long before the magic starts to turn the living? Are you going to spend your last days washing blood off the stones until there's no one left to do the same for you?"

Mari stood up from her seat, trembling and pale. She fled the library with a suppressed sob, her feet pattering down the steps.

"Tamsin . . . ," Emrys said. "Maybe now's the time to take a well-earned break from your usual heart-crushing fatalism?"

I ignored the furious looks of the others. I didn't need a morality lesson from people who refused to swallow even a small dose of the truth.

Caitriona started after Mari, but Olwen stood and held up a hand. "I'll check on her after we finish here."

"Look," I said, but couldn't bring myself to apologize. "Without the ring, the only thing I can do now is try to find the next relic or spell or sorceress that might be able to help Cabell."

"And you don't think the answer could *possibly* be here?" Neve said, sweeping an arm around us.

"You still have not spoken of how you came to this land," Caitriona said. "How, then, will you return?"

I spoke before Neve could tell the truth. "Neve opened the path. I'm sure she can do it again."

"That's only if I agree to go with you," Neve said with the sort of deserved resentment that only made me like her that much more.

"Then one of the priestesses can send us back on our merry way," I shot back.

"No," Caitriona cut in. "Contrary to your lies, it is impossible for a sorceress to open the path after the Forsaking, and no priestess shall take you. There is not enough daylight to make the journey, and I will not risk any of my sisters' lives for yours again."

A blazing swell of fury and outrage rose in me. "There has to be another way—"

A bell tolled harshly, its frenzied *clang-clang-clang* a desperate summoning. My pulse sped to meet it.

"What now?" I asked.

Caitriona's armor rattled as she ran past me toward the back wall and pulled aside a tapestry, revealing a row of arched windows. We gathered behind her, searching the darkness beyond the tower's walls.

Caitriona gripped the crumbling sill, her breathing turning ragged.

Below us, the parched moat was an inferno of fire. The flames cast a sinister light on the hundreds—thousands—of Children of the Night who had gathered at its edge.

Some threw themselves at the flames, testing whether they could pass. One flung itself from a nearby tree, clawed hands somehow catching the fortress's wall, only to skid down and be devoured by the shimmering heat. A second made it farther up but was picked off by an archer before it could scale the curtain wall.

There was a clattering of footsteps on the stairs. Betrys burst through the door a moment later, her brown skin glowing with sweat.

"What's happened?" Caitriona asked, going to her side.

"They're—" Betrys sucked in a deep breath. "They came all at once. They've surrounded us completely. I lit the moat—but they're not fleeing from it, the way they have before. How did they get through the protection wards in the forest?"

A whisper of fear crossed Caitriona's face before she steadied it into its usual mask of calm control. "Their magic has finally failed. It'll only be a matter of time before those on the tower's walls do as well. You were right to light the moat."

"What do you mean, their magic has *failed*?" I demanded. "How is that possible?"

"Dark magic is corrupting," Caitriona said. "The presence of the Children weakens the isle's oldest and strongest spellwork."

I caught Emrys's eye.

"Should we light the secondary fires on the upper walls?" Betrys asked.

Caitriona shook her head, taking her sister by the arm. "Wake the rest of the tower guard. We'll need to search the lower levels and springs to ensure none have gotten inside—" Their voices disappeared as they passed through the door.

An image of the ravenous Children lingered in my mind long after Caitriona and Betrys had departed. "How much brush and wood do you have to keep the fires burning?"

"It's burning with magic," Olwen explained. Her words were meant to be reassuring, but the way her lips trembled with her smile didn't instill much confidence. "The Nine will take turns feeding it until first light, when the Children retreat."

"And if the Children never leave?" I asked.

Olwen didn't dare answer, but I already knew.

We'd be trapped here with them.

And when the last protective magic burned itself out, and claws met the cold stones, we'd die with them.

Without any sort of agreement, let alone acknowledgment, the others followed me to the room Emrys and Cabell shared. The heavy oak door was already ajar, as if my brother had been expecting us, or at least wondered about the bells still clanging.

He sat on his bed, his knees curled up against his chest, his arms wrapped around them. His shoulder-length black hair had fallen forward as he stared at the opposite wall. Cabell didn't look over as we came in and Emrys shut the door behind us.

"You told them?" Cabell asked gruffly.

"I had to," I said.

He lifted a shoulder. "You could have at least waited for me to be there."

"I know." And because it was all I really could say: "I'm sorry."

He nodded, then rose to sit at the table in front of the hearth. The fire of the salamander stones flickered with the shifting air. At the edge of my vision, both Neve and Emrys took an unconscious step back at his approach.

The widening chasm of numbness inside me immediately filled with white-hot anger.

"I don't bite," Cabell said, and my heart broke just that little bit more as he forced his tone to stay light, joking. His white teeth flashed in the firelight. "At least not as a human."

"Tough luck with the curse, Lark," Emrys said, sounding like his usual arrogant self again. "I suppose that explains why your old man was after the ring in the first place."

He claimed the seat across from Cabell at the table—a round table not so different from Arthur's, where we all had equal status, and equal ability to eye one another suspiciously. My mouth twisted into a humorless smile.

"What happened outside?" Cabell asked, turning to look at me.

"The Children have surrounded the tower," I said. "The Nine are holding them off with fire."

Cabell frowned. "Is that going to be enough?"

"Olwen told me fire is the only way to truly kill them," Neve offered, rubbing her finger along a knot in the wood. "The creatures fear it, and hate light."

"The bigger issue is that they're blocking our way back to the portal," I said. "We need to find another way back to the mortal world, otherwise we're little more than a feast for the undead."

"You'd really leave?" Neve asked in disbelief. "You don't even want to try to help them?"

"What am I supposed to do about any of this?" I asked.

Her gaze hardened. "I don't believe you're that heartless."

My nerves prickled. "Could that be because you barely know me?"

"We can do *something*," Neve tried again. "This can't be the end of Avalon."

I knew she wasn't just angry with me for having a realistic take on the situation. There was at least some misplaced anger over keeping the truth about the ring from her—someone who clearly prided herself on being self-taught and knowledgeable. Which, fine. It felt good to fight. To release some of that painful pressure that had been building up in me since we entered the watchtower.

"I came here for the Ring of Dispel, and now the trail isn't just cold, it's dead," I said, not bothering to soften my tone. "I'm not going to risk my life or Cabell's scouring the forests for a relic that may no longer even be here. I'd rather get back to our own world and find another solution, and I suggest you do the same."

"This is about more than the ring now," Neve protested. Her face was the very portrait of noble-minded compassion that had been getting heroic people killed for thousands of years. If ever there was a time for her to be selfish, to trust the impossible odds, it was now.

"Did *you* forget the whole reason you wanted the ring?" I asked. "What makes you think the Council of Sistren will accept you for saving the very place they were banished from?"

Neve looked down, her expression tightening. Clearly, that was exactly what she'd been thinking. "It's not—it's not just that."

"You want access to the priestesses' texts so you can learn more about magic?" I suggested. "Including that light spell you cast?"

"The one that saved your life?" The fierce expression she turned on me made me sit back in my chair. The fire seemed to suddenly roar at my back, echoing the heat of her words.

"Tamsin's right—" Emrys said.

I looked over, brows raised.

"Yes, for once I actually agree with you, Bird—"

"Stop calling her that," Cabell interrupted.

Emrys continued, ignoring him. "We still have the portal waiting for us. If we travel by daylight, we can probably survive long enough to use the one trip back the hag promised."

"Yeah, let's just hope one of the Children doesn't find it and try to climb out into our world first," I said.

The three of them looked at me with varying degrees of horror.

"Can you please tell whatever chaos gremlin lives in your brain to be quiet?" Cabell asked, pained.

"I'm just saying that time is of the essence," I said.

"You're right," Neve said, pushing her chair back. "Which is why I'm going to stop sitting here spiraling into deeper and deeper panic and head back to the library to look for solutions."

I shook my head, casting a quick glance at Cabell, but his troubled expression had only deepened.

At the door, Neve stopped, and didn't bother to turn around as she said, "I'm sorry about Nash."

Then she was gone.

Emrys stretched his arms up and rolled out his neck. "On that note, I'm off to get some food and start poking around the place to see what I can find."

After he was gone, Cabell rose and sat again on the edge of the bed. I moved to sit beside him, feeling the silence between us like a third presence in the room. All at once, the anger, the resentment, hurtled through me. My hands curled into fists in my lap as I leaned my head against Cabell's shoulder. He leaned his head on top of mine.

"He's really gone, huh?" Cabell said after a while.

When I closed my eyes, I saw Cabell there—the Cabell of seven years ago, small and frail, soaked to the bone with freezing rain after searching Tintagel for Nash. Telling me what I already knew. *He's gone.*

When it became just *us.*

"He's been gone for seven years," I said. "It's just that now we know for sure he's never coming back."

"You've always thought that," Cabell pointed out.

"Doesn't mean I wanted to," I heard myself admit.

He sat up, craning his neck to look at me. "Maybe we'll find another journal of his. And it'll have answers about what he was thinking, coming here with the ring. Or your birth parents' names."

My jaw set, and I resented the way my eyes prickled with heat. "It doesn't matter. We're all we need, right?"

Cabell sighed, and it was a while before he could bring himself to say, "If it happens again . . . if I shift . . ."

"It won't," I said, straightening. I gripped his forearm, forcing him to look at me. "It won't happen."

"If it happens," he continued, looking down at his hands, "don't let me hurt anyone, especially not you. I couldn't live with it. Do whatever it takes to stop me."

"It's not going to happen," I said.

"Tamsin," he said firmly. I met his dark eyes, hating the haunting way the shadows painted his face. "Whatever it takes."

I leaned my head against his shoulder again, welcoming the quiet back into the space.

"It's not going to happen," I repeated, because I never made promises to my brother I knew I wouldn't keep.

The endless night stretched into what Olwen called the resting hours, when most of the surviving Avalonians tried to sleep, however impossible that was.

I ate a few bites of the bread and barley stew I was offered by Dilwyn and went to bed early, relieved to find Neve wasn't there.

I left the room's hearth cold; my thoughts were clearer in the dark, where their only competition was fear and memory. I lay on my side, staring at the wall until my eyes had adjusted enough to count each stone and my ears no longer noticed the screeching of the Children gathering along the edge of the burning moat.

Trapped. The word was on my tongue like bitter dandelion greens. Every plan I conceived—flying, digging, fighting—collapsed under the weight of its own implausibility.

I turned onto my other side, feeling every bit of the ache in my back and legs.

You'd really leave?

I would, and in a heartbeat, if it meant saving us. Even Emrys. This wasn't our world. We had no responsibility to it, or anyone in it.

Blowing out a sigh, I rested my cheek against my hands. I knew I should be grateful for the breath in my lungs, and for the fact that we'd made it this far. But everything dissolved into simmering anger beneath my skin.

Come on now, Tamsy, it's not so bad.

In the stillness of the moment, hundreds of questions rose into a poisonous swarm in my mind. But the crushing truth lay beyond these walls, scattered among his bones.

His remains were the last answer we'd likely ever get. Nash was dead. Nash was dead, along with everything else we deserved to know and now never would. Nash was dead, and he'd taken our pasts with him beyond our reach, into the dark wilderness of death.

I couldn't even be angry at him for it, not when I was so furious at myself. *I'd* brought us here. In chasing his ghost, I'd killed us all.

Somehow, impossibly, I must have fallen asleep. The next thing I was aware of was the scuff of the door sliding over stone and the bed dipping with Neve's weight.

"You weren't going to tell me about how the ring is claimed, were you?" Neve whispered into the darkness.

"No."

"Because you thought I was a fool and that by the time I'd found out, it would be too late."

"I never thought you were a fool," I whispered. "But I am sorry."

I didn't explain the rest. That it was different between us now. That I'd never thought it would turn into this. None of it mattered now, and all I wanted was the silence. The cold expanse of nothing that used to exist between us.

The only safe place there'd ever been to hide.

23

That night, I dreamt of the woman in the snow for the first time in years.

It was as clear as the day it happened. Cabell and Nash had left me on our borrowed riverboat so they could search a nearby vault for Arthur's dagger. I'd heard her voice, how the longing in it had somehow harmonized with my own. As if I had been looking for her, and her me.

She waited for me in the open field, the falling snow giving shape to her translucent form as she hovered over the ground. Her hand stretched out toward me, and I went to her, desperate for that touch. To be wanted.

The White Lady was beautiful, but her face grew pained as she took in the sight of me.

Something had stirred in me as I approached her. A thought. A tale, told by Nash months before. Of women who died by their own hand before they could reveal the location of a treasure. How they were meant to guard it until they killed another to take their place.

But the thought melted away, and then there was only her. Her hand, reaching out to touch my chest, just above my heart.

And pain. Pain sharper, and crueler, than any I'd ever known. As if she had taken a knife and plunged it there, again and again. I tried to pull back, but my body was too weak. I couldn't even scream. Her face, so serene, turned monstrous with delight in my suffering.

But the wind called, icy and imperious as it cut over the field. The snow turned frenzied with the words it sang.

Not her. Not this child.

And the shivering light of the spirit obeyed, fading like the last stroke of sun into night.

The dream shifted.

I was back on the path leading to the tower's imposing gate, following a white horse with no rider. As I walked, the thick mist around us parted, and the world changed. Glowing green with unstoppable life—birds, fish in the glistening moat, small fairies gathered along the walls. The Mother tree's branches were thick with leaves and tendrils of adoring mist.

The horse's hooves echoed on the stone. At the steps to the tower it turned, as if to ensure I was still following.

I saw my face reflected in its black eye. A spiraling ivory horn rose from its head. An effervescence moved beneath my skin as it bowed its head at the base of the tower steps, touching its horn to the ground. And there, a single white rose cleaved up through the dark earth, through the stones. Its trembling face unfolded.

I jerked awake, gasping. I pressed my hands to my clammy face, but the phantom smell of petals lingered on my skin. I pushed out of the bed, relishing the feel of the freezing stones under my feet. That was real. That was true.

I wiped my hands against my shirt, the blanket, anything to rid them of that smell. I only stopped when I saw that the other side of the bed was empty, but politely half made.

Neve was already gone for the day. I didn't blame her.

The cracking ache in my skull sent the bedchamber swirling into shadows. A gray light filtered through the window behind me.

Daylight.

I didn't bother to put on my shoes or straighten the clothes I'd slept in. I bolted from the room, running up the stairs to the library. I was certain I'd find Neve at a table, buried behind a stack of books, but the room was empty.

I slowed in the doorway. With all the tapestries pushed aside, steely light pierced the window glass like blades. The tables and rugs looked worn and morose.

I was almost afraid to look as I stepped close to the cold glass. People moved in the courtyard below and flanked the fortress's walls. My heart leapt. The moat fire was out, but the creatures had clustered beneath the trees, suffering the dim light by building hideous mounds and lurking behind the boulders for shelter.

There was a gasp behind me. I spun around, raising my hands defensively. Olwen stared back at me, clutching a small cauldron, three candlesticks, and a wreath of dried greens to her chest. Her dark blue curls seemed to float at her shoulders.

"You startled me," she said with a shaky laugh. "I wasn't expecting anyone but Flea up here."

I glanced at the objects she set down on one of the tables. "Lessons?"

Olwen quirked a brow. "If I can draw her out of hiding."

The smell of lavender and lye washed over me as she crossed the room toward me.

"The Children never retreated," Olwen said. Close up, her exhaustion became plain: the skin beneath her eyes was bruised and hollowed, and she seemed to sway with the effort it took to stay on her feet.

"How is that possible?" I asked. "Have they ever done this before?"

Olwen shook her head. "We have no notion of what it might mean, but I suspect nothing good."

I gave her a wry look. "You think?"

Suddenly the idea that she would be spending hours teaching Flea instead of preparing for the Children's next attack seemed ridiculous.

I waved a hand toward the table. "What's the point of teaching her anything when you can't even guarantee her a tomorrow?"

Olwen's expression shuttered.

"You know, Tamsin," she began, "our High Priestess, Goddess restore her soul, used to say that if you expect to fail, you invite failure with open arms, because you can't bear the ache of hoping, or the possibility of success. But tell me, does being right make it hurt any less when it happens?"

"No," I told her, the ache pounding in my head worse and worse with each breath, "but at least you're prepared."

In the short time I'd been gone from the bedchamber, someone else had already slipped in and out. My old clothes—just a sweater and shirt, given that my pants had been left a shredded mess—had been laundered as promised and were neatly folded on the table in front of the fireplace.

There was something else sitting on top of them. I squinted at it, working out the cricks in my neck. I leaned closer.

It was a small wooden bird. A finely carved figurine, hardly bigger than my thumb but precise in its details. The crest of feathers on its head . . .

It was a lark.

Its wooden eyes stared back at me with a strange kind of intelligence, its beak shaped to be partly open, as if it were drawing a breath before flight. It felt warm at the center of my palm, its edges digging into my fingers as I closed them around it, bringing my fist to rest against my forehead.

I needed to find Cabell, then gather the others to continue our conversation—to convince Neve to abandon the ridiculous idea that this land could be saved. Find a map of the isle and figure out where the hag's portal had dumped us. Work out a plan to escape the Children, then a backup for when the first plan inevitably failed. See what extra food and supplies I could find to stow in our bags, and hope no one else would notice their absence.

But neither Cabell nor Emrys was in their bedchamber, nor were they in the main hall of the tower—there were only men and women set up with looms, weaving simple cloth or making blankets.

The clatter and clang of metal on metal finally drew me out into the courtyard, where the air still smelled of smoke.

I spotted Cabell's dark head of hair first, then the dark leather of his jacket. He stood alone, bracing his forearms against the training ring's fence. He watched intently as Bedivere led a group of men and women through a series of drills with their wooden swords.

The old knight demonstrated with his steel sword, swinging the blade one-handed with precision and confidence. He still wore the metal glove over his lost hand, and used that wrist to brace the sword's hilt.

I glanced at the uncertain novices as I came to stand beside Cabell; they all looked bewildered at whatever Bedivere was explaining. They fumbled with their practice weapons as if they had spent their lives carrying harps and flutes, not swords.

Just beyond them, Caitriona and a few of the others were having their own training sessions. I watched, stunned, as Arianwen decimated the center of her target with four perfectly aimed arrows.

Behind her, Betrys somersaulted, rolling over the ground and throwing a quick succession of knives at her targets—roughly human-shaped dummies. They'd already been in a sad state, with hay jabbing out of the cloth covers, but she managed to behead one and disembowel another. Straw rained on the ground as they collapsed.

Caitriona was working with a gleaming long sword, her face flushed crimson and dripping with sweat as she moved the heavy blade in smooth figure eights over and over, only adjusting the height and speed of her attack. Her feet were light and nimble, leaving spiral patterns on the dusty stones.

"I don't suppose you have another thermos of coffee stashed anywhere?" It was as much a plea as a question.

Cabell gave me an apologetic look. "Didn't you bring any packets with you?"

"They got ruined in the rain and sludge," I moaned.

"Maybe they have some tea?" he suggested.

I looked at him, too disgusted to dignify that with a response.

"Anything interesting happen this morning?" I asked him.

"I saw Neve helping in the kitchen earlier. Then I met Lowri—one of the Nine. She has the strawberry-blond hair and is even taller than Caitriona."

I nodded. I'd seen her in the tower. Her shoulders and arms were incredibly muscled.

"Lowri works in the forge with Angharad the gnome," Cabell said, as if reading my thoughts. Then added, sardonically, "No one else has even come within arm's length of me. I can't imagine why."

"You do smell like you slept next to a wet donkey," I told him.

He didn't laugh.

"They'll come around." My throat ached as I spoke. "They'll see who you really are."

"Yeah?" he asked, fiddling with the stack of silver rings on his right middle finger. "And what's that?"

"A wonderful person who was dealt a bad hand," I said with a look that dared him to argue with me. "Who may smell of donkey, but possesses a heart of gold."

He managed a small smile. "Thanks, Tams."

"Now," I said, keeping my voice low, "we need a plan."

Cabell turned his back to the training, scuffing the heel of his boot against the ground. "What we really need is what we always need at the start of a job—information. About the tower itself, and if there's a remote chance of taking longer trips outside the walls."

I preferred when it was just the two of us working alone, but he was right. In this case, it was impossible.

"Is that what you're doing out here?" I asked.

"I was going to try to talk to Bedivere about yesterday," he said, crossing his arms over his chest. "About how he managed to pull me back from the edge."

I nodded, ignoring the way my stomach tightened at the mention of what had happened. "That's a good idea. Actually, it wouldn't hurt to get close to him. He might know of other ways to get out of here."

"What about you?" Cabell asked. "Do you need any helpful pointers on how to make friends?"

"Ha ha." I rolled my eyes.

"Cabell!"

We both turned toward the training area. Bedivere was motioning to him with one of the wooden practice swords. "I've a blade for you, my lad."

"Oh—no," Cabell said, shaking his head. He took a step back. "Really. I'm fine watching."

I elbowed him in the side, calling back, "He's been waiting all morning for you to ask."

The knight left his novices and made his way to us, his smile partly hidden by the wiry tufts of his beard.

He wore a leather chest plate today and smelled of the oil he'd used to soften it, with the faintest bit of horse sweat mixed in.

"Come on, lad. We're short one for dueling drills, and I've a suspicion it'll help to clear your mind of worries."

Bedivere tossed the practice sword to him. Cabell caught it with ease. He stared at it as the old knight returned to the group, calling out, "Assume your stances!"

"Information," I reminded Cabell. "Your idea."

With a groan, Cabell shrugged off his jacket and left it hanging on the rail beside me. He pulled the sleeves of his tunic down over his tattoos and secured them at the wrist with their ties.

"Get after 'em, tiger," I said, giving him a pat on the back. "Do the Lark name proud."

"I'm going to flush all of your instant coffee when we get home," he said through his clench-jawed smile.

For all the confidence and ease my brother had navigating our world, it was strange to watch him tentatively join the others like a nervous kid trying to make friends on the playground.

"Good lad!" I heard Bedivere cheer. "Everyone, this is my friend Cabell."

There was a soft pressure at the pocket of my jacket. I reached down just in time to snatch the small hand before it could slip back out.

"Better," I said, turning. Flea's bottom lip jutted out as she handed the carved bird over. "It's usually best to try for flat or smooth objects until you get quicker with it."

The girl pretended to ignore my advice as she leaned against the fencing. "Is that yer brother over there? The one looking like a fop-doodle who's got himself into too much o' the mead?"

"*I'm* the only one allowed to call him a fopdoodle," I said, taking an educated guess on what the word meant. "Besides, he's not that bad . . ."

Both of our gazes drifted back toward the group. Cabell just wasn't as practiced as the others. And the uncertainty meant he always hung back, staying one step behind so he could follow their lead.

"If ye says so," Flea said, tugging her knit cap down over her ears.

With her dirt-smudged face, wavy white-blond hair, and bad attitude, I had to admit I felt a certain kinship with Flea.

"Shouldn't you be out there with them?" I asked, nodding to the other priestesses.

"Cait says I'm still too young," Flea answered sullenly, then, with another impressive imitation of the elder priestess, added, "*You have to learn with your eyes before your hands,* she says."

"Oh, that's a load of"—I caught myself—"dung. The best way to learn is hands-on."

Flea nodded vigorously. "That's what I always says!"

"Have you talked to Bedivere about it?" I asked, sensing an opportunity. "What's his story, anyway?"

"Sir Beddy?" Flea glanced back over her shoulder, considering him. "He's fine when he's not tootin' his trumpet about servin' that old arse-faced corpse in *glorious* battles and snot."

I let out a shocked laugh. "Is that story true?" Realizing she might not know the mortal world's versions of the tales, I explained, "About

King Arthur being brought here as he lay dying, and kept suspended in enchanted sleep?"

All so he could one day return in England's time of need.

She nodded, biting at her already well-bitten nails. "Got a fancy tomb in the forest and all. Don't know about him coming back, though. He looks right rotten to me. Surprised he didn't turn with the rest of the dead, but there's some magic protecting him and keeping him just alive enough, says Olwen."

"How is Bedivere still alive?" I asked.

"Some spell," Flea said, waving a hand. "He'll stay living as long as the king needs him, see."

I did see. "Has Bedivere always lived here at the tower?"

She swiped her sleeve against her nose. "No. He lived himself alone in some little house near to the tomb for hundreds of years and only came two years past."

For the first time, Flea looked like the child she was. Her bottom lip trembled as her fingers reached out to grip the fence rail.

"When the Children first appeared," I clarified.

Flea sniffed. "When the Children first rose hungry, they came for the people in the orchards and villages that used to be. And . . . the school."

There was once a school. The thought crept up on me, weaving through the horror of the words like a thread of ice. I hadn't been completely conscious of it until she'd said it.

Flea was the only child left at the tower.

There could be a nursery tucked away in one of the tower's many buildings, but I hadn't seen a baby or heard its squalls. There were no toddlers toddling about, either. Not in all the time we'd been here.

I hoped like hell I was wrong because the thought was almost too much to bear. I might have had a hard heart, but it was still beating. It made sense to me that no one had dared to welcome another child into this world. Not as it was.

"And . . . you weren't at school that day?" I asked her carefully.

She shook her head. "I didn't wanna go. It was dull and the others were better at everything. So I came to the tower to watch 'em set up for the harvest festival. And then . . ."

Flea trailed off, rubbing at her runny nose. "And then there was no harvest. Me mam and papa were there in the sacred grove and now nothing's left of 'em. And that's the whole of it."

The force of her words pressed down on my body until it felt too heavy to move. As bad as my childhood had been, it hadn't been . . . *this.* The tattered remains of a life that Flea could only cling to as the last vestiges of her world crumbled around her.

"That's not the *whole* whole of it," I said gently. "I'm sorry about your parents and your friends. It must be hard, missing them."

Flea frowned. "'S fine. I've got me sisters. I'm not alone now. None of us are."

"I'm glad about that," I said, looking back at where Arianwen was nocking another arrow on her bow. "And their families . . . ?"

"Gone," Flea confirmed. "One by one. The dark was so thick it could strangle ye, but Cait got us through it. The others are always jokin' about how, with her hair that peculiar shade, she wasn't born, but made in the forge, but I know she once had a mam and papa too."

I nodded.

"Mari's got her auntie and uncle here. Old Aled and Dilwyn," Flea said. "But the rest of us, we've got each other to care for, and it only hurts sometimes, when it's quiet enough to be thinkin' of it."

I nodded, working my jaw, trying to think of what to say to that. I was too scared of my words coming out as bitter and sharp as they always did.

"And ye have yer brother, even if he turns into a beastie?" she said, looking up at me with a surprisingly solemn expression. "I'm sorry 'bout your own papa."

It didn't make sense why *that*—out of everything that had happened—brought an unwelcome sting to my eyes. I needed to change the subject.

"When were you called to be a priestess?" I asked.

Flea sniffed. "Just before our High Priestess got herself clawed a few days after the orchard and schools. 'Twas just there—"

She pointed to the area beside the kitchen.

"The Children actually got into the fortress?" I asked, horrified.

Flea nodded. "She was old as stone and died quick-and-bloody protecting Mari and the others 'cause only a few guards knew how to fight—Avalon being peaceful and the like. Gave Mari a bad fright and she was never the same—or so says Olwen, but she knows these things."

I wanted to say something comforting, but I'd never been good at this sort of thing. All the words I had for it felt wrong.

You don't owe them anything, that same voice whispered in my mind, *even kindness.*

"That's why Caitriona and the others learned how to fight?" I asked. And why Bedivere helped them, once he'd come to seek refuge at the tower. "They didn't train like this before?"

"Oh no," Flea said. "They all flounced about in gowns, blessing the grounds for the Goddess, having the festivals, singing daft songs, and making them wee flower crowns. But it's not so strange, I suppose. There was the Lady of the Lake, 'course."

"I thought the Lady of the Lake was just another name for the Goddess," I said. "It was someone else?"

" 'Twas the title given to all the priestesses over the ages chosen to defend the isle with sword and magic," Flea said dreamily, "when it was still part of yer world, and there was need of it. Excalibur was the sword each Lady of the Lake used, until they gave it to Arthur to be Avalon's protector while he ruled. That's why he had to give it back when he got skewered."

"Really?" I could understand how I'd misinterpreted the title Lady of the Lake in the texts I'd read, but this version of Excalibur's origins was utterly new to me.

"There hasn't been a Lady of the Lake since the isle became its own realm. The last one stayed behind in the mortal world with her love, who was a smithy of some sort, says Mari. A bunch of tosh if ye ask me." Flea's nose wrinkled. "Cait says we've got to show the others there's still hope, so we fight. It's why they should be teaching me how to use a blade, but they say I'm too little, and they think I'm stupid. Rhona and Seren agree."

I hadn't met Rhona and Seren, but I'd seen the two priestesses walking arm in arm between chores. Rhona with hair as dark as a raven's wing, and Seren's like spun sunlight.

"Actually, your sisters seem to think you're too clever for your own good," I told her.

Flea beamed at that. "I just have to come into my magic, is all. Then I'll be full clever."

"You were called, but you can't use magic yet?" I clarified.

Flea's brow creased in understanding. "I forget you don't know nothing."

"Explain it to me like I'm a baby," I told her, amused.

"Well . . . I was sleeping with the others in the tower and 'twas like I felt a warm glow come into my mind. It whispered a song only I could hear, and it tells me to sing, so I did. The warmth filled me like a hot bath, making me feel good and nice, and it made my feet bring me to the hall, to the image of the Goddess there, and Cait and the others heard the song and they came too. One priestess dies, one gets called, see?"

I did see. Avalon was once a place where there was no sickness and suffering. But even though magic could extend a life by hundreds of years, it couldn't vanquish death. Eventually, everyone met their end.

Flea scratched at her nose in thought. "Except not me. I got called too soon, and everything's been wrong since. Olwen thinks I'm just too young, that it'll happen when I'm thirteen like the others. All I know is, the great stonking well of magic won't open to me, and we don't got years to wait."

"So with the old High Priestess gone," I said, "who becomes the new one?"

"Cait," Flea said. "The others willed it so, 'cause she's Cait."

Flea turned to look back at where Cabell and Bedivere were working together, clacking practice blades over and over in different positions. Cabell was almost smiling. Beyond them, Caitriona and Betrys were dueling, demonstrating something to Arianwen.

Betrys stepped back, but Caitriona, glowing with sweat and vigor, held out a hand and said, "I'll go again."

"No," Betrys was saying, "there's no need—"

"I'll do it again," Caitriona said, assuming her stance. Her arms strained to lift the sword. "And I shall do it better."

"All you'll do is knock yourself on your arse," Betrys said in her usual matter-of-fact way. "Rest, Cait."

The conversation interrupted whatever Bedivere had been saying to his students. The old knight looked over and assessed the situation with impressive speed.

"Caitriona," he called, catching her attention. "Will you assist me? I've need of your skill."

She hesitated, breathing hard. He held out his hand and the priestess finally nodded, drawing in a deep breath.

She returned her long sword to the rack and went to join him. Cabell and the others followed along intently, leaving Bedivere to step back with a look of obvious pride.

"In a battle, whether it be against one foe or a hundred, it is imperative you remember this," Caitriona was telling them behind us, her voice ringing out clear as a bell. "If you drop your weapon, you will die. Fight to keep it in your hand, even if it means battling your own fear first. Now, ready your blade."

Cabell, a few feet away from her, nodded and glanced down at the practice weapon in his hand.

"I've a question for ye."

Flea paused, and the pensive expression on her face had me dying to know what she was thinking. I wasn't disappointed.

"Do ye think Arthur'll still look like he does now when he comes back to life? All waxy and withered like a sun-dried grape? 'Cause he sort of smells, if I'm being honest."

"I hope not," I said with a laugh. "An undead king is already going to be a hard sell to the modern world without him looking putrid. Have you actually seen him?"

She shrugged. "Before the Children rose. 'Twas a dare. Mam was none too 'appy 'bout it. A long walk, that was."

Before I could respond, a sly grin spread over her face.

Flea held up a penny—a modern penny that had apparently hitched a ride to this Otherland in my jacket pocket. My jaw dropped, but I was laughing, and so was she.

"I have nothing left to teach you," I told her.

"Do I want to know what you're teaching her?" came Neve's voice.

We both turned to find the sorceress watching us, brows raised and arms crossed. She was in a simple dress with an apron that was splattered with what might have been food or dirt. It was almost impossible to tell for sure in the gloomy light.

"Oh, you know," I said. "Just my musings on human nature and the great big world."

"What I'm hearing is that you enjoy giving children nightmares," Neve said, her hands on her hips.

"Some say 'giving them nightmares,'" I replied. "Others say 'building character.'"

"Yeah, you're a real architect when it comes to that," Neve said.

I glowered. "Sarcasm is *my* thing. You get access to ancient magic, and I get stinging ironies."

Flea looked between us, thoughts whirring behind her eyes. "What's the matter with the two of ye?"

I looked right at Neve as I said, "Neve wasn't told the truth about something and she's angry at me."

"Tamsin," she said, staring right back, "doesn't quite know how to apologize yet and needs to learn to trust and open up to others."

"And Flea," the little girl said, "thinks both of ye are batty."

"Flea!"

The girl straightened at Olwen's sharp voice as the other priestess came around the tower. She would have bolted if I hadn't gripped the back of her tunic and held her, squirming, in place.

"Ye traitor!" she snarled, still trying to fight her way free.

"*Ye* shouldn't have taken my coin," I told her.

"You are an hour late to your lesson," Olwen said, arms crossed.

"I don't need lessons," Flea said. "Not your kind, anyway."

"Oh?" Olwen said. "You don't need to learn how to call your magic or perform our rites?"

Flea's lower lip jutted out.

"I'd like to learn how you do those things," Neve said. "I'm sure it's different than the way I learned."

The priestess smiled. "Of course, Neve. You're always welcome."

"I'm so behind in my studies," Neve began, "it would be helpful to have a second, equally knowledgeable priestess to help me . . ."

"Ah," Olwen said, not missing the way Flea's head lifted at Neve's words. "My sisters are all at work or training, and so I do not know where we might find such help . . ."

Flea made an *och* noise at the back of her throat. "Well then, it'll be me that 'elps."

"Really?" Neve asked. "You'd do that for me?"

The girl gave her a look. "Don't make a fuss 'bout it. It's only 'cause yer so pitiable."

"Flea!" Olwen admonished. "Apologize to Neve."

"It's all right." Neve's gaze slid over to me. "At least she's honest."

The girl lifted her shoulder. "We going or not?"

I watched them until they had disappeared into the tower, delaying my next task as long as I could. The little carved bird in my pocket seemed to grow heavier as the lessons continued behind me.

I found Emrys in the walled garden next to the infirmary. He was on his knees, working something into the dark soil there. His hair was tousled, and there was a streak of dirt across his cheek. As he leaned forward, the open neck of his tunic gaped, revealing a hint of the muscle there, but also the gnarled ropes of scarring. Absently, he shooed away a few of the sprites swarming around his head.

A small smile touched my lips as I leaned over the stone wall, trying to get a better look at what had him so wholly absorbed.

Soil sniffer, greenthumbie, leafkisser. There were so many contemptuous names among Hollowers for Emrys's Talent. Greenworkers were believed to be largely worthless in our line of work, and most were thought to be eccentrics who tottered around greenhouses cooing at flowers. The way Emrys used his power was much more considered—meditative, almost.

Emrys set about replanting the unrecognizable shriveled greens around him. Every now and then, he'd stop, holding their thin white roots in his palm—nodding to himself, or to them, I wasn't sure. Next he added something to the soil, or dipped the plants into a small pail of water, before returning them to the ground.

"Oh, you must be Tamsin," came a voice from behind me. It was Seren. Her golden-blond hair had been braided, but loose strands clung to the sweat on her face. Her dark brown eyes fixed on me as she shifted the basket of linens to her hip. "I was wondering when we'd meet."

Emrys startled, the shell of his ears going bright pink as he looked up and found me watching.

"I'm like a bad penny," I told her, "wait long enough and I'll eventually turn up."

Seren paused, processing those words.

Even in the gloomy daylight while they should have been at rest, the Children never stopped with their chittering and screeching. I wrapped my arms around my middle, trying to fight off the chill.

"Can I ask you something?" I began.

"Of course," Seren said.

"If you all have magic, and at least some weapons," I began, "why not try to kill the Children of the Night with fire while they're exposed like this? Or at least attempt whatever spell Neve performed that first night?"

"We haven't yet identified the spell she used, and as for the Children . . ." Seren shifted the basket again, her mouth in a tight line. "They were once our friends and family. Somewhere inside them, they still are, and if we can destroy the darkness plaguing the isle, there is still some hope that they may return to us."

"Do you actually believe that?" I asked her. "You've seen how thoroughly the magic, or whatever it is, has corrupted them. What exactly are they going to turn back into?"

Seren's expression hardened, and I knew there'd be no answer for me. "As you missed the morning's meal, I wanted to make sure you knew there was bread in the kitchen."

And with that, she walked away.

"As determined as ever to make friends, I see," Emrys said, standing. He wiped his hands on a rag, then tossed it back onto his shoulder as he came to the other side of the wall from me.

I held up the carved bird, letting my irritation shine.

"You got my message," he said, grinning.

"Is this your idea of a joke?"

"Oh, it's no joke," he said. "The tree was a bird many lifetimes ago, so I set it free."

I stared at him, trying to work out if he was actually serious. In the end, I didn't want him to think I cared enough to ask.

Emrys braced a hip against the wall and crossed his arms over his chest. His gray eye was as pale as the sky, his green one like the flecks of leaves still clinging to his shirtsleeves. He no longer seemed to feel the need to hide his scars. For a moment, all I could focus on was the way he smelled like mint. That must have been what he was replanting.

"Listen," he said, his voice low. "I found something last night."

"What?"

"I couldn't sleep after . . . well, after the whole thing with Nash and Cabell, and I decided to have a look around. I think you're right, and there might be another way out of the tower. At least one that won't put us in the direct path of the Children."

I think you're right. The most beautiful words of any language, and the very ones I'd been desperate to hear.

"Okay," I said slowly. "What did you find?"

Emrys shook his head. "It's better if you see it. Meet me in the great hall after the others have gone to bed. Oh, and bring your crusty friend, too. We may need him—that *is* a Hand of Glory, right? Your hobby isn't making decorative wax sculptures of dismembered body parts?"

"No, it's not," I confirmed. "What are you doing, anyway?"

"This?" He looked over his shoulder at the garden. "How about we make a wager? If you guess—"

"If you make me guess, I'm walking away," I told him.

"Well, that's no fun."

"Yeah, because that's me, Tamsin Fun-and-Games Lark."

"Why not Tamsin-on-a-Lark?" he asked. "I could add a little fun to your life—"

"Keep talking and you'll end up buried in the same dirt you just turned over," I warned.

He laughed. "Fine, fine. The soil here is about as starved for nutrients as the people are. I'm putting eggshells and ash in—to add some potassium and raise the pH of the soil. We'll see if it works."

I raised a brow. "Emrys Dye . . . you're a bit of a nerd, aren't you?"

"Had you fooled, didn't I?" he said, the cocky smile slightly undermined by the specks of dirt splattered on his face.

"So, back in the guild library, you weren't bragging about dating three girls at once," I said, "or about how you can talk your way into any bar in Boston, or how you've crashed three of your father's priceless cars street racing? I hallucinated all that?"

"I don't see how any of those things are a contradiction. A guy can contain multitudes, can't he?" His grin only deepened, and when he leaned closer, I didn't pull back. For whatever wild, stupid, or stubborn reason, I didn't want to. "I didn't realize you'd been keeping an eye on me."

I put a hand on his chest and pushed him away, desperately hoping I hadn't flushed. "What's the point of doing all this gardening? It's just wasted effort."

He cocked his head, considering the neat lines of herbs. "Is it?"

I blew out a harsh breath through my nose, my fingers curling into fists at my sides. "Why is it so hard for them to accept the truth of what they're up against?"

"You're not telling them anything they don't already know, Tamsin. They're just trying not to let it crush them."

"But what are they doing about it?" I asked. "What are they actually *doing* to reverse any of this?"

"Maybe that's why we're here," he said. "Maybe Neve's right and it's our job to figure it out for them."

"That's absolutely *not* why we're here," I told him, "and you know it. How are you going to explain this to Madrigal?"

"Still working that one out, but I'm sure there's another rare bauble or weapon she'll want." He ran a hand through his hair. "Hopefully."

"Did Madrigal ever tell you why she wanted it?"

I don't know why I asked him; he hadn't been forthcoming about anything before now.

Emrys frowned, absently trying to twist his missing signet ring. "No. Neve has no idea either?"

I watched him a moment longer, trying to sense any trace of deceit. "Neve's had limited contact with the Sistren."

"Makes sense" was all he said. It was like watching a fox slowly retreat into its burrow. His face was carefully blank. That wall inside me added another layer of stone.

"Why did you take the job from Madrigal?" I asked him again. "And why can't you tell your father about it?"

"There's no story there, Tamsin," he said. "At least nothing like what you seem to be thinking."

"Yeah?" I shot back. "And you know my thoughts?"

The look he gave me blurred the world around us. "I know you."

My gaze met his for a long moment, and like everything between us, it became a fight—a refusal to be the one who looked away first.

A startled cry shattered whatever feeling had kept me rooted in place. Several people rushed past the garden and around the tower. Emrys and I exchanged a look, and then he was jumping over the wall and we were following them to whatever awaited us ahead.

A small crowd had gathered just at the base of the steps leading up into the tower. They were murmuring, not with worry or concern but excitement. As we wove our way up through them to the front, I took in their awestruck, reverent faces with a growing alarm. A few dropped to their knees, bowing their heads. Even Emrys stopped suddenly beside me, his face transforming with wonder.

"It's singing," he whispered.

I turned back toward the steps and saw it.

A single white rose, risen through a split in the stone step, its lovely, delicate face full and laced with tendrils of white mist.

24

That evening felt like a basilisk venom dream—dark and illusory. My mind drifted between sharp moments of awareness and the shadows of my own thoughts. The great hall was a blur of motion and candlelight around me, but I couldn't stop staring at it.

The rose.

The priestesses had placed it in the pale, upturned palms of the Goddess's statue. The pale flower stayed there throughout the evening meal.

"Okay, what's wrong with you?" Neve's voice cut into my thoughts. "You look even more irritated than usual. Like an angry toad."

Cabell snorted, but at my look, he wisely kept his thoughts to himself.

"Angry toad?" I repeated, mentally comparing my features to the warty little beast that had shown up to collect the Sorceress Grinda's locket. It was strange to think that had been less than a week ago—the memory felt so distant, it might as well have been a past life.

"Trust me, you don't want to meet one," Neve said, taking another sip of her wine. "They are *very* rude."

Her dark eyes were glassy. In fact, she looked incredibly relaxed despite the suspicious stares still fixed on her from all over the room. As she brought the goblet to her lips again, I put a hand over it and gently guided it back down to the table.

"Can't you be happy just this once?" she asked, clutching my arm dramatically. "It won't kill you. Olwen says a rose hasn't bloomed in Avalon since the Children appeared. They think it could be a sign the isle is healing."

I almost told her then, but what would I have said—*I dreamt it would come?*

"Even Sir Bedivere seems to think it's a sign," Cabell offered.

"Not you, too." I glanced over at Emrys, but he was looking at the rose himself, contemplating it. "Is it still singing?"

"Singing?" Neve's eyes lit up. "What was the song? Did you recognize what it was saying?"

He scratched at the stubble along his sharp jawline. My gaze drifted toward his mouth as he spoke. "It was more of a humming, but . . . it's fading now that they've cut it."

Emrys turned toward me, brows raised as he caught me looking. His eyes glittered with recognition that felt instantly dangerous.

I flushed, grateful for the hall's shadows as I threw back the last drops of my shallow pour of wine. The Avalonians around me conversed animatedly, and there was a palpable but almost hesitant sense of ease about them as they started in on the watery broth of barley and dried meat.

Everyone had been given a small round of bread that reminded me of a soul cake; the one in front of me was spiced with cinnamon and nutmeg, with a star cut into its top. It was the best thing I had eaten in days—and judging by the empty plates around me, the feeling was unanimous. Dilwyn, our elfin cook, beamed with pleasure at the compliments she was receiving.

A harpist sat at her instrument beside the Goddess's image and began to play. After a moment, the other Avalonians sang, too, their voices naturally flowing together in a stream of emotion.

Born of the spring that ever comes new
Born of bright starlight, undying and true
Born of the mists, the mountains, the dew

253

Fair isle of her heart, I sing to you
As the bud blooms to flower
As the moon passes to mark the hour
As Lord Death rides upon his cold power
So the Goddess built the tower . . .

"*Is* there a moon here?" I whispered to Neve as the song continued. "Or a sun, for that matter?"

"I read in one of the library's books that the sky here is a mirror of our own," Neve said. "Reflecting the heavens above the land it used to occupy in the mortal world. Though I don't think they've seen any celestial bodies since the Children appeared."

"They haven't," Emrys chimed in. "You can feel it in their vegetation and soil. Any sunlight they're getting is provided by magic, and it's a pale imitation."

"Oh!" Neve nearly knocked over both of our goblets as she turned to him, her face lit with excitement. "Did you talk to the others more about turning part of the courtyard into a garden? I can help you find mushrooms around the tower—"

At the word *mushrooms,* I turned back to face the statue.

The Nine were gathering around the image of the Goddess. They chanted quietly, laying down offerings of herbs and filling the bejeweled chalice that sat near the Goddess's foot with glowing water from the sacred springs. All were focused on their task, save Caitriona, who was watching us.

Not us.

Neve.

Catching my eye, Caitriona whirled back around, body bracing as if for a strike.

"You do seem upset," Cabell said quietly from my other side. "Everything okay?"

I gave him a look. "When was the last time anything was okay?"

There weren't many things I didn't tell him, but this—whatever *this* was—felt like more trouble than it was worth.

"Just tired." After glancing around to make sure no one was watching us, I lowered my voice to add, "Emrys thinks he found something and wants us to meet tonight."

Neve had been swaying dreamily in her seat to the ballad, but that caught her attention. "I told Olwen I'd meet her in the library for more research. I'm worried she'll get suspicious if I back out."

"And I told Bedivere I'd walk the wall with him on tonight's watch," Cabell said, his expression all apologies. "You got this one?"

If I said no, I knew he'd come with me. I also knew we needed what information we could get out of Bedivere. "Yeah. Of course."

"Let's catch up in the morning." Cabell eyed Emrys like a crow did a worm. "Behave."

Emrys ignored him, leaning back around Neve to whisper, "Looks like it's just you and me tonight."

I raised my goblet, only to remember it was already empty. "Great."

After the light and song of dinner, the shadowy great hall seemed brooding by contrast. The long tables were barren now and only the candle at the center of the Goddess's idol was still burning. The white rose, with its creamy petals, beckoned from the heart of her palms.

I moved toward it slowly, my hand reaching for the achingly perfect petals. The candle flame shivered, causing the statue to glow as if it were alive.

"It's the *Rosa × alba*."

Emrys peeled away from the shadows near the hall's entrance. I jumped, bumping the offering table hard enough to splash myself with the bowl of springwater.

"Do you make a habit of lurking, or is it a special thing you save for me?" I hissed.

"Only for you, Bird," he said, slinging his workbag over his shoulder. "Got to say, I didn't take you for a flower type, but you've spent all night watching that rose like it's about to burst into flames."

I sidestepped that and asked, "Where's this thing you just have to show me?"

He brushed his hair out of his eyes with a secretive smile. Without another word, he looked back over his shoulder, searching the entrance for any movement on the steps or in the courtyard. Satisfied, he moved past me, toward the statue.

"Where are you . . . ," I began, trailing after him.

There was a small space between the altar and the back wall, just enough for him to crouch down. Pressing both hands to one of the wood panels on the statue's platform, he slid it to the right, revealing a hidden set of steps leading down into darkness.

"God's teeth," I whispered, crouching to stick my head through the opening. It was impossible to see what was below. Behind me, Emrys donned his head lamp and clicked it on.

"I knew you'd like it," he said with an infectious grin.

"I have been known to appreciate a hidden passage from time to time," I allowed. "Provided there aren't curses trying to behead me along the way."

"I swear on the sainted soul of my grandmother that your pretty little neck is safe," he said. "After you . . ."

"Necks aren't pretty," I said after a too-long pause. "How did you even find this?"

"I saw someone go in," he answered. "And naturally I had to follow the mysterious cloaked figure to see if they were up to no good."

"A cloaked figure? What a cliché," I said. "You didn't see a face?"

"They had a hood up," he said, crawling in behind me. The smell of green life and pine still clung to him. "Like I said, it was mysterious, and I don't particularly enjoy mysteries."

Ironic, I thought, *given that you are one.*

The door scraped shut behind him, trapping us in the shadows.

I took my own flashlight out, thumping it until the batteries rattled and the beam stopped flickering. It was a tight squeeze those first few steps down, but the deeper we went, the more breathing room we gained. The air bore the stench of age and something like damp mulch, but the source didn't reveal itself until the last of the steps.

Heavy roots spread over the ground, gripping the stone like straining fingers. The hallway was cocooned in them; they knotted and wove through one another, some as thick as my arm, others no wider than a string of yarn.

I looked to Emrys, eyes wide.

"I know," he said. "And this isn't even what I wanted to show you."

"Are we really deep enough in the ground to see the Mother tree's roots?" I asked, carefully stepping onto the roots.

"I'm guessing these are secondary roots," Emrys said. "They feel younger to me—they're probably attracted to the damp down here."

"You're guessing?" I shot him a narrow look. "Shouldn't they be telling you the secrets of the ages or something?"

"I wish," he muttered, reaching out to steady me as my heel slipped on a root. "They're not speaking a language I can understand."

I squinted at him in the dark. "How is that possible with the One Vision?"

"Because like the rose, it's more of a humming . . ." He hummed a melody to imitate it, the depth of the notes strangely appealing—and somehow familiar.

"Come on," he said, "it's still a bit of a walk."

We followed the trail of roots until they thinned. I backed up several steps, aiming my flashlight at a spot on the wall where the roots were so thick, they formed a solid mass. I took another step back, dropping onto a knee to see it from a different angle.

"This is another hallway," I told Emrys, shining the flashlight where just a sliver of the joint in the paths was visible. "The roots seem to be coming from down there."

257

I brought a hand close to one of the roots, letting my fingers run along its rough skin. It throbbed, sliding forward.

I jumped back, knocking into the solid warmth of Emrys's chest. He reached out from behind me, touching the wall of roots himself. They twined around his fingertips, his wrist. He tilted his head, as if listening to something. Glimmers of cerulean light laced through the roots.

Emrys's eyes lost their focus and his smile fell away. A single root slithered up his sleeve, winding itself around his skin.

When Emrys didn't pull away, I did it for him, tugging him back by the elbow. "What are you doing?"

He shook his head. "Sorry, I just—we can't go that way. We shouldn't."

"Good," I told him, "because I don't want us to go that way either."

Any bit of wildlife that had survived the isle's darkness had likely only done so by absorbing its malevolence.

There was an odd look on Emrys's face, as if he hadn't fully re-joined me in the present.

"Seriously, are you all right?" I asked him.

"Yeah, I'm fine." Clicking his tongue, he nodded toward the main path. "This way."

As the roots thinned and our boots found the stone floor, some of the tension bled out of me. But now and then I looked back, aiming my flashlight behind me. Just to be sure—completely sure—that the sound I was hearing was the scuff of our footsteps and not the slow slide of roots trailing after us like an obedient servant.

Or the most patient of hunters.

25

We'd been walking the tunnel's winding path for so long that the chamber startled me with the suddenness of its appearance.

Emrys pushed the heavy oak doors open a crack, using his head lamp to peer inside before propping them open for me. I swept my flashlight beam over the cavernous space. It was vast but cluttered with furniture, rugs, and stacks of trunks that had been left down here and—intentionally or not—forgotten.

"You've brought me to . . . basement storage?" I asked.

"This is where the cloaked figure came last night," Emrys said. "I managed to hide behind one of the doors while they were inside, but I couldn't see what they were doing, and I didn't want to risk coming in alone in case I got locked in."

"Dying alone down here where no one could hear you scream *would* be a drag," I noted. "Were they looking for something?"

"No, that's the weird part," he said. "It didn't sound like they were rummaging around, and they weren't holding anything as they came out. All I heard was the sound of stones shifting."

"Were they building something?" I asked, touching the dusty top of the nearest trunk. Silver stars were inlaid in the wooden lid, but it was otherwise in shambles. The damp air was drowning in the stench of rot.

"Or they were moving something out of the way," Emrys said,

scratching at his chin. "I think there could be another passage or door-way hidden in here."

I whirled around. "A doorway out into the forest?"

Now I understood his request to bring Ignatius.

Putting my flashlight between my teeth to free up my hands, I retrieved the bundle of purple from my bag. Darkness wove through my thoughts like ink in water.

Clutching the Hand of Glory in one fist and returning my flash-light to the other, I asked, "Are we even outside the tower's walls?"

"That's the question," Emrys said. "It feels like we should be, right?"

"Let's hope not."

"And why is that?" he asked.

"Because why would someone need secret access to the forest when it's overrun by Children?" I said. "There's nothing out there—no crops, no fresh water, no animals—that they would need to risk their lives to get, especially while it's dark out."

"You never disappoint, Bird," Emrys said, shaking his head. "You always find a way to make things even more terrifying."

I ignored him. "I think we can all agree that what's happening here is some kind of curse, but why did it only rear its head two years ago?"

"It might have been cast to start on an anniversary of something," Emrys pointed out. "Or someone might have accidentally triggered it."

"Accidentally?" I scoffed. "What's more likely—that, or this curse being an inside job?"

"You think someone in this tower cast the curse." Emrys turned toward me fully, all traces of humor gone from his expression.

"Don't tell me that thought didn't cross your mind," I said.

"I'd be lying if I said it didn't," Emrys said. "But what's missing is the *why*—because they were sympathetic to the druids? Or secretly worship Lord Death? We don't really have proof of that, do we?"

"There is one thing," I said, surprised at how easy it felt to bounce theories off him. "I didn't notice it the first night—"

"That tends to happen when you're running for your life," Emrys said magnanimously.

"—but the creatures," I continued sharply, "seem to work together to hunt. And look at how they've coordinated themselves around the moat. I don't think they have enough sense or awareness to function as a pack, you know?"

"So you think someone is controlling them," he finished.

I set Ignatius down and pulled out my lighter.

"Hold your breath the first few seconds," I warned Emrys. "Unless you want to fill your lungs with the smell of burning hair."

He did as I suggested, his face a mixture of alarm and curiosity as Ignatius cracked his stiff knuckles and the skin over his eye slid open. It gave a bleary look around before narrowing as it fixed on me.

"I'm just staying alive to spite you at this point," I told him. "Come on, time to earn your next lard bath."

The Hand of Glory cast a halo around us. Picking him up by the handle, I wondered how I had ever been satisfied with the glimpse of the hidden world of magic it had given me.

"We're looking for passages to unlock, Ignatius," I said.

"You . . . *named* that thing?" Emrys stayed a step behind me, watching the Hand of Glory from over my shoulder. "Does it actually understand you?"

"As much as anyone can." I brought Ignatius to the nearest wall, letting the light fall upon the stones and slowly walking the length of it.

"I always wondered how you managed to work without the One Vision," Emrys said. "I guess I just assumed that Cabell was very careful about telling you where to step. Obviously, you have it now, even if it meant almost recklessly killing yourself in the process."

I *did* have it now. It was strange to have Ignatius's light reveal nothing more than I was already seeing. The gloom of our situation was clearly getting to me, because I felt the first stirrings of fond nostalgia when Ignatius rolled his eye at me.

"It did change your eye color, though," Emrys said, still searching the wall.

My face scrunched. Granted, it had been a while since I'd seen a mirror, but . . . "No, it didn't."

"They used to be a darker blue. Like sapphire," he said, still running his hands over the stones.

I slowed, chewing at my bottom lip as I tried and failed to figure out how to respond. He looked back and our gazes clashed in the soft, warm light.

"That thing's a bit peevish, isn't it?" Emrys said, turning away quickly. "He looks like he wants to strangle me."

I hissed as Ignatius dripped hot wax on my hand. "You don't know the half of it."

We went over the walls twice, but if there was a doorway, either it wasn't locked, rendering Ignatius useless, or the cloaked figure had been extremely careful in disguising it. Eventually, the call of the scavenge became too tempting for two Hollowers to resist, and we turned our attention to the room's waiting treasures.

"I can't get over the fact that you've been using a Hand of Glory this whole time," Emrys said as he flipped a trunk's lid open. "Those things are incredibly rare. Sorceresses find them so abhorrent, they don't make them anymore—and believe me, my father has asked. Many times."

"Nash gave it to me when I was little," I said, something in me bridling at the memory—at the fact that I was even talking about this, and to Emrys. "And before you ask, I don't know who he stole it from."

Emrys set the decomposing blankets he'd pulled out back in the trunk. His forehead creased. "Why do you always do that?"

"Do what?"

"You always seem to assume the worst," he said, "and you expect everyone else to do the same. But all you're really doing is punching at phantoms the rest of us can't see."

262

"Can't imagine why I would do that," I said, the words tumbling out of me before I could stop them. "It couldn't possibly be based on years of experience driving that point home again and again."

"Is it that," he said, "or is it just another excuse to push people away?"

The darkness caressed his face as he watched me. A whisper in my mind finally put a name to the uncomfortable heat swimming beneath my skin.

Shame.

"You don't know a damn thing," I told him, hating the way the heat was building in me again, the uncontrollable burning at the back of my eyes. "About me or my life."

Get a grip, I told myself. *Calm down.*

He let out a faint, almost rueful laugh as he opened a tarnished silver box with nothing inside. "Sometimes I wish that were true, Bird."

He knows the color of your eyes, that same voice whispered.

"I realize your life hasn't been easy," he continued, "especially after Nash disappeared, but at least—"

"Please tell me you're not about to find the bright side of child abandonment and neglect," I snapped. "Because I assure you, it does not exist."

Nash was dead. I didn't want to talk about this. About him. About anything. But it was like I was unspooling, and each turn only spun me faster.

"I would never say that," Emrys said, moving on to another metal chest. Inside were books bloated and unreadable from water damage. "But at least you can do whatever you want. You can be whoever you want. You think my life is so easy, but you have no idea. You just . . ."

He trailed off.

"Poor little rich boy," I sneered. "It's so hard having everything handed to you, isn't it?"

It felt good to unleash the words on him, to get the festering heat, that anger and resentment that burned like the worst bile, out of me.

"At least you don't have to worry about *legacy*." He spat the word out like a bitter taste in his mouth. "There are no rules, or boundaries, or expectations you could never live up to. And there's sure as hell no—"

"No what?" I asked. "Don't stop there. You were just about to tell me how much harder you have it within the walls of your mansion."

"See, that's what I'm talking about!" he said. "You're the only person I know who ever notices or cares about money."

For a moment, I was so stunned I couldn't speak. "The mere fact that you don't *have* to care is a privilege not afforded to the rest of us."

I tracked every cent coming and going. Every night, as I tried to force myself to fall asleep, I was swarmed by thoughts of how I would find more, and what would happen if I didn't.

"You have *everything*," I told him, hearing the hoarseness in my voice. He didn't have a dead guardian, or a cursed brother. He had stability, a mother who doted on him like a prince, houses scattered across the world, friends, cars, new clothes, the very best Hollower tools and supplies.

I wasn't going to feel sorry for him just because the trade-off was living up to his last name, or having a life laid out for him from birth.

That was called security. He had a future.

And a past, I thought, squeezing my eyes shut. Some of us didn't even have that. I would have killed to know anything about my parents. Even just their names.

"Listen," Emrys said after a while, looking up from where he was thumbing through a waterlogged tome. "We've had a textbook case of a rough start, and, frankly, it's beneath us. If nothing else, can we at least agree to be professionals? The ring is gone, Avalon is a festering hell, and we're surrounded by strangers. Can we call a truce?"

"Fine," I said. I could admit that our best chance to survive and get back to our world was working together. I could even admit that some of what Emrys had said was true. Day by day, I could decide what I wanted to do, and I had no one other than Cabell to answer to.

264

We worked in silence, careful to put everything back exactly where we'd found it. There were vases that looked as if they had come from other ancient lands, a helmet crowned with stars, and a shield shaped like a dragon. I picked up the tarnished helmet, studying the strange constellations etched into it.

"Maybe we should bring those up with us," he said quietly, "and leave them outside the forge. They have no mining here, and they don't have enough raw ore left to keep making new weapons and armor."

"And how do you know *that*?"

"I asked," he said, shrugging. "They're just melting down what metal they have on hand and repurposing it."

"You and Neve just made yourselves right at home, didn't you?" I said.

"If that's what you want to call *asking questions as you think of them*, then sure, I'm right at home." Emrys blew the dust off something in his palm. "I'd recommend trying it, but, fair warning, it might actually lead people to believe you care."

I set the helmet back down. "Yeah. Wouldn't want that."

"Is this . . ." Emrys held the small piece of coppery metal up toward Ignatius's light. His eyes shot over to a large armoire, where several wooden staffs, their tops curled into different knots and spirals, leaned. "I think this is a druid spoon—is that possible?"

He passed it to me, then wove through the maze of broken statues and chests to take up one of the staffs.

"It looks like part of a spoon," I said. "Nash had drawings of them in one of his journals. Usually there's two halves . . ."

The shell of the spoon was like a leaf, with a short flat tab at the end to hold. Four quadrants had been etched into the patinaed metal. The other half, a mirror image of this one, would have a small hole for blowing in blood, or bone dust, or whatever they used for divination. The divine messages depended on where those bits landed in the quadrants—not completely unlike reading tea leaves.

"Oh, what's *this*?" I heard Emrys say.

I'd noticed the towering object shrouded in a drooping tapestry when we'd come in—the size of it, even next to the large armoire leaning crookedly to the left, made it impossible to miss. Emrys gripped the tattered and faded fabric, and down it came with a sharp tug.

I took a step back, my gaze drifting up over the pale stone.

The body of the statue was massive, broad-shouldered and thick with corded muscle. A horned crown of real antler, moss, and holly leaves was somehow preserved on its head, radiating a seething malevolence that made me not want to touch it. Worse, the statue's face had been smashed, and what remained was monstrous. A cloak, carved to resemble animal skins, draped over its shoulders and dipped across its chest, where there was a hollow. A candleholder like the Goddess statue's, I realized.

But my eyes kept returning to its ruined face, where all the answers to unspoken questions had been crushed into obscurity. This kind of damage was an act of rage.

"Tamsin?" Emrys said. "What's wrong?"

"Who is this?" I asked. "It looks like—"

Nash's voice echoed through my memory, his face lit by our campfire. *He rides on a fiery steed as the Wild Hunt scours the Otherlands, searching for the wandering dead, but he loves no world so much as our own . . .*

I couldn't bring myself to finish, but Emrys had figured it out for himself. "Lord Death. This was probably meant to be a pair with the statue of the Goddess in the great hall. Or, more likely, to replace it."

I forced myself closer, trying to imagine the two of them side by side. One of the statue's arms was outstretched, palm up, as if to cup the Goddess's from below.

"Lord Death. Rarely mentioned in Immortalities, let alone legends, as if his name itself was a curse." Emrys circled it, humming. "Sometimes called the Holly King, the—"

"—manifestation of darkness and winter on the Wheel of the

Year," I finished. "Forced to fight the Oak King of light and summer for the hand of the maiden they both desired. For each year, for all eternity, a cycle of the seasons."

"Show-off," Emrys said, laughing. "Still, must have been quite the lady."

"That legend's just a metaphor for the changing seasons," I said, shaking my head. "None of it explains why they didn't destroy the statue altogether after the Forsaking."

"Superstition, probably," he said. "Would you want to risk destroying an icon of a powerful deity? They may not worship him, but they still believe he exists."

I ducked beneath the statue's hand, noticing something carved on the back of it. It looked like a fragment of some kind of sigil. Or a crescent moon? No—I tilted my head. It looked like part of a knot design.

"Do you recognize this mark?" I asked, wondering why my memory was failing.

Emrys ducked under it. "Maybe? Could just be a crack, though?"

I shook my head. "No . . . there's something about it . . ."

What was wrong with me? It couldn't just be the stress or exhaustion of the last few days. It was like each time I reached for it, the memory that would have filled out the rest of the symbol evanesced into mist.

"I can't believe these words are about to pass through my very own lips," Emrys said. "But it does make you feel a bit sympathetic to the sorceresses. They were the ones willing to fight for what they believed in—even against a child of the old gods who ruled the damned."

A chill crawled up the back of my neck. I shook myself, trying to escape the sensation. "They must have been afraid worshiping Lord Death would cause their souls to go to Annwn. The Goddess is the one who initiates the cycle of life, death, and rebirth."

"Right," Emrys said, rubbing the back of his neck. "Annwn. The

Otherland no living mortal can reach, and wouldn't dare try, save a brave few—I'll bet you a truth or dare that you can't name who."

"Arthur and some of his knights," I said in a bored tone, "either to rescue a prisoner or to steal the cauldron of the ruler of Annwn, as described in the Book of Taliesin."

And by Nash, who had loved every version of the legend that saw the great King Arthur travel to the land of the dead and live to return to his own.

"Wow," Emrys said after a moment. "Walked right into that one. Cabell always said you had a perfect memory . . . You were going to let me keep making stupid bets with you forever, weren't you?"

I lifted a shoulder. "Just wanted to see how much I could get out of you."

He shook his head. "You really broke the mold, Bird."

"Can we . . . ?" I began, still staring up at the statue's crushed face. "Let's cover him. I don't want to look at him anymore."

"Not that you'll be able to forget it," Emrys said, almost apologetically. We threw the tapestry back over it, and as surely as if Emrys had cursed me, the image of it was seared into my mind like a photo negative.

"I choose truth," I said, playing with the frayed edges of the fabric, unraveling a row of crimson thread.

"What?"

"You said I can choose a truth or dare," I said. "I choose truth."

Emrys stilled beside me. "Right now?"

"Right now," I said. "Why did you take this job?"

He shook his head.

"You're the one who wanted to make the bet," I reminded him.

After a moment, he let out a small noise of frustration.

"Because . . . I don't know," he said, running a hand through his hair. "Because my whole life, I've never done anything for myself without help. I've never worked without my father. I've never accomplished anything that lives up to the legacy of the great Endymion Dye or the ancestors all lined up on the walls."

"Do you *want* to accomplish something like that?" I asked. "Or do you feel like you have to?"

His brow furrowed. I wondered if anyone had bothered to ask him that question before.

"As far as I can tell," I continued, "a legacy is just a tool parents use to control their kids."

"You wouldn't understand," Emrys said, leaning against the armoire.

"No, I wouldn't," I agreed. "I surpass Nash's existence just by not regularly drinking myself into a coma."

I heard the bitterness in the words, tasting that bile again. Seven years, I'd lived without the man. I'd accepted that he was never coming back. And now that he'd gone and died . . . he'd upended everything all over again, and here I was, giving him control. Letting him reopen that raw part of me I'd seared shut.

I hated him. I hated Nash beyond words and worlds. Better him dead and Cabell and me on our own.

You, on your own, came a dark whisper in my mind. *Cabell will leave you, too, in the end.*

My fingers curled into fists at my side as I drew in a sharp breath.

"What's the story with that?" Emrys asked. "You told the others about how he found your brother, but how did you end up in his care?"

"*Care* isn't the word I would use for it," I said, forcing myself to look through another stack of trunks, searching their engravings for any familiar symbols. That spinning feeling was back, faster and faster, pulling up all of the memories I'd kept locked away. Each a knife.

"That wasn't an answer," Emrys prodded.

The humiliation of it still stung, all these years later. I didn't care if it made me a hypocrite. The thought of telling him made me want to vomit.

"You don't have to tell me," Emrys said softly. "Really."

"How generous of you."

"No, I just—" He shook his head. "Sorry."

I breathed in the cold air, running my hand along the battered shield in front of me. All at once, the spinning stopped, and that thread ripped free from the spool. There was nothing left to tether that control to.

There was nothing but the need to be known, to be seen.

"My family abandoned me in Boston and Nash took me in," I heard myself say. "So, let's just say I know what it's like to grow up *without* a legacy, and I wouldn't recommend that, either."

The words felt like they were reaching down and drawing my lungs out through my throat. I let him fill in the story's gaps the way he wanted to. That was what everyone did anyway.

"There's something I've always wondered," he said, sitting on one of the trunks. "What happened to you in the years between when Nash left and you joined the guild? Where did you go?"

I knew that six-year stretch, from the time Cabell and I were ten to when we could officially claim Nash's membership at sixteen, had always been a source of speculation among the guild. Our silence on it wasn't just that they didn't deserve an answer—it was what would happen if they found out.

"If I tell you," I said, "you can't repeat it to anyone. Your father especially."

Emrys let out a soft hum. "Now I'm even more intrigued."

"I'm serious," I told him. "If you repeat what I'm about to tell you, I'll come down on you harder than any curse."

"Only increasing said intrigue," Emrys said.

I shook my head, taking in a deep breath. "The library's attic."

"The—" He actually did a double take. "The guild library's attic?"

I carefully put the shield back. "Librarian broke the rules and let us inside, even though we weren't members ourselves."

"I didn't realize Librarian *could* break rules," Emrys said, amazed.

"He hid us up in the attic, along with some of the lesser relics not on display, and let us come down at night to eat and play with the cats," I said. "He'd bring us Immortalities and guides to read, and food and water until we were old enough to get it ourselves—though I'm still not sure where he got the food."

"From everyone's lockers. Nicodemus Lot and Astri Cullen had a four-year war break out between them because each was so sure the other was stealing their food stores," Emrys said. "I thought it was the cats being tricky but . . . apparently not."

His brows lowered, as if trying to imagine Cabell and me up in the cramped crawl space. "Why didn't you just go to one of the guild members?"

My top lip curled in disgust. "What makes you think we didn't?"

That was the simple truth of it. Librarian didn't have a human heart or mind, but even he somehow knew to protect and care for two vulnerable children.

"Anyway," I said, "it was fine once we learned how to speak ancient Greek and we could actually talk to him. Well, *I* learned. Cabell had the One Vision."

"It's a good thing you had Cabell," he said after a while. "You're lucky."

It had always surprised me that Endymion and Cerys Dye only had one child, but when all you needed was a son to continue the family name, there was no reason for more, I supposed.

"Yeah," I agreed. "I wouldn't have survived without Cabell."

That wasn't exactly true, though. I wouldn't have had a reason to survive without him. And if the curse stole him from me, it would take that piece of my heart, too.

"I'm sorry," Emrys said. "About what happened. All that stuff I've said about Nash and you and your brother over the years . . ."

"It's fine," I said, putting the conversation out of its misery. "Not like it's your fault."

A sound came from the hallway outside—skittering, rattling, almost like—

The roots are moving, I thought.

The quick clip of footsteps echoed down to us, slipping through the crack we'd left open between the chamber doors. I blew Ignatius out with a single breath, waving the smoke away and shoving him in my bag to smother it. The smell of it would give us away—

Emrys grabbed my arm and yanked me toward the armoire. The shelves inside had either been removed or collapsed long ago, leaving barely enough room for two people to stand after he pulled the doors shut behind us.

I switched off my flashlight and tapped his head lamp off just as the chamber's heavy oak doors swung open.

My heart thundered in my ears, and I held my breath. My legs were tangled with Emrys's longer ones, my body fitted against his side. The fabric of his tunic was soft against my cheek, and for several moments, all I heard was the galloping pace of his heart, faster than my own.

I hadn't realized he had an arm around my shoulder until it shifted as he leaned forward, trying to see through the sliver of space between the doors. I hadn't even realized I'd looped *my* arm around him for balance. My fingers were splayed against his waist, and the heat of his skin radiated through the thin linen, sending a bolt of warmth through my core.

The new arrival stepped inside, lifting the candle on its iron holder. Emrys was right—the dark hooded cloak was so oversized that it completely engulfed their face and form, making it impossible to see who they were. They turned toward the abandoned possessions, toward the armoire, and sniffed.

We froze, my fingers digging into the hard muscle beneath them. Emrys's breath caught.

But the figure only turned back toward the wall opposite us. A pale hand reached for a cluster of three white stones I'd barely noticed before, pushing each twice in turn. The stones around them seemed to come alive, pulling back like scurrying mice to create an opening in the wall. As they shifted, they exhaled a cloud of mist into the chamber.

The figure stepped through the opening, and in the darkness of the armoire, Emrys's eyes found mine.

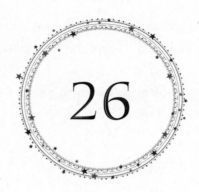

26

"Tamsin."

The inviting darkness breathed my name. It rose and fell in tandem with my own slow breathing. I stayed in that slow, honeyed pull of exhaustion until I felt the band of heat around my back give a gentle squeeze. My eyes shot open.

Emrys's pale face hovered at the crack in the doors, and somehow, the fact that he wasn't looking at me, wasn't acknowledging that I'd dozed off on him, made it all the more humiliating.

"We've officially waited them out," he murmured.

There was no sense of how much time had passed, only the sound of the stones shifting again. The cloaked figure emerged moments later and made for the entrance. Finished with whatever lay beyond the wall.

The great oak doors lumbered shut, hinges whining in protest. The chamber was thrown into unyielding darkness. I counted back from two hundred in my head, waiting to see if the steps would return.

But even as it became clear they would not, neither of us moved.

I closed my eyes again, trying to think of anything other than the way my cheek was pressed to his chest, his heartbeat the only sound in my ears, the way his fingers were absently stroking down my side, seeking and granting comfort.

In that dark, warm place, we'd become shadows ourselves. Breathing in unison, bodies intertwined until each point of contact felt like a burst of sparks across my skin—there was nothing outside of that sensation. No magic, no monsters, no world at all.

The cedarwood had turned the air sweet, but woven through it was the smell of him. His fingers tightened around my waist, and somehow, impossibly, I drew closer. I couldn't remember the last time I'd been held this close by anyone. When I'd wanted to be.

If he turns his face . . . The thought whispered through me, warming my blood like a shot of whiskey, curling low in my belly.

No.

I pulled away so quickly, it made lights dance in front of my eyes. I pushed out of the armoire and staggered forward, unsteady after crouching for so long. The chamber's damp chill coiled around me, as if all too eager to have me back in its shadowed grip. I shivered, switching my flashlight back on.

After a moment, Emrys followed, keeping his back to me as he shut the armoire's doors.

"Let's—" I cleared my throat. "Let's see if we can open it."

He nodded, his Adam's apple bobbing.

Standing in front of the white stones, I stole another quick look at him, then opened my bag, taking stock of what supplies I had left, mentally running through my list. No crystals, tonics, or rope. No axe, either, but I did have my dragonscale work gloves and pulled them on.

"You think whatever's back there is cursed?" he asked, surprised.

"I think we don't know what we're going to find," I said, "or who created the passage, and it doesn't hurt to be cautious. What do you have on you? Any crystals?"

Emrys opened his own workbag—monogrammed in gold with his initials, of course. He pulled out a small sack of amethyst, quartz, labradorite, and tourmaline, as well as a collapsible hand axe he opened with a flick of his wrist. He passed it to me, then pulled out a black velvet pouch.

The long silver chain dropped into his palm first, followed by a black crystal point—only, as he picked up the chain and let the point hang in the air, the black inside it moved, swirling like water to reveal the tiniest of white blossoms inside.

It was a crystal pendulum, usually used to answer questions or detect energy vibrations caused by magic or the presence of malicious spirits. I had never been able to get one to work, and with Cabell, I hadn't needed one.

The crystal didn't move.

"No curses," Emrys said, pulling the stone up to eye level. The black liquid inside thrashed, creating a whirlwind around the flower. "But a lot of magic, as you might expect."

"What kind of crystal is that?" I asked as he held the chain closer to the wall. Seeing the smile growing on his face, I added, "If you tell me to guess, I will punch you."

His smile turned mysterious in the most annoying way. "Family heirloom."

I let out a noise of irritation and reached up, switching on his head lamp.

"You want to do the honors?" he asked.

I passed him my flashlight and turned toward the stones, closing my eyes and bringing to mind the touch pattern the figure had used. The stones felt like ice beneath my fingertips, and I could have sworn they shivered with each touch.

The stones around them pulled themselves back, clattering and scraping against one another to crawl out of our way. Reclaiming my flashlight, I took a deep breath of mist and stepped through the opening.

Into a stairwell. The wall closed behind Emrys. I turned, making sure the white stones were visible from this side, too. There was only one way to go now—up.

"Where are we?" I whispered. "Is this still the tower?"

The beam of Emrys's head lamp moved up the stairs. "Let's find out."

So, we climbed. I kept count of the landings between each steep and shallow set of stairs. One, two, three, four, five, six, seven, eight . . . nine.

"It can't be the tower," I said, recalling the image of the tower from the courtyard. "It has five levels, and the library is at the top."

"We went down three stories too," Emrys pointed out. "Maybe the main stairwell only goes to the fifth floor because that's all the other Avalonians are allowed to see?"

"Or no one alive remembers there's another floor, or how to get there," I said, winded from the climb. "Except our cloaked friend."

The last set of stairs was shorter than the others, lending some credence to our theory that there was a smaller, hidden floor above the library. The dizzying and winding trail led to exactly what I had expected: a locked door. Black iron, with a door pull inside the metal mouth of what looked like a screaming human skull.

The door was locked, but there was no keyhole, making it impossible to pick. But a fastening spell had never stopped my persnickety companion before.

Ignatius, still clearly petulant about the rough treatment I'd given him earlier, took forever to open his eye once his wicks were burning.

"Sorry to catch you at a bad time, but if you aren't too busy . . . ," I said to the churlish hand, gesturing toward the lock.

As his light fell upon it, misty, golden webs of magic appeared, as if the glow had peeled back a layer of shadow to reveal the locking spell's structural bones. It was only when Emrys reached out to stroke one lightly with his fingers, amazement dawning on his face, that I realized it was anything unusual.

The bolt inside it slid open and the heavy door swung out.

"You've got a complicated relationship with that thing, don't you?" Emrys said.

I pushed him forward, forcing him into the room first. As he stooped to pass through the doorway, he stopped, blocking it.

"What?" I asked, standing on my toes to see past the expanse of his back. Every muscle there seemed to tense at once. "What is it?"

A strange vibration moved through my left hand and down my arm. It was Ignatius. The hand was trembling; the filmy pale eye was wide open.

Finally, Emrys moved out of the way.

The walls on either side of us were lined with wood shelves, each burdened with small objects, white as fired porcelain. But as I stepped inside, letting Ignatius's light fill the small space, unease ran its cold, clammy hand over my chest. The shapes—the sculptures—were grotesque. Agonized in their forms.

And made of human bone.

"Holy gods," I breathed out, risking a step closer to the nearest shelf. Emrys's fingers skimmed down my back, as if instinctively trying to grab my shoulder and keep me from it.

"Have you ever seen anything like this before?" he asked.

"No," I said. "Not in books, or vaults, or tombs, or anywhere else."

"This is . . ." Emrys, for once, truly seemed at a loss for words. A noticeable shiver moved through him as he rubbed at his arms. "Who do these bones belong to? What kind of sick mind would desecrate them like this?"

"It feels like a collection, doesn't it?" I said.

"Is it possible whoever made them killed this many people?" Emrys asked faintly.

I shook my head. "Even before the curse, there weren't enough beings living here for someone not to notice people dying or disappearing. I think someone's been digging around in graves."

Setting Ignatius on the ground, I brought my flashlight close to the first sculpture in the line of them. The upper portion of the mouth, just behind the teeth, had been carefully cut to fit against a pelvic bone. Both were etched with tiny, almost unreadable markings.

"Are they curse sigils?" Emrys asked, leaning over my shoulder. The warmth of his body caressed my back, his breath stirring the loose hair near my cheek.

"No," I said. "The shapes are rounder, more intertwined. I've never seen some of these before. Do you think they're left over from the days of the druids?"

"The sorceresses created their own language to control magic," Emrys said. "It makes sense there might be others. Or the marks are purely decorative."

The sculpture beside it was a rib cage balanced on two femurs, secured in place again by precisely cut slits in the bones that allowed them to fit seamlessly. A hand hung down from the center of the ribs, its finger bones melded together with silver knuckles. All covered in the sigils.

Bile burned its way up my throat as I turned, taking stock of them all. They were vile and horrific; I could barely stand to look at them without feeling the cold swell of some deep, innate fear that had been bred and nurtured across the thousands of generations of my family line.

I bent to retrieve Ignatius, then froze. The light from his small flames had bled into the nearest sculpture on the bottom row of shelves, throwing the shapes of the carved sigils onto the stone floor in illuminated patterns. As I knelt, the sigils shifted and began to spin.

"Tamsin," came Emrys's sharp voice. I looked up, only to realize I didn't see him—he'd gone around to the other side of the stairs climbing up from the center of the room. As I made my way toward him, I passed a tarnishing suit of armor and a glass-faced cabinet full of vials and withered black herbs.

The narrow staircase—hardly better than a rickety ladder—led up to the open air, and near its base sat a large cauldron. The first gray light of Avalon's dawn broke over it, glinting off silver clawed feet and causing its etched sides to shine like polished blades.

Emrys was staring down into it, his face sickly pale. I came to stand beside him, bracing for whatever grisly thing waited inside.

Instead, I found myself staring into a glistening pool of molten silver.

It churned with some unfelt wind, swirling with eddies. The metallic smell was emanating from the cauldron, but when I floated my hand over it, there was no heat. Only blistering cold.

As I stared into its depths, fragments of memories rose unbidden and splintered further. The pale face of the White Lady in the snowy field, calling me forward to join her in death. A flash of darkness and stone and the steel of a small blade. The unicorn, standing beneath a dead tree, collapsing as an arrow pierced its chest.

I took a step back, forcing myself to look away. Emrys looked awful, worse than I'd ever seen him, his skin bloodless and clammy.

"Are you all right?" I asked. "Emrys?"

It took a moment for him to look up, his eyes filled with a wrenching, pure terror. He didn't seem to know where he was, moving from the cauldron until his back hit the wall.

"Emrys?" I asked more urgently. "What is it? What did you see?"

He held up a hand, his throat working hard as he doubled over. "I'm fine—give me—give me a second."

He wasn't fine at all. I looked back at the cauldron, my mind bursting with thousands of thoughts. I searched through that storm for a memory—for any passage of a book, or a story, that had mentioned a cauldron in Avalon.

"What is this?" I whispered.

The liquid silver simmered as I leaned over it. An unnameable feeling passed through my body from scalp to toe, an animal instinct that there was something beyond that mirror-like surface. That someone was watching from the other side.

Before I could stop myself, before I could tell myself what a stupid idea it was, I dipped the very end of Ignatius's candlestick holder into the surface.

Nothing happened for several heartbeats. Then came the tug.

It pulled down, sucking at the holder even as I tried to lift it free. Small shapes spiked in the liquid, rising from the surface like—

Like reaching fingers.

The Hand of Glory's eye bulged, its burning wicks squealing as if in terror, guttering wildly at the tips of the fingers. Emrys was there in an instant, helping me rip my arm and Ignatius free.

"What are you doing?" Emrys choked out.

A hard gust of wind billowed down the steps, sweeping past us and blowing Ignatius out completely. I held up the end of the holder between us. It was coated in solid silver.

"The bones of the Children . . . ," Emrys whispered.

They were the same.

I stooped, walking around the cauldron, trailing my fingers along the basin until I found a slight rise in the rim. It almost looked as if it had been scratched off, worn down until it was nearly impossible to tell what it was.

Nearly.

I'd seen it before.

I reached into my bag, retrieving Nash's journal. For the first time in my life, I wanted to be wrong. My hands shook, just that little bit, as I flipped through the pages. I found the page of symbols that Nash had sketched and labeled, and held it up beside the mark.

It was a spiraling knot pattern with a crude sword slashed straight down through the serpentine twists. No wonder I'd felt the stir of recognition at the mark on the statue's hand—it was a section of this very one.

"Tell me it's not what I think it is," Emrys said, his voice barely above a whisper.

"It's the emblem of the king of Annwn," I said.

He looked a bit queasy. I looked around the room—at the horrible sculptures, at the curse sigils—and felt the chill creeping along my skin turn my body numb.

Neither of us seemed to want to say the name aloud now. *Lord Death.*

The familiar sound of scraping stones echoed up from far below. With one last shared look of horror, Emrys and I spun around, searching for any place to hide. There was no room behind the armor or in the cabinet. The shelves were too open and pressed to the wall. The only way out was up.

I led the way, switching off my flashlight and returning Ignatius to my bag. The upper deck was enclosed by a roof and four walls with large open windows that overlooked the courtyard below. We were at the very top of the tower—what I had thought was merely a decorative embellishment.

The door's lock clanked open. I dropped down onto my stomach on one side of the stairs, moving far enough away from the edge to avoid being seen from below. Emrys did the same on the other side of the opening.

Don't come up, I thought, *don't climb the stairs . . .*

A light patter of footsteps was accompanied by the whisper of fabric dragging over stone. Because I apparently hadn't had my fill of stupid for the night, I inched closer to the opening in the floor, trying to see who had come in.

It was the same cloaked figure as before. The brightening sky revealed the deep blue tone of the fabric sweeping behind them as they stepped up to the cauldron. Closer now, I could see other details, too.

Raising a small, curved dagger, the figure pressed its vicious tip against their palm and, with a hiss of pain, slashed down. Blood dripped from the pale hand into the waiting pool of silver.

In the forest, the howling of the Children of the Night turned to screeching. It knifed at my ears, piercing every thought until I was desperate to clamp my hands over my ears.

They're being controlled. The thought hammered in my skull. And if they could be compelled, what was to say they hadn't been made—born of the dark chamber below us?

The cloaked figure lingered by the cauldron, listening. Clearly satisfied, they started toward the door. As they passed by the suit of armor, the movement was enough to shift the bottom of the hood, revealing a hint of a braid.

It took me a moment to realize why it was so difficult to see reflected in the surface of the breastplate. It was the same color as the cloudy metal.

Silver.

Cold, deadly silver.

27

Knowing another uninviting dawn was upon us and there would soon be people working in the great hall, Emrys and I waited only a few minutes before rising and silently making our way down into the gallery of death. My heart was thundering in my chest as we followed the path out through the storage chamber and into the tunnel.

The back of Emrys's hand brushed mine again and again as we hurried along the corridor and over the roots. I couldn't seem to pull away any more than I could put words to what we'd seen.

We emerged from the hidden doorway just as the first of the women arrived at the great hall with their looms. Their eyebrows rose at the sight of us alone together, but I was beyond caring or trying to explain it away. It didn't matter. None of it mattered, except getting us back to our own world.

Our eyes met one last time on the steps leading into the courtyard, an unspoken promise passing between us. The Children had quieted with the coming of daylight, but the relative silence felt all-consuming without the calls of birdsong to comfort us. It left a different kind of ache in me, a longing for the ordinary I'd never appreciated before.

"Oh—I was just coming to find you!" Olwen's bright voice was jolting after the dark hell we'd crawled out of. She seemed to appear out of nowhere, her gray dress and white apron blending into the colorless morning. Her inky-blue hair waved around her, as if drifting in water.

"We're about to pull up the stones to see if the earth beneath will take crops," she continued. "That is . . . if you feel well enough for it?"

Emrys hesitated but plastered a smile on his face. "Of course."

"Are you certain?" Olwen's dark eyes narrowed with consideration. "You look a bit peaky."

"Just didn't sleep very well," he assured her.

Or at all, I thought.

"The Children were restless last night, and something was amiss with them this morn," Olwen said, shaking her head.

"Did they . . . do anything?" I asked.

"They've not moved at all, I'm afraid," she said. "Cait suggested we try to dispel them with fire and arrows if they still haven't gone by nightfall."

"And that's not an option now because . . . ?" I prompted.

Olwen's face hardened. "Because we've not got many arrows to spare."

A pathetic "Oh" was all I managed.

"I'm ready to dig in, figuratively and literally," Emrys intervened smoothly. "Do you have an extra shovel for me?"

"Of course," Olwen said, leading him away. "I've asked the others to gather what ash they might have . . ."

Her voice trailed off as they went to join the growing cluster of men and women gathered near the forge. Emrys glanced back one more time, mouthing, *Later?*

I nodded.

Cabell and Neve, I reminded myself, turning back toward the tower and the many steps between me and the bedchambers. They needed to know what we'd found—and maybe Neve would have some idea of what the sculptures were used for.

The clash of metal drew my attention back outside. Taking a chance, I made my way toward the training area. I'd expected to see another batch of anxious novices, or at least some of the Nine, but Cabell and Bedivere were the only ones there. My brother worked through a series of blocking and parrying moves, this time with a broadsword, not one of the blunt training weapons.

I stared, almost not trusting my eyes. Cabell had always thrived at night, and, on more than one occasion, had come home from a night of reveling through the streets of Boston or a guild gathering as I was getting up. His idea of an early start was noon.

Yet he'd been out here long enough to have worked up a heavy sweat. There was real color in his face—real emotion in his eyes as he grinned at something Bedivere said.

The older man gave an encouraging "Yes—good, *good*! Well done, lad!" and pounded him on the back as Cabell stopped to catch his breath. The hunger for approval on Cabell's face, the way he smiled in turn, was almost painful to see.

I felt oddly unmoored watching them, like I was drifting in the mist, insubstantial and fading. As he raised his sword again, Cabell happened to look my way, and stilled. His face tensed with concern.

I pressed two fingers against my upturned palm. *Later.* Then formed a small square with my hands. *Library.*

He nodded, turning back to Bedivere to resume practice. The old knight raised his hand in greeting to me, and I returned the gesture, struggling to muster a smile.

I could try to confront Caitriona, or at least shadow her steps, but that might only turn the others fully against me.

No, the best thing I could do right now was continue to gather information and bring Cabell and Neve to see the room with their own eyes. That might finally be enough to sway them into finding another way out of Avalon.

Opportunity came in the form of a soft gasp of surprise behind me on the steps. Mari's leaf-green face leaned around the mound of folded linens in her arms. "My apologies, I did not see you there."

"I don't know how you can see anything at all," I said. "Can I help you?"

Mari's face pinched in a way that made me wonder if she was replaying my harsh words from the other day.

"I was rude to you in the library," I continued, thinking quickly. "I'd love to make it up to you . . . ?"

After a moment, her expression relaxed and she nodded, but still didn't meet my eyes as she let me take half the sheets from her teetering pile. They were still cold from the line they'd been pinned to high on the southern wall.

Mari wasn't one for empty words. It became obvious within minutes that my usual tactic of letting the other person nervously talk to fill the silence wouldn't work; Mari seemed to relish the bit of peace it provided. I'd have to engage her where she was willing to be met.

"So . . . ," I began, racking my brain for something to say as I scurried along after her. For someone so small, she moved with the speed of a cat. "What do you know about unicorns?"

The dream had been hovering at the back of my mind, begging to be acknowledged, but it was slightly mortifying that this useless question was the best I'd been able to come up with on the spot. This was why I didn't do small talk.

Mari's eyebrows rose. "Have you come across one?"

"No," I said, fumbling in a way that annoyed me. I was better than this. "I just thought that—in the library, you seemed to know so much about legends. I just wondered if they were real. Or something invented out of—well, you know, dreams."

"A dream of a unicorn is a wonderful omen of good fortune ahead." Mari started to turn away, only to pivot back, unable to resist elaborating. "They were alive once. One of the Goddess's most beloved creations, as gentle as they were fierce."

"Once?" I repeated. "What happened to them?"

"No one is certain, only that eventually, they stopped appearing to the priestesses, and were no longer there to aid in healing the sick," Mari answered, starting down the hall again. "The dragons came to the same fate."

It took me a moment.

"Hang on—dragons?" I called, hurrying after her.

After stripping the beds in the hall and leaving clean sheets, we brought the soiled linens down to the sacred springs. They were washed in a different set of pools, deeper into the cavern. And there I saw my first real opportunity for answers.

"Are there any other rooms or tunnels hidden beneath the tower like this?" I asked Mari as we climbed the steps back up to the courtyard.

"Certainly," she said, voice airy and melodic. "As many as the body has veins. Some have collapsed with time, and others simply forgotten, waiting to be found once more."

"There's no record of them anywhere?" I asked, trailing after her through the courtyard. She was so slight—a mere seedling to the rest of us. It was little wonder the other Avalonians barely seemed to take notice of her as she hurried by them, keeping her head down.

"Oh, but I wish," Mari said. "That knowledge died with High Priestess Viviane. She was . . ." She paused, collecting her thoughts. "She was the High Priestess when the sorceresses rose against the druids and taught me nearly everything I know of magic, ritual, and Avalon's history."

"Flea says that Caitriona is your new High Priestess," I said. "Was she able to learn from the last one before she died?"

"Yes, but not for very long." A curious transformation came over Mari. She stood straighter, her shoulders back as she led us up the stairs. Even her voice sounded clearer. "Cait was the first called of our Nine, but we chose her because she is the best of us."

"Nobody is perfect," I managed.

"Cait is," Mari said, looking back at me with defiance. "She is the bravest soul I know, and the kindest."

"She hasn't been kind to Neve," I pointed out.

"That's only because . . . because she knows the old stories so well," Mari protested, tucking the streak of white hair behind her ear. "The betrayal of sisters is not easily forgotten, nor forgiven."

"Do you think the High Priestess ever taught her anything about Lord Death's magic?" I asked.

Mari stared at me, her wide-set eyes the very portrait of bewilderment. "What makes you ask that?"

My stomach curled in on itself, cramping with everything else I should have said. It felt wrong not to tell her, knowing what was at stake for all the priestesses. I'd only wanted to plant that suggestion in her mind, to let it fester enough for her to find her own answers, but it suddenly felt breathtakingly cruel.

The Nine were fiercely loyal to Caitriona and one another, perhaps unbreakably so after what they'd faced together. For the first time, looking at Mari, I started to doubt my own eyes.

Why *would* Caitriona want to do any of this, knowing it threatened her sisters and had killed hundreds, if not thousands, of Avalonians?

She could be serving another, I thought, *and this is all their design . . .*

But that only brought up more questions my mind was too exhausted to handle. Instead, I asked, "What's next?"

"I'm afraid if I tell you, you won't want to help," Mari said with a smile.

I was already intimately acquainted with the garderobes— essentially medieval lavatories that jutted out from the back of the tower. They were nothing more than a hole on a wooden bench that opened to the reeking, stagnant moat below, and to my eternal joy, I got to see every one of them as we emptied out the chamber pots and dumped used wash water into them.

Mari had a way of always staying at the very edge of things: the stairs, the walls of rooms, the courtyard. It was growing clearer to me by the moment that she was the unseen engine at the heart of the tower, quietly assigning the day's tasks to all the others and shouldering the most thankless, invisible work herself. It was in the elfinkin's gentle nature to tend to animals, and it seemed that extended to the human variety as well.

Hours later, Mari moved to her final task of the day: tallying their stores of food and other supplies and distributing the daily allotment to those assigned to cook the evening meal, including, as it turned out, Olwen, who had come to collect it herself.

The larder was in a room tucked away at the back of the sleeping hall, where many people were still milling about, greeting Olwen as they rolled the bed pads and folded the blankets to store at one end of the room.

The priestess's smile grew at the sight of me. The simple dress she wore was the color of a faded rose and hugged her full curves; its draped bell sleeves rolled and pinned to keep them from interfering with her work.

"Just taking in the sights," I said lightly.

Olwen passed a small basket to Mari, who lifted it with a look of obvious pleasure. The scraggly gray kitten inside examined her with equal interest, taking in her face with his unusually vivid blue eyes.

"I thought you could use a new mouser for the larder, or just a friend to join you as you go about your day," Olwen said, smiling. "I'm not sure what's happened to his mother and siblings. He just wandered into to the kitchen and took a bit of goat's milk."

"Oh, what a darling you are," Mari cooed, lifting the kitten out of the basket. "Does he have a name?"

"Rabies?" I suggested. But the sight of his adorable little face made me miss the fiendish felines in the guild library to an almost unspeakable degree.

"That's an unusual name," Mari said, visibly relaxing as she cuddled the kitten beneath her chin. The creature happily accepted the attention with a soft purr. "I think . . . yes, you look more like a Griflet to me. Thank you, Olwen!"

"Don't forget to eat something before this evening," Olwen said. "The both of you. I'll hunt you down and feed you bits of cheese if I have to."

"Just so you know, you're invited to do that anytime," I said.

The larder was lit by three glass windows, which gave a clear view of the disaster inside. I turned. And turned again.

The room was as large as the bedchambers and smelled sweet with dried fruit, but there was food only on one wall of shelves. My stomach turned over at the sight.

"Where do you keep the rest of it?" I asked.

Mari set her kitten down to allow him to explore. Olwen quickly shut the door behind us, pressing a finger to her lips.

"They don't know?" I asked, the words bursting out of me. I turned to survey the shelves again. "This is food for weeks, not months."

"Now you understand the importance of the crops they'll be growing in the courtyard," Olwen said, glancing at Mari as she fussed with a nearly empty jar of dried berries. Seeing them reminded me of the almost decadent sweet bread they'd given us the night before.

Dread crept over me like a shadow. There was no way this would last until they had viable crops to eat. Unless . . .

"Can you use your magic to grow crops faster?" I asked.

"Yes," Olwen said. "Though we've been reluctant to do so, with the magic of the isle feeling so . . . unpredictable."

I did the math in my head, working out how much about two hundred people would need each day. "Do you think they'd be fully ripened within two weeks—a fortnight?"

Why are you doing this? my mind whispered. *This isn't your problem . . .*

Wasn't it, though? I wasn't about to have any of us starve to death before we carved a path back to our world.

"Possibly," Olwen said. "Why?"

"You're in luck," I told them, reaching for the first basket of grain. "Because if there's one thing I know how to do, it's stretch a little bit of food to make it last."

And, if it came to it, lie and lie until every last hope they had was extinguished.

28

Unsurprisingly, Neve had returned to the library at some point during the day. By the time I'd managed to drag my tired bones back up the stairs to talk to her, the pile of books beside her had grown so high, I almost missed spotting her at the table.

She had her headphones on, and her dreamy synth music seemed to be wandering through the rows of shelves, as if curious about what books it would find there.

I collapsed into the chair directly across from her at the worktable. With a sigh, Neve paused her CD and lowered her earphones.

"I feel like I need to brace myself whenever I ask you this," she said. "But is everything all right?"

"Get excited," I told her. "It's even worse than what you're imagining."

"I'm imagining you found out the Mother tree is going to die within days, starving the world of its last bit of magic and reducing us to a feast for the Children and whatever worms might live in the soil," Neve said.

"Okay," I managed. "Wow. I'm . . . not actually sure it's worse than that."

"Are you going to tell me," Neve asked, "or am I supposed to guess? Because the sacred pools drying up is next on my list."

The story tumbled out of me so quickly that I struggled to catch my breath by the end of it. All the while Neve stared back, her frown deepening.

"What do you think?" I asked her.

"I think you *believe* you saw someone with silvery hair," Neve said. "And you assume it's Caitriona, just like you assume it has something to do with the druids and Lord Death."

"Did you miss the part about the literal human bone statues?" I said. "And the mark of the king of Annwn?"

"Those 'statues' could be used for anything, including to commemorate the dead." Neve took a book off the table's towering stack. "And the cauldron could have been a gift."

"You didn't *feel* that room," I said. "There's something wrong about it. Something dark. And the cauldron . . ."

"Here's the thing—there are a number of legendary cauldrons, as I suspect you well know," Neve said. "Not all of them serve darker purposes. One can produce endless food, for example. Actually, I wonder where that one is . . . Do you think it could produce, like, sour gummies? Or macaroni and cheese? I would give up a toe for some mac and cheese right about now. Not the big one, though."

"It has to be her," I insisted. "The height, the way she moved . . . it's her."

"Why are you so set on it being Caitriona?" Neve asked.

"Why are you so certain it's not?" I countered. "I don't understand why you're defending her when she treated you so horribly."

"Why not?" Neve asked absently as she returned to her book. "I still defend you to the others."

She realized what she'd said a beat later, looking up.

"Don't you dare try to soften it or take it back," I told her. "I deserve it. And for the record, I *am* sorry we didn't tell you the truth. But knowing how the ring is claimed, can you blame me?"

"I don't blame you for wanting to protect your guardian, and I certainly don't blame you for trying to help your brother," she said, letting the book slam shut. "But I do resent being made to feel like an idiot, which you and I both know is the furthest thing from the truth."

"I understand," I told her.

"And what somehow makes it worse is that even after you got to know me, you still thought I was capable of killing Nash to get what I wanted," Neve continued. "So which is it? What am I—the clueless weakling you can use, or the cruel, ruthless sorceress?"

My hands clenched beneath the table. "Neither. I know I can be—"

"Difficult? Prickly? Mulish?" she suggested.

"All of those things," I agreed.

"And you're proud of it," Neve said, shaking her head. "Why? I know you think I'm too trusting—too softhearted, or whatever—but where's the bravery in pushing everyone away the second they get too close?"

"I think it's a mistake to try to help *everyone*. You have to put yourself first because no one else will," I protested. "And while there's nothing wrong with being as kind as you are, everyone has to develop a thick skin eventually, otherwise the world will keep finding ways to cut at them."

"Tamsin, you don't have thick skin, you have *armor*," Neve said. "And while armor can stop some blows, it also means that no one ever really gets to see who you are beneath it."

"That's not true," I protested, feeling my heart batter my ribs.

"After a while, they all stop trying, don't they?" she continued. "They think you're indifferent to them. They get tired of the negative takes. And what does that give you? A sense of safety? Or does it leave you with nothing at all?"

I wanted to push back from the table, to walk out of the room, but it was as if her words had turned me to stone. I couldn't draw a deep enough breath. Cold sweat broke out on my chest and back.

"I know you'll find this hard to believe, but I do get it," Neve said.

"Showing that you care about something or someone makes you vulnerable, because it gives the world another way to hurt you. But there comes a time when you have to decide if feeling empty is really any better than the risk of being broken."

She stretched her arm across the table toward me, palm up. After all I'd done, still offering.

I hesitated, but did the same, gripping her forearm as she gripped mine.

Neve smiled. The green flecks in her hazel eyes were bright in the candlelight. "You are a clever, loyal, and caring person."

Her hold on me tightened in a playful way, and her smile blossomed as I tried not to fidget. "That's right. You're going to have this earnest, heartfelt moment and you're going to suffer through it even though you're dying a little inside, aren't you?"

I winced. "Uh-huh."

"Good," she said primly, and, with one last squeeze, released me. "As penance, you'll have to bear more of these tender moments with me, and accept that you are my friend."

"Have mercy," I begged. "Can't I just steal something else for you to take back to the Council of Sistren and we can call it even? Maybe one of the creepy bone statues will impress them—"

"Tamsin!" She threw her quill at me. "Absolutely not."

"Why?" I asked. "I've never been caught. Well, except for that one time, and it was only because a parrot ratted me out."

"Listen," she said. "I know you're worried . . ."

Neve trailed off, seeming to struggle for her next words.

"You want to know about the parrot, don't you?" I asked.

"Yes," she said sheepishly. "I can't help it. Tell me everything."

"His name was Carrot, and he lived in an antiques shop in Prague," I said. "And he was a handsome traitor."

Neve closed her eyes, sighing happily. "Carrot the Parrot. It's perfect."

"Offer still stands," I said, crossing my arms as I leaned back against the chair.

"Answer is still no," Neve said. "But I appreciate you offering up your services as a Hollower—" She caught herself too late. "I mean, not that I think Hollowers are thieves, exactly, it's just . . . you know . . ."

"Hollowers are thieves," I said. "We just gave ourselves a different name to feel better about it."

Neve shook her head, returning her attention to the book she opened in front of her.

"Can I ask you something?" I began.

"Not if it's about leaving Avalon before we find a way to help them," she said blithely, turning the page.

"Why do you want to be accepted by the Council of Sistren so badly?" I asked. "I understand wanting to further your education—believe me, I respect that ambition—but you've been so successful at teaching yourself, and now you have the Nine helping you. From what I know about the Council, I'm just afraid they'd try to crush all of the creativity and kindness out of you. I know you're not afraid to go your own way, so why does their approval matter?"

"It's not that simple," Neve said, her fingers tightening almost imperceptibly around the book. "In that world—our world—I'll be no one."

"You'll never be no one," I said sharply. "You don't need their draconian rules and outdated spells."

"No, that's not what I mean," Neve said. "I'll really be no one."

I leaned back against my chair, letting the words settle in my mind, trying to understand them. Instead of elaborating, Neve reached into the bodice of her dress, lifting the chain over her head, revealing what she'd managed to keep hidden all these days.

A pendant.

She set it down between us, eyeing it like an asp. A simple silver setting held an oval white stone at its center. No—not white, but opalescent, a rainbow of colors hidden in the depths of its smooth surface.

"The stone's called a Goddess Eye," Neve said, her voice faint.

My memory helpfully supplied the rest. "An incredibly rare stone capable of amplifying magic."

I had to fight the urge to pick it up from the table and study it more closely.

"It was my mother's," Neve said. "I found it while I was cleaning the attic with my auntie—and I knew, I *knew* by the look on her face that I wasn't supposed to find it, just like I wasn't ever supposed to learn what I was."

Shock barreled through me. "She hid the fact that you were a sorceress?"

"Not exactly. I was left on her doorstep as a baby—that old cliché." Neve shook her head. She was smiling, but it was undercut by the obvious hurt in her eyes. "Auntie claimed she had no idea who left me, or even who my mother was. She could tell I had magic, but she wasn't sure if I would manifest full powers. I could have just as easily been one of the Cunningfolk, like her."

"But then you turned thirteen," I said softly.

She nodded. "It's hard to explain what happens to you—you wake up one morning suddenly feeling like you've been electrified. If that magic isn't tamed or directed into spellwork, it can explode out of you. Fires. Blown-out glass. Cursing someone you hate with a pox."

"You said that last one *very* casually." I gave a nervous laugh. Neve didn't join in.

"My auntie basically thought . . . I don't know what she thought," Neve continued. "That if I ignored it, the power would disappear? But even after I put the pendant back, it called to me. It felt like it was supposed to be mine. I swear I could hear it whispering to me through the walls."

I said nothing, waiting for her to continue when she was ready.

"I didn't want to upset Auntie in any way, and I resisted it for a year, telling myself I didn't need it or want it. But one day, when Auntie went to work, I couldn't lie to myself anymore. I went back up into the attic to get it. And I didn't just find it again. I also found some of my mother's old books and her wand."

She didn't have to say it for me to know. It was the wand Caitriona had taken that first night we were here.

"And I realized Auntie had lied to me," Neve said, her voice growing smaller. "Not only did she know who my mother was, they were friends. I found letters she had sent, including one explaining my father had died, but she hadn't signed them with a name, only the letter *C*. It was the last in the pile that made me sure they had come from her."

My eyebrows rose. "What did it say?"

"*Her name is Neve. Don't let them take her.* 'Them' could have been anyone—my father's family, whoever they are, the Sistren, the State of South Carolina . . . All I knew was that Auntie had kept all of it from me, and it was mine," Neve said. "So when she left for work, I would work, too. I went through my mother's books, trying to learn more about her, trying the spells she'd known. The pendant made it all so much easier."

"Do you think it might have played a role in the protective spell you cast when we first got here?"

"Olwen thinks it helped amplify it," Neve said. "But also . . . I've read countless times that magic is something that has to be tightly controlled, and carefully directed into a spell. Magic is so untamed and endless that the practice of memorizing an established set of sigils has always felt restrictive to me. It never made sense until Olwen explained that the priestesses' way of calling magic *is* more intuitive and personal to each caster."

I frowned. "Personal in what way?"

"You call the magic in whatever way feels good, or natural to you. The magic responds to your will, and how you picture it," Neve said. "The spells don't always come out exactly as you imagined, though. I think that's why the sorceresses developed their language—so everything would be more specific. And predictable."

"Makes sense," I said. Personally, I'd take the certainty of the sorceresses' method any day.

"Olwen uses humming to call it, others use song," Neve continued. "Mari prays directly to the Goddess, and Lowri—the sister who works in the forge—she uses hand signals."

"You screamed," I said, remembering.

"Yeah, exactly," Neve said. "I knew the kind of spell we needed and the scream just came out of me—there was no thought to it, just instinct. I created the spell."

"That's . . ." I almost didn't have a word for it. "That makes it even more impressive. But knowing there's another way to practice magic—a way you seem pretty good at—why do you need the Council of Sistren?"

Neve's whole body heaved with her sigh. "It's so stupid, I know it is. I shouldn't want their acceptance, but I do."

She closed her eyes, as if needing to see the memory play out again.

"A few weeks ago, Auntie came home early from work. And we fought. Fought like we never had before . . . ever," Neve said. "I love her more than anyone in the world, and I said *horrible* things to her—that she was trying to hold me back, that she wanted me to be as weak as her . . . She claimed all of the lies and half-truths had been to protect me, but wouldn't say from what. She begged me not to go to the Council of Sistren. To just let it all go."

"But you couldn't."

Neve shook her head and opened her eyes. "I left that day to take the admission test to their school of sorcery. I told you the truth before. They wouldn't even let me try—they barely let me speak. What I didn't tell you, though, was that it wasn't just my lack of apprenticeship."

"What do you mean?" I asked.

A quiet anger flickered in her expression; it was the kind of fire that turned iron to steel. "It was because I had no known lineage. I had no documentation of my maternal line. I couldn't even tell them my mother's name. I can still see them at that table, laughing . . ."

My jaw was clenched so tightly, I couldn't speak. I felt it then, as if I'd been standing there beside her. The humiliation. The desperation of being wholly alone in your story, with no way to piece together a past. The need for approval.

There was so much about Neve's life I would never truly understand, but that . . . *that* I understood.

"They can rot in the infernal abyss," I told her fiercely. "You don't need them—you're too good for them in every way."

"I do need them, though," Neve said. "It's not just about acceptance, or even trying to master my power more fully. I think . . . Something Auntie said before I left makes me think the Council of Sistren may have my mother's Immortality in their archive."

And the answers about who I am inside it.

She didn't need to say it. I had lost my past, but she had a chance. Neve could still find the answers to the questions burning in her, and she'd been willing to do anything, including venture into an Otherland, to get them.

I understood that, too.

"Maybe it's stupid," Neve said, sighing. "I don't even know her name. How could I even begin to look?"

"Well, you now have a friend who is fairly skilled at finding things," I pointed out. "I'll even give you the friends-and-family discount."

Neve snorted, but the sadness in her eyes only deepened as she murmured, "Wheel of Fortune reversed, Five of Wands, Three of Swords."

It took me a moment to realize she was talking about her last tarot reading at Mystic Maven. For all Neve's talk about not giving up, some part of her had internalized the cold reality check of the cards.

Her question echoed in me. *Am I going to find what I'm looking for?*

I understood it then—really understood the reason for her belief in things working out. It wasn't because she lacked uncertainty or doubt, or that she was naïve; it was that she was strong enough to hold on to her beliefs and hopes, even in the face of loss or rejection.

"What happened to *That's just the cards' opinion*?" I asked. "Let's not forget I have zero magical ability here. You would have gotten the exact same answer if you'd asked if you were getting a pony for your birthday."

That, at least, got a laugh out of her. "I do love ponies."

"I never would have guessed," I said. "But listen, I have some contacts with sorceresses I've worked with in the past. I can't promise that any of them will be willing to help, but it would only take one to search the archive for your mother's Immortality."

"You really think they might?" Neve asked. She leaned forward, a look of false shock on her face. "Tamsin . . . are you being hopeful?"

I pretended to shudder. "You'll have to come with me. They'll be a lot less likely to kill me for my insolence if you're there too."

"I'm sure that can be arranged," she said, trying to smother her smile. "Assuming we make it back to the portal alive."

"Assuming." I studied the stack of books in front of her for a moment and pulled one over to me. *The Healer's Journey.*

"What are you doing?" Neve asked.

"Maybe it'll help to have a fresh set of eyes on the problem," I said.

"I've already been through that stack."

"Then I'll go get some more," I said. "Or just sit here and admire you for being so smart and studious."

Neve laughed and slid another book across the table. "This one's an account of the shapeshifting creatures of the Otherlands."

My chest clenched. "You've been researching Cabell's curse?"

"Yes, and Olwen has too."

I opened the cover of the leather-bound volume, relishing the smell of old parchment. "But you haven't found anything useful?"

"Not yet." Neve paged through the book in front of her. "But I had the thought that maybe he's another type of being, and his human form is the curse."

I stared at her, an endless, ringing pressure expanding in my skull.

At my silence, Neve looked up from her page. "Did you ever explore that possibility?"

"No," I croaked.

"Well, I guess that's a point in favor of getting a fresh set of eyes on things," Neve said. I must have looked skeptical because she quickly added, "It's just a theory. I have no proof either way."

I was still shaking my head as I gripped the edges of the book.

"Would it really be so bad?" Neve asked. "It would bring him a measure of peace."

"Breaking his curse would bring him peace," I insisted.

Neve's eyes softened as they met mine again. "I can't begin to tell you what it feels like to know that you're meant to be something else than what you are—it gnaws at you every day, even if you refuse to acknowledge it, until there's a void in you that nothing but the truth will fill."

"He's human," I told her. He had a human heart and a human mind.

And if he didn't, it would mean he belonged somewhere else, in a different world, and a part of him might always yearn to go there, even if he never knew why.

29

The minutes gathered into hours. Each turn of the page brought me deeper and deeper into the manuscript I was poring over; I was so captured by my reading, it took someone clearing their throat to pull me away. When I looked up, it was to find Emrys standing in the library's doorway, his face like thunder. Cabell hovered behind him, visibly confused.

"What's wrong?" I asked.

Neve emerged from her own reading trance, blinking. "Is it the soil?"

"Oh, the soil beneath the stones was fine and the seeds are well on their way to sprouting, thanks to a little infusion of magic from Deri," Emrys said, shifting his weight from one foot to the other. "But I think I found something. Something else."

His eyes were overly bright, almost feverish, contrasting harshly with the sunken shadows beneath them.

"*Something else* implies that I'm already behind," Cabell said. "Anyone want to fill me in? I tried to get here earlier, but Sir Bedivere needed help."

"Speaking of Sir Bedivere . . . ," I said. Cabell's expression fell into pure horror as I quickly, and quietly, told him what Emrys and I had found last night.

"So what's Bedivere's connection to all this?" Neve asked.

But Cabell, of course, had understood. He remembered Nash's stories about Arthur's journeys to Annwn as well as I did. "Sir Bedivere was said to be one of the knights who accompanied King Arthur to Annwn. But I thought the cauldron they recovered had something to do with food?"

"See!" Neve said.

"Could you try fishing for some information about it?" I asked. "Just . . . feel him out."

"*Feel out* an immortal knight of the Round Table," Cabell said, rubbing his hands over his face. "Sure. Why not."

Emrys had been all but vibrating with impatience as I caught Cabell up, and it was clear he'd reached the end of his fuse. "Can we please get going? It's really important you see this."

"Have you slept at all since we got here?" Neve asked, cocking her head to the side as she studied him. "Maybe you should take a nap first. I have a potion that could knock you out in a few seconds. It tastes like bat hair, but, you know, night spells from night creatures and all that."

Emrys sent a pleading look my way, and a part of me, one I didn't want to acknowledge, went soft. I'd been steadfastly avoiding the memory of our interlude in the wardrobe, but now it came rushing back.

"All right." I sighed, closing the book. "Whatever it is can't be worse than last night."

It was clear from the emptiness of the tower that the hour was even later than I'd thought. The doors to the sleeping hall were partly shut, but I could see well enough inside to spot Olwen, Flea, and Arianwen huddled up nearby.

Emrys led us down to the tower's entrance, waiting for Betrys and the others on watch to turn their backs before we darted across the courtyard. I surveyed their efforts from the day; half of the stones were gone, revealing a dark belly of soil that had been carefully sowed in neat little rows.

Cabell glanced at the guards overhead one last time. "Coast's clear."

Emrys motioned for us to follow him to the armory.

The small building was surprisingly well lit and, if I had to guess, had likely once been a gatehouse. Now the air was perfumed by the animal fat and linseed oil used to polish tools and blades.

Beside me, Cabell wrinkled his nose. "What now, Dye?"

A battered full suit of armor, blood-red with rust, kept silent watch over the room. Emrys moved Neve and me into position directly in front of it. He watched us, waiting for something, and a moment later, I felt it. A cold draft of air exhaled from the floor beneath us. Neve jumped as it ruffled her skirt.

"What is that?" she asked.

"That was my question as well," Emrys said. "Anyone want to make—"

"No one wants to make a bet," I told him. "Or play a game. We are tired."

"All right, all right," he said. He lifted the visor of the rusty armor and reached into the emptiness behind it. He pulled on something—hard—and the floor rattled beneath us.

Cabell offered a steadying hand to Neve and me as the section of floor beneath us lowered.

"What in hellfire . . . ," he breathed out. My whole body tensed as the platform sank into the darkness of a tunnel—as ancient and crudely hewn as the tunnel beneath the great hall.

"Oh, wow," Neve said, trying to see down the length of it to the shadows ahead.

As we stepped off, the floor rose again of its own accord.

"Should we be worried about that?" I asked faintly.

"There's another lever down here to lower the platform," Emrys assured me. "I spent a precious hour of my life finding it."

As the platform slid into place, blocking any trace of light from above, I realized what I'd forgotten in all our hurry.

"My workbag," I said, pressing a hand to my forehead.

"Have no fear, ladies and gent," Emrys said, pulling on his head lamp and clicking the light to turn it on. "I've got us covered."

Beside me, Neve closed her eyes and drew in a gasp like the last soft breath before a kiss. Her lips were moving, but it was a moment more before I heard the song: the words that had no translation, the humming that seemed to be born from the deepest chamber of her heart. It harmonized with her echoes on the stones around us, until Neve's voice became a thing of pure power, and the power became her voice.

The melody was otherworldly and filled with promise, like a revelation. Wisps of pale blue light gathered at her fingertips. She brought her hands to her mouth and blew on them, scattering the shivering lights like dandelion seeds down the length of the tunnel. Their glow made me feel like I was floating in one of the pools in the cavern below.

"Incredible," I told her. And she hadn't needed a sigil, let alone her wand, to do it. She had done what had felt natural, and the result was astonishing. Neve beamed, tracing a finger around one of the lights.

With what dignity he could muster, Emrys reached up and turned off his head lamp. "Well, that works too."

"Where are we going?" I asked. "I can't imagine you just wanted to show us this paradigm of a cold, drippy cave tunnel."

"It's really more of an ancient path into the bleak never-dawn," Emrys said, starting down said ancient path. "But it is indeed drippy and cold."

The damp passage was short, but it reeked of the isle's decay in a way the other tunnel hadn't. The air was thick with moisture, and we churned up foul odors with our every step. My ears strained, listening beyond our footsteps and the dripping water that seeped from the walls.

At the end of Neve's trail of lights, I could make out a grotto of some sort. I was so focused on it, I overlooked the antechamber that opened into it.

Dread brushed along my spine, cold and quivering, as I turned to my right. There, an iron-grated door barred entry to a crypt; through the rusted metal, I could just make out the shape of three plain stone coffins. It was a lightless crevice, lacking any color or adornment beyond the names chiseled into their lids.

The one closest to me read MORGAN.

"Can we assume this is the Morgan we know as Morgan le Fay?" Emrys asked.

"Yes," Neve said, her voice hushed. "Olwen told me about this. While the surviving sorceresses were exiled, High Priestess Viviane didn't know what to do with the bodies of the priestesses who died getting revenge on the druids. She decided not to bury them in the earth, to keep them from being reborn, but couldn't bear to burn them."

I nodded, feeling something heavy settle at the base of my throat. After everything, the High Priestess had still loved her sisters in spite of their betrayal. She hadn't left them to rot into the ground, the way I had with Nash's remains.

"Someone's been down to visit them," Cabell said. He slid a hand through the bars, pointing at the bouquet of dried roses placed at the head of Morgan's coffin.

Neve squinted, trying to see for herself. "That's impossible. Olwen said she wasn't even sure where the crypt was."

"*She* might not be," I said. "But someone remembered."

"I agree this is all very unsettling and mysterious," Emrys said. "But believe it or not, this isn't what I wanted to show you. Follow me."

Past the antechamber, the stench thickened until I could barely draw breath without becoming queasy. We stood on a wide stone platform, overlooking a section of the tower's moat. It ran through the length of the grotto, its murky sludge filtering through grates.

"*This,*" Emrys said, "is why I brought you down here."

I glanced back over my shoulder and stilled. Neve stepped in closer to my side, her breathing turning ragged.

The platform spread out around us, filling the cavernous space. There, on either side of the entrance we'd come through, were cages.

Four of them, made of crudely shaped iron. Two looked as if they had been torn apart from the inside, the bars twisted as if made of twine, not metal. A pile of silver bones waited in the third.

And the ground around the fourth's was painted with dark, dry blood.

That very same blood had most likely been used to daub the symbols on the ground near Neve's feet. There was something desperate, or frenzied, about the way they'd been painted.

Cabell noticed the markings too, and gently pulled Neve away from them. His nostrils flared as he took in the scene.

"So," Emrys said, leaning against one of the cages. "Anyone want to venture a theory?"

"Maybe they kept a few of the Children down here when they first started turning, to see if the dark magic was reversible?" Cabell suggested.

"I thought that too, but look," Emrys said, moving into the cell with the bones. With a grimace, he picked one up—a very human femur, not coated entirely in silver, but mottled with specks of it, as if the transformation had somehow been interrupted. "Is it possible someone was experimenting on turning people into Children—that it took time to perfect whatever curse they used?"

"No," Neve said sharply. Something about the way she refused to look at us tugged at me. "There's no one here capable of that kind of spellwork—to will those creatures into being would require a truly dark soul."

There were few areas of magic the Council of Sistren restricted, resurrection and other death magic among them. The threat of accidentally—or intentionally—creating violent ghosts was all too real.

"That's true for the magic you use," I said. "But what about Lord Death's magic?"

Neve said nothing, and suddenly, a new suspicion bloomed in me.

"You recognize those sigils on the ground, don't you?" I asked.

"Neve, if you know something . . . ," Cabell began.

Finally, Neve turned back toward us. "I saw it in a book I wasn't supposed to be looking at in Olwen's infirmary—it didn't have any sort of title on it, and she'd hidden it behind some of her jars, and I really didn't mean to betray her trust but—"

"You are talking to three Hollowers," Emrys said. "This is a judgment-free space when it comes to snooping."

Neve looked like she might be sick. "It's a druid mark. Like sorceresses, they used a written language to control the magic Lord Death gave them. It's meant to sever a soul from a body."

My whole body recoiled.

"You're sure?" I asked. "Absolutely positive?"

"Beyond a shadow of a doubt," she rasped out.

My head pounded, blood storming through my veins.

"Then we're right," Emrys said. "Someone in Avalon is still using death magic. Whatever was done to the isle was done intentionally. The only question is why. Because they're sympathetic to the druids, or because they serve Lord Death?"

My heart sped until my body felt strangely hollow. An overwhelming nausea swept through me, and I had to lean against Cabell to keep from bending over.

"You okay?" he asked, gripping my arm.

I waved him off, but he didn't let go.

"And you think Caitriona is behind it?" Neve said, shaking her head. "You're piecing all these so-called clues together, but what's her motive? Why would she destroy Avalon?"

"Maybe Lord Death promised her something in return," Emrys said, "to finish what the druids started."

"Caitriona isn't behind this," Neve said. "There's no way."

"I can see that you hate this theory," Emrys said, "and believe me, I do too, but I don't think we can discount the idea that Caitriona is controlling the Children, or at least working with whoever is."

"How do we even know they're being controlled?" Cabell asked, scratching at the stubble on his jaw.

"They're still out there, doing nothing," Emrys said. "Not hunting, not digging, not scouting, just waiting. Waiting for an order."

"There's just no way," Neve said, but her words became muddled in my ears, then thinned as Emrys replied, and I felt my consciousness slipping . . .

My body felt as if it were in an icy coffin, without even a scant bit of space to move in. The cavern around us revealed itself, blanketed in mist, but a horn pierced it. The glossy black eyes of the unicorn stared back at me from the other side of the moat's sludge. For a moment, we only watched each other, and I didn't dare breathe for fear of breaking the spell.

But still, it shattered.

The unicorn reared up, and the vision shifted behind my eyelids, each detail more horrific than the last. The unicorn faded back into the mist, and in its place came hairless gray scalps, then long, spidery limbs. Claws embedding themselves in the wet stone.

Tamsin? I thought I heard my name from somewhere nearby.

Children rising from beneath the thick mire of the moat, dragging themselves onto the platform, galloping on their strange, spidery limbs down the tunnel, toward the hidden entrance—

I gasped, my eyes snapping open.

"Tamsin?" Cabell had me by both shoulders, his grip like iron as he shook me.

"What's wrong?" Emrys asked.

The bile was too thick in my throat to speak. I shook my head, dropping into a crouch.

"Come on," Neve said as she and Emrys helped me stand again, supporting me from either side. "Let's head back up and get some fresh air. I can get Olwen—"

I shook my head fiercely, but when my eyes slid shut, I saw that same scene play out again. The Children's rancid breath fanning over my face . . .

I forced my eyes open to find Emrys's face hovering nearby.

"You look like you're about to be sick," he said. "Neve's right, we should go."

"When are you going to realize that I'm always . . ." Neve trailed off, looping one of my arms over her neck. She looked around us, searching the shadows. "Do you hear that?"

Behind us, where the sludgy moat lapped against stone, the dank water began to gurgle. Roil.

Mist rose, sweeping past us with stunning force. And within the depths of it, four shadows emerged, scaling the edge of the platform.

30

The moment turned gauzy around me. As surreal as my waking nightmare just moments before.

No. This was—it was—

"Run," Emrys breathed out. *"Run."*

We made it all of five feet before the first of the Children screeched, scrabbling after us. Ten before Cabell realized I couldn't keep up and stopped to throw me over his shoulder.

My body ached as it was jostled, but my attention was fixed behind us. The Children broke ranks as we passed through the antechamber back into the tunnel. They clawed their way up and over the walls, crawling along them. Rather than being repelled, their jaws snapped around Neve's lights, devouring them one after another. That threw the tunnel behind us into complete darkness and made them appear to ride the wave of an unnatural shadow.

The tunnel dead-ended where the platform was meant to lower down from the armory. Cabell slid to a stop, and to my left, I saw Emrys dive for an iron lever on the wall. The platform rumbled as it started to lower.

"Now, Neve!" Cabell shouted.

Her scream pierced the pathway a breath before the spell's lights did; they roared across the stone, tearing through the Children until there was nothing left but ash.

As soon as the floor was low enough, Cabell dropped me on it and turned back toward the others. The sorceress swayed, her face graying with exhaustion from the spell. Emrys caught her arm, and he and Cabell lifted her and themselves onto the slowly rising platform.

"Thank you, thank you, thank you," Cabell told Neve.

"How . . . ," she gasped out between heavy breaths, "did . . . they get in?"

"There must be some kind of gap in the walls around the moat," Emrys said, running a hand through his hair and clenching it. "We have to tell the others. *Now.*"

But as the platform finished its ascent and leveled out with the armory's floor, the Children's screaming didn't stop. It only amplified into a roar, engulfing us like a thunderstorm.

I pushed to my feet and ran to the nearby window. Betrys was visible through the rippled glass, a sword clutched between her hands, her back to the building. She ran into the courtyard with a ferocious battle cry.

"Holy gods of night." Cabell ran to the doorway, throwing it open before I could stop him.

My mind finally grasped what I was seeing.

The racks around us had been emptied, and the courtyard was on fire.

Lines of flame blazed on the fortress's walls and between the buildings, dividing the open space and trapping Children within flaming cages. Some threw themselves forward, undaunted, trying to get to where Caitriona, Arianwen, and Rhona were defending the main entrance to the tower, hacking and slicing through any of the Children who tried to enter.

Emrys helped a stumbling Neve forward. I looked to her, desperate.

"I need . . ." She held up a hand, visibly anguished. "I need a few minutes before I can cast the spell again . . ."

"Stay in the armory," I told her, tossing a glance toward Emrys. He nodded, his expression fierce with resolve. "We'll buy you some time."

314

We ran forward into the raging chaos of the fight, searching for a torch or weapon to defend ourselves.

"Flea!" Caitriona's shout drew my attention to them again. The girl bolted from the tower. Dragging a sword nearly as tall as her, she ran to join the fray on the ramparts.

Horror punched me in the chest as Caitriona broke from the others, chasing her. The other Avalonians were spread out between the infirmary, the kitchen, and the stables, fighting desperately with fiery arrows and staffs.

A single word rang through my mind as I searched the smoke, the fire, the darkness. *Cabell.*

I spotted him again near Bedivere, who blocked the entrance to the stables, defending the horses and goats from the ravenous creatures dropping like spiders from the roof.

The dead, Children and human, were everywhere. The sheer carnage brought me up short. A flaming arrow singed the air to my right, piercing the skull of a creature I hadn't seen coming.

Seren's sunshine-gold hair was splattered with dark blood as she nocked another arrow and shouted down to us. "Get to the tower!"

"Tamsin!" I turned just as Emrys tossed me his axe. He knelt to pick up a dead man's sword.

"Can you buy me a few minutes?" Neve gasped out, her breathing hitching again. "I can try to figure out what I did before, but I need time!"

Without a word, Emrys and I moved into position around her. My eyes stung from the smoke and the wall of heat radiating from the fires, but the stench of blood and roasting flesh was worse. With a cry, I swung the axe into the darkness around me, striking stone, striking monstrous flesh, striking, striking, striking until it felt like my body was burning too.

A terrifying growl rose at my right. I whirled around, the blade of my axe cutting into the darkness, but I wasn't met with the gray face of the undead.

It was the snarling mouth of an enormous black dog.

I released my grip on the weapon just in time, narrowly avoiding its head. The hound's teeth were white knives as it dove for my ankle, locking its jaws around my boot. The breath blew out of me as my back hit the ground. I tried to twist, to claw at the stones, but it dragged me forward—away from the other predators that threatened its prey.

"Tamsin!"

Emrys ran forward, but I threw my other hand out to stop him. The hound yanked me toward a break in the fire line around the newly planted crops. The Children were there tearing up the soil, polluting it with their foul blood.

"No, Cabell, please!" I shouted. "Please!"

Emrys leapt forward, trying to grip the hound's jaws and pry them off me. When that didn't work, he picked up a loose stone and threw it at one of the dog's red eyes.

The hound whimpered, releasing me as it retreated. Emrys hooked his arms around my chest and lifted me. I gasped as I tried to put weight on my ankle, my vision blacking out with pain.

The hound howled as it sighted new vulnerable prey. Neve, her eyes closed. Concentrating. Undefended.

Cabell's quiet voice flooded my mind, drowning out the desperate voices around me. *Don't let me hurt anyone.*

"No!" I screamed. I dove forward, but the hound was too fast, too strong—it leapt over fire, over bodies, its gaze never wavering from the sorceress.

Someone else got to her first.

Caitriona jumped down from the wall, landing in a crouch before Neve. Her armor glowed gold in the fire of battle. She raised her sword, her face rigid with determination.

I couldn't live with it.

"Cait!" Flea screamed from the wall.

"Hold her, Seren!" Caitriona called back.

Do whatever it takes to stop me.

Seren shouted something down to us, but I couldn't hear a word over the blood roaring in my ears.

Whatever it takes.

"Don't kill him," I begged. "Don't kill him!"

Caitriona showed no signs of having heard me. Her gaze was sharp and assessing. When the hound sprang, she drew in a hard breath.

And let the sword fall from her hand.

The full weight of the beast slammed into her, tackling her to the stones beside Neve. Her armor clattered as it rolled, but it wasn't half as terrible as the hound's victorious howl, and Caitriona's agonized cry.

The hound had clamped its teeth around her steel gauntlet. Emrys and I tried to lock our arms around its shuddering frame, to pull the hound away from her, but it was thrashing, baying, impossible to hold. Heat radiated from its fur as its pulse rose with killing intent.

Caitriona slammed a fist into the side of the creature's neck and it howled in rage. Claws extended from the paw that was pinning her chest to the ground, piercing the metal.

Whatever it takes.

Reaching down toward her boot with her free hand, Caitriona tried to pull free the dagger there. Emrys cut at the paw pinning her, but the hound was lost to its bloodlust. It released her chest and I watched in horror as it bit down at the place where her neck met her shoulder, puncturing the armor to rip into the skin and muscle below.

Caitriona screamed.

An arrow slid into the hound's back, but not even the pain loosened its jaws as it thrashed her around like a doll. Blood streaked Caitriona's face as she tried to pound against its snout, its eyes.

Whatever it takes.

A strong arm shoved me out of the way, and then Bedivere was there, gripping the struggling beast around its middle and lifting it from Caitriona's prone form.

The moment fractured around me.

Seren and Flea ran toward us.

Emrys pressed his jacket to the priestess's shoulder to stanch the flow of blood, shouting for Olwen.

Bedivere shouted, "Master it, master it—"

The hound began to shift into something like a human.

And the light of Neve's spell flooded the courtyard, incinerating the Children, washing all of it, and all of us, away.

31

The darkness returned like a smothering hand. Motion blurred around me.

Flea sobbed as she pressed her face to Caitriona's chest, her breath fogging the armor where it wasn't already wet with blood. She kicked and screamed as a stone-faced Lowri pulled her away. Lowri hugged the girl to her tightly, allowing Rhona, Seren, and Emrys to lift Caitriona's limp form.

Olwen was already directing the wounded into the great hall. She cried out when she saw their group coming, rushing down the steps to meet them. Others screamed in disbelief or began weeping at the sight of Caitriona.

"Start searching the tower and the underpaths," Betrys shouted up to the men and women watching in terror from the wall. "I'll get Ari and meet you in the springs."

The magic that had fed the lines of fire across the courtyard released with a hiss. Through the smoke, I saw Betrys and Arianwen pull their swords from the twitching body of one of the Children, Arianwen crying as she gently touched one of its grotesque limbs.

A low moan of terror rose behind me. Cabell was white as milk in the dark, fighting to stand as his legs shook. His breathing turned erratic as his shock set in, and through the storm of death around us, his eyes found Neve.

The sorceress took several steps back, her face stricken.

"No," he moaned again. Cabell tore at his face and hair, his clawed fingers cutting angry red welts over his skin, until it became impossible to tell if the blood on his hands was Caitriona's or his own. His clothing hung in tatters from the shift.

"It is all right now, lad," Bedivere said, his voice low and soothing. "It's done."

"Cab—"

His head shot up, and the look was so accusatory, so terrible, it stole the breath from me.

Whatever it takes.

Bedivere's hand came to rest on Cabell's shoulder, but the touch sparked something. He wrenched himself away and ran through the shuddering clouds of smoke.

I followed, weaving through the wreckage of the battle, gasping for a deep enough breath to fill my lungs. The living moved around me like sleepwalkers, limping toward the tower. Ahead, Cabell disappeared into the stables. I followed.

The animals inside were in a state. The horses kicked at their stalls, unable to see that the threat had passed. Terrorized goats raced around in dizzying circles, bleating with the same animal desperation I'd felt in the courtyard. The sound of Cabell's ragged breathing led me to an empty stall at the back.

He slid down the wall into a crouch.

"No . . . no . . . no . . ." The word was hysterical, an agonized prayer. I approached slowly from behind. Until I smelled the blood.

He was frantically digging his nails into the cut Emrys had given him, ripping at the skin as dark blood poured down his arm.

"Stop—*Cabell!*" I dropped to my knees in front of him, trying to pull his injured arm away. He fought me hard enough that I was knocked onto the ground. "Stop!"

"I have to see—I have to see—" He chanted the words, teeth chattering. There was still blood around his mouth and chin.

I scrambled over to him, gripping his blood-slicked wrist again, trying to wedge my body between his arms to block his clawed nails. "You have to see what? What is it?"

When I turned his face toward mine, his eyes were empty. The waves of remorse and pain that had racked his body quieted and he was suddenly still. His eyes deadened, and I knew, I knew without him saying it, that I had witnessed the last light in him gutter out.

"To see if it's silver," he whispered hoarsely. "If I'm one of them."

My heart surged in my chest. I wrapped an arm around his shoulder and pressed my hand against his open wound, trying to hold the skin together. To hold *him* together.

"No, you're not," I said. "I swear, I swear you're not."

"I killed her." It wasn't a question.

"No, you—" I wanted to protest, but the truth was I didn't know. I didn't know what would happen next, or what they might try to do to him, and that was what scared the hell out of me. I didn't have a weapon to protect him, or the training to. I couldn't even sneak him out of the tower without drawing him into worse danger.

If the Avalonians believed that the darkness was slowly corrupting all magic on the isle, would they deem Cabell just as tainted as the Children?

Who's to say he isn't? came the dark voice at the back of my mind. *He's losing control more and more . . .*

"Your ankle," he rasped out, seeing the blood, the bite mark. "I hurt you again . . . I . . ."

I held him tighter, trying to keep him there, with me. But it didn't matter. None of it mattered.

"You promised," he said, agonized. "You *promised.*"

"We'll fix this," I whispered, holding him as he shook. "We'll fix you, I swear, we'll fix you."

"Lass."

I looked up to find Bedivere watching us. The battle had painted his face in cuts and bruises, but his expression was soft. He tilted his head away, toward the other end of the stables. I resisted, searching Cabell's face one last time for any sign of emotion amid the bleak nothingness in his eyes. Ripping the bottom of my tunic, I used the strip of fabric to bind the wound on his arm the best I could.

He didn't react, not even a flinch, as I knotted it tightly where the flesh was coming apart.

"I'll be right back," I promised.

As the old knight moved to the entrance of the stable, he brushed a hand over each of the animals, soothing them into a settled quiet. The horses watched us with dark eyes.

Bedivere looked out into the courtyard, where Betrys was helping a man with a gashed leg struggle toward the tower.

I gripped his arm, drawing his attention back to me. I didn't care how desperate I looked or sounded. "He didn't mean to do it. He would never have wanted to hurt her or anyone else—"

He covered my hand with his own. The skin was heavily callused and surprisingly cold to the touch. "There's no need to convince me, lass. I saw with my own eyes how he fought the shift."

I understood in an instant why the Nine looked to Bedivere with such adoration and trust. His unflinching calm was a ballast to the storm raging in me. He neither tried to hide the problem nor offered false assurances. His long life, and all that it had shown him, had shaped him into a rare source of dependability in Avalon.

"I don't know what to do," I said, my throat thick.

"I see your pain," he said quietly. "You have cared for him all these many years. He has spoken of how you have protected him, and how honorably you have tried to find the answers to his struggles."

"He's my brother," I said. "He's my responsibility."

"Yes," Bedivere said, nodding. "But I've been working with him these last few days and I see potential in him. I believe, with more time, I can help him find some measure of control over his magic until the blessed day comes that his curse is broken."

I knew better than to hope, but it was so hard not to cling to the idea of what he was offering. *More time.* "How?"

"It is fear and pain that spark his transformations," Bedivere said, "and both can be conquered. I will teach him what I know of these things."

I hesitated, glancing back toward Cabell.

"You have been alone in this for so very long," Bedivere said. "If I may relieve you of some of this weight, if only for this small measure of time, please allow me that honor. I care for the lad, and I believe this is what he himself desires."

Maybe that's what was bothering me. That Bedivere had been the one to truly help Cabell, and not me. Not after years of trying and searching.

I'd failed him, but maybe Bedivere wouldn't.

"What if he shifts again?" I asked. The adrenaline had faded and now exhaustion battered me from all sides. "What if the others want to kill him for what he's done?"

"I swear to you, lass, on my life and on that of my lord and liege, that I will let no one harm him," Bedivere said, kneeling with his oath. "I believe I may be able to suppress most shifts with what small magic I possess. That will ease the fears others may harbor."

It would. The others, even Caitriona, listened to him. Respected him. They would never hurt Cabell so long as the knight was there, defending his humanity. If I couldn't get us out of this hell, I could at least give him the best chance of surviving it. I could do *that*.

"It's his choice," I forced myself to say.

Bedivere bowed his head, drawing his hand across his chest as he rose. "I shall speak with him, then." When I started to follow, he held out a hand, stopping me with an apologetic look. "I think it best I speak to him alone."

My stomach clenched but I nodded. Nothing felt more wrong than this—entrusting someone else with the care of the only person who truly mattered to me. "His wound . . ."

"I'll see to it," Bedivere promised. "The others will need you as they clear the courtyard and tend to the bodies."

I left the stables in a daze, feeling as if my body might fold in on itself and collapse before I reached the tower. Gray smoke twined with the mist, turning it as silver as the bones of the dead creatures around me. It thinned, revealing Emrys standing a short distance away, his face soft with worry. Waiting for me.

I moved toward him, needing to feel something—anything—other than the sharp ache in my chest and the cold gathering on my skin. Yet when he lifted his hands as if to reach for me, I stopped. I forced myself to.

Ash fell around us, catching in the waves of his hair. Hopelessness bled into his expression, darkening even his bright eyes. Sweat and blood molded his tunic to the muscles of his chest; I knew by the look of some of the deeper cuts that the night had added to his collection of scars.

Emrys gave a weak shrug, his throat bobbing as he swallowed hard. A dangerous feeling rose in me, terrifying in its clarity. I wanted to comfort him as much as I wanted to be comforted by him. The thought of being so exposed, and in front of him, made the lingering nausea worse. I was Tamsin Lark and he was Emrys Dye, and whatever the moment could have been passed.

"Is Cabell all right?" he asked carefully.

"Do you know where Caitriona is?" I countered.

He blew out a breath and nodded.

They'd gathered the dead beside the forge. The bodies were maimed to such a degree that some weren't even recognizable as human. There were twelve in all—fewer than I'd feared. Lowri, Betrys, and Arianwen worked silently with a handful of men to lay them out, to wash them in one last act of tenderness. Some had already been covered in shrouds of white linen.

"They have to burn the bodies," Emrys said quietly, pulling me toward the great hall. "To keep them from turning."

"They're supposed to be returned to the earth," I said, "so they can be reborn. That's what the Immortalities say."

"I know," came his soft reply. "I know."

The wounded numbered in the dozens. Most were up and walking, tending to the more critically injured, who were laid out on the long tables. Neve moved among them with water and bandages. Mari brought a basket of herbs and tools to Olwen, staying close to the healer's side as she bent over a man who'd lost the lower part of his leg.

Flea sat at Caitriona's head, as if to stand guard. She was still crying, stubbornly wiping tears away against her sleeve. She stroked Caitriona's blood-caked hair and bandaged cheek. It wasn't until Caitriona's eyes fluttered open that I knew for sure she was still alive.

The tenderness of the moment turned my lungs to stone. It seemed impossible that Caitriona could have been the one to bring this darkness to the isle, but I couldn't shake the sickening misgiving that her plans had been derailed by Cabell's transformation.

But she didn't kill him, I thought, *when she was completely capable of it.*

That meant something, didn't it?

Rhona and Seren had taken up positions on either side of the table. Rhona gripped one of Caitriona's hands, stroking it.

"You'll look a fair bit more ferocious now," Seren was telling her. "The scars will only enhance your magnificent glower."

"It will be simply tremendous," Rhona agreed.

"Like the heroes of old," Seren continued.

"And the greatest of Sir Bedivere's companions," Rhona finished.

"Will I . . . lose . . . the arm?" Caitriona rasped out.

"Olwen didn't think so," Rhona said, then paused.

"Tell me . . . all of . . . it . . . ," Caitriona said.

The raven-haired priestess sighed. "She cannot be sure you'll have the full use of it once it heals. Time will tell, as it does with all things."

Caitriona wheezed, her breath wet, considering this. It was Flea who looked up at our approach.

"Get out of here!" Flea snarled at me. "Ye do not belong and never 'ave!"

The focus of the room fell on me, the pressure gathering like a thundercloud from all sides. Emrys edged in closer at my side and Neve came to stand with us, smoothing her hands down the bloodied apron she wore. Tear tracks had dried in the soot and dust on her cheeks.

"Flea, enough," Seren chided.

"I . . ." Words abandoned me. I moved to stand beside Caitriona, but Rhona instinctively shifted, as if to block me.

Caitriona's hair streamed out on the table under her, having broken free from its usual tight braid. The entire right side of her face was covered in some sort of tincture and bloodied bandages that wrapped down the length of her throat and over her mauled shoulder. They'd stripped off her ruined armor to bind the shallow claw marks across her torso. Her eyes tracked my movement.

"I'm sorry," I told her, torment welling up in my chest until it was almost too tight to speak. "I'm so sorry."

"Is your brother . . . all right . . . ?" Caitriona asked.

"Don't do that," I said. "Be terrible to me, please. It's the only thing I can stand right now."

"Not . . . ," she managed. "Not . . . his . . . fault."

Her gaze shifted to Flea. The girl let out a huff, her bottom lip trembling as she cleaned the blood and dirt from Caitriona's silvery hair with a wet rag.

Neve drew close to kneel beside them. Some of the rigidity in Caitriona's body eased as she looked to Neve. The pale, freckled hand resting on her stomach curled.

"Thank you for saving my life," Neve told her. "You were so brave."

What was visible of Caitriona's pale skin flushed. All of us pretended not to see.

Caitriona squeezed Rhona's hand to get her attention.

"Her . . . wand . . . ," she said, the words failing as her mind drifted back toward unconsciousness. "Get it . . . for her . . ."

"Really?" Neve asked, looking between the two of them. "Are you sure? What's changed?"

Caitriona's eyes closed as she breathed out a single word. *"Everything."*

32

I don't know why I didn't tell anyone what had happened in the tunnel.

There were plenty of opportunities throughout the rest of the night and into the gray morning.

When I helped Mari scrub the blood off the tables and floors of the great hall.

When I passed Emrys, Deri, and the others trying to replant the section of the courtyard that had been ravaged by claws during the fight.

When I sat beside a near-catatonic Cabell and tried to get him to eat.

During the funerary rites for the dead, watching their bodies turn to ash and their souls release with the rising sparks.

Part of me insisted it was nothing more than a hallucination brought on by exhaustion and stress; another feared it was something worse. But until I could explain it to myself, I couldn't explain it to anyone.

That next morning, I found myself outside the bedchamber Emrys and Cabell shared, leaving the small carved bird balanced on the door's latch. Hours later, after the pulse of the tower had slowed with sleep, I made my way down to the great hall. Emrys was already there, perched on one of the long tables. For a moment, I just watched his strong hands work as he whittled.

He caught me staring and bit back a smile. I hoped the darkness covered my flush.

"Got your message," he said, putting his knife and the small piece of wood away. "What's going on?"

After shadowing Mari and helping her with her tasks, I'd gone to the library to help Neve research the curses. I should have relished the fact that I was getting to read texts that no one in the mortal realm had even heard of, but instead, I'd come to resent their uselessness.

"We have to get out of here," I begged him. "We have to find a way out of the tower and back to the portal."

"I know," he said, rubbing at his face. He looked haunted by his exhaustion.

"There's barely ten days of food left," I told him. "And the Children can attack again at any time!"

"I know," he said. "Tamsin, I know."

I sat beside him on the table, staring at the statue of the Goddess with a growing bitterness. It wasn't just that the situation was out of control—so was I. My emotions were spiraling again, and it was becoming harder to get a grip on them.

Emrys ran a hand through his chestnut hair. It was wilder than I'd ever seen it, unkempt and curling at the edges.

I liked it.

Reaching up, I plucked a small green leaf from the coarse strands, holding it up into the light of his head lamp.

"Sage," he said reflexively. "For colds and coughs, but also tasty in a stew."

I laughed despite myself.

He cocked his head, the corner of his lips quirking. "Am I growing on you, Bird?"

"Like one of your beloved weeds," I said.

But I hadn't pulled away, and neither had he, and both of us seemed to want to do anything other than acknowledge it. The serene darkness of the room, so sheltered from the outside world, made it all too easy to forget why we had come in the first place.

"What if we tried to catch the cloaked figure?" I asked, voice low. "Whoever it is. I think that's the only way anyone will believe us, and we can find out once and for all if they're actually controlling the Children."

He grinned. "You know me. Can't resist a good game, even if it's just hide-and-seek."

So that was what we did, scouring the tower and its outer walls until our bodies grew tired and we stole a few hours of sleep. The next morning, I woke to find the little bird at my door once more, and I placed it by Emrys's the next, that same message passing between us, the hope it carried as delicate as a feather. *Tonight? Tonight.*

There was an unexpected comfort to our explorations. Sometimes we whispered about things we had seen during our days: he'd update me on how the crops were faring, and I'd tell him something interesting I'd read while researching with Neve in the library. We even talked about past Hollower jobs.

Mostly, though, we shared an easy silence, the kind that didn't need to be filled with nervous chatter, or anything other than the knowledge that we weren't alone.

The rhythm of our days reminded me of being little and learning to swim. As the gray light faded each afternoon, we took one last deep breath before submerging into the dark and whatever it would bring. Dragging ourselves through the churning unknown of the resting hours until, finally, first light came and it was time to surface once more.

On our third night of searching, I arrived in the great hall earlier than I'd intended, and Emrys wasn't there.

There was only a smattering of wood shavings dusting the floor under his usual spot at the table. The scant trail led to the hidden door, carelessly left open a sliver.

He went ahead without me.

The thought left me hollow at my core. I didn't know why I was surprised, either. Emrys might have called a truce, but this wasn't a partnership. It never had been, and it never would be. Clearly, he'd found something he had no intention of sharing with me.

My thoughts sputtered in futile circles as I slipped inside and shut the door behind me.

I didn't have my flashlight, but I now knew my way down over the steps and roots well enough to navigate them. My eyes slowly adjusted to the darkness, but there was no need. Up ahead, the lone beam of Emrys's head lamp turned the corner.

I followed, my steps quick and light as I took each curve. Once or twice I was tempted to call out to him, to let him know he hadn't managed to pull a fast one on me, but each time I stopped myself.

More than anything, I wanted to know what he was doing down here alone. What he hadn't wanted me to see.

Rather than continue along the hallway to the storage chamber, Emrys turned to the corridor choked by roots. Turned, and stretched a trembling hand out toward them. And this time, instead of reaching back, the roots receded, inviting him into their depths.

He stepped through. The roots braided themselves together behind him.

A strangled noise escaped my throat as I rushed forward, contorting my body to push through them. Their rough skin slid against mine, squeezing in on all sides. The branching limbs wove around me, blocking the way forward. The sight of Emrys became smaller as the living wall closed between us, and for one terrifying moment, I thought the roots would crush me alive.

"Emrys!" I shouted.

A root slid around my throat and tightened—only to release. The roots cracked as they twisted and lifted away, revealing a shocked Emrys. I shot forward, colliding with him. He caught me with a gasp of surprise.

"What are you doing here?" he asked.

"What am I doing here?" I croaked, shoving him back. "What are *you* doing here? I thought we were—"

I couldn't get the words out, but they were there in my throat, aching. *I thought we were doing this together.*

He shook his head, and for the first time, I realized he looked dazed, the way he had the first night he'd brought me down into the passage. "I just . . . I heard something . . ."

"You always hear something, right?" I asked. "The Mother tree must be talking to you every second of every day."

"No," he said, gripping my arm again. Stilling me. "No, I heard a voice. A man's voice."

My lips pressed together in a tight line, and I cocked my head to the side, studying the deepening shadows beneath his eyes again. "Have you slept since we got here?"

Emrys said nothing, leading me forward. He put a hand out, and the roots that had knotted together in front of us fell to our feet and drew back, rattling over the stones.

The beam of his head lamp swept out. The floors and walls were scarred with burns and pocked with missing stones, as if some tremendous fight had blistered them. Ahead, the hall ended abruptly with a bulging mass of rough wood.

"Is that . . . ," I started to say.

"Part of the Mother tree?" Emrys finished, taking a step forward. "I think so."

Exchanging a quick look, we moved toward it. From the shadows, the raised edges of bark at its center began to take shape. Two hands, pressing out, as if desperate to escape. A twisted torso. What might have been a head.

"I've seen some creepy things in my day," I said. "This looks like it came out of their nightmares."

Emrys took another step forward.

And the being opened its eyes.

Flakes of bark fell to the ground as it—the creature, the monster, whatever *it* was—tried to turn to us. To open its mouth.

I gripped at Emrys's arm, drawing him back. He didn't move. He didn't seem to be breathing.

The creature's lips parted with a horrifying *snap,* and gleaming beetles spilled forth through the stringy sap. I pressed in closer to Emrys, watching in horror as the insects scattered around us.

"Who . . . comes . . . here . . . ?" the creature rasped. *"Who . . . seeks the knowledge . . . of the ages . . . ?"*

Neither of us spoke.

"One who seeks what must . . . remain . . . forgotten . . . ," it continued. *"And one whose heart . . . he has stolen . . ."*

I flushed with heat, taking a step away from Emrys. "No one has time for bullshit riddles."

"Who are you?" Emrys demanded.

"I am one of three . . . three who sleep . . . but do not dream . . . ," the creature continued, its terrifyingly human eyes fixing on me. *"One who dies but might yet live . . . one who lives but yearns to die . . . and one left behind, waiting . . ."*

"One left behind?" I repeated. "Are you talking about a sorceress? Or a druid?"

"When the paths turn to ice . . . when the world shakes and weeps blood . . . when the sun is devoured by darkness," it rasped, closing its eyes again, *"the worlds will sing of the coming, chains of death broken . . . new power born in blood . . ."*

In the dim light, Emrys went rigid. "What in hellfire is that supposed to mean?"

"When the sun is devoured by darkness . . ." The memory came whip-quick, a lash of sudden understanding. "Like what happened at Tintagel?"

And the reports of roads freezing in Britain before I'd ever left home.

"What do you mean by the chains of death being broken?" I asked.

"*She did this . . . ,*" the creature wheezed. "*She thought . . . to master death . . . but became its servant instead.*"

"Who?" I asked.

"*It is fate . . . ,*" it rasped, hardly above a whisper, "*but what is fate but an unwelcome bargain . . . with time . . . ?*"

The creature went still. Silent.

Emrys flew toward it, trying to wake it with touch. "Who are you? *What* are you?"

The roots rippled back across the floor, creaking and snapping in protest. I whirled around, only to find a shadowed figure there. They raised their candle closer to their face.

Bedivere.

"If we are to be answering questions," he said, "perhaps the two of you might tell me what it is you're doing down here?"

33

It took more than a moment for my heart to start beating normally again, but even then, I couldn't muster a good lie.

"We heard a voice and followed it," Emrys said smoothly.

Good. That was good. And technically true.

The knight crossed his arms over his chest. "I suppose it has nothing to do with your nightly excursions scurrying about the tower while everyone else is asleep? Do not insult me with falsehoods—your own brother told me it was so."

Your own brother told me. The words were like a knife between the ribs. My hands curled into fists at my side. Cabell would have no reason to tell him that. To betray our confidence.

"Are you looking for a way out of the tower as he said?" Bedivere asked. It might have been the shadows of the tunnel, but there was an ugliness to his expression then, as if he was revolted by us. Our cowardice.

Disbelief stole through me.

Cabell did tell him. I hadn't realized they were close enough for that.

"Hello?" a voice called down the tunnel. "Who's there?"

"'Tis Bedivere, my lady Olwen," Bedivere called back.

The priestess appeared a moment later, carefully stepping through the labyrinth of roots. Her gaze moved between our faces, taking quick measure of the situation as always. "I saw that the doorway was open . . . What is amiss?"

"I came upon our guests skulking where they shouldn't, and was about to hear their explanation for it," Bedivere said.

Olwen drew in a deep sigh. "I'll take care of this, then. Thank you, Sir Bedivere."

"My dear—" he said in protest.

She held up a hand. "It's all right. They mean no harm, and I'm sure you're missed on watch."

The old knight wavered, but eventually nodded and turned back the way Olwen had just come. The priestess waited for the sound of his steps to fade before speaking.

"Now," she said, putting her hands on her hips. "What in the Great Mother's name do you think you're doing?"

In the end, we told her everything.

I hadn't meant to, and I didn't think Emrys had either. But the longer the look of betrayal remained on Olwen's face, the more desperate we became to find the right detail to erase it.

"So I'm to believe," she said, "that the two of you suspected someone—possibly Caitriona—created the Children of the Night, and neither of you thought to tell a soul about it?"

"We told Neve and Cabell," I offered weakly.

Olwen shook her head and pulled a torch off the wall behind her. "Come with me, you jobbernowls."

She led us down the tunnel path. The roots that had covered the ground pulled back at her disapproving *tsk* of the tongue, retreating like scolded puppies.

"*That,*" she said, gesturing back toward the tangle of roots, "was Merlin you were speaking to."

"Merlin?" I echoed, wondering why I was so shocked. "But I thought . . . wasn't he a druid? Why wasn't he killed with the others during the Forsaking?"

"Oh, they certainly tried," Olwen said, picking up her pace. "He was once the most powerful of that lot, always with the most pressing prophecies and wisdom, generously shared. He dueled with Morgan, and before she could kill him, he joined his body to the Mother tree to ensure his survival, knowing she would never cause it harm."

"He seemed . . ." Emrys searched for the right word.

"The magic has gone somewhat feral in the years since he became one with the tree," Olwen said. "And most of what he speaks now is mindless babble. Don't let it trouble you."

"But he said there were three like him," I pressed. "Three who sleep. I think he was referring to himself, and then there's King Arthur suspended between life and death, but who's the third?"

"We would know if there was another enchanted sleeper on the isle," Olwen said. "As I said, the thinking part of him vanished centuries ago. He stirs restless dreams into nonsense. *Chains of death* are a recurring theme, and the story changes with each telling."

I drew in a deep breath, looking to Emrys. He seemed satisfied with Olwen's explanation, but I wasn't.

"He rambled on about a *she* trying to master death but becoming its servant instead," I said. "Couldn't that be the person behind the curse on Avalon? Why are you so sure it isn't Caitriona?"

"Oh, you wee fools," Olwen said, shaking her head. "Follow me."

Rather than bring us back to the great hall, Olwen drew us down the familiar path to the chamber of abandoned objects. She muttered something to herself, shaking her head, as she pushed the massive doors open.

When we reached the hidden doorway to the bone room, she whirled around, giving us both a hard look.

"Know that I would never show you this for any other reason than to prove my sister's innocence," she said. "And if I hear a whisper of you repeating this, it'll be hemlock tea for the both of you."

As she turned to press on the white stones, Emrys leaned over to me. "Hemlock is—"

"—a poisonous plant," I finished. "Yeah. Threat received."

The stones pulled back, allowing us passage up the stairs. We climbed in silence until, as we reached the last steps, we heard it.

A song.

Intoned by a rough, despairing voice—one that begged as much as sang. The hair on my arms rose at the breaking words, the sobbing that turned the Goddess's language from a prayer to a lament.

Beside me, Emrys's Adam's apple bobbed as he struggled to swallow. The rawness of Caitriona's emotion was unbearable. Olwen stood on the step beneath us, blocking any instinct I had to turn away from it.

Hear this, her eyes said. *Witness it.*

After a few moments more, she relented. We followed her down the steps and into the chamber beyond.

"Caitriona comes every night she is able to in her role as High Priestess to give the Moonlight Prayer, which thanks the Goddess for her blessings and asks for protection in the coming day," Olwen said. "You have found the inner sanctuary of the tower. Secret to all but the Nine—and now, it seems, the two of you and Neve."

"It'll stay secret," Emrys promised.

"I know that Cait may seem as unbending as her blade—that when she speaks to you, she cuts to the heart, rather than using pretty words to soften the blow," Olwen said. "But I beg you to understand her position. She feels the burden of responsibility for our way of life, and all of it is slipping away, no matter how hard she fights to save it. She blames every death on her own failings."

Guilt left a sour taste on my tongue. I wondered if it was the same every night she came here—if this was the only place she allowed her pain to show. I'd thought they were in denial about what was happening to them, that it was a sign of their weakness, but the strength it must have taken to just make it through each day without shattering was almost unthinkable.

"What about the sculptures?" Emrys asked. "And the cauldron and the cages?"

The stones pulled themselves open behind us and Caitriona emerged, lifting her hood with her uninjured left hand. She stopped at the sight of us, and her entire being seemed to tense as if preparing for a fight.

"We've had some curious mice running through the underpaths," Olwen told her.

"It was you that night, wasn't it?" Caitriona asked, her voice hoarse. "I knew I smelled smoke. There are some secrets that are not meant for you. You had no right coming here!"

"We had every right when we—correctly, I might add—assumed you were keeping things from us," I said.

"You question our honor?" Caitriona asked.

"No one doubts your honor, or your honesty, but they have seen everything," Olwen said. "All of it. And even you must acknowledge how dark it might appear to the uninitiated."

Caitriona drew in a wheezing breath, clearly resigned. "Do you still have it in the infirmary?"

"Yes," Olwen said. "I've yet to finish with it."

"*It?*" Emrys asked, looking between them.

Caitriona started toward the great oak doors. "Come along and I'll explain."

As it happened, we weren't the only ones who wanted a word with Olwen. Neve was already there, pacing the short length of the infirmary. A large tome, *Rituals of the Realm,* sat beside the small rack of bottles and vials on Olwen's worktable. Candles flickered around her, tracking the shifts in the swirling air.

At the moan of the door opening, Neve pounced. "Olwen, why didn't you—wait, what's going on?"

"A good evening to you as well, Neve," Olwen said dryly. "How fortuitous you're already here."

Neve looked between Emrys and me, but her surprise was reserved for Caitriona, who shut the door firmly behind her.

"Come out, Flea," Caitriona said.

Neve jumped as the girl crawled out from beneath the lower shelves.

"How long have you been there?" Neve asked, clutching her chest.

"Long enough to hear you muttering and fluffing up your courage like a goose," Flea said. She glowered at the older priestess. "No way ye saw me, Cait!"

"No, in truth, I did not," Caitriona said. "But Betrys complained to me that one of her prayer stones vanished, which happened to co-incide with you disappearing from your lesson with her."

The girl stuck out her lower lip, crossing her arms over her chest. "Wasn't me."

"Must we do this every night, Flea?" Caitriona asked, some of her exhaustion breaking through to the surface.

"Only 'cause ye make me," Flea countered.

"Empty your pockets and prove that your word is good," Caitriona said.

The girl only hung her head, sulking. "I'll give it back."

"Thank you," Caitriona said. "Please do so now and apologize to her. This is not a courteous way to treat anyone, let alone your sister."

"But—" the girl protested.

"*Now,* Flea," Caitriona said, opening the door for her.

Flea sent one last look my way, some smugness slipping into her smile, but did as she was told. Caitriona locked the door behind her, her shoulders slumping as she leaned back against it.

"I know what I'm doing here," Neve said, looking at each of us in turn. "But what are the rest of you doing?"

"We're about to get an overdue explanation," I said, taking a seat on the edge of the worktable.

"So you finally got caught snooping around?" Neve said.

"That would be the negative spin on the events of this evening, yes," Emrys said.

"Where would you like me to begin?" Olwen asked. "Perhaps with the bone sculptures, as you called them?"

"Fine by me," I said.

Olwen crouched, lifting the curtain of fraying fabric that covered her lower shelves. She retrieved a basket and set it down on the table next to me. Inside, wrapped in layers of linen, was one of the sculptures.

An inverted skull formed the base of this one, with an array of long, thin bones fanning out around it like the petals of a great and terrible flower. Neve gasped at the sight of it, and it was impossible to tell if what she felt was surprise or delight. She leaned forward, studying the etchings.

"If I may?" Caitriona asked quietly.

Neve stepped back, allowing Caitriona to lift the sculpture and place it on a wooden pedestal covered in wax drippings. Olwen handed her a small candle, which Caitriona carefully placed inside. The wick flared as she passed a hand over it.

She ran her fingers along the edge of the pedestal and a trail of mist appeared, wrapping around it, spinning its top. The flame inside the bone flickered wildly, casting fluttering shadows and glowing sigils on the walls.

"Our memories dwell in our minds, yes, but also in our blood, and in our bones," Olwen said. "Upon the death of an elder druid, a vessel like this would be made of his bones, so that his memories could be preserved and consulted for the ages to come. After it is shaped and carved, it is placed inside the cauldron you saw so that it can be imbued with more memory and magic. This is the vessel of our High Priestess Viviane."

"It was made by the last descendant of the druids to learn the craft," Caitriona added. "And by the Great Mother's mercy, he taught us how to use it only days before he himself was killed."

I turned, trying to take in the sigils as they streamed around us. "The symbols . . . they're different than the sigils used by sorceresses. What do they mean?"

"Alas, I haven't the slightest idea. It is the language of magic used by the druids," Olwen said. "They brought it and the cauldron here when they left the mortal world."

"Do the bones in the sculptures belong to druids, then?" I asked.

"Yes," Caitriona said. "We've kept them because they hold important memories of both the isle and your world."

"But Viviane's is the only vessel belonging to a priestess," Emrys clarified.

"Yes," Olwen said, her eyes soft as she looked to it. "It is not as elaborate as the other vessels, because I feared preserving more of her bones might be enough to transform this—her mortal remains—into one of the Children."

Neve leaned over the vessel, her shadow intruding on the flickering lights. "How does a vessel work?"

Olwen answered with another question. "What would you like to ask Viviane about her lifetime?"

"I don't know . . . how she became High Priestess?" Neve said.

"Close your eyes," Olwen instructed. "All of you."

As we did, a deep humming emerged from her, becoming a language I'd never heard before. It was a low, guttural tone that seemed to emerge from deep in the ancient earth, rather than one girl's throat. A shiver passed through me as an image painted itself in my mind.

A young girl, as fair as moonlight, woke from her bed as if in a trance, singing a song of her own. The image of her shimmered with milky brightness as she passed her sleeping parents and moved toward the waiting door. Outside, an emerald forest waited, the trees bowing to her—

My eyes snapped open as I gasped. Emrys and Neve stayed in the memory a moment longer before joining me in the present moment.

"We refer to witnessing a memory as *echoing*," Olwen explained. "And though many of our rites are recorded in the written word, we sometimes consult the past through memory."

"I'm guessing you've already asked the vessel to show memories of a possible curse on the land?" Neve said.

"I have examined all of her memories around the time of the Forsaking," Olwen said. "I have also searched her memories of Morgan to no avail. She was the one who led the rising against the druids, and I thought she might have shared something about the druids' magic with Viviane."

"Anything Morgan might have known died with her," Caitriona snorted. "She truly turned her back on the Goddess and her sisters."

"She's a hero for stopping the druids from taking over Avalon," Neve shot back. "She should be remembered for that."

"Please," Olwen interrupted, holding up her hands between them. "Let me finish."

Caitriona and Neve looked to opposite ends of the infirmary, mirrors of each other.

"After she nearly destroyed Merlin, Morgan was killed by another druid in the final battle," Olwen said. "She died in the arms of Viviane. Our High Priestess never truly recovered from that terrible day—she and Morgan were lovers, you see."

I nodded. Dark magic had been born from lesser horrors.

"Our problem now," Olwen continued, "is that the vessel is missing several years of memories, including the battle between the sorceresses and druids. The last memory we have before it is an argument she had with Morgan."

Olwen stopped the spinning pedestal with her hand and blew out the candle inside. After removing it and setting it aside, she carefully turned the vessel upside down. There was a jagged hole at the bottom of the skull that had been partly plugged by the candle's wax.

"When did this happen?" Neve asked.

"Impossible to say, really," Olwen said. "I only know it's been like this since our first attempts at echoing with it."

"Just as it would be impossible to say if it was damaged accidentally by the now-dead person who created it, or on purpose by someone who didn't want those memories revisited," I said.

The others looked at me with varying degrees of alarm.

"Please don't tell me I'm the only one who had that thought," I said. "Merlin mentioned a *she* who tried to master death, which feels like a riddle-me-this way of saying someone tried to learn the death magic of the druids. Caitriona may not be the one controlling the Children—"

The priestess's entire being seemed to swell with outrage. "You thought *I* was controlling them?"

"We did," I confirmed.

"Sorry," Emrys added.

"I didn't," Neve offered.

Caitriona's eyes flashed over to her, then away just as quickly. She shook her head, forcing herself to draw in a deep breath.

"Again, I must tell you, Merlin is little more than a wagging tongue," Olwen said. "He may be referring to Morgan, as she ultimately did die in her attempt to defeat the druids."

"The vessel's final memory of that dark time is of High Priestess Viviane telling Morgan that there's no magic stronger than that of death," Caitriona said, turning to address Neve. "While you may think her a coward, Viviane truly believed in her heart that confronting the druids would be a losing battle."

"Then how did they prevail?" Emrys asked, circling around to look at the vessel closely again. "How did the future sorceresses defeat the druids so soundly?"

"We can't say for certain," Olwen said. "When it came to it, the sorceresses overpowered their greater numbers with ease, as if the druids couldn't draw upon their death magic quickly enough to repel them. That, or it was merely the force of these women's rage."

"A truly powerful force," Emrys said. At my look, he added, "What? I'm being serious."

"I have another question," Neve said. "As you heard, Tamsin and Emrys believe that the Children are being controlled by someone still alive in Avalon. It couldn't be that Merlin is the one who created the Children . . . right?"

"No," Caitriona said. "The Mother tree's grip is too powerful to be overcome by a weak man."

"But we saw a druid symbol—" I protested.

"If you are referring to the cages in the underpath, I assure you, there is an explanation for that as well," Olwen said. "One far less sinister than you seem to believe."

"Try me," I said.

"The first of the Children were captured and kept out of sight to avoid causing unnecessary fear," Caitriona said. "High Priestess Viviane tried, with every scrap of knowledge she possessed, to transform them back into the people they had once been."

Emrys crossed his arms over his chest. "Why would she try to sever their souls from their bodies?"

"When Viviane understood that our magic was incapable of transforming them back to their original forms," Caitriona said, her posture turning defensive, "she called upon what she knew of the druids' death magic to release their souls from their monstrous confines and return them to the Goddess."

That may be what she told you, I thought, *but it doesn't make it true.*

"And you're certain the missing piece of the skull isn't buried with the rest of her?" Neve asked.

"No," Caitriona said. "When she was . . . when she—" She made herself take in a deep breath and look up at us. "When Viviane was killed, we were forced to burn her body so she would not become one of the Children."

The grief on Olwen's face was staggering; the pain of the High Priestess's death would have cut like a serrated blade to the heart, aggravated by the need to burn her body, rather than bury it in the soil to meet her Goddess and begin life anew.

In the eyes of the Nine, High Priestess Viviane's entire being had been destroyed, and the isle would never know her soul again.

"I know Olwen explained that blood can hold memory," I said to Caitriona, "and what I saw you doing in the bone room makes sense now, but if no one can make a vessel, why are you cutting your hand and bleeding into a big creepy pot each night?"

She seemed less sure of herself than usual when she answered. "I believe another vessel maker will come, born with the sacred knowledge whispered in their mind. The cauldron will keep my knowledge until the day my own vessel may be prepared, and what we have faced will not be forgotten."

"Here's what I still don't understand, though." I licked at my chapped lips in thought. "You were so certain the sorceresses were behind the curse. It really never occurred to you that the druids might be to blame when you were dripping your blood into a swirling vat of silver the exact same color as the Children's bones?"

Caitriona bristled at that. "There's no silver in the cauldron."

"Did you forget the part where Emrys and I saw it with our own eyes?" I asked her.

Olwen's brow wrinkled. "No, Tamsin, Cait is correct. The contents of the cauldron, if there are any, are unseen to the eye. Even our blood disappears into its darkness."

Alarm rang out in my mind, trilling down the length of my spine. The worktable creaked beneath me as I shifted, looking to Emrys.

"It wasn't empty," he confirmed, moving to stand beside me. His words and his nearness steadied me in a way I hadn't expected. "The liquid inside it was silver, as if piles of it had been melted down."

Caitriona and Olwen shared a look. Something silent passed between them.

"You both must have been exhausted," Neve said. "And you were already upset and confused about the vessels . . ."

"We did *not* experience a shared hallucination," I told her. "I know what I saw—in fact, I have proof."

I undid the latches on my workbag and retrieved Ignatius inside his silk wrappings. I unwound the strips around the handle and thrust it out for them to see.

But the iron was as black as it had ever been.

"I don't . . ." The words drifted away with my certainty. "I don't understand . . . I dipped this into the cauldron. It came away silver." I looked between the others, feeling strangely desperate for them to believe me. "It was *silver*."

Emrys gripped my wrist, drawing my eyes to his. The belief in them gave me something to anchor myself to. "I know what we saw."

"You are welcome to join me tomorrow so I can convince you otherwise," Caitriona said.

"Then I'll go too," Neve said. "Neither Tamsin nor Emrys would lie about something as important as this."

Caitriona bowed her head. "If you wish."

"That's what we were doing here," I said, turning back to Neve. "Now, why were you waiting for Olwen?"

"Because I had a question of my own," Neve said, retrieving the book she'd left on the table. "Why haven't you attempted a ritual cleansing of the isle?"

Caitriona's lips parted, but she was interrupted by a shuffling sound outside the infirmary door. Olwen quickly bundled the vessel away into its basket, and when it was out of sight, Caitriona opened the door.

Bedivere stood a short distance away, scratching at his gray beard. For the first time since I'd met him, he looked indecisive.

"Sir Bedivere," Caitriona said. "What's amiss?"

"Ah, I'm sorry, I let my worry get the best of me," he said. "I only wondered if the interlopers needed escorting back to their rooms to put an end to the evening's wanderings."

Caitriona gave a faint smile. "You are too kind, but we have the situation in hand."

"Come in," Olwen urged him. "This conversation affects you as well, and we've need of your wisdom."

My grip on the table tightened, just a little bit, as the old knight entered. Emrys strayed closer to me, his hand warm and soothing as it moved over my shoulder and ghosted down the ridge of my spine.

"Neve was just asking why we haven't tried a ritual cleansing of the isle," Olwen supplied.

The knight made a slow lap around the room as she spoke, stopping abruptly when she mentioned the ritual. I couldn't see his face but could feel the burn of his eyes behind me.

"Yes," Caitriona said, staring at Olwen. "And what a remarkable coincidence that the book describing the ritual found its way back to the library, where anyone might have stumbled upon it."

"Indeed," Olwen said serenely. "Truly remarkable are the workings of the Goddess."

"And the scheming of Olwen," Caitriona muttered.

"What does the ritual do?" Emrys asked.

Neve opened the heavy book to a page marked with ribbon. "*When dark power stains the land and hope retreats from shadow*—sounds like a place we're all acquainted with, doesn't it?"

"It's painting a familiar picture, yes," I said.

"*The isle must be restored through the invocation of the maiden, young and blooming, waking that greater power which ever slumbers in the mists,*" Neve read. "*Only Her renewal shall drive out all that is cursed and ailing within the soil and those who walk upon it, for there is no power greater than rebirth.*"

My pulse stammered in my veins.

"Is that saying what I think it is?" I croaked out.

"Yes." Neve met my gaze, determination blazing in her eyes. "This ritual wouldn't just heal the land—it would break every curse within it."

34

Every curse.

Not just the one upon the land and the Children of the Night. Every curse.

Even Cabell's.

Neve must have seen those thoughts play out over my face, because she nodded, fueling my hope. Bedivere came around the worktable to face us, his expression inscrutable.

"It seems to be saying that the isle has to be purified through a kind of rebirth," Neve said. *"This ritual summons the Goddess back to the isle to restore it to a new cycle of life."*

She and Emrys blurred at the edges of my vision as I looked from Olwen to Caitriona. A burning desperation rose in me again, and I didn't fight it. I was beyond caring. "Why haven't you done it, then?"

Olwen was uncharacteristically silent, her face turned toward the window of her infirmary.

"Neve has not told you what is required for the ritual," Caitriona said.

The attention of the room swung back toward the sorceress. Neve glanced at Caitriona before reading aloud. *"Join hands with your Sisters, and be whole of heart and power once more. Await the full blessings of the moon to bring forth Her three gifts entrusted to you, and cleave yourself to Her anew with blood and mist."*

She looked up as she finished, brows lowered in thought.

"What did this person have against writing clear instructions?" Emrys asked.

"Viviane transcribed the messages of the Goddess that came to her in dreams," Olwen explained.

"But when you break it down, it all seems doable," Neve said, turning to Caitriona. "The incantation is here in the book, and you must know what she means by the 'three gifts.' What's the problem here?"

"We are not whole of power," Caitriona said. "We need nine sisters to attempt the ceremony."

Neve's face went ashen as she understood what I didn't. "And while Flea was called by the Goddess, she hasn't come into her magic yet. That's why your High Priestess lived so long, isn't it? Why the magic of her vow wouldn't allow her to pass into her next life?"

"We will not be whole of power until then, whether it be days or years," Caitriona said. "It weighs heavily on Flea's heart, but it is not her fault. And we lack one of the three gifts besides."

Neve tilted her head in question.

"The wand and chalice are with us, but the athame, our ritual knife, was lost many years ago and no amount of searching has brought it back."

Bedivere drew in a harsh breath, but said nothing. He fiddled with a pair of shears hanging from a hook on the wall. My gaze lingered on him. If it had been anyone other than the chivalrous knight, I would have called the flicker of emotion that crossed his face guilt.

"Couldn't a new athame be made in the forge?" Neve asked.

Caitriona and Olwen looked horrified at the thought.

"Why not just see what happens?" Emrys asked. "What do you have to lose at this point?"

"Please . . . ," I breathed out, the sting of hope, the lance of knowing better, almost stealing the words from me.

"It will not work," Caitriona said. "We have not been successful in any other ritual since our ranks were diminished—not in blessing the earth, nor clearing the skies, nor freeing the souls trapped within the Children. We are eight, not nine. Until Flea comes into her power, we are not whole."

Neve made a small noise of frustration, shaking her head.

"Well, you could wait years for that to happen, or you could, you know, hold your nose and ask the sorceress standing right in front of you for help," Neve said.

I heard myself gasp, but I wasn't the only one. Caitriona sat heavily on the edge of the table, her face tightening with unspoken emotion.

"Before there were only nine priestesses left in Avalon, there were many," Neve continued. "I'm descended from one."

Bedivere lifted his head again, turning to the priestesses. Olwen bit her lip, as if to force herself to stay silent as she looked to Caitriona. The words she'd spoken on the night of our arrival rose in my mind: *If I am absolutely certain of anything, it is this: the Goddess led you here to us. All of you.*

Caitriona's long silver braid glittered in the firelight as she turned to her sister.

"You and the others have fought me every step of the way, and it"—she drew in a choking breath—"it is . . . not easy to stand against you all alone and feel as if I am difficult—and to be resented . . . to be *hated* for it. I only know what our High Priestess taught me, and she—if I cannot do what she asked of me, then I have failed her."

"No, my dear heart." Olwen dropped to her knees in front of Caitriona and gripped her hands. "Never think that. You are our sister. Even when there is nothing left of this world, our love for you will still remain, because there is no power capable of destroying it."

"I have disappointed you all," Caitriona said desolately.

"Never," Bedivere swore, pressing his hand to his chest. "Nothing could be further from the truth."

"It is as the High Priestess said," Olwen told her. "*Only deep roots survive harsh winds,* and you have kept us steady these last years. We only ever wanted you to see our perspective—that it may be time to open ourselves, and the isle, to a new season, with new ways. The Goddess will meet us there."

"There is only the way that is written," Caitriona said. "And the rituals require priestesses to be pure of heart and intention because we are asking the Goddess to use her more powerful magic on our behalf. I don't doubt Neve's power, but the High Priestess said that the magic practiced by sorceresses poisons their souls."

"How dare you—" I began.

Neve put her hand on my shoulder, giving it a squeeze to cut me off. The hurt had vanished from her face, leaving only deep resolve.

"The Goddess will be my judge," Neve said, "not a High Priestess who never laid eyes on me. Not even Caitriona of the Nine."

"Cait," Olwen started again. "I know the war in your heart, and that you only wish to respect our ancestors and honor the Goddess. But if we do not do what we must to survive, the old ways will not merely cease to exist, they will pass from memory forever. If Neve is willing, there can be no harm in trying."

"There is harm if it fails," Caitriona rasped out. "For then we will truly be without hope."

"No, my lady Cait," Bedivere said. "We will know we have fought with all our might, and there is only honor in that."

For a long while, they listened to the crackle of the fire in the hearth and the howling of the creatures in the dead forest.

Emrys was lost in his own thoughts. He finally sat on the table beside me, bracing a hand near my hip. The weight of his shoulder pressing into mine was like a ballast against Caitriona's words. Unconsciously, his little finger began to stroke my thigh, the feather-light touch turning the skin beneath the fabric hot. Something in me shifted as I realized I wasn't the only one craving the comfort of touch. The need to feel anchored to something—someone.

"All right," Caitriona said at last, bowing her head. "We shall try and see if the Goddess will recognize Neve as her own. And if it should come to naught, then may we be forgiven."

Olwen broke out into a smile, sharing a look of relief with Neve.

Caitriona struggled to rise from the table, accepting the arm Olwen offered. "I will speak to Lowri and the others, then. We will search for something suitable to forge the new athame."

"You need to explain it to Flea first," I heard myself say.

They turned to me, surprised.

I swallowed. "It'll hurt her if she feels like she's not needed."

If she feels useless.

Caitriona hovered in the doorway, giving me a long look of what might have been approval. "Yes. I will speak to her."

Olwen ushered the rest of us out with her. "Until then, no more lurking about. Rest. All of you. By morning, the way—the new way—will be clear."

I trailed behind the others as we walked toward the tower, trying to work through everything I'd learned. Bedivere wrapped an arm around Caitriona's shoulder, saying something I couldn't quite make out about resting. Ahead, Deri was still at work patching and pruning the Mother tree. Emrys stopped to speak to him, pointing out something I couldn't see.

"Meeting without me?"

I startled at Cabell's voice cutting through the darkness. I turned, searching for him among the shadows, only to find him leaning against the rickety fencing of the training area.

"There you are," I said. "I tried to find you earlier. Where were you?"

His arms crossed as I came toward him, and there was a hardness to his expression I hoped was the night playing tricks on my eyes.

"You think people really want to see me wandering around after what happened?"

I knew the sting in his question wasn't aimed at me, but I still flinched. His words from the stables twisted like a knife in my chest. *You promised.*

"They know it's not your fault," I said. "It was the curse."

"Yeah," he said, looking down. "I'm sure."

I hopped up onto the fence beside him, turning to face the tower. "Were you with Bedivere? Did you ask him if the stories about Arthur going to Annwn were true?"

"Oh, are we still working together on this?" he said. "Mind filling me in on whatever your midnight meeting was about first?"

"Yeah," I said, remembering my shock from earlier. "After you tell me why you ratted me out to Bedivere for searching the under-paths."

"It made me feel bad to keep lying to him when he was helping me," Cabell said sharply. "And answering the questions *you* wanted answered. Maybe if you'd ever thought to tell me what was going on, I would have given you a heads-up."

I released a soft breath.

He was right to be upset. I should have tried to find him, to make sure he was aware of all the pieces of this story finally shifting into place. I would have been hurt too.

"I'm sorry," I said. "Tonight happened so fast, and I wasn't thinking. Your sister can be an idiot sometimes too, you know."

"Runs in the family, of course." Some of the stiffness in his posture eased. "What happened, though?"

He stared down at his boots as I recounted the story, only nodding now and then, as if he'd suspected some of it himself. I wondered at that, but worried more about his utter lack of reaction to hearing about the ritual.

"What do you think?" I asked him. "If Neve can help them pull it off, it could be the answer to everything. It could fix you once and for all—it could make everything right."

"Fix me." His lips pressed into a bloodless line. "Yeah."

I opened my mouth to clarify what I meant, but backed off when I saw the way his shoulders hunched. I really was an idiot—it was way too soon after losing the trail of the ring and enduring another trans-formation to try to lift his spirits. There were only so many times you could get your hopes up.

"You really think a *sorceress* could perform the ritual?" he asked. "Their magic is as treacherous as they are."

For a moment, I was speechless. "We're talking about Neve here. Neve, who loves cat drawings and fungi and learning and created a spell of pure light. Why would you say that?"

Cabell blew out a hard breath through his nose. "You're right. Neve is different. I just keep thinking . . . the sorceresses are responsible for all of this. None of this would have happened without them killing the druids."

Including, my mind filled in, *Nash's death.*

I bit my lip until I tasted blood. "Cab . . . do you want to go back home? We can leave all of this behind. I'd do it in a heartbeat for you."

He didn't respond. The leather of Nash's old jacket creaked as his arms tightened over his chest, and his fists clenched in the material.

"Do you remember," he said after a while, "that night in the Black Forest when Nash put on a whole shadow play retelling the story of King Arthur's final battle?"

I laughed despite myself. "God, he had the most horrible sound effects for the battle. His dying-Arthur voice was pretty dismal, too."

Cabell hummed in agreement.

It was a rare telling of the Battle of Camlann; Nash had never liked endings, especially when his heroes died. After Arthur had left to fight on the Continent, his nephew Mordred usurped the throne, forcing his return to Britain. The battle mortally injured Arthur and killed nearly all of the remaining knights. Only Bedivere was left to accompany the dying king to Avalon.

I rubbed at my arms, trying to ward off a chill. The Children, at least, were quieter now that the brief daylight was coming.

"What made you think of that?" I asked.

"Being around Bedivere, I guess. Wondering how much of the story is true, and how much strength it took for Bedivere to stay here all these years." Cabell swallowed. "Do you think Nash regretted his choice to look for the ring?"

"Nash never regretted anything in his life," I reminded him.

"That's not true," Cabell said. "He always regretted leaving you that morning. When the White Lady called out to you. I've never seen him so scared."

The mark over my heart ached, burning with its own cold, as if to answer.

"I've been thinking a lot about Nash," I admitted. "Not that I want to, but I feel his presence."

"Yeah?"

"Mostly the stories he told us," I said. "It's weird, isn't it? It's almost like they've all come alive now that we're here."

Cabell considered that. Then, catching my shiver, pulled off Nash's jacket and draped it over my shoulders.

"Thanks," I said. "Are you sure you don't need it?"

"I like the cold," he said. "It helps clear my mind."

I pulled the jacket tighter around me, wishing I had thought to put on my flannel coat before meeting Emrys.

"Do you think Olwen could be right, and we were supposed to come here?" Cabell asked quietly. "That Nash told us all those stories for a reason?"

"I think he told us partly to explain the relics we were looking for," I said, "but mostly to amuse himself."

Cabell looked down at the silver rings on his hands.

"I mean . . . maybe?" I offered. "Maybe there is more to all of this. Like with all of the stories that had so many variations, we can choose which version we want to believe."

"And which version of ourselves," he said.

"Yeah, I suppose," I said. "What is it you want to believe about yourself, Cab?"

He didn't answer.

"Sometimes I envy your memory," he told me then. "Because it's a place where nothing dies."

"Your story isn't finished yet, Cab," I promised him.

"Maybe," he said. "But whatever happens, at least you can find me there."

35

The dance of flame was as terrifying as it was hypnotic.

In the lean times between paying jobs, Nash had us camp out under the stars. Long after I was meant to be sleeping, I would lie awake and watch the campfire thrash and flicker. I'd try to count the sparks as they rose through the darkness, fading like stars in the morning. And when the flames finally subsided to smoldering ash, I'd sleep.

Tonight, by the time I'd made it back to our chamber, Neve was deep asleep, sprawled out on the mattress. Eventually, I gave up on trying to follow her lead and climbed out of bed. I paced as if I could shake the thoughts loose that way.

When that didn't work, I settled into the chair in front of the hearth and found my way back to my own ritual, nudging the salamander stones together to create a small fire. Crossing my legs, I propped my elbow against my knee and my chin against my palm. The flames rose from the cold stones, golden bright.

I let thoughts stream through my mind without trying to grasp any of them. Old memories of vaults and primordial forests. Cabell and me in the library. My knife slicing Septimus moments before he was torn apart. The Children rising from the mists. The gleaming bottles in Olwen's infirmary. The hound racing toward Caitriona. The white rose. Nash's yellowed bones . . .

It was the last image that lingered long after the others had settled.

That picture of quiet, anonymous death after such a loud and infamous life.

For the first time since he'd vanished, the thought of Nash didn't bring anger. It only brought an aching at my core. Regret.

Let the dead die, Tamsy, he told me once. *It's only memory that truly pains us, and they release it when they go.*

Nash's memories had come in song, in fireside stories, over the clink of pints, but they were silent now, and always would be. Unlike the sorceresses and the priestesses, who strove to crystallize their memories, who refused to let their lives be forgotten, he would have welcomed the unburdening. He'd always been selfish like that.

Let the dead die.

And any memory of my parents along with him.

My eyelids grew heavy. I didn't fight the insistent pull of exhaustion.

The air turned to dark water around me as my mind sank deeper and deeper into unconsciousness. Flurries of bubbles streamed toward the retreating light at the surface until, finally, I reached a soft bed of earth. Silvery shells rose as the dirt dissolved beneath me, pearly and sinister.

Not shells. Bones.

I tried to scream, but water filled my mouth and lungs. I pushed away, but they were everywhere, shivering and clattering as they started to assemble themselves. Their pieces fitting together into monstrous forms that crawled forward, grasping at my legs.

My fingers brushed ice beneath the silt and I gripped it, tearing it free.

A sword. In my hand, the blade blazed with blue fire, the fire that burned in the hearts of stars. It roiled the water until it became a barrier of light against the shadowed world.

I surfaced from the dream, my lungs burning with a harsh gasp.

Clutching at my head, I squeezed my eyes shut, trying to stop the dizzying spin of the room before I vomited.

A soft knock sounded at the door. I looked up, bracing myself—uncertain if the dream still had me in its grip.

Neve sighed softly in sleep behind me. I looked around, taking in the familiar sight of the room with growing composure. Real. This was real.

There was another knock, as faint as the first.

I forced myself onto unsteady legs and went to unlatch the door.

Bedivere stood in the darkness, clutching a lantern. He had dressed fully in armor—far more than he wore while on watch—and had a sword at his side.

"What's wrong?" I whispered, stepping into the hall and shutting the door behind me. "Is it Cabell?"

He inclined his head toward the stairs and I followed, surprised at how quietly he moved, despite the metal that covered his body.

"I am sorry to have woken you," he said, his voice low. "I would not come to you except in grave need. I must ask you to do something for me."

"I don't like the sound of 'grave need,' " I whispered.

He let out a soft breath that might have been a laugh in any other circumstance. "I long to believe the ritual could save the isle."

"What do you mean?" I asked, my pulse jumping. "How do you know it can't?"

"High Priestess Viviane," he said. "She came to visit me when I lived away from the tower, keeping watch over my king. In that time, she told me of the need for rituals to be performed as written. They are commands from the Goddess, and must be followed, or else they are doomed to fail."

My hands felt numb with the cold. With dread.

"So . . . what? You're saying it's pointless to try?"

"No," he said. "They must try, only with the true athame."

"But it was lost . . ." My voice trailed off as I saw his look of guilt. "You know where it is?"

The old knight closed his eyes. "To my great shame, I was the one who took it. I had no knowledge of its importance, only that the High

Priestess carried it with her always, and I thought it hers and cherished so deeply that it should be buried with her as well."

Realization flared in my mind. "Caitriona said they burned her body."

"Some of it, yes." Bedivere's expression turned tortured. "I have lied to them and forsaken my own honor in doing so. I could not abide the idea that her gentle soul would not be reborn. I pulled her bones from the fire as the others slept and buried them in the place where all High Priestesses are borne back to the Goddess."

The athame isn't lost. The words lit a flame in my chest. *The ritual will work.*

"You're going to get it," I said, "aren't you?"

Bedivere nodded. "I must. If I tell the priestesses, they will try to go themselves, and it is my wrong to put right. And so I come to you with one request. If I do not return, tell the others what's become of me. Remind Cabell of his strength."

My mind raced. This couldn't happen. Bedivere was needed here, in so many ways, by so many. His fighting ability, his guidance, his work with Cabell. My brother was already walking along a cliff's edge, and if the one person who could help pull him back didn't return . . .

He would never recover.

And I would never forgive myself.

A calm surety took hold of me. Everyone had a role here. The Nine and Neve needed to perform the ritual. Emrys needed to help them grow what food they could. Bedivere was an experienced fighter who could keep them alive. Cabell needed the chance to learn control over his curse. The Avalonians needed to keep the tower secure and themselves alive.

No one was expendable enough to take this risk.

No one except me. One of the few people here who had experience opening and searching tombs.

The Goddess led you here to us. All of you.

I didn't believe in fate—it seemed like an excuse to blame your troubles on something bigger than yourself. But I couldn't deny how the others had fallen into place here, serving some greater purpose as surely as if they'd been led to it by the hand.

This . . . *this* was meant for me.

"Will you do me this service?" Bedivere asked.

"No," I said. "Because I'm going in your place."

His shock was palpable. "I cannot let you go. It must be me. There is no other choice."

I wasn't above using his guilt against him. "How would you feel if there was another attack while you were gone and you weren't here to help them? Where's the honor in that?"

He was still shaking his head.

"You must know a way to get out of the tower without having to go through the Children," I said. "And you must think you'll be able to reach the burial site before nightfall. That means I can do the same."

And faster, given that I wouldn't be traveling in a full suit of armor or with such a heavy load of emotional baggage. But this was the problem with honor—it poisoned you against reason.

Still, Bedivere held firm. "I cannot . . ."

"If they wake and find you gone, they'll send out people to search for you," I told him. "No one will even notice I'm missing."

His remaining hand curled at his side, his eyes closing.

The knights of Camelot followed a strict code of chivalry; Bedivere would never put his burden on another without cause. It played out time and time again in the stories Nash had told us of life in Arthur's court. Of quests and challenges accepted.

"I am *begging* you," I whispered, my throat raw from the effort it took to not cry. "Please let me accept this challenge on your behalf. Please don't leave Cabell. I can do this. I can."

"I do not doubt that—" he began.

I had one last card to play. "You have to stay alive to protect your king until the mortal world needs him again."

The words struck at him like an icy fist. He staggered back.

"You made a vow to him," I said. Another strike. "Just as you made a vow to help protect the tower." Another. "Please, Sir Bedivere. Let me go."

In the silence, my heart thundered with a single refrain. *He won't. He won't. He won't.*

But then he bowed his head, and a rush of purpose, of gratitude, broke loose.

"I cannot bear this, yet I must, and may I be cursed for it," Bedivere said, his eyes pale as they bored into me. "If you truly desire to do this, then ready yourself. First light is nearly upon us and there is not a moment to tarry."

36

Clever Emrys had missed one hidden passage, it seemed.

While I quietly dressed and gathered what supplies I had left in my workbag, Bedivere went to the armory to find me a breastplate of woven leather and a dagger he deemed me capable of using without accidentally slicing off my own thumb.

Avoiding Deri curled in repose at the base of the Mother tree, then the eyes of those keeping watch on the walls, I met Bedivere at the kitchen. The air was beginning to lighten and the Children to quiet—a fact Bedivere had not missed either.

"We must hurry," he said, holding the door open for me. "Dilwyn is an elfin, and it is in her nature to race dawn to be the first to work."

I was barely inside before he tossed me a sizeable chunk of bread and his skin of drinking water.

Relieved of his heavy armor, the old knight moved with surprising nimbleness to a cabinet on the back wall, holding his lantern up to one of its panels. At the caress of candlelight, the invisible markings there illuminated. Bedivere made as if to trace them with the metal glove that covered his lost hand, only to correct himself and use the other.

"The night comes," he said.

The cabinet swung away from the wall at his words, scraping over the well-worn stones. The hole hidden beneath it was just wide enough for us to take to its ladder one at a time.

I went first, carefully making the steep climb down. Bedivere followed after ensuring the cabinet was pulled back into place.

With the benefit of his lantern, the underpath revealed itself in all its refined beauty. Unlike the other tunnels, this one was a marvel of arched ceilings and stone columns, the walls painted with wildlife and creatures both familiar and new.

"What is this place?" I asked, trailing after him. A few sprites slept in the alcoves at the top of each pillar, their glow brightening and dimming with each breath in and out.

"This was once the fairy path, used by the Fair Folk shy of humans but eager to trade with the tower," Bedivere said. "It leads all the way to the sacred grove."

I felt a twinge of victory at having been proven right. There was at least one way to leave the tower and pass under the Children gathered around the moat.

"Why wasn't this one sealed?" I asked.

"It is protected by wards born of ancient magic that have yet to fail." Bedivere turned, holding his lantern higher. "But more vitally, this is the last hope of Avalon. Should the tower fall to ruin, it is the path we will take to the barges, and the mortal world beyond."

He tore through the thick lace of spiderwebs ahead, clucking his tongue in dismay when they clung to him like a second, filigree skin.

"Do you ever miss it?" I asked.

Bedivere looked back again.

"The mortal world," I said.

He was silent for a long while, his shuffling steps the only sound between us. "I can scarcely remember it well enough to desire it."

"What about King Arthur?" I asked, unable to help myself. "What was he like?"

The knight made a gruff noise at the back of his throat. "As righteous a man as they come, but vainglorious. Always seeking more than he was due at the expense of what he was given."

I blinked.

Bedivere slowed. "He was a king of good humor and skill, deserving of memory beyond death."

It wasn't exactly the sort of praise I would have expected from someone who had agreed to watch over a man for a thousand years, but maybe a few centuries of isolation and monotony could sour even the sweetest milk.

"You've been stuck watching the guy sleep for a thousand-odd years—you're allowed a few gripes," I told him. Then, sensing an opportunity, I added, "I don't suppose you could give me some directions on where to find whatever's left of Camelot—"

"We must be quiet now," he said with a slight edge. "We are not so far beneath the ground that the creatures cannot hear us."

For once, I did as I was told.

We walked for what felt like a small eternity. Rather than a growing light, the end of the tunnel revealed itself with another ladder. This time, the knight was the first to climb, unlocking a heavy iron chain that barred the hidden door.

"Wait here a moment," he told me, lifting the hatch and climbing out. My pulse throbbed inside my skull as my fear finally caught up to me.

A moment later, he leaned over the opening and motioned for me to follow. I climbed quickly, trying to keep the contents of my bag from rattling, and emerged into a small fissure between several towering rocks. The mist hung in a morose curtain across the expanse of rotting trees that lay just beyond the entrance.

"I shall ask once more—are you certain of this?" Bedivere said, his voice hushed.

I swallowed hard, nodding. The mist was undisturbed by any movement. The way was clear. For now.

"Where am I going?" I asked him.

"Good lass," he said, briefly clasping a hand on my shoulder. "Run straight across the grove from where we stand, and you'll find a deer path between two oaks. Follow that way for a league, until you reach the river, then head east until you find the lake. The burial mound is at the center of it, its entrance hidden on the northern face. I marked the grave with a pale stone."

I nodded. The chill in the air gripped me, squeezing my chest until it was hard to draw a deep, steadying breath.

"Travel swift as an arrow," he said. "Stop for no reason, not even to rest. I will lock the path behind you and return within three hours. You will have little more time than that to complete your task before the dark comes."

Not that I had a way to track how much time had passed. I'd have to keep an eye on the sky and go by my gut.

I hugged my workbag and waterskin close to my body. "I'll see you then."

I burst out from between the spiky boulders at a full run, sucking in deeper and deeper breaths of the sickly sweet rot of apples withering on the forest floor.

Beads of ice clung to the bare branches like forgotten diamond necklaces. Overhead, the gray sky seemed to hang lower than usual, as if to greet the ghostly mist. I had the suffocating sense that I was being bottled in. A buzzing filled the air, almost like cicadas in the summer.

Between two oaks had very little meaning when the trees had that identical look of putrid death. All the trunks in the grove were twisted into anguished spirals, as if they'd tried to pull themselves free from the ground.

In the end, it was the oaks' size that gave them away. The two giants were bent toward one another. The heavy lower branches were draped along the ground, bracing their towering bodies as the upper branches wove themselves together over the path. The image of them, like lovers collapsing into death together, held me there a moment longer than it should have.

Shaking myself, I climbed through a gap between their intertwined bodies and continued.

In the years before the curse, the deer had cut such a deep groove into the earth that the path was still visible beneath the wet skin of decaying leaves and black mold—without it, I would have been lost within moments. The trees, stripped bare of life, all had the same gaunt look as they faded in and out of the mist.

My heart hammered in my chest and I winced as something—brittle bones or twigs—snapped underfoot. I swung my gaze around, scanning to see if I'd drawn any unwelcome attention, but it was impossible to see more than a few feet in front of me. Every waiting shadow in the mist became a potential threat, the creaking of the trees a sign that something was watching me from above. My body felt electrified with awareness as I started moving again.

The mist churned around me, drawing me deeper into the isle, past the festering open sores that had once been gleaming pools, around the homes turned hollow, through fields of crops that had died on the vine.

The buzzing only grew louder. The river. I should have reached the river by now—

One moment my foot was pounding through the reeking mulch, the next the ground was gone and I was falling forward.

My body was quicker than my mind to react. I sat hard, rolling my weight back to land on my tailbone and back ankle. Pain shot up my left leg, and somehow, I caught the curse before it slipped past my lips.

At least my instincts and timing hadn't failed me yet. I had, indeed, reached the river.

The bank dropped sharply into the muddy bed. Netting, fish bones, and leaves piled high in the place of water. Here and there, other debris emerged from the wasting foliage. Shields. Shreds of fabric. A wooden doll.

I backed away from the edge, giving my ankle an experimental roll. I grimaced; it was twisted. I thanked every god of luck I hadn't broken it, but this wasn't going to help my already lagging speed.

I'd only gone a few steps when something moved at the edge of my vision. Slithering.

With a sinking fear, I turned back toward the riverbed.

Dried leaves slid toward me, skittering like startled roaches, as beneath them something moved. More leaves fell away as it rolled, worming forward. I bit my tongue hard to keep from making a noise as a gray, hairless head turned up from beneath the mulch and released a shuddering breath. Another moved beside it. Another.

Hellfire, I thought.

Two facts crystallized in my mind as I slowly backed away. The first, that the Children of the Night made that buzzing sound as they slept, a horrible mockery of a purr. The second, that they'd turned the length of the river into a nest. They had burrowed down to avoid the light.

Which I was losing with every second I wasted here.

I pressed a fist against my mouth, holding my breath, and used the other hand to clutch my bag tight to my body.

Slowly, so slowly it was almost agonizing, I limped my way along the river as it curved through a grove of young trees, all denied the chance to thrive. My heartbeat throbbed in every part of my body, and my knees were threatening to turn to water. I couldn't tell if I was on the verge of throwing up or pissing myself in terror, or both.

You're all right, I told myself over and over. *You're okay. This is for Cabell.*

The mist seemed to take pity on me, stretching itself thin enough that I could see the way ahead. Finally, the rounded top of the burial mound came into view, and I could feel my body again.

Unlike the river, the small lake, no more than a mile across, had retained some of its water. It had thickened at its edges with slime and moss that gave it a boglike appearance.

The burial mound—the barrow—was massive, taking up the entirety of the small island at the center of the murky water. After the endless parade of gray, the shock of bright green grass covering the mound's rise took my breath away. There had to be some sort of old protective magic on it. Somehow, impossibly, it had held.

I walked along the edge of the lake until the mist revealed a small rowboat caught on the bank. Pulling it free from the grasping mud, I moved it along to clearer water and pushed down, testing it for leaks.

"Sinking would be the least of your problems," I muttered, climbing inside and seizing the oars. Both they and the long neck of the boat were carved to look like dragons.

Pushing off the bank, I paddled forward as quietly as I could, my hands shaking until I could barely grip the oars. My breath was harsh in my ears. A fresh sweat broke out along my back and chest.

The silence of the lake was worse than the Children's purring had been. It possessed all the terrible potential of the unknown.

The boat bumped up against the island and let out a miserable creak as I stepped ashore.

"This is the part you know how to do," I whispered to myself. "This is the easy part."

I reached into my workbag, feeling for crystals at the bottom of it. Depending on the wards, I might need magical assistance to get inside.

As I made my way around the barrow to the north side, the grass faded to yellow and then a desiccated brown. Still, there was a simple, primal beauty to the mound—so unlike the cold stone of the tombs beneath the tower. I wondered then, running my fingers along the side of the structure, if Viviane would have preferred to be interred with Morgan. At least then they wouldn't be separated in death as they had been in life.

The flowers that had once bloomed around the stone doorway lay scattered like shriveled tissue. I pushed the brittle leaves on the wall aside, revealing a muddy handprint.

The hair on my body rose like needles against my skin. I crouched and closed my eyes for a moment, saying a prayer to the gods of luck. Switching my flashlight on, I aimed it into the barrow.

There was no pale stone.

The earth was split and overturned from front to back, bones and decomposing corpses exposed to the damp air.

Behind me, the water gurgled. The slime on its surface bubbled up, carrying with it long, stringy dark weeds.

But then there were eyes, white and lidless, over the water.

A face.

A body.

I fell back against the entrance of the barrow as she rose to float over the lake, a rough creature of silver bone and mud and rotting flesh. Not at all like the Children.

A revenant. It had to be. An unsettled spirit that fought to reclaim a body through whatever means available.

She lifted her hand toward me, so much like the White Lady in the snow all those years before that I choked at the sight. Mist gathered at her feet. Clumps of black moss dripped from her arm, but a metallic glint at the end of it caught my eye. There was a ring on the finger pointed at me, its large stone flat and a grayed brown.

The Ring of Dispel.

A strange, cold spell stole over my body and mind. Everything faded to darkness beyond it. My own hand rose, straining for it.

Metal sliced the air between us, blazing through the skin of my arm. I let out a strangled scream, dropping my flashlight to clutch the vicious wound. The revenant screeched in victory, lifting her arms toward the sky, as if in prayer.

One hand had the ring, but the other wasn't a hand at all. It was an untarnished knife melded with her wrist—the athame.

Terror and adrenaline surged as the creature drifted toward me, her feet floating above the ground. Mud dripped from her expressionless face, revealing patches of silver bone. Hot blood poured out between my fingers to the ground as I staggered back. The thought came suddenly, as if someone else had whispered it.

I have a blade. I have a weapon.

I had to use both hands to lift my dagger, the edges of my vision going dark with the effort. But not so dark I couldn't see what lay beneath the torn flesh of my own forearm.

Bone, gleaming silver in the low light.

I screamed and the creature lunged, knocking the dagger away and dragging me into the murky water.

PART III

BLADE
&
BONE

37

The cold depths knifed at my body.

I gasped, inhaling icy water into my lungs until I choked. The creature's hold tightened, strangling, as we sank. Floods of white bubbles and dark blood rose around us. At the surface, the gray light dimmed until it disappeared altogether behind the creature's body.

This has happened before, a voice whispered in my mind. *Wake up, Tamsin.*

I hit the silt at the bottom of the lake, something sharp digging into my back. I pushed at the creature, turning my head. White bones in the mud. A halo of them around me.

This has happened before.

The mud melted away from her face, revealing a skull as silver as the bone of my arm. Her jaw unhinged like a snake's. Jagged, broken teeth flashed in the gloom.

This has happened before.

The white rose. The monsters in the mist. The flaming sword.

The dream.

Gathering power whispered in the darkness. *Wake up.*

I felt along the ground until my fingers brushed freezing steel. Through the cloud of inky blood, through the black haze overtaking my vision, I gripped the hilt and swung.

The blade of the sword flared to life, its blue flames heating the water into a fury. The creature screamed as I sliced across her front. Mud and rancid skin broke away from her body, but she had no blood to bleed.

Starved for air, I kicked off the bottom of the lake, swimming with desperate strokes for the surface. The athame slashed through my boot to my ankle.

The blade—I needed that blade. For Cabell. For everyone.

I pushed through the pain, the heaviness of my body, and brought the sword down again. At the last moment, the creature reared back, and the burning sword passed through only water.

I lurched forward, trying one last time to get the athame, but the creature shrank back toward the bottom of the lake, wailing with rage, her weedy hair trailing after her like watersnakes.

I swam. The gray light at the surface appeared again, calling me toward it. With a hard kick, I burst through, coughing as I vomited up dank water.

But once I was there, my body had nothing left to give. Blood flowed out of my arm, draining those last embers of strength from beneath my skin. The water closed over my mouth, my eyes, and I slid under again. I no longer felt the blade's steel grip in my numb fingers. Its fire dimmed.

In the cold thrall of death, a murmur of consciousness begged, *Don't let go.*

The thick morass thrashed behind me, whipping up a torrent of loam. A painfully hot arm wrapped around my belly and yanked me *up*.

The cold air made me gasp until I choked, unable to get the water out of my lungs. I drove my head back, trying to slam it against the monster. My hand clenched reflexively around the sword's hilt again and the blue fire returned, boiling the black sludge on the water's surface. I didn't realize the blood was roaring in my ears until I heard a muffled voice right beside my ear.

"Tamsin! Tamsin, stop!"

I twisted my neck back, my stomach clenching as the dark splotches cleared from my sight.

Emrys.

"Not here—" I choked out, coughing. *You can't be here.*

His face was pale with fear. "Just hang on!"

His grip on me tightened as he swam us not to the island but to the far shore. The muscles in his body worked hard, his heart racing and racing. The heat of him was almost enough to drive out the ice that had crystallized around my bones.

The strap of my bag twisted around my neck as he dragged us both up onto the muddy bank. My arm screamed with pain as the bitter air met wounded flesh. The silver bone had a sinister gleam in the low light, a truth I couldn't outrun.

He'll see, I thought desperately, trying to tuck it beneath me. It was already too late. He swore viciously at the blood streaming from it, rivers in the mud. Frantically, he gripped the wound with one hand and brushed the soaking-wet hair off my face with the other.

"Tamsin?" he rasped. "Can you hear me? *Tamsin!*"

He hugged me close to his chest, rubbing and pounding on my back until I vomited up the rest of the water.

"What is this?" he asked, trying to pry my fingers from the hilt of the sword. Its heat whined and crackled as it fired the mud of the bank to hard clay.

But I only saw what was crawling out of the shadowed forest behind him.

The Children crept over the boulders and through the trees, staying in the heavy shadows of the forest, just outside their hated light. Dead moss and lichen rained silently to the forest floor as they scaled the branches with terrifying grace. Others perched on knobby roots that clawed into the ground. They chittered with excitement, huffing and sniffing.

No, I thought. It couldn't be . . . Olwen had said . . .

Olwen had only said they weren't as active during the day. That they hated the light. Not that they all slept. Not that none would try to attack us.

Emrys turned slowly, slowly toward the stench of vile death. The Children's panting breath became the mist, and the mist their breath.

He released me gently back to the ground with a heart-shredding look and rose onto his haunches.

The sword slipped from my hand to Emrys's and I moaned as the flames flickered out to hissing smoke. He looked down at it, bemused, as he stood to face the Children alone.

One crawled out in front of the others, spittle flying as it growled. One of its long, bony limbs reached out through the mist, slick with sour sweat and scaled.

It tilted its gray hairless head at an unnatural angle. Its eyes were lidless and wide, and the thin, pallid skin around them was puckered. But past the exaggerated and sunken features, there was something disturbingly familiar about the way its lips curled into a smirk.

I knew that face. Those eyes with their wolfish gleam.

It was Septimus.

Or what remained of Septimus.

My nails tore at the dead grass and cattails. I tried to push myself up. To stand.

Emrys swung the sword in wild arcs to hold the Children back, but without the threat of fire, they were undaunted, clambering over one another with cracking bones and snarls to be the first to get to him.

A screech echoed across the lake. The monster—the revenant—rose from the water and drifted to shore. Mud, twigs, and dead grass floated to her outstretched arms and the exposed half of her rib cage. Sickly mist amassed around her feet as the creature was restored to her full form.

Pressure built in my ears. My chest. More Children appeared in the darkness of the spiky bramble around her.

"What the hell is that?" Emrys gasped. "Is that—is that the High Priestess?"

Her head swung around at those words, and when she screamed, the sound rent the air. I clutched at my ears. Emrys staggered down to one knee.

The revenant called again, scaling the rocky hill of the opposite bank, vanishing into the woodland at such speed it stripped the bark from the black craggy trees. The Children around us moved back, deeper into the forest's darkness. They barked and growled as they circled the wide body of the lake at a gallop. Chasing her.

Or summoned to her side.

Summoned to her side.

She's controlling them. The words drifted through my mind, trying to take root. *High Priestess Viviane is controlling them.*

Emrys dropped the sword and fell into a crouch. "I don't know what the hell just happened, but we're losing the light. Can you—?"

He gripped my shoulder, his voice faded beneath the slow drumming of my heart. My whole body throbbed with each beat.

He'll see. I drew my wounded arm beneath me, hiding it. *He'll know.*

Blackness overtook my vision, and there was no fighting it. As my body released into numb exhaustion, one last ghost of a thought was left to follow me into the dark.

He'll know I'm one of them.

38

There was something about the watery light that made it impossible to tell if I was awake or dreaming. It was shifting, swelling against mossy stone walls. Caught, for a moment, like smoke in a bottle.

It would have been easy, so easy, to drift back into the blessed nothingness. To not feel the way my arm throbbed and my skull seemed poised to split open like a clam.

Instead, I forced my eyes to focus through the satin blur around me. I licked at the gritty dirt between my teeth, my tongue dry and heavy. A wind howled as if searching for its lost brothers.

My mind, ever the survivor, took an inventory of my surroundings. Dirt floor, woolly blanket beneath me, the rough arch of a low ceiling. A shadow in the doorway, coaxing a fire from a snarl of twigs.

The smell of sweet, earthy greens so foreign to this hellscape.

My memory was slow to return, as if it knew it was unwelcome. Tears burned at the corners of my eyes as my gaze fell to my arm.

A thick, shimmering ointment speckled with flecks of dried petals and herbs oozed out around the long leaves used to bandage the gash.

Emrys turned from the fire, letting its smoke drift out through the open doorway. Seeing me stir, he came to sit at my side.

"How are you feeling?" His voice was rough. A cold towel pressed

380

to my cheek, gently wiping something away. My stomach curled at the sight of his worried face.

It's not worry, came a dark voice in my mind. *It's pity.*

"Another favor . . . I owe you . . . ," I rasped out.

"Bird, don't you know I stopped keeping score?" he whispered. "It was never about that."

He leaned over me, his beautiful eyes still assessing as he brought the towel to my forehead.

"Then . . . why?"

"I wanted you to . . . I guess I just wanted you to . . ." He swallowed hard. "To change your mind about me. Not because of anything I'd done, but because you finally . . . Because you saw me. *Knew* me."

My heart seemed to rise with my breath.

Emrys pressed a hand to his forehead. "Sorry. I'm not making any sense."

I looked around again, desperate for anything other than the sight of his all-too-handsome face. "Where . . . ?"

"One of the watch outposts, not far from the lake," he said. "The fire's still burning above us and I set another one at the door. I had to use both your wards and mine to surround this place. I hope that's okay. But I'm not sure it's going to be enough to stop the Children once the light is completely gone."

A chill found its way into my blood.

"What?" I whispered. "You don't want to make a bet?"

His mismatched eyes were soft. I wondered if he was as afraid as I suddenly felt. "Not about this."

Go, I wanted to tell him. *Go back to the tower.*

But the weaker, worse part of me couldn't. I hated it—*hated* it. He deserved to be safe. To stay alive. And yet it was always there, that push and pull. The fear of getting close straining against the fear of being alone.

"You shouldn't . . . have come," I said, letting my eyes drift shut. "Why . . . ?"

"I couldn't sleep, so I decided to go to the springs. I saw you and Bedivere go into the kitchen, but only Bedivere come back out," Emrys said. "I was worried something had happened, so I confronted him and made him tell me where you were going. I may have punched him."

I gave him a look of disbelief.

He held up his bruised knuckles. "I may have also sprained my hand and shattered my remaining pride in the process. And while I wouldn't dream of lecturing you—"

"Good."

"But for a *very* smart person, leaving by yourself to do this was very stupid," he said. "Really. You wound me, Bird. I thought we did all our clandestine searching together."

Emrys said it lightly, in his usual way, but there was real strain around his eyes. He was angry—maybe more than that.

"Not. Sorry," I managed to choke out.

"I know, you absurd human." Emrys was fading at his edges, splitting into two like the opening of butterfly wings. "Do you want some water?"

"I can . . ." *Do it.*

I didn't need help. I didn't . . .

He retrieved the waterskin from my things, wavering a moment beside me. I tried to lift my hand, but it was as if my blood had turned to lead. After a moment, he slid a strong arm beneath me and slowly propped me up, bringing the water to my lips.

I spat out the first of it, needing to rinse the foul taste from my mouth, then, too tired to feel self-conscious, I drank greedily. The smell of him, evergreen and warm skin, wrapped around me.

Emrys had taken off both of our jackets and hung them near the fire to dry. When he lowered me back onto his blanket, the one that smelled like him, the cold crept over me again.

A strange sound, one I hadn't caught in weeks, drifted in through the doorway. I turned toward it, not quite believing my eyes as the first drops of rain pattered down. After a few moments, it fell harder, rattling the dead leaves on the nearby branches and slanting against the watchtower's walls.

And for once, I could barely hear the Children at all.

The fire burning at the head of the tower hissed viciously, but it would hold as long as the salamander stones touched one another. Our wards would offer another layer of protection from the Children. For a moment, I could almost believe we were truly safe.

"Try to rest," Emrys murmured, tucking a loose strand of hair behind my ear. He seemed to realize what he'd done a moment too late and flushed.

But I had liked it, that touch. What it said without speaking. What it could have become.

His hair was redder in the dying light, and the shadows made him seem older—a hundred years, not seventeen. "You lost a lot of blood. I had to utilize my extremely limited first-aid training and stitch the cut on your arm."

The quiet peace of the moment splintered into thousands of jagged shards.

He saw.

Olwen's voice sang with the rain. *Three magics to be feared . . .*

"Emrys," I whispered with what urgency I could muster. Already, the shadows were returning for me. "When I die, burn my body. I'm one of them."

He gripped my hand tightly, leaning his face over mine again. I tried to focus on it. On his eyes, gray as a storm cloud, green as earth. "No, you're not."

Three magics to be feared . . . curses born of the wrath of gods, poisons that turn soil to ash, and that which leaves one dark of heart and silver in the bone.

"Dark of heart," I said, my thoughts fracturing, my tongue turning lazy. "Silver in the bone."

"There is nothing dark about you," he said vehemently. *"Nothing."*

"I killed Septimus . . ." Maybe that had left a mark on my soul. A brand on my very bones.

"The Children killed him," Emrys said.

My eyelids sank again, and I tried to hold on to his words, to believe them.

But there, in the darkness, I only saw Nash's bones returning to the earth. Laid out the exact way I was, in an identical tower. Lost and nameless.

Alone.

The sight of him faded like twilight into night.

"Don't leave," I begged. "Please don't leave . . ."

"You're the bird," Emrys whispered. "You're the one who always flies away."

Liar, I thought. Emrys Dye was a liar, his words as smooth as a snake's underbelly. He'd leave if it benefited him. If he knew what I'd seen.

He'd leave like everyone else.

Don't tell him, I thought. *He'll go and it's too dangerous. She'll kill him . . .*

But if clever Emrys wanted it, he'd find a way. He'd find it, and I wanted to know.

I needed to know.

Because you saw me.

"She has the Ring of Dispel," I whispered, disappearing into the flickering dark. "The High Priestess . . . she . . ."

Because you saw m . . .

When I opened my eyes again, I did see him.

Emrys sat beside me, one arm wrapped around his knees, his perfect face soft as he watched me through his lowered lashes. His fingers were still clasped around mine, and they tightened, as if to say *Rest.* As if to promise *We're still here, the both of us.*

My eyelids fluttered shut.

The daylight was gone, but he wasn't.

39

The rain turned to snow.

I woke in time to see the silent, dreamy transformation. The curtain of rain slowed, and in its place came tufts of white, falling through the night air like a shower of stars. Emrys leaned against the doorway watching, his scarred arms crossed over his chest.

Scars.

He'd stripped off his heavy wool sweater and wore only a plain T-shirt. One, like mine, that had seen better days. The muscles of his arms and back were taut beneath the fabric, as if he was bracing for something to emerge from the trees.

Near his feet, the small fire was struggling. The pile of deadwood he'd gathered had already dwindled to its last few branches. The cold seeped inside the watchtower like an uninvited guest, and now, like the cries of the hungry Children that surrounded us, we would never be rid of it.

I shivered, my teeth chattering painfully. Reeling in that last bit of consciousness that seemed to want to slip away again, I tried to curl my legs up closer to my middle. An unexpected but comforting weight shifted over me. Our jackets and his sweater were tucked in tight around my body.

Emrys reached out to catch some of the snow in his palm, his faint smile fading with some unknowable thought.

Something in me softened as I watched him—it had no name, but it was new and strange and dizzying as the sensation spread. My arm throbbed painfully as I moved it, filling with needles as I tried to curl my fingers, remembering the feel of my hand in his bigger one.

I should have been horrified at the thought of him having to take care of me again when I'd always fought so hard to take care of myself.

Yet all those thoughts turned to ash in the wind as Emrys looked at the remaining firewood, then back out to the woods. Weighing the risk. The cost of trying.

Panic fluttered in my chest.

"Don't," I croaked out.

Emrys's expression shifted to that easy lightness that seemed to carry him through life on a gilded cloud. His posture relaxed as he knelt beside me, adjusting the coats.

"I'm thrilled you think I'm brave enough to go out there right now," he said, his voice scratchy.

"*Br-brave* wasn't ex-exactly the word I was thinking," I said, trembling hard from the cold.

He clutched at his heart. "Ah, her aim strikes deadly and true."

There was a luminous, hazy quality to him, like a creature who'd escaped from a dream. The rakish hair and those vivid eyes only added to the effect. My thoughts came warm and flushed with something I didn't want to examine too closely.

"D-do I have a fever or something?" I asked. It was the only explanation for why I leaned into the touch of his palm as he pressed it gently to my forehead. Why it felt so good to have him brush my loose hair off the sticky skin of my face.

"Nah, I just have that effect on people," he said with a wink. "Well, everyone but you."

"Th-thanks to N-Nash, I ha-have an immunity t-to charm," I managed to get out.

Careful to avoid my injury, he rubbed my upper arms beneath

the layers of fabric, trying to create some heat. His smile drifted away again, and like a pathetic soft-in-the-head idiot, I immediately wanted it back.

"You have a little bit of a fever," he explained. "The herbs are doing their work, though. Think you could eat something? I have some bread that didn't go for a swim with us."

I shook my head. My stomach was as tight as a drum.

"H-how are you not fr-freezing?" I asked.

"If you were to ask my dear mother, she'd say it was because I was born with gentle fire in my heart," he said with a strained look in his eyes. "But I think there's just something wrong with me."

The heat from his hands felt like it was radiating through our jackets. My jaw locked from the force of the shivers racking my body. Emrys's face fell with concern.

"That bad?" he whispered.

I nodded. It felt like my lungs had frozen and the silver coating my bones refused to loosen its grip on the cold.

Emrys closed his eyes, turning his face up toward the ceiling of the watchtower, where a winding staircase led to the flat roof. "I am suggesting this in a way that is devoid of anything other than concern for your well-being, and with the full knowledge that you are less likely, in this moment, to be able to punch me for it . . ."

I stared up at him, exasperated.

"Yeah, I do deserve that look, but . . . I could warm you?" The words came out in a rush as he looked back up at the ceiling, his throat bobbing hard. "I mean, for your well-being. Not any other reason. I said that already, didn't I? I'm just trying to make the point that it's only weird if we make it weird, and we don't have to make it weird. At all."

The thought was enough to get the blood back to warming my face.

It won't be anything different than when you and Cabell were kids, I told myself. In the days we had to sleep outside in the cold, we'd huddle together under the blankets to stay alive. And there was nothing there between Emrys and me to make it any more than that.

There wasn't. And I was so cold.

To keep him from seeing the way the flush was spreading up from my neck to my ears—and to get him to stop talking—I turned onto my uninjured side, facing away from him. Creating space for him beneath the makeshift covers. It wasn't fair for me to keep them all to myself, anyway.

His hesitation made my stupid heart give a kick. I stared at the dark stones across from me, my body tensed with a held breath. The firelight flickered away like the sun past the horizon.

There was a soft rustle of fabric. As I drew my next breath like the last one before a deep plunge, the jackets lifted and he slipped in behind me, fitting his body to mine.

Heat enveloped me like a summer day, spreading slowly across my every sense, turning my body from stone to skin again. He inched closer still, until my head was tucked beneath his chin, and I let out a shuddering breath as one of his impossibly warm arms wrapped around my waist.

"Is this okay?" he asked, barely a whisper.

I nodded, closing my eyes at the feeling of his heart pounding against my back. His breath stirred my hair, sending a shiver down my spine. I flushed as warmth pooled low in my belly again.

"Still cold?" Emrys's voice rumbled in his chest.

His arm tightened around me until I brought my own down over it. Every thought, every nerve in my body, narrowed to where my bare skin touched his. Long legs wove through mine as if they belonged there. I wondered, as his hand spread over my belly, if he could feel the honeyed heat pooling in my core.

I breathed in deeply, no longer able to hear anything over the sound of our hearts racing one another to some unknown end. I felt almost drunk with it, the way his breathing hitched when I traced a vein from the top of his hand down over his wrist. I'd never had any other power but this.

It would be reckless to do it again. Absolute madness to let my finger drift farther through the light dusting of hair, tracing over him like a map to someplace unknown. My hand stilled as the soft skin became rough. Scarred.

Emrys turned his cheek to rest against my hair. "I lied to you before."

A whisper. A secret.

My eyes opened.

"I didn't get the scars on a job." I could barely hear him over the pounding of his heart. He breathed the words as if he were scraping them from his soul. "My father gave them to me."

It took a moment for me to understand what he'd said. Careful to tuck my wounded arm close to my body, I rolled over and pulled back from his chest to look at his face.

"What?" I whispered.

The tendons of his neck strained as he tilted his head back, closing his eyes. The scar there made my breath catch again. "The things he believes . . . He's always been fixated on strange ideas, I guess, but in the last year . . . it's gotten so much worse. This was . . . this was punishment when I refused to do what he wanted me to."

My mind was too quick to fill in the blanks of what had happened to him. I didn't dare ask any of the questions racing through my mind. I didn't know what to say. What *could* I say to any of that?

Nash had warned me about Endymion Dye years ago, and as with most of his stories, I'd assumed it was exaggerated. The man had always been rigid and harsh, but never, in all my worst thoughts of him, could I have imagined him giving his own flesh and blood such cruel and lasting injuries.

Wordlessly, I drew Emrys close again; I wrapped my arm around his waist and pressed my face to the warm spot between his shoulder and neck. My hand stroked down his spine, and every rough ridge of a scar brought me closer to tears, imagining.

Emrys shuddered, his arm around me tightening. "That's the real reason I took this job. I have nothing of my own. He controls everything and everyone in my life. I needed money to find a way to get me and my mom out of his reach. Out of his life."

Stripping away the charming gloss, that beautiful polish of wealth he'd once worn as proudly as his signet ring, what was left was this real boy whose life had been little better than a cruel secret. One who'd been alone inside that gilded cage of pain and blood and quiet terror.

I breathed in the scent of him, my nose and lips skimming over his skin, trying to give comfort my words felt too clumsy to convey. His fingers drew drowsy circles on my back, leaving trails of fire behind.

"I wanted you to know," he whispered. "I wanted to tell you before so you'd understand, but I was ashamed—"

"No," I said vehemently. "There's nothing to be ashamed of."

"There is," he said thickly. "Because I was too much of a coward to leave before things got this bad. I was scared to let go of everything I'd grown up with, and what I was supposed to be. And then there were other fears, including if I'd ever see you again . . . and I wasn't ready for that."

My hand stilled on his back, but my heart climbed.

"I don't want to make you uncomfortable. I know how you feel." He swallowed. "There's nothing you have to do or say, and I'm not telling you all this because I want you to feel sorry for me—gods, that's the last thing I want, especially knowing how much worse you've had it. But if we're in this freezing hell and everything is upside down and nothing's certain, I can at least be brave enough to tell you. I can tell you that to me, you've always felt like spring. Like possibility. I admire you, and respect you, and I want to be near you as long as I can. As long as you'll let me be."

The shock of his words exploded like stars inside my skin, somehow as inevitable as they were unexpected. My lips formed his name against his collarbone. *Emrys.*

"So . . . ," he said with a trembling laugh. "There. I've said it now."

And maybe, for him, I could be brave enough to say it too.

My throat worked hard to clear the lump from it, and when I spoke, there was an unexpected huskiness to my voice, one I'd never heard before. "I lied to you, too."

Where to start? Where to begin when I had no beginning at all? His hand stroked up my back to the place where my neck held all of that tension. Years of restraint.

"Or not a lie, but not the truth, either," I whispered, closing my eyes. "You asked me how I came into Nash's care, and . . ." Cabell was the only other person who knew this humiliating story. "It was a misunderstanding."

"What do you mean?" he murmured.

"He . . . he was playing cards and thought the *Tamsin* being staked was a boat," I managed to get out. "Imagine his horror and surprise when it turned out to be a little girl he had no use for. Another mouth to feed."

"What?" Emrys breathed out. "Your parents just . . ."

"Gave me away," I finished hoarsely. I drew my injured arm closer to me, almost relishing the fresh sting of pain. "Didn't care about who it was or what Nash would do to me. Maybe they knew what I was . . . what was under my skin. Maybe Nash figured it out and that's . . . that's why he left."

"No," Emrys said fervently, "no way. There is nothing wrong about you. We don't even know what it means."

"Don't we?" I whispered. "Cabell was right about why I wanted to look for Nash. He's always been right. I just didn't want to believe it."

"What do you mean?"

That hairline crack in my heart that I'd fought so hard to keep from splitting finally broke open, and all that was left was for the shame and pain to flow out in a drowning tide. For the first time in years, I started to cry.

"I wanted to break his curse," I said. "If I lose Cabell, I really will be alone . . . but I wanted proof that Nash hadn't meant to leave us. I wanted to know that he hadn't discarded me too. Even after years of knowing I wasn't wanted, I didn't want it to be true."

The muscles of his arm flexed against my back, his hand weaving through my hair to tilt my head up. As I opened my eyes, the last of the firelight disappeared, and it was only the two of us intertwined in the warm darkness.

"You are," Emrys swore. "You are wanted. God, I want you more than anything."

A new heat gathered in my core at his words, but my whole body braced for him to take it back. To dash it all with a joke. But Emrys refused to back away from the words he'd put between us, and now they hovered there, all promise and anticipation and aching vulnerability.

Emrys had become a friend to me in the last couple of weeks, a partner, even, in the long hours of night. And now . . .

What was this?

I watched him watch me, his other hand rising between us to gently thumb the tears away from my face. To cup my cheek. His face was so serious then, handsome and shadowed, and somehow, for a moment, mine alone.

When all of this was over, he'd disappear, and this would be only a memory. The look and feel of him imprinted on my mind for as long as I lived. I turned my head to press my lips against his rough palm so I would remember that, too.

Emrys inhaled. His eyes burned with a longing that echoed in my body.

"I have to go after the High Priestess," I whispered. "I have to somehow get the athame and ring away from her."

He leaned down so our faces were perfectly aligned, our breath as one.

"But," I said, "I think you should probably kiss me first."

His lips brushed softly over mine. "Any guesses on how much I want to?"

I closed that last whisper of distance, capturing his mouth with my own.

For a moment, I felt like I was back at Tintagel, standing at the place where the edge of the rough land met the cold, harsh sea. The water crashing, crashing against the ancient earth, trying to make it yield. The vast, sweeping power of that collision, of those two halves each trying to withstand as much as consume the other.

It was the feeling of the first glimpse of the One Vision, the unseen hidden within the known. The shafts of light breaking through the thick canopy of a forest. A dream and waking.

The hardness of his body turned soft and yielding against mine, and there were no more thoughts but the feel of him, of his skin and lips and coarse hair as I kissed him and he kissed me.

Hands touching and searching. Lips languid and soothing. Desperate and promising.

Alone together, until sleep finally claimed us both.

40

The next morning, I was the first to wake and meet the gray light pouring through the door. My body ached, but my head was surprisingly clear. I felt rested, riding a pleasant wave of heat.

I was still tucked against the warmth of Emrys, our legs hooked together in a tangle. It took every last trace of willpower I had to pull back from the slow rise and fall of his chest, that center of warmth, and sit up.

The air was cold and sharp in my nose, the chill made all the worse by the absence of him. Through the doorway, a thin blanket of grayed snow had begun to creep into our sanctuary, burying the evidence of our fire.

Realization, icier still, set in. The snow had likely buried the revenant's trail, too.

Bracing a hand against the dirt floor, I leaned toward Emrys, stealing one last look at him. My heart was painfully tender at the boyishness of his face in sleep. I touched my lips, remembering . . . only to grimace at how saccharine my thoughts had become.

I reached for the waterskin and drank, using a little of it to wash my face and hands before taking some of the bread Emrys had offered last night. It had gone stale, but I was ravenous.

When I finally worked up the nerve, I brushed a light finger down

Emrys's cheek. It was rough with the stubble coming in, so different from last night.

My cheeks heated. He let out a groan, burying his face into the blanket beneath us and stretching an arm out, as if searching for me. I placed the other half of the bread in his upturned hand, and he laughed.

"All right, all right," he said, rubbing his face with his other hand as he sat up. He flushed, adjusting the blankets over his lap. "Let me just . . . pull myself together."

He angled away from me, taking a long drink of water. In the silence, a self-consciousness I hated began to ferment. I reached for my boots, which Emrys must have removed, grateful to find that they were mostly dry now, and the wound on my ankle only hurt a little as I laced them up.

"Hey," Emrys said softly.

"Hey yourself."

As I looked back, he caught my face with his hand and leaned forward, pressing his lips to mine. I lingered there, relaxing a bit, simply feeling the new texture of his stubble. As he pulled back, a grin on his stupid handsome face, I realized why he still had yet to move, why he was holding on to his jacket for dear life in his lap, and I burst out laughing.

"Ah," he said, half groaning, half laughing. "I'm but a man, and you have an effect."

"Come on," I said, shaking my head. "We need to get going."

"Let me look at your arm first," he said, "then we'll fly, Bird."

His touch was skillful as he removed the dried leaves from my arm and reapplied the ointment, but there was a new intimacy to it now. His fingers stroked and smoothed as he examined the neat line of stitches he'd put in the skin. The wound itself looked furious, but no longer throbbed unless I touched it.

Ever so lightly, his fingers skimmed up to my shoulder and across my collarbone, then pulled down the neckline of my shirt to reveal the edge of the hideous death mark over my heart. His brow creased as he looked at it, and I forced myself to remain still. To not flinch and pull away as he traced its starlike shape.

"What happened?" he whispered.

I couldn't. Not that.

I drew my injured arm between us. Emrys returned his attention to it immediately.

"How do you get the bandaging leaves to stay so green?" I asked, studying the way his dark lashes curled. "How did you figure any of this out?"

"I'll meet your deflection with one of my own." He gave me a sly smile, stealing one last quick kiss.

Carefully, he eased us both off the hard floor. The world spun, just for a moment, but he held us steady and pulled his sweater over my head.

"You need it," I protested.

"You need it more," he answered, and helped me with my jacket. We reassembled our meager belongings but paused in the doorway before removing the wards. Icy wind kissed my cheeks as I gazed out into the desolate forest.

"How do you want to do this?" he asked.

Heat climbed up my throat again, washing over my face. "Could . . . could we not tell the others yet, before we figure whatever this is out? People complicate things, and I . . ."

I trailed off, noticing the way his smile bloomed into a full-out grin.

"I was talking about the High Priestess," he said, leaning closer. "But good to know I seem to have an effect on you, too."

Now it was my turn to groan. I pushed him away, embarrassment lighting a fuse in me.

"We have to see if there's any sort of trail," I said. "She seemed to be heading north, but who knows where she is now." As I remembered the strange grace with which the creature—the revenant—had floated over the water and land, a new thought occurred to me. "We might have better luck trying to find the tracks of the Children. She called them to her, didn't she?"

"It sure seemed that way," Emrys said. "Do you think she's the one who created them? She did know something about the druids' death magic."

All it took to create a revenant was unfinished business and the presence of magic in the body. Unlike the creatures, her form could shift and remake itself. Killing her would be difficult.

But not impossible.

"Maybe." But Neve's words drifted back to me. *I'm still not seeing any motivation on her part.* "Didn't Merlin say there were two others like him on the island—couldn't she be the third, the one . . . waiting, right?"

"He also said that a *she* tried to master death but became its servant in the end," Emrys said. "Could mean she got in over her head and caused the curse by mistake."

"Or," I said, "she came around to wanting to serve Lord Death and give the isle to him."

Emrys's expression turned pained. "Have we decided to believe the unstable, prattling druid trapped in the tree?"

"Yes. No. I don't know." Clutching the strap of my workbag, I took a step out of the watchtower, letting my boots crunch in the snow. The sight of the landscape mottled with decay drew the memory of Nash's bones to the front of my mind. "I guess the more important question is how the High Priestess—the revenant—got the Ring of Dispel. Was she the one who killed Nash?"

"Unfortunately, I'm not sure we'll be able to figure that one out," Emrys said. "But . . . maybe Nash brought it to her? Or she found it after becoming a revenant, drawn to its magic. She clearly had a number of secrets—here, don't forget this." He held out the sword from the lake. "Its party trick seems to only work for you."

My breath grew ragged as I stared at it. The hilt was inlaid with ivory that not even the mire of the lake water could stain. And the way its blade had burst into flame . . .

"You hold on to it," I said, unknotting our protective wards.

Emrys knew how to wield a blade. It was right that he carried it. Used it. That thing had been in my dream, and I didn't want to look at it if I didn't have to. Didn't want to think about what any of it meant.

We went opposite ways around the watchtower, gathering the sigil-carved clay tablets in neat stacks. When we met in the middle at the back of the tower, he took both garlands and stowed them in his bag. Not for the first time, I wished they had the power to protect bodies as well as places.

"Hey, Tamsin," he said, linking his fingers with mine. "I'm okay with this just being ours for now, too."

I nodded, and, together, we headed north.

The powdery snow was as much a help as a hindrance, silencing our steps but slowing them in turn. The isle couldn't have been more than a few miles long and wide, but it had never felt bigger as we trudged forward.

Somehow, impossibly, the forest had taken on a more sinister appearance. Half buried in snow, the fallen trees were indistinguishable from the creatures burrowing below. Icicles, black with sooty moss and decay, hung from the skeletal tangle of branches like barbed fangs.

Now and then, clumps of snow crashed down, startling us as they crusted in our hair or slipped beneath the collars of our jackets. My toes and fingers were stiff with the cold after only an hour of walking, and I was so focused on the ground directly in front of me, I almost missed the tracks at the edge of the barren riverbed that ran alongside our northerly path.

Tracks that looked as if someone had crossed the open field on the other side of the water and disappeared not into the trees but over a snow-dusted hedge maze.

Tracks that were nothing like those of the Children, who clawed the ground on hands and feet. A fine line cut through the snow, too clean for any earthly being. It reminded me of the way the revenant had floated just above the ground, as if the heat or force of her magic had marked the ground where she passed.

I gripped Emrys's arm and pointed. He squinted, following my line of sight. His lips parted, but whatever he might have said was cut off by a steaming glob of bloodied saliva dripping onto his cheek.

Emrys reared back with a sharp inhale, swiping at it. I turned my gaze up.

Children clung to the highest branches of the old trees, shadowed and covered in a thick rime of snow. A curtain of it drifted around us as one shook itself, snorting as it settled again, leaning more heavily against the trunk. Its leg dropped down, kicking the creature perched on the branch beneath it.

A lightning bolt of adrenaline fired through me as the second creature snarled and took an irritated swipe at the first. My grip on Emrys tightened. The two of us stood rigid, not daring to breathe.

The wind whipped at the trees. As it died, the sound of rattling purrs rose to replace it. All around us, the mounds of snow shifted.

Emrys took a step back, carefully retracing his steps. I did the same, trying to make as little noise as possible in the crunchy snow. When he looked at me again, the question was plain on his face. *Run?*

I shook my head. *Not yet.*

I eyed the river, my mind spinning with possibilities. The leaves and debris had been concealed by the snow, but I had no doubt the Children slept beneath. Edging us carefully out of the trees and along the riverbank, I leaned forward, looking back and forth along the river—and saw our opportunity. A half mile or so ahead, a narrow stone bridge connected the forest beside us to the field and the strange, rounded hedge beyond it.

We shared another look.

Ready? I mouthed.

He nodded.

The Children in the trees spat and hissed at one another, mauling those around them awake until they became a thrashing knot of gray skin and claws. The Children that were knocked to the ground immediately climbed back up to rejoin the squabble, squealing with unbridled glee as the fight spread and turned savage.

Rent limbs and blood splattered the white expanse of snow. My pulse beat a terrible song in my veins. Emrys and I stayed low and hugged the edge of the bank as we ran past the growing melee of Children. I didn't dare look at them, or so much as draw breath, until the din faded and my hand touched the frost coating the bridge's stones.

Then we ran, harder than before, fighting through knee-high drifts until my legs and ankles throbbed from tackling unseen rocks below. We followed the trail of fresh footprints to where the hedge wall beckoned. The moment it was in reach, we darted behind it, keeping our backs to the browned leaves and snarled branches. My ears strained, trying to pick up on any indication that we'd been scented and followed.

None came.

I blew out a hard breath, lungs burning. Emrys placed a hand to his chest and gave a shaky laugh. His grip on the sword turned his knuckles white.

As white as the massive sun-bleached bone he leaned against.

Seeing my expression, he looked back, only to stumble away. "What in hellfire is that?"

"I don't know," I said. "But at least it's dead." Then, because that had a different meaning in this Otherland, I added, "*Dead* dead."

The bones were all around us, each arching over the hedge to meet at a knobby joint almost like . . .

A massive skeleton's spine and ribs.

"Should we . . . ?" he asked, using the sword to point at the tracks.

The hedge fed into a labyrinthine enclosure, but there wasn't far to go to find its center, and what was hidden there.

I'd been right. A gigantic creature had curled up and died there, its body giving life to the hedge. Behind us, the delicate bones of the folded wings were still there, supported by the gnarled growth. The skull, nearly as large as the stone cottage next to it, was filled with rows of serrated teeth.

Dragon, I thought faintly. Mari hadn't been teasing me.

Emrys and I crouched as we came around the last corner. A cottage with its snow-dusted thatched roof, like something out of a fairy tale.

The trail of steps led to a firmly shut door. With its lone window covered by fabric, it was impossible to tell who, if anyone, was inside.

I caught Emrys's eye and shrugged. He shrugged back but slid the sword across the snow to me with a meaningful look.

I hesitated, motioning that we should try to approach the cottage from the side, but he only pointed to the sword and drew his collapsible axe out of his workbag.

My fingers closed around the hilt, and blue flames roared to life along the blade. Emrys stared at it in wonder, shaking his head.

Before either of us could lose our courage, we charged at the door. Emrys readied himself to kick it in and I assumed the best fighting stance I could—but we never had the chance to strike. The door swung open and there was a knife at my throat.

Not a knife—a wand.

41

Neve and I both yelped, dropping our weapons. The sword's flames extinguished themselves in the snow and the wand rolled to Emrys's feet as we threw our arms around each other.

"What are you doing here?" I demanded, my voice tight with shock.

Caitriona hovered with a sword a step behind her, and Olwen twisted a misty snarl of magic between her hands a step behind that. Both relaxed at the sight of us, but only just.

Neve took a step back, keeping her grip on my upper arms, and gave me a look of utter disbelief. "We came to find you. Both of you."

"Why?" I asked, alarmed. "What's happened?"

Olwen pressed a hand to her face in either dismay or amusement.

"I'll make some tea, shall I?" she murmured.

"What's happened is that you left the protection of the tower, you utter ninny," Caitriona said, her voice even raspier than usual. "Come inside, the both of you. *Now.*"

It took me a moment to understand. "You came to find us."

"Yes!" Neve said, exasperated. "What else did you think we'd do when you didn't come back before nightfall?"

Nothing. The word clanged in my mind. I only stared at her as she shook her head. My life wasn't worth trading theirs. Neither Emrys nor the others should have followed. I tried to tell them, but something was happening in my chest, in my throat, and the urge to cry suddenly became too much.

Emrys bent to retrieve the sword, then put a gentle hand on my shoulder, guiding me inside so the door could be shut and latched firmly behind us.

The inside of the cottage was surprisingly homey, with a bed in the far corner, a dining table set up in front of the hearth, and a pair of stuffed chairs near a bookshelf jammed with what appeared to be record books of some kind.

"What is this place?" Emrys asked, all but collapsing into one of the chairs.

"This home belongs to the keeper of the orchards," Caitriona said, sheathing her sword. Softly, she corrected herself. *"Belonged."*

"Talk about burying the lede," I muttered. "Is that really a dragon?"

"It was Caron, the last of her kind," Olwen explained. "She was a dear friend to a keeper of the orchards years and years ago."

Neve sat me in the other chair, putting her hands on my shoulders to push me not so gently down into it. I made a face at her assessing look and she returned it, twice over.

You shouldn't be here, I thought desperately. *None of you should have left the tower.* The whole point of my mission had been to keep everyone safe, and now they were in far more danger because of me. This was the last thing I'd wanted.

Neve's expression turned serious, as if she could see the flow of thoughts passing through my mind. "You really thought we wouldn't?"

I looked down. "You shouldn't have put yourselves at risk."

"Too bad," Neve told me. "You don't get to decide that. I'm sorry to inform you that, despite your best efforts, people care about you, myself included."

Turning back to where Olwen was using magic to heat a small pot of water, Neve said, "I'll finish that, Olwen. I think you'd better have a look at these two."

"Start with Tamsin," Emrys said, "and don't judge me too harshly, Olwen. I did my best."

I shrugged out of my jacket, turning my arm up for the healer to assess. She washed her hands and came toward me, her eyes narrowing as she knelt and took in the sight of the stitches and the ointment. She sniffed at it.

"Echinacea and yarrow?" she asked approvingly.

"And a touch of oregano oil," Emrys confirmed.

"Your stitching needs work," Olwen informed him after inspecting both my arm and ankle. She gave me a soft pat on the hand. "I'll clean it properly and apply something that should help it heal. How did you come by such a deep wound? Was it one of the Children?"

"Not . . . quite," I said faintly.

Behind her, Caitriona stopped pacing, allowing Neve to pass by with a steaming cup of something that smelled divine. Dried apples and herbs bobbed at its surface.

"Bedivere told us about the athame, but the storm set in as we reached the lake and we lost your tracks," Caitriona said. "Did you find it?"

Her bandaged face made it difficult to read her expression, but the thread of hope in her voice was enough to make my lungs squeeze. I hadn't thought of this part—of having to tell them what had become of their beloved High Priestess, and how she had cursed them all.

As I took my first sip of the tonic, I got to experience what Neve had that very first night. A warm, golden glow seemed to pass through me, easing the soreness of my body and the ache in my stomach instantaneously. That restorative effect had to be Avalon's famed apples, healing and nurturing all at once. It gave me that last bit of courage I needed.

"I found it," I told them. Olwen looked up from where she was bandaging my ankle, drawing in a breath of surprise. Her relief was just as terrible as Caitriona's hope. "But you are *really* not going to like where it is."

When I finished, Olwen was in tears and Caitriona had slumped into one of the chairs at the table, bracing her head in her hands. I could practically feel her mind working, running through the story I'd presented—weighing if she could trust it.

"How could this be true?" Olwen asked, dashing the wetness from her cheeks with her hand. "A revenant, from so few bones—who could have cast such a curse on her?"

"Only herself," came Caitriona's dark reply. She sat back against the chair, misery etched on her features.

"No," Olwen said. "It cannot be."

"Who else, then?" Caitriona asked, bereft. "Our High Priestess was the only one in all of Avalon we know for certain called upon death magic. I've denied the possibility for years, but knowing this . . ."

"Could it have been a mistake?" Neve asked softly. "She could have misunderstood one of the druidic spells."

"Or she was no longer a servant of the Goddess," Caitriona said, her long body curling up into the chair. "And accepted the greater magic of death."

"No," Olwen said. "No. There are many things I'd believe, but that is not one of them."

"Olwen," Caitriona said. "You know how she spoke of her longing to return Morgan to life, to have but one more day with her. Perhaps she sought the magic to resurrect her, and it led to our ruin."

The other priestess shook her head. "*No.* She would not upset the balance in such a way."

"Did the High Priestess tell you how revenants form?" I asked.

Olwen pushed her thick, dark curls over her shoulder. "Very little, though I have gleaned pieces from memories."

"All that's needed for a revenant to form is the presence of strong magic lingering in the body, and a desire to go on," I said. "Sometimes revenants aren't even malicious. They're just determined to see some task through and won't let anyone stop them."

Emrys nodded. "If this wasn't intentional, her desire to go on could have been nothing more than a wish to protect Avalon."

"Or," I said, "she really was a servant of Lord Death, and she knew that becoming a revenant would make her nearly unstoppable."

Olwen pressed her hands to her face, struggling to contain herself at the thought. Behind her, Neve let her head fall back in exasperation.

"Your mind is intolerable," Caitriona told me.

"Look." I tried again. "I don't like the idea either, but it did seem like she controlled the Children at the lake. I think we have to accept the possibility that she allowed the transformation so she could continue her work in secret or become closer to invincible."

"Blessed Mother," Olwen said, pressing a hand to her chest.

"What if it was the Ring of Dispel?" Emrys said suddenly. "I've been wondering all day how she came to have it. What if Mari was right, and the ring has a corrupting influence? Could it have caused her to do all of this?"

Olwen shook her head. "The only ring she wore was one of moonstone . . . but . . . perhaps she kept it hidden on her? I will not deny that she had secrets, or that she enjoyed collecting those of others."

"Or it played no role in all of this," Neve said. "And the revenant happened upon it somewhere in the forest."

My own theories were still too thin to voice, and, ultimately, they didn't matter. The athame and ring were within reach, and now it was just a matter of figuring out how to find the revenant and take them from her.

Which, as my wounds clearly demonstrated, was easier said than done.

"A revenant is a parasite. It has to feed on magic to maintain a

physical form," I said. "Is there someplace north of here that's still protected by old, strong magic? There's such a thing as high magic, right?
A spell you ask the more powerful Goddess to cast on your behalf
through ritual?"

Olwen and Caitriona exchanged a look.

"Yes," Caitriona said cautiously. "Why?"

"Because that's the kind of magic she'll want, and most likely where
she's headed," I said.

"So to destroy a revenant, you first have to cut it off from that
magic?" Neve clarified, intrigue and horror warring in her expression.

"Right. You'd have to remove the old spellwork." I turned back to
the two priestesses. "Is that site far from here?"

Caitriona rose from her seat. "That is none of your concern, as
you'll be returning to the tower with the others."

"What?" I said. "No!"

Caitriona pulled the various pieces of her steel and leather armor
back on, stubbornly refusing to look at the four of us. Neve sat on the
arm of my chair with a sigh, shooting me a worried look.

"You are not leaving here without us," Olwen told her.

"Who will stop me?" Caitriona asked with a haughtiness that was
truly earned.

"No one, you wonderful, glorious fool," Olwen said. "I know where
it is too, and I'll just bring them there myself."

Caitriona's braid whipped around as she whirled on Olwen, eyes
flashing. Olwen didn't so much as flinch.

"I am not so delicate, Cait," Olwen told her softly. "And she was
my High Priestess, as well as yours. You should not have to face this
alone."

"It was my mistake," Caitriona said roughly. "I should have—"

"Stopped Sir Bedivere from doing something he kept secret until
yesterday?" Neve offered. "How? Tell us, and we'll let you go alone."

Catriona's grip on her gauntlet tightened, her jaw working.

"Everyone here understands the risks," I said. "And between all of us, we can figure out how to stop the revenant and get the athame and the ring."

"You still desire the Ring of Dispel?" Olwen asked, surprised. "Knowing what you know about it?"

"If the renewal ritual doesn't work as intended, it may be my brother's last hope," I said.

Caitriona's nostrils flared with her next hard breath. "Come if you must, then. But only after Olwen finishes her work and restores herself with water."

"I don't need to, I promise," Olwen said. "I don't feel weak or even tired, and I'm not about to haul in a tub of snow to melt."

"You will," Caitriona said, a gentle order. "I'll not have you or anyone else hurt."

She returned to her armor, wincing as she shifted her bad shoulder. She lifted her arm to her mouth in visible pain, trying to use her teeth to tighten the gauntlet.

"Here," Neve said, coming toward her. "Let me help you."

Caitriona suddenly looked like a fox caught by the tail. "No, truly, I can . . ."

Her words trailed off as Neve gently turned her wrist up and began to work the leather laces as if she had done it a thousand times before.

With her head bent over her work, Neve was too focused to notice the way the other girl had stilled, or the way the hardness of her expression had eased. For a moment, it didn't seem like she was even breathing—as if Neve were a feather that might drift away with even the smallest stirring of the air.

Olwen's finger prodded the stitches in my arm, sharply drawing my attention back to where she knelt in front of me.

"*Ow!*"

"Dear me," she said with a pointed look. "A thousand apologies for my rough handling."

I raised my brows. She raised hers back.

Emrys leaned over my shoulder, watching as she dabbed oil on the wound—oregano, by the pungent smell of it—and then a waxy ointment that she warmed between her fingers before gently massaging it into my skin.

"This is a deep wound," Olwen began, a small tremor in her voice. "It must have been terribly painful when she . . . when the revenant cut you." She drew a breath and looked up. "Viviane never would have done this if she were—if she were still herself. I'm so very sorry."

"I know, and there's nothing to apologize for." I caught Emrys's eye. He gave me a small, reassuring smile, and I knew I couldn't keep withholding the other important piece of information I'd learned at the barrow. "There's something else you should know. About me."

The others listened with varying degrees of horror as I spoke. Once or twice, Olwen seemed on the verge of bursting with some thought or question, but managed to hold it in—until she couldn't.

"Your bone was silver? It wasn't merely a vision?" she asked, eyeing the stitches.

I tensed. "As shiny as a polished coin. Just rotten to the core, I guess."

Emrys gripped my shoulder, but Neve cut in before he could speak.

"It doesn't mean what you clearly think it does," she said sternly as she came toward us. "So stop feeling sorry for yourself about it."

My lips parted in indignation.

"Yes, you are, and it's understandable, but it doesn't make all of your worst thoughts true," Neve continued. "And here I was thinking that finding a mystical fire sword would have cheered you up."

I sighed. "Well . . . there's something else I have to tell you about that, too."

Olwen nodded as I explained about the dreams, absorbing the information with the same imperviousness I'd come to expect from her. Caitriona hung back, an odd expression on her face I couldn't quite read.

"Why didn't you say something about this before?" Emrys asked, troubled.

"I don't know, I just . . . didn't know what it meant or if it meant anything at all." I looked at Olwen. "You don't think it's related to the silver, do you?"

"I think it has a far simpler explanation," Olwen said, exchanging another knowing look with Caitriona. "The Goddess uses the mist to speak to us in different ways. Song, dreams, even visions. Perhaps she, in all her great wisdom, has need for you to listen, and is speaking to you the only way she knows you will hear her."

"By sending me visions of unicorns?" I asked, pained. "She needs to work on her communication skills."

"Perhaps that is merely how she chose to appear to you," Olwen said.

"I have to admit, some part of me was afraid I was dreaming these things into existence," I said hoarsely.

Olwen glanced over to the door, where Emrys had leaned the sword I pulled from the lake. "A fascinating thought. Objects may be born from the mist in rare cases, but I believe that sword has been in existence far longer than you've been in Avalon."

"Do you recognize it?" Neve asked.

"It reminds me of a story Mari told us once, though I cannot quite recall it all now," Olwen said.

"You must ask her when you return to the tower," Caitriona said. "Such a treasure will delight her."

"I do have a suspicion about the silver, if you'd like to hear it," Olwen offered, reaching into her bag for a rolled bandage.

Emrys's hand was still on my shoulder, warm and reassuring. I had to tuck my hand under my leg to keep from reaching for it. "All ears."

"Well," she said, eyes shining with an excitement I might have appreciated more under different circumstances. "I believe bone turns silver when you come across a great deal of death magic. You're certain you never happened upon a curse or spell—perhaps in an object you touched?"

The ghost of the woman in the snowy field flashed through my mind. The icy fire of her touch as she'd tried to drag me into death with her. The mark over my heart burned with the memory.

Neve touched my shoulder, guessing my thoughts. By the look on Emrys's face, he'd figured it out, too.

I breathed in deeply, nodding. "That's probably it."

Olwen tied off the bandage. "Does that feel all right?"

I nodded. "Thanks. But here comes the hard part—are you both really willing to do what it takes to destroy the revenant, knowing she has some small piece of your High Priestess in her?"

"There is no other choice but to uproot her dark magic," Caitriona said simply. "We must get the athame to perform the purification ritual."

Olwen nodded. "If the ritual can restore the land and return the Children to their original selves, some good may yet come of this pain."

"Well, it should be easy enough to destroy the magic the revenant is feeding on, right?" I said.

Caitriona and Olwen exchanged a long, horrified look.

"Right?" I repeated.

"Is it possible to merely . . . trap and relocate the revenant before killing her?" Caitriona asked, a pleading note in her tone.

"Is that your way of telling us you can't remove the high magic attached to her new source?" I asked.

"Both Cait and I have the ability to do so," Olwen said. "Only a priestess of Avalon may cross the wards protecting it."

"Again, what's the problem?" Emrys asked.

"The location in question," Olwen said faintly, "is the living tomb of King Arthur."

42

The words seemed to inhale all the air in the cottage.

Caitriona began to pace again, hugging her injured right arm to her chest to stabilize her shoulder. Her face was tight with thought as she tried desperately to untie the knot Olwen had just presented us with.

"It is an obligation of the Nine to protect the sleeping king," Caitriona said, more to herself than to us. "Inherited from our sisters of ages past. If we remove the protective magic around the tomb, Arthur will die once and for all."

Emrys swore beneath his breath.

I was the only one willing to ask the obvious question. "Does it matter?"

"What do you mean?" Olwen asked.

"Does it matter if he finally dies?" I asked. "The whole reason he was kept alive was to come to the aid of the mortal world in their time of greatest need, and the guy couldn't even be bothered to wake up and help Avalon. Maybe we don't want his help."

Caitriona's back was to us, her body rigid with the war no doubt raging inside. "You do not understand. You cannot."

Olwen looked at us, her eyes pleading. "It's one of the few duties we've been able to fulfill since the isle fell to darkness. We took a vow."

Caitriona was only partly right. I might not have understood the point in keeping Arthur alive in the face of all we were up against, but I did recognize he meant something to them, just as he had meant something else to Nash, and to all those who longed for the legends to be true. The role the Nine played in protecting him was one of the few pure things that hadn't been corrupted by the decay spreading through this wasteland.

"Fine," I said, glancing at Emrys and Neve to make sure the three of us were in agreement. "Then we'll try to lead the revenant away from the tomb. If we can't, we'll have to remove the magic she's feeding on, even if it means letting Arthur go. Can you at least agree to that?"

"Cait?" Olwen looked to her, waiting.

When Caitriona faced us again, she was as pale as the snow outside.

"We're losing the light," I reminded her.

"Then . . . ," Caitriona said. "We had best hurry north and see the plan through."

"You're certain?" Olwen asked.

"The past cannot hold more worth than the future," Caitriona said, her voice thick. "Nor can one man be prized above the whole of the isle."

Olwen visibly relaxed as she pushed up off the floor. "I'll gather our things."

Caitriona nodded, retrieving her sword from where it lay across the table. She said nothing more, but I knew how much it would cost her to destroy a piece of something she had sworn to protect and serve.

And if she could escape the grip of all that she'd ever believed, perhaps there was hope for me, too.

The trudge north was an uphill battle through bone-chilling icy snow for the better part of an hour. The dead trees we'd used for cover dwindled in number the higher we went, until only craggy boulders were left to judge our slow progress.

My boots were soaked through, my toes, fingers, and face numb, when we reached what seemed to be the crest of the rise. Caitriona slowed, dropping onto her belly to crawl the rest of the way. We slithered up beside her, forming a line along the rocky edge.

The other side of the hill dipped a few feet before leveling out into flat earth. With a jolt, I realized we were at the northernmost point of the isle, and there was simply . . . nothing beyond it. Here, the edge of this Otherland ended abruptly, with a sheer drop down into the misty black void.

Between that darkness and us stood a handsome gray stone structure that looked to my eye like an open-air cathedral.

"Are you kidding me?" I whispered. "Every High Priestess gets buried in the same hunk of dirt and this guy gets a whole damn temple?"

Neve shushed me with a sharp jab of the elbow.

"Do you see anything?" Olwen asked, her voice scarcely above a whisper.

On cue, Emrys reached into his bag to pull out a pair of binoculars.

"The rocks," Caitriona breathed.

I shifted my gaze west of the tomb, where spears of dark stones jutted up from bare soil and formed a natural barrier to the cliff. A humble cottage sat among them, its thatched roof buckling into its single room—it must have belonged to Bedivere before he took shelter in the tower.

But that wasn't what Caitriona had spotted.

They were sprawled over the ground, clustered in the shadows of stones and trees. The coloring of the Children had made them nearly indistinguishable from the rocks and dead grass until they roused at the sound of a shrill, wordless call. I recognized it instantly.

The revenant.

The Children turned their faces toward the tomb in anticipation, barking and howling, foamy saliva dripping from their maws. They shivered and hissed as they crept out into what remained of the day-light.

It was all the proof I needed that the revenant was controlling them—instinct alone would have kept them in the shadows. Only their master could compel them to do the thing they most hated.

"Both plan A and plan B just got significantly harder," Emrys whispered.

He passed me the binoculars. I counted a dozen or so Children, all speckled with mud and crusted with leaf litter. I followed their line of sight over the uneven ground, over the ring of green grass that sur-rounded the tomb, clearly marking the edge of the protective magic. One by one, they prowled forward to that living line, pacing along its length, until, finally, she came.

The revenant emerged not from the rocks but from the tomb, her body formed from dirt and dead leaves. Olwen's sharp inhale faded beneath the eager howls of the Children as they saw what she was dragging forth by the ankle.

"Is that . . . ?" Emrys whispered.

Neve pressed her hands to her mouth to smother her horror.

And there was nothing we could do but watch as she threw the sleeping body of Arthur Pendragon to the Children as if he were a mere slab of half-rotten meat.

43

Before any of us could move or speak through the strangling horror, the Children had devoured everything but the bones, scattering the final remains of Arthur Pendragon on the snow in bloodied ribbons of flesh.

Emrys gripped my wrist, trying to draw my attention to something, but I would never know what. Time wound itself as if on a spindle, tighter and tighter, until at last the thread snapped and it unraveled in a frantic spin.

"Guess we're going with plan B," I choked out. There was no point in trying to lure the revenant away now. The protective magic had to be removed.

Caitriona rose with a cry of pure rage, struggling to unsheathe her sword with her wounded shoulder. The harsh song that poured from her turned the eddies of mist below into streams of fire. She charged down the hill, her sword at the ready, leaving us, and the tatters of our plan, behind.

The rest of us had one heartbeat to decide what to do.

"Blessed Mother," Olwen groaned, pushing up from the snow and darting right to make a wide circle around the tomb.

Neve turned to Emrys and me, her voice low and urgent. "Please be careful. I'm not sure I can call the light more than once . . ."

"We will," Emrys swore. "Good luck."

I nodded, an invisible fist closing around my throat as Neve rose, the image of grace and power, and followed Olwen. Her long wand was clutched in her fist—ready to protect the priestess in every way she could. But neither would make it if we didn't draw the attention of the revenant and her Children away from them.

Emrys squeezed my wrist one last time and picked up the sword to follow Caitriona down the hill. My hand closed around the cold handle of Emrys's small axe.

"Go," I told myself, shoving off the ground. *"Go!"*

Terror made me feel strangely weightless as I ran forward, half sliding down the hill's icy slant. The scene spread like a nightmarish painting by one of the old masters. The vividness of the fire, the blood, Caitriona's silver hair, Emrys's jacket as he raised his sword—every color was intensified against the blank canvas of the snow.

The revenant stood at the boundary of the protective magic, the emotionless shell of dirt and skin that was her face taking in the Children before her with glowing eyes. They formed a scattered line between her and us, knowing only one instinct—to protect their mother.

The creatures at the front threw themselves into Caitriona's magic blazes, screeching as they were reduced to smoldering lumps of char.

The High Priestess growled like a thundercloud and the others were unleashed in all their bloodlust, using the burned bodies to vault themselves up over the flames. They hurtled toward where Caitriona stood alone. Her foot slid back in a defensive stance as she fought to raise her sword, her face screwing up in agony. Her armor glowed in the maelstrom of fire she'd unleashed.

Emrys moved to stand at her right, and I took my place beside him, adrenaline and terror pounding in my blood. The creatures galloped on hands and feet as they circled us, their spidery limbs tangling, their hooked fangs chattering with excitement.

"Stay close!" Emrys shouted, turning so his back was to mine. Whatever else he might have said disappeared in a chorus of barks and yelps as the Children leapt, launching themselves at us with teeth bared.

I gagged at their rancid breath but held my ground. I swung the axe wildly, hacking at anything that tried to slash or grab me. My chest burned and it was several moments before I recognized that I was screaming, the sound ripped from somewhere primal inside.

As she cut an expert path forward, her blade slicing through soft skulls, legs, claws, Caitriona called back to us, *"With me!"*

We tried to follow, but the Children flooded between us and swarmed her from behind. Claws pierced the back of her metal breast-plate.

"Cait!" I screamed.

The girl took two staggering steps forward and then dove. As she rolled over the protective boundary of magic with a cry of raw pain, the Children clinging to her were thrown back with a tremendous pulse of light and magic. They yelped and stilled as they crumpled to the ground.

"Tamsin—*trade!*" Emrys called, and I turned. In that split second, he had already tossed the sword to me, and I had no choice but to take it and throw the axe toward him. He caught it by the handle and swung it up, but the heavy sword hit the ground, and I had to rip one of the Children away from it with my bare hands.

It clawed back, slashing through my already wounded arm. Pain lanced through me as the creature bit into the back of my neck. I choked with the pain and terror, falling to my knees.

"Tamsin!" Emrys shouted.

I grabbed the sword hilt. Fire ignited along the blade with a furious *whoosh.* Twisting back with a scream, I rammed it through the head of the creature, and only then did it release me.

Hot blood spilled down my front as Emrys fought his way back toward me, but my eyes stared ahead, where Caitriona was facing the High Priestess.

The revenant darted forward, the athame aimed at Caitriona's bare throat. Deflecting it with her sword, Caitriona spun around, slashing down across the creature's chest. The movement tore open her healing wound, flooding the front of her armor with blood. Pieces of grass, wood, and mud fell away from the revenant, only to rise again as she re-formed.

"Cait!" I panted out as we finally fought our way to the edge of the protective magic. She had to get the revenant to cross the barrier, otherwise we wouldn't be able to help her.

Caitriona's dark eyes widened, sweat dripping from her face. She turned, looking past us, but her shouts were lost in the tumult of monstrous shrieks. I followed her gaze to where more of the Children had appeared at the top of the hill.

She threw out her left hand, the other limp at her side, struggling to hold on to her sword. Her lips formed the words of a song I couldn't hear. Mist rose on the hill, thick and churning, but before it could ignite, the revenant struck again, gripping her by the neck and throwing her toward the ground.

Caitriona hooked her legs around the revenant and twisted, sending the creature flying toward the edge of the barrier, her head and arms falling across it. I lunged toward her with my blade, swinging it down, but the creature was too fast, and the flaming sword hissed as it severed only one of the revenant's hands.

I brought my foot down hard on it to keep it pinned there. Frustration tore at me when I realized it was the hand with the ring, not the athame.

The revenant's screech was like a knife in the brain. I screamed with her—all of us did—and even the Children shrank back from it. The revenant rose to her full, terrifying height and turned to me with burning eyes.

A voice like midnight slashed through my mind, drowning out the high-pitched keening.

I know you.

I gasped, dropping back onto my knees. The sword fell from my hand.

I saw you born in my dreams.

"St-stop—" I managed to choke out. My hands squeezed against my head, trying to drive the words out. *"Stop it!"*

He does not know what you are . . .

The air between us brightened, shimmering, then faded to nothing.

I heard Olwen's voice as if it had traveled across worlds. "Now, Neve!"

"Wait—" I tried to say. "What does that mean?"

The wave of blistering light had already been unleashed.

Sensing that the magic was gone, the Children sprinted toward Caitriona as she fought to rise from the ground. Neve's magic threw them back, incinerating them.

The revenant stood before us, her back to the throbbing power, letting it burn away her edges. A flicker of humanity appeared on her face.

"Caitriona." The voice that emerged from it was as sweet as the first day of spring, and achingly tender. *"My Cait."*

The revenant reached out to her with the athame, her body cracking and tearing as the light broke through it. The young priestess stumbled forward, tears streaming down her face as she reached out a hand.

"Why?" she begged. "Why did you do this?"

In her final moment, the revenant whispered, *"The power . . . I could not stop . . . what had already begun . . ."*

Her body disintegrated, crumbling back into bone and earth. As Neve's light faded and the air cooled, the athame fell to the ground, glowing with heat and power.

Caitriona cried out into the sudden silence, her sob catching in her throat as she dropped to the ground.

My body felt hollow as I slowly knelt beside her. Hesitating, I wrapped my arm around her shoulder.

Instead of pulling away, Caitriona curled into me, sobbing against my shoulder. My throat was painfully raw, but I didn't know what I would say if I could speak.

Neve and Olwen ran toward us and wrapped their arms around our small huddle, alive and whole and trembling. I clung to them, letting the insistent wind cool the sweat on my skin and the blood in my veins. But there was a warmth in me like the sun, rising and rising until I thought I might burst with it.

I pulled away from them, looking over my shoulder to seek out Emrys's gaze.

But there was only ash and mist swirling in the air.

I unwound my arms from the others, fear slamming through my chest like a spike. "Emrys? Emrys!"

There was no answer.

I ran toward the hill, searching the remains of the Children that hadn't burned to dust.

"Emrys!" If something had happened while I wasn't looking—

I heard the others calling for him, their voices echoing through the silence, growing in pitch and fear.

Neve came to my side, shaking her head. "I don't understand . . . The spell wouldn't have harmed him. Could one of the Children have carried him away?"

The thought came like a blow to the stomach. I bent at the waist, trying not to vomit.

"Wait," Neve said, grasping my arm and pulling me up again. "Look."

Behind her, Olwen's face drained of color. My heart rose into my throat as she and Caitriona came toward us.

A trail of footsteps led back up and over the hill, heading away from the tomb and us—heading, I knew, to the portal back to our world.

I *knew*.

The Ring of Dispel was gone, and so was Emrys Dye.

And that sun I had felt in me, the one that had burned so bright, sank back below the dark horizon.

44

The light was failing by the time we started our return to the tower. Caitriona had initially suggested waiting out the darkness in one of the watchtowers—but that was before we came across the first of the Children among the trees.

They lay scattered where they had fallen from the branches. Their bodies were whole, but unmoving, as if the spark of life had simply been plucked from them.

Maybe it had.

My companions stopped, dropping behind the broken body of a hollow log, but I continued forward.

"Tamsin, wait—" Neve tried to grab hold of me, but I pulled free.

I wasn't afraid. I wasn't curious.

I couldn't feel anything at all.

I moved like I was at the bottom of the lake, each step forward taking more strength than the last. Each bit of ground a fight to keep underfoot.

Caitriona had fashioned a sheath for the sword so I could carry it on my back, rather than wield the heavy weapon like a torch. Between Neve and the priestesses, with their command over the mists, they were able to create enough light to guide the way.

I walked toward the nearest monster and stared down at it. Robbed of life and the terrifying instinct that had compelled it, the creature was almost pitiful. Its tongue lolled out of its mouth and its limbs drooped as I used my foot to roll it onto its back.

Its empty sockets stared up at me. Scavenger beetles had already made quick work of the eyes.

Olwen dropped onto her haunches beside the creature, her forehead creasing as she touched the shriveled gray skin of its chest.

She looked back at Caitriona and shook her head.

"The High Priestess—the revenant—gave them life, then," Caitriona said, looking exhausted. The bandages on her face were soaked with sweat and grime. "And the curse, or whatever power sustained them, ended with her."

Neve drew in a sharp breath as she touched one of the creatures with a single finger.

"What troubles you?" Olwen asked.

"Curses *can* outlive their caster," Neve explained. "But I don't think that's the case here. It's like we cut the head off from the rest of the body."

"Is there still a chance the ritual could restore them?" Caitriona rasped out.

"I believe the best we can hope for . . ." Olwen swallowed. "The best that we might hope for is that the ritual will release whatever piece of their souls might still be trapped inside these bodies."

My top lip curled back at the devastation in their faces. If they'd been stupid enough to believe the ritual would restore everything to the way it was, they deserved the pain it had won them.

"There's never been any hope for them," I said acidly as I continued forward through the wasted forest, stepping over the bodies in the trampled snow. The air was sharp and icy in my chest. "You just couldn't accept it."

With my eyes fixed on the corpses, I nearly crashed into Neve as she stepped in front of me. Her face was pinched with worry. When I moved to go around her, she moved with me, mirroring the action.

"Move," I told her coldly.

She didn't.

"Move," I said again, a pressure rising in my ears.

Neve stepped forward, and before I could pull away, she gripped my shoulders. I tried to shift, but she was surprisingly strong, locking me in place. Forcing me to be still. To feel it—all of it.

I had never felt as exposed as I did then, stripped of a lifetime's worth of lies and careful performance. The humiliating truth was bared for all to see. Hidden beneath all those cynical, cold layers wasn't a core of strength. It was fear. It was the little girl even I'd tried to leave behind.

I slumped against Neve, my face buried in her shoulder.

"I'm sorry," she said softly, wrapping her arms around me. "Please don't turn away from us."

Every part of me felt like it might snap. For a moment, I smelled pine and realized I'd never taken his sweater off. I pulled away, ripping it off me and letting it fall over the creature. The cold was better than having it touch my skin.

"I'm so stupid," I said in a ragged voice. "I let it happen again."

Alone.

Discarded for something more important. And it *was* more important—saving his mother, getting away from his father, all of it had outstripped whatever trust had grown between us.

If he was even telling the truth at all, that familiar voice whispered in my mind. *Clever Emrys Dye, always quick to hide and lie.*

The thought was enough to leave me raw. I'd told him my truth. I'd told him things not even Cabell knew.

"He is the only one who should feel shame," Caitriona said, anger simmering in the words. "He deceived us all."

Olwen stroked my arm, her fingers skimming over the gash she'd hastily rebandaged. "You do not have to keep the thought of him from your heart, but do not let the love in you harden because of him. He was not worthy."

"What do you mean?" I asked.

"I should have said something of it before, but I did not want to wound him." Her smile was tinged with sadness. "I do recognize that sword you carry, and I do know its story. Mari told it to me years ago."

"Then . . . ," I said. "What is it?"

"I believe that blade is called Dyrnwyn, or White-Hilt. It was forged in Avalon and once carried by a king, Rhydderch Hael," Olwen explained. "It was said that the blade would burn with flames when held by someone worthy and well born."

I stared at her.

"Are you certain?" Caitriona asked.

"Thanks for the vote of confidence," I said dryly, but a little laugh bubbled in me at her expression as she realized the implication.

"No, I did not mean *that*," she said. "Of course you are worthy."

"I'm really not," I said, "and no offense was taken. Should we test the theory?"

I held the sword toward them, hilt-first, but all three stepped back.

"Really?" I asked.

"I don't want a piece of metal to pass judgment on me," Neve said, holding up her hands.

"I am content with my own sense of worth," Olwen said simply.

Caitriona eyed it several moments longer than the others but in the end still turned away. "Tamsin, are you sure you don't wish for us to follow him? The snow will allow us to track him with ease."

Neve gripped my hand, watching me. Waiting for the choice to be made.

I could follow Emrys. I could probably even take the Ring of Dispel back before he presented it to Madrigal. The portal might still be open.

But there was the ritual to think of. There was Cabell and Neve and Bedivere, and the priestesses who had become friends even as I'd fought to push them away. There were the survivors at the tower, still fighting against all odds. There was Avalon—the place of beauty and life it could become again.

"No," I said. "He's already gone."

"How does he plan on returning to your world," Olwen asked, "without any of us there to open the path for him?"

Neve and I exchanged a look.

"About that . . . ," I began.

Olwen's eyes widened in wonder at the story of the Hag of the Mist, the offering, and her instructions that the portal could only be used once to go into Avalon and once to return to the mortal world.

"I believe we'll be able to open the original path back to the mortal world for you, even if the ritual isn't successful," Olwen said.

"It won't fail," I told her. *It can't.*

"Are you angry with us for keeping it from you?" Neve asked, glancing at Caitriona.

Her silvery hair shimmered with the snow falling from the trees. "No, for even now, with your path home open, you have chosen to stay. With us."

Neve smiled.

Caitriona cleared her throat, turning her back to us. "We should continue on. I do not want the others to worry more than they already have."

I raised my head and began to walk, letting the chaos in my chest settle and a new calmness take hold. Neve smiled at me when I glanced over, and there was nothing in her warm gaze that was pitying or wary. The quiet stillness of the isle gave me the gift of sudden clarity. An understanding that the pain I'd feared for so long was the very thing that told me I had survived the loss.

We kept pace with one another as the shadows around us deepened to welcome the long night.

We stopped once to rest, giving Olwen the opportunity to check our bandages for signs of infection, but it was only for a few moments.

With the athame back in their possession, they were eager to perform the cleansing ritual, and I was growing more and more eager to get back to Cabell. After what had happened with Bedivere . . . I couldn't imagine how he was feeling.

Finally, the tower came into view, its highest stones illuminated by the fires still burning in the moat. The lines of Caitriona's face eased at the sight of it, and she doubled her pace.

But as we emerged through the last stretch of the forest, I found myself slowing.

"What is it?" Neve asked.

"Where are they?" I asked, looking around. Before we left, the Children had formed a ring around the perimeter of the tower, one we should have crossed by now.

"The revenant must have called them to her," Neve said as we finally caught up to Caitriona on the path. She stood at the tree line, taking in the sight of the tower in the near distance, its ancient stones aglow with flame. Long streams of red flowed down the nearest wall, reflecting the light like silk. Mist lingered over the mile-long path leading down to the moat. The drawbridge, to my surprise, had already been lowered.

The Mother tree looked darker from this distance. Its upper branches were covered in white, masking what little green remained.

Olwen's steps crunched through the snow behind me, but as she came to my side, she froze midstride. Her breathing grew ragged, the white puffs mingling with the mist. For the first time, I realized I wasn't just smelling fire smoke. Something bitter underscored it—burned cloth, maybe.

And something worse.

"It looks like they've started the celebrations without us," Neve said, squinting. "I wonder why they used red banners, though."

And then I understood.

Caitriona gave a hoarse cry, bolting down the hill to the lowered drawbridge. Olwen was close behind her, stumbling through the snow and rocks in their way.

I couldn't move. The darkness curled around me, pressing down on my shoulders with its icy hands, trapping me in place.

"Those aren't banners, Neve," I managed to choke out. "That's blood."

45

The silence of the dead had its own power, great and terrible. Like a dark pane of glass, it swallowed everything, and nothing, not even the light, reemerged.

The courtyard had become a battlefield, the arena for one final, desperate stand. A place that only swarming flies and foul wind dared to enter now.

The lower half of the Mother tree was charred black, its remaining leaves trampled into the bloodied snow. Deri was a pile of kindling beside it, still gripping the massive trunk. The bodies of sprites ringed it like a halo of death.

Every part of me strained, desperate to turn and run. I forced myself to stand there at the edge of the slaughter. I forced myself to see.

To see it all.

Betrys, fallen just before the gate, the first line of defense between the monsters and the innocents inside. Her sword gripped tight even in death. Arianwen lay near her, her body draped over Lowri's. Seren and Rhona lay across the white steps of the tower, their hands reaching for one another amid the carnage around them. Rivers of blood had flowed over these stones and dried into rust-colored streams.

It was that stench, of death, of decay—that was the only thing that felt real. Olwen was moving, stumbling, among the bodies, screaming and sobbing as she desperately checked them for life.

Caitriona ran for the tower, climbing through the remains of everything she had known and loved. The once-mighty doors to the great hall were splintered and torn from their hinges. And when her anguished shouts echoed across the courtyard, I knew no one inside had survived.

Neve said something behind me, her voice ragged and breaking, but I was selfish. I could only think of one thing. One name.

Cabell.

My brother . . . he . . . It wasn't possible.

None of this was possible. It wasn't real.

I took off at a run, searching the bodies, turning them over to reveal the agony of their deaths, ravaged faces, torn and devoured. I knew I was screaming when it became impossible to draw a breath, calling his name, pleading with whatever gods might actually exist.

The dead were inescapable, the echoes of their sheer terror in those final moments hovering around us in the mist. The animals lay slaughtered in the stable. The men and women were draped over the walls, bodies broken and skin gaping. Aled and Dilwyn were in Olwen's garden. Angharad and countless others were in the courtyard field, where a few sprouts had emerged from the dirt to be baptized in gore.

Where was Cabell? *Where?*

I ran to the dungeons, to the springs, to the path beneath the armory, until, finally, I saw that the door to the kitchen had been torn off, and a memory of Bedivere's voice broke through the searing panic in my mind. *The last hope of Avalon.*

I clambered over the bodies of Children and Avalonians alike to get inside. The cabinet had separated from the wall, blocked by a man's body, and I ripped it open the rest of the way, sliding down the blood-slicked ladder.

And after everything I had seen, what lay below in the fairy path was what brought the bile burning up my throat.

Gore rose above the top of my boots, black and thick in the

darkness. I pulled my flashlight out of my bag, my hands trembling so badly I nearly dropped it as I surveyed the bodies around me. What was left of them.

Anyone who had dared to come down here had been trapped. The door leading up into the grove was shut. Locked. And with no hope of escape, they'd been torn to shreds.

My flashlight beam swept over the massacre, and I held my breath so I wouldn't have to take in the overpowering stench of death. Pieces of Bedivere's familiar armor were scattered among the bodies. The cold snaked around me as the light ran across a piece of worn brown leather.

I saw my hand reach down to the blood-drenched ground, my fingers dipping into the dark, grisly pool to retrieve it. The piece of leather was the size of my palm, still recognizable as a jacket collar. I saw myself turn it over, saw a child's careful stitching, once yellow, now crimson, and the letters *LAR*. Beneath it, like a hidden curse sigil, was a tattooed patch of pale skin.

I leaned over and vomited up everything in my stomach. Gasping, retching, until I lost all feeling in my hands and dropped the cloth and the flashlight.

The darkness swallowed me, and I didn't know where to turn, didn't know which way was out. A pain like nothing I'd ever felt before split me in two, and all I could do was hold on to the wall behind me to try to keep from drowning in what was left of the dead.

Of Cabell.

I cried, the sound echoing on the stone walls, my whole body heaving. Everything . . . everything for *this*. For the person I loved most in the world to have suffered this—the pain and fear in this dark, that moment of knowing he wouldn't get out, of being reduced to nothing more than memory and this . . . *this* . . .

I couldn't find my way out, and I had no place to go. So I stayed, the tears pouring out of me, hoping and praying I would just die of the pain, until Neve at last came and led me out.

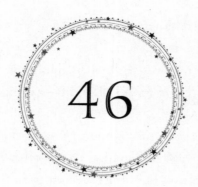

46

I stood alone on the curtain wall, gazing out into the dark forest. Time was playing games with my mind, and here, in a place of almost endless night, it seemed to matter even less. A part of me hoped that if I just stood here, letting the cold wind do what it would to me, I'd become stone too. I wouldn't have to untangle the bonfire of thoughts in my mind, or ease the throbbing in my chest.

My eyes watered from the cold, but tears wouldn't come. The well deep inside me had emptied in an almost frightening way. When it filled again, it was with a familiar poison. One I deserved every burning drip of.

You did this.

You brought him here because you thought you knew best.

It was all for nothing.

You got what you deserved.

And he died hating you.

My brother—the sensitive, brilliant, talented, charming one. The best not just of the Larks but of any world. Avalon had brought him nothing but pain and death. I never should have asked him to come with me.

I never should have gone looking for Nash.

The weight of the loss hit again, knocking the breath from my body. Cabell had been so close to the end of his nightmare. So close to breaking free of the darkness that had tried to smother every last trace of hope he'd had. To devour him.

I couldn't close my eyes without imagining it. How quickly and savagely death had come for all of them—within hours of the isle's salvation.

A sickening fury crept through me, bringing the taste of bile to my mouth again. There was no Goddess or any other god. There was no fate. There had only ever been the cruel uncertainties of life.

The isle's mist roamed between the trees, spreading its long, searching fingers toward the tower. The last of the Nine's magic had dwindled, and the fires inside the moat were no longer burning. I stared down into it, eyes skimming over the bones, the charred wood, the swords and shields that had fallen in and become distorted with heat.

What was I supposed to do? There was hardly anything left of my brother to bury. The way to the barge, to the human world, was clear now and there was nothing to stop me or anyone else from leaving, but what was left for me there? A small life riddled with painful memories of being left behind and made to feel useless. A job I'd inherited, a guild that had never wanted me, no friends to lean on, no place to go but back to a home that was meant to be shared, full of things my brother would never need again.

At the end of everything, what was left?

Quiet weeping filled the gloaming, and a faint light rose below. With stiff muscles, I pulled myself away from the wall and looked down into the courtyard.

Olwen was laying the bodies out alongside one another, tenderly arranging even the most grotesque of them. She tried to clean their faces, their arms and legs, but when she came to Betrys, she began to shake. She pressed her face into her bloodied apron to muffle her cries.

This.

The word sang through me, as clearly as if someone had whispered it in my ear.

This. This was what was left.

Them.

I made my way along the wall, stopping to hook my arms beneath the body of a man slumped over his broken bow. I brought him down the stairs, struggling beneath his weight, and laid him out beside the others. Olwen looked up, but I had already started back toward the stairs, where more of the dead waited.

We worked in silence, and I found that the movement, the focus, stilled my thoughts. At some point, Neve joined us, washing and preparing the dead as Olwen and I brought them to her. Neve, who had once been so intrigued by death, had lost the last trace of light from her eyes as the grim reality overtook her.

Then Caitriona came, carrying Mari's frail body out of the tower. She laid Mari beside her sisters, her face rigid with barely suppressed emotion.

She brought Flea out last, but as she came near us, she stopped. Her grip on the girl tightened, her face strained beneath her bandages.

"Cait," Olwen said softly, lifting her arms.

"No," the other girl said roughly, cradling Flea.

"She's already gone, dear heart," Olwen said. "There is nothing to be done now."

"No." Caitriona closed her eyes, pleading.

Neve rose and went to Caitriona, placing a gentle hand on her back and guiding her forward. I wiped the sweat and grime from my face with the sleeve of my jacket, barely able to look as the little girl was placed with the others.

Flea looked almost peaceful, and somehow that made it worse, because I knew her final moments had been anything but.

I crouched beside her, touching her hand, studying her like I had the others. I didn't want to forget any part of her. Her small-boned frame. The thin blue veins on her eyelids. The white-blond strands tucked up into her knit cap.

I took her left hand and cleaned it with a new rag. Olwen took her right, placing a small bundle of herbs and dried flowers in it, as she had with all the others. Caitriona hung back, tears streaming down her face. Neve stayed close to her side, giving me a helpless look as she hooked her hand around Caitriona's elbow.

Gently, gently, I placed Flea's hand over her stomach, but as I pulled back, my fingers skimmed over something tucked into the waistband of her breeches. Frowning, I lifted the blood-stiff fabric.

"What is that?" Neve asked, leaning over my shoulder.

The others crowded around me as I held the flat, palm-sized rock toward the nearest wisp of glowing mist.

No. It wasn't rock at all, but bone. And the etchings . . .

Olwen rose, disappearing into her workshop, only to reappear a few moments later with a basket holding the vessel of High Priestess Viviane. She turned the sculpture upside down and I brought the shard of bone to the hole there, adjusting its angle until it fit perfectly in place.

"Where did she find that?" Caitriona breathed out.

"Or who did she steal it from?" I said, my words scratchy.

"We were checking her each night for missing belongings," Olwen said, resting her hands over Flea's smaller ones. "She must have come across it while we were gone."

"Can the vessel be repaired?" I asked. "If someone broke it intentionally, I want to know what memories they were trying to hide."

Olwen shook her head. "There is no one alive who can repair it and rejoin it magically."

A thought slithered through my mind, hushed and coiling with anticipation. "Not in this world. But what if there was someone in the mortal one?"

The Bonecutter had been crafting keys for skeleton knobs for ages and could procure anything, even basilisk venom. If they couldn't repair the vessel, maybe they would know someone who could.

I tucked the bone shard into the basket and covered it with the cloth. It would be coming with us on our journey.

Caitriona stroked Flea's cold cheek.

"What should we do?" Neve asked after a moment. "Bury them?"

Caitriona shook her head. "We cannot. We have to burn them, as we did the others."

"But the curse—" Olwen began.

"We do not know if the curse is still upon the land," Caitriona said. "Better their souls release forever to death than risk them turning into the very creatures that killed them."

"Tamsin and I can do it," Neve told them.

"No," Caitriona said. "Honoring the dead is one of the most sacred duties of a priestess of Avalon. It must be our final act as such."

"You're still a priestess of Avalon," I told her.

"I am the priestess of nothing," Caitriona said, rising. "That is all I shall ever be."

We placed the bodies on the field within the courtyard, where crops might have grown, if there'd been time. Caitriona sang for the fire, the words gritty as they emerged from her throat. Yet when Olwen took her hand and began to hum a low tune, Caitriona pulled away.

Sparks gathered among the bodies, nurtured into small flames by the debris we'd used for kindling.

"I will not pray to a goddess who allowed such a thing to happen," Caitriona said.

Olwen looked as if she wanted to reach for her, but in the end, she only bowed her head and sang the prayer alone.

"To you, Mother, we send the beloved of our hearts . . ."

Her song vanished beneath the *whoosh* of fire as it caught and spread, climbing higher and higher over the broken pieces of furniture, over the hay, over the bodies, encasing them, just for a moment, in pure light.

The four of us stood together, watching as the smoke turned silver against the darkness and merged into the looming mist. Out of the corner of my eye, I saw Caitriona take a step forward, as if to climb onto the pyre.

"If we were to die . . . ," she rasped out. "If we were to die, it should have been together. This pain . . . I cannot bear the thought of never meeting them again."

The air shimmered with heat. Across the sea of flames and smoke, a pale creature stood, watching us. Its horn glinted as it bowed its head. I swiped the ash and grime from my eyes in disbelief and looked again, but only the fire remained.

Olwen hooked her arm through Caitriona's, for comfort or to hold her there, I wasn't sure. Neve looked at me, wearing her shattered heart for all to see.

Them.

I hadn't been able to save Cabell, or any of the others. But I could help them. Take care of them.

"Choose me."

The words were raw, born from some deep part of me I'd worked so hard to push back. From the child given away. The girl left behind over and over.

"Choose me," I said again, the words scratchy with desperation as the others turned to me. "Choose me, because I choose you."

"Tamsin . . . ," Neve whispered.

"I can't be who they were to you, I know that. And I've never been a good person," I said, feeling the heat billow past me. "But I'm trying, and I know that whatever comes, I can stand it—I can survive it—if the four of us stay together. So please, choose me . . . just . . ."

I stepped back, pressing my hands to my face, but someone was there to pull them away—Caitriona. Her hands were rough and callused as she gripped mine.

"I chose you the moment I discovered you had left for the athame," she said. "That you risked yourself for all of us was an act of courage and hope. For all my life, as long as I live, I will be your friend. What we vow here, let no one tear asunder."

Olwen and Neve stood on either side of us, and Olwen's arms were soft and warm as she wrapped them around us both. Neve clasped her hands around our joined ones. Something in me settled then, easing its grip on my chest. My lungs, my heart, my whole body seemed to swell with some greater emotion, as if we had sealed the promise with magic.

"If we are together, we will survive this," Olwen said, her voice breaking. "But we must decide what to do."

"Will you come back to the human world with us?" Neve asked, looking between them. "You could open the path. We'll cross with you."

I was surprised when Caitriona said simply, "Yes. I think . . . I think there is no other choice now."

"What about the ritual?" I asked.

"What of it?" Olwen asked.

I knew my shock must have registered on my face because I saw confusion on theirs. "After everything, shouldn't we try?"

"The Nine is not whole. It will never be again," Caitriona said.

My grip tightened around her hands, not letting her pull back. "It *is* simple. I'm not entirely sure the instructions say what you think they do. Nowhere does it state you *have* to have a specific number of priestesses to perform the ceremony."

"*Join hands with your Sisters, and be whole of heart and power once more,*" Neve recited. Her expression turned thoughtful. "The two of you would know better than us, but I can see Tamsin's point. It may simply be that those performing it have only to be together in purpose."

"*Whole of heart and power once more,*" I recited. "That just sounds like a poetic flourish to me."

Caitriona was still shaking her head, her face tormented.

"It would restore her land at least," Olwen said. "And purify the mists."

"The Goddess has already left us," Caitriona said. "She has left Avalon."

"I do not believe that's true," Olwen said. "How else would Neve be here? How would Tamsin? They were brought to us for a reason, and I have to believe that this is that reason."

Caitriona wore the struggle plainly on her face, but she was softening to the idea, I could feel it.

"Please . . . ," Olwen begged. "They can't have died for nothing."

And finally, in the glowing light of the pyre, Caitriona turned toward the tower and led us to the great hall in a silent procession.

47

While Olwen and Caitriona prepared the altar in the great hall, cleansing it with incense and oils, Neve and I returned upstairs to change into clean clothes and gather our belongings. The sky was beginning to brighten with first light, and all I could think was that it was the same color as the smoke still rising from the pyre. The smell of the bodies burning turned my stomach, but there was nothing left in it to expel.

Neve shut the door behind us one last time and watched as I moved toward the chamber that Cabell and Emrys had shared.

I stopped, feeling the words well in me. The story that finally wanted to be told.

"You were right," I told her. "I do have a death mark."

"Tamsin—" she said softly.

"Nash and Cabell had left me behind at our camp. They'd gone to search another sorceress's vault for Arthur's dagger, and they had no use for me." I swallowed the knot lodged in my throat. "And then I heard her . . . I heard a voice on the wind. I thought she was calling for me. It was a White Lady."

A woman who'd been murdered by her lover and left to guard her lover's treasure until she killed another to take her place.

"I was just a stupid kid, and I was so angry and hurt they'd left me," I whispered. "Even though I knew better, even though Nash had

441

told us so many ghost stories, all I could think was *She wants me.* I know this is going to sound absurd, but . . . there was a part of me that even wondered if she was my mother, and she'd finally come to get me."

We'd stood alone together on the open, snow-dusted field, and even as she'd reached out to touch the skin over my heart, to freeze it, I'd wondered if the look on her face was love.

Neve wrapped her arms around me from behind, pressing the side of her face against my shoulder. Instead of pulling away, I leaned into her.

When she released me, she waited for me to look back before saying quietly, "I'm going to go up to the library for a little while. Have one last look around."

I nodded. "I'll meet you there in a minute."

I waited until her footsteps faded on the stairway before facing the door again and pushing it open.

The neighboring chamber was a mirror image of our own. The icy bite of the air had set in deeper with its emptiness. Aside from Cabell's workbag sitting on the end of the bed, there were no signs that anyone had been sleeping there.

A fresh bitterness filled me. Emrys couldn't have known that we would find the ring, but the fact that he'd left no trace of himself here—it made me wonder.

I don't care, I thought, picking up Cabell's bag and hugging it to my chest. *I don't.*

I reached into the pocket of my jacket, my fist closing around the piece of smooth wood. I gripped it tightly against the swell of emotion in me, until its edges cut into my skin.

And then, with a deep breath, I placed the small carved bird on the pillow and walked away.

I found Neve not wandering through the oaken shelves of the library, but at the very back of it, contemplating the tapestries that covered the windows. On one, a man wreathed in branches raised his sword to face the knight on the other, draped in holly.

Neve glanced back as I came toward her.

I touched the woven figure sprouting with oak leaves. "Have you heard this story? The Holly King and the Oak King?"

"No," she said. "But I can make a guess—they represent the turning of the seasons?"

"Basically," I said. "They're personifications of winter and summer, or the dark half of the Wheel of the Year, and the light. They duel one another again and again, their power waxing and waning as their season comes and goes. Some versions say the Holly King is Lord Death and that they're dueling for a woman they both love, or the Goddess herself."

It was surprising to see it represented here, but given the size of the library and the variety of manuscripts in it, I figured the Avalonians had collected stories from all over the world.

"Should we go down?" Neve asked, struggling to pick up her fanny pack. While the spell expanded its capacity, it didn't do much to lighten the load.

"Yeah," I said, and seized by a strong impulse, I touched her arm. "Thank you for being my friend, even when I didn't deserve it."

"You really didn't make it easy," she said. "But then, nothing truly good ever is."

Footsteps echoed up to us from the staircase. I angled back toward it, expecting to see Olwen or Caitriona there—but no one came.

I frowned, moving to the stairs, but there was no one there. Neve and I exchanged a look, continuing down the steps and searching the darkened hallway of the level below. There was movement there, all right.

"Oh," I whispered, dropping to a crouch. "Come here, you rascal."

A trembling gray kitten, his fur matted with blood, darted out of the shadows and all but leapt into my outstretched arms. His claws snagged the front of my jacket as he tried to wrap himself around my neck.

"It's Mari's cat," I explained to Neve. His tail flicked my face and made me think of home.

Neve reached out, stroking the kitten's soft head. "Where have you been hiding, little Griflet?"

And what have you seen? I wondered.

"How would you like to live in a library?" I asked the kitten as Neve and I made our way down to the great hall. "With many other cute and devious friends?"

Olwen met us on the stairs. "I was just coming to find you."

I pushed my hair back so she could see the kitten. Olwen's expression became a watercolor of emotion, none strong enough to hold for more than a moment. "Oh, Blessed Mother."

Carefully, she extracted the kitten's claws from my jacket and tucked him into the crook of her arm. He purred contentedly.

"Are you ready?" Neve asked.

"Yes." Olwen scratched between Griflet's scruffy ears. "The ritual has to be performed at daybreak, so we haven't a moment to spare."

The great hall still reeked of blood, and dark stains were still visible on the floor, even after we'd tried to clean it. The statue of the Goddess loomed above the altar, her white stone body speckled with blood. At the center of her chest, a candle still burned.

Caitriona stood with her back to us, staring down at the items before her: the athame, the wand, the chalice, a bowl of what looked to be dirt, and a carafe of glowing springwater. At Griflet's quiet mewling, she turned, her eyes widening.

"How?" she rasped out.

"Tamsin and Neve found him hiding upstairs," Olwen explained. She brought him up to press his soft face to her cheek, then stowed him away in the basket with Viviane's vessel. Griflet nestled into the soft blanket covering it.

Neve and I set our bags down beside it and accepted the thin wreaths of greens and twisted wood that Olwen placed upon our heads.

"I don't have magic," I said, understanding.

"Trust me" was all Olwen said.

Caitriona motioned us forward to gather around the altar. When I hung back a step, Olwen gently nudged me into place between her and Caitriona. I froze, my pulse thrumming in my veins as I stared down at the glossy black top of the altar. The flecks of gold and silver in the polished stone looked like stars in a night sky.

The athame's blade glinted. The chalice was silver, simple in its form but rimmed with glittering sapphires and emeralds. It was the wand that caught my eye, though. Longer than my arm, longer than even Neve's own tool, it looked like a straight branch capped with a silver point.

While Olwen donned ceremonial robes, Caitriona did not. She bent down to retrieve the massive tome that she had placed near her feet.

I drew in an unsteady breath as she thumbed through the pages, revealing glimpses of color and glorious illuminations. Neve shifted, clearing her throat in the silence. Out of the corner of my eye, I saw her decide—she set her wand down near our bags, freeing her hands to let the magic come naturally.

"Hail Mother of All, the heart of the world—" Caitriona's voice choked, but steadied again as she began to chant. The words were grave and edged with no small amount of anger. *"Earth of your body."*

"Earth of your body," Olwen repeated, licking her cracked lips as Caitriona added a handful of dirt to the chalice.

"Water of your blood."

Olwen echoed her again, pouring water into the chalice.

"Breath of your daughter."

Olwen leaned forward and breathed into the chalice.

Sickly mist rolled up and over the steps, as if called forth by the chanting. It spread through the great hall like roots in dark soil, feeling its way toward us.

Caitriona used the statue's candle to light another. *"Fire of your soul."*

"Fire of your soul," Olwen said. And then, together, they said, *"We call upon your power."*

Caitriona shut the book and picked up the athame, chanting as she sliced her palm and squeezed blood into the chalice.

"Let that which dies know your light and be born again."

Olwen took the ritual dagger next, cutting her palm quick and neat, before adding her blood to the gaping mouth of the cup. At our feet, mist gathered.

"Let that which dies know your light and be born again."

Neve was next, repeating the words.

"Let that which dies know your light and be born again."

And then it was my turn. I felt their eyes on me as I brought the fine tip of the blade to my hand. My arm ached in memory, and an image of the High Priestess flashed behind my eyelids until I forced them open. With one last deep breath, I sliced down. The blade was sharp enough that my skin only stung for a moment.

"Let that which dies know your light and be born again."

I added my blood to the chalice. The damp touch of the mist crawled up my legs, my hips. There was a tingling at the center of my chest that spread, sparking like the firecrackers Nash used to buy Cabell and me at the start of the new year.

"Deliver your heart from darkness, as you have delivered us. We call upon you, Mother, to be reborn." Finished, Caitriona took up the wand, closing her eyes. As she drew the instrument up, the mist followed like a spiderweb caught on its silver tip, glittering with the light of the statue's candle. She held it there, silent and still.

Until her arm started to shake.

Until Olwen closed her eyes, crushed.

I didn't know what was supposed to have happened, but it was painfully obvious that nothing had. The ritual hadn't worked.

Caitriona set the wand down on the altar, looking as if she'd love nothing more than to break it into splinters against the stone.

"I told you," she said derisively. "The Goddess will not lend us her power. Her heart has turned away from Avalon, if she ever possessed one at all."

She walked away from us, moving toward the bags we had gathered for the journey, and stood there, an expectant look on her face that only partly masked how close she was to tears. I started toward her, the blood dripping from my palm onto the altar and floor.

"Wait."

Neve's voice hooked me, drawing me back. She was staring at the chalice, transfixed by what she saw inside.

The dark liquid whirled within the belly of the cup. Threads of mist rose from its center, growing as they wound through the air, twining between us. Caitriona slowly drifted over to the altar, clearly uncertain, even as the liquid rose from the chalice, billowing out with a sudden fury to stain the mist.

"What's happening?" I shouted.

The mist became a hurricane of pressure and wind, spiraling faster until it tugged at our hair and clothes. Instinctively, I reached for Neve's hand. She gripped Olwen's, and Olwen Caitriona's, until, finally, Caitriona reached for my free hand, and we formed a linked circle around the altar.

The ground trembled, rattling the chandeliers and tables. I held on to the others, fighting the pull of the violent air around us. The column of dark mist rose to tower over us, spreading through the great hall, tearing banners from the walls, upending chairs.

There was a voice in the wind outside the tower, desperate to get in. I closed my eyes, trying to focus on it, to make out what it was saying.

A song. The voice was soft, fair and low, like a mother's lullaby. It grew in strength and loveliness, at odds with the maelstrom around us. It was the voice of warm sunlight, the refreshing water of a clear pool, of dew on petals, and the breath of trees. It was outside me, and in me, urging me to sing.

Sing.

The others gave voice to the phantom song—struggling at first with the unfamiliar words, to capture the blood-thrumming perfection of its melody. It was intoxicating, irresistible even if I'd had the strength to fight it. The foreign words, words with no translation, only a feeling that tasted like honey on my tongue.

The wind and mist swelled with our song, and the world trembled with it. My whole life, I had never felt power like this—magic, true and pure magic. It blazed through my body like lightning, electrifying every sense until I became it.

This was what it felt like to be caught in the palm of a god. To call their magic down and unleash it into the world, to be reborn along with it.

The ritual was working. I shouted the song now, desperate for it to rise above the harsh winds and stormy pressure gathering around us. Tears streamed down my face, and I was overcome by the magnitude of everything I felt. The joy, the pain, the release.

I forced my eyes open, trying to capture it all, let it live in my memory until breath left my body. The glimmering ribbons of white shot through the wild haze of expanding darkness. The power lifted us at the heels, until I was balanced on my toes, then off the ground altogether.

Through the squalling air, faces emerged, glowing and iridescent. Their features sharpened the longer I watched, fighting the need to shield my eyes from the whipping of the mist. Lowri. Arianwen. Rhona. Seren. Mari. Betrys.

Flea.

My heart felt like it would explode at the specters. I squeezed Neve's and Caitriona's hands, trying to get them to look, my throat aching.

But the ghostly eyes were fixed on me; their lips were moving but no sound emerged above the song in my ears, and the wind that threatened to carry us away. Singing with us. Joining their power to ours.

No. As quickly as it had come, the elation evaporated. Their faces weren't ones of love—they were ones of terror. All of them were screaming. Shouting the same word.

I forced myself to stop singing, pulling hard on Caitriona and Neve again, but it was too late.

With a roll of ear-piercing thunder, the isle erupted beneath us.

48

The air filled with strange light.

Silvery and elusive, its shafts broke through the cover of dust and mist, falling over me like cool fingers. I stared down at the dirt and blood caked onto my jacket, not understanding. The ringing in my ears was painfully sharp as I tried to sit up, only to find that I couldn't.

My arm was caught beneath a pile of crushed stone. With a grunt of pain, I managed to slip it out, dislodging a large piece. The chunk of white marble rolled down, coming to a stop beside me.

I turned my head to find a pale white face staring back at me. Its serene expression was at odds with the splatters of blood dripping from it. A small candle burned on the ground nearby, its flame struggling until, at last, a gentle breeze blew it out.

As the mist and dust were gathered and pushed away by the wind, I realized where the light was coming from.

The moon.

It was full and lovely overhead, crowned by stars that sparkled like cut jewels in the black velvet of the night sky. I stared at it, my mind as bruised as my body, until I remembered.

The ritual.

I was in the great hall, but no ceiling or tree branches hung above me. Only sky. The Mother tree and the upper levels of the tower were gone, as if they had been ripped clear off by some great and terrible hand.

Horror flooded me, tasting of bile and blood. I ignored the flare of pain in my back and neck as I tried to twist around, searching for Neve, Olwen, and Caitriona.

"Hello?" I rasped out. The chalky air coated my mouth and throat, making it almost impossible to speak. "Is anyone there?"

The world spun as I got onto my hands and knees beside the broken statue of the Goddess.

The walls of the great hall were like a mouth of broken teeth, clattering as chunks of stone crumbled onto the mountains of debris. A section of one of the long tables was still standing, its other half buckled under the massive stone arch that had splintered from the ceiling. I crawled over the stones and debris, gasping for breath, trying to call out for the others.

They'd fallen like petals where they had stood. A slab of the ceiling had crashed down onto the altar, but the stone had caught it and shielded my friends from being crushed by the rubble.

Still disoriented, I crouched down and stumbled forward, reaching Olwen first. I turned her onto her back, pressing an ear to her chest to check for a heartbeat. She groaned, shifting stiffly. Her skin and ink-blue hair were caked in a thick layer of dust and soot.

"Tam . . . sin?" she whispered.

"You're all right," I told her around the lump in my throat. "Don't move. I'm going to check on Neve and Cait, okay?"

Neve was out cold, but Caitriona was already starting to rouse herself. A cloud of dust exploded from her hair when she shook her head. Her eyes blinked rapidly as she tried to focus on me. She brought a shaking hand to her split lip and started to say something, but a different voice reached us first.

". . . said she wouldn't be hurt!"

I swung toward the place it had echoed from, near what had been

451

the entrance of the hall. My heart slammed into my already aching ribs.

It couldn't be.

Another, lower voice answered. "I said she would not die, and she has not."

Their outlines appeared in the mist, faces shadowed. I rose again on shaking legs and struggled through the maze of crushed stone. Splotches of black floated in my vision at the suddenness of the movement, but I drove myself forward, desperate to prove it wasn't a dream. That I wasn't dead.

The haze pulled back, and I cried out. Confusion warred with pure, burning joy at the sight of Cabell standing in front of me.

Alive.

He was wearing unfamiliar clothing, and other than a bandage on his forearm, he looked clean and whole. His dark hair had been tied back neatly at his nape. His eyes widened a fraction at the sight of me.

"How is this possible?" I staggered toward him.

But Cabell stepped back, his expression hardening. I stopped in front of him, and the euphoria I'd felt spoiled into unease.

The second figure came alongside him, surveying me with a dispassionate look. He had shaved his beard and—my lips parted in disbelief—his two flesh-and-bone hands were visible as he crossed his arms over his chest.

But somehow, it was Bedivere.

They were both still alive.

I turned to my brother, feeling like I might be sick. "What's going on?"

He only looked to Bedivere, waiting.

"You . . ." My mind couldn't grasp what was happening. "You were dead. Was it the ritual? Did it bring you back?"

A muscle feathered in Cabell's jaw, his gaze still turned away.

"Look at me!" I rasped out. "I thought you were *dead*. Why would you pretend—why would you fake it? Unless . . ."

My stomach turned so violently I almost doubled over.

"Did you have something to do with the attack?" The words came out scarcely above a whisper, pleading. I knew he had heard me by the way he flinched. "How are you alive? *How?*"

Bedivere looked utterly bored by my horror. The wind tugged at his overcoat, hissing as it blew between us.

"Sir Bedivere—" I began.

"I am not Bedivere," the man interrupted, his voice like the most brutal of winter winds. "He had the honor of the first death at my hand. I took the body of the king, as is only right."

"You're . . . ," I choked out. "You're . . . Arthur?"

His smile was all teeth. "Not quite. I was in need of form, and came to wear his skin well."

The answer echoed in me. Tasted like smoke on the tongue.

I took a step back.

He took a step forward, and I hated myself for falling back again. Ice seemed to radiate from him, turning the air around me to freezing needles. The horned crown, the very same one I'd seen on the statue below the tower, materialized from the mist and shadows to rest on his head—as if it had always been there, secret and unseen.

"Say my name," he said, his voice as smooth and cold as a blade.

Merlin's voice echoed in me. *I am one of three . . . One who dies but might yet live . . . one who lives but yearns to die . . . and one left behind, waiting . . .*

King Arthur. Merlin. And . . .

One left behind, waiting.

Cabell was the one to answer. "Lord Death."

He smiled, all teeth. "And how have I come to be here, when the paths between worlds were sealed?"

The answer wove together in my mind. "The druids."

"No," he said. "Shall we play a game, child? I'll tell you another piece of the tale for every question you answer correctly, and deny you the rest should you make another mistake. Do you wish to try again?"

My heart pounded painfully against my ribs.

"The priestesses," I heard myself say. "Morgan and the others brought you to Avalon."

"That's right," he said, the words reeking with condescension. "In the mortal world, I had given the druids the knowledge of how to call on the magic of Annwn, the greater power of death. I thought the women were finally prepared to renounce their pathetic Goddess to seek the same knowledge. That they wished to serve me."

"They would never," I said fiercely.

Lord Death tilted his head in dark amusement. "No indeed. They offered me a bargain: if I removed the druids' access to Annwn's magic, they would give me the one thing I truly desired. Something no one else could."

So that was how Morgan and the others had been able to kill the druids—not by wielding death magic themselves, but by having Lord Death cut off the druids.

"You turned against your own loyal disciples?" This went beyond the fickle whims of gods. "What could you want that badly?"

"I'm asking the questions, am I not?" Lord Death's eyes bored into me, and there was no spark of life in them. "When it came time to collect on their promise, the treacherous snakes instead tried to destroy me. Tell me, child, what happens when you burn away a god's temporary flesh and splinter their very essence? Do they die?"

"No." Dread roiled in me as I understood. "You've been here all along. You never left the isle."

A deadly seed, waiting to bloom.

"It took centuries to reassemble my scattered soul. *Centuries* of appalling weakness, unable to exist as anything more than a specter watching from the shadows of the forest." Lord Death's words were edged with barely suppressed rage as he touched his crown. "In time, I regained my strength and magic returned to me. I remade the isle to my liking and created my Children to hunt those who had betrayed me. You can imagine my displeasure in discovering the traitors were either dead or had fled into another world."

My pulse rioted in my veins. I looked at Cabell, trying to draw a breath that wouldn't come. His impassioned look was unbearable.

"We *were* brought here for a reason, Tamsin," Cabell said fervently, as if begging me to believe him. "The ritual would only work if it was performed with a sorceress. Sisters joined again in purpose. High Priestess Viviane knew that, but she didn't think the ritual could ever be performed."

Something in me hesitated before asking, "Why not?"

"The Nine were wrong," Cabell said. "They were *all* wrong. There was never a protective spell barring the sorceresses from Avalon."

"What are you talking about?" I asked, trying to reach for him again. "You're not making any sense . . ."

"The sorceresses barred the entrance to Avalon from our world, not the other way around," Cabell said. "They didn't want Lord Death to come for them. He *had* to do this to the isle. He couldn't call the Wild Hunt to Avalon and pass through the worlds that way—there are protections here against it. He'd foreseen that a sorceress would come one day, and he knew the ritual was his only way around the sorceresses' spells. And now he can truly punish them."

"Poor child," Lord Death said to me, clicking his tongue in false sympathy. "For all your cleverness, you do not yet understand. You cannot see how you came to my aid."

"I didn't," I rasped out. "I—"

But I knew. I *knew*.

"Yes," Lord Death said, the very portrait of arrogant disdain. "The athame. The High Priestess suspected me, and what I had planned. She hid the athame in a place I could not enter so no ritual would ever be performed."

The way the athame had become an extension of her, as if, even in death, Viviane knew she needed to keep it close to protect it. That was the will, the desire, that had manifested the revenant.

"I could not cross the barrow's protection spell, nor could I send one of the Nine without arousing suspicion. I was at quite a standstill, until young Cabell had the most excellent notion to send you," Lord Death continued. "I was pleased to repay his favor with one of my own—ensuring that you would survive to see the ritual performed, and be offered the very same chance to join him at my side."

I turned again to my brother, feeling like I was back in the lake. Like I was drowning in icy water. The darkness closed in over me, stealing the last trace of light. "Cabell—look at me. *Look.*"

He wouldn't.

"All of those people died—did you just stand there and let it happen?" I said, voice breaking. "Please . . . I don't know what he's told you, but—"

"He showed me what I am," Cabell said. "After all these years, I know who I am. He can help you discover your own path, Tamsin. All you have to do now is come with us."

I stared at his outstretched hand, sick to my soul. For all those who had died. For the role that he had forced me to play in this. "No."

Cabell's expression darkened with pain as he pulled his hand back. His black eyes pierced me to the bone. "For years, I told myself there was something wrong with me. That I was a problem that had to be fixed. Do you know how it made me feel to have you and Nash treat me that way? You made me feel like I was a monster. Always walking me back from the edge because you both were too afraid to let me truly control my power. It made me feel like I had to be afraid of myself, too."

"That's not true," I protested.

"It was never a curse," he said, his voice ragged. "All along it's been a gift, and one I'm meant to use. My lord helped me see that. He can help you, too. Please. Come with us."

I searched the ancient king's face, his eyes, but there was nothing human left in them. Lord Death had stolen that from Arthur.

"What have you done to him?" I demanded.

Cabell's top lip curled, his expression flashing from pain to anger at the rejection.

"I have done nothing to your brother," Lord Death said, "but reveal him."

A dagger, carried on a scream of fury, flew past my head—not toward Cabell, but toward the man who had claimed to be Bedivere.

Lord Death leaned to the left, allowing it to strike the scarred wall behind him. He clucked his tongue in mock pity, taking in the sight of Caitriona barely restrained by Neve and Olwen.

"How could you?" Caitriona raged. "Why did you let them die? We were going to perform the ritual—so why? *Why?*"

"When young Fayne—Flea, as you called her . . ." He said her name with such disgust that my whole being lit with fury. "When she discovered the fragment of the vessel I'd taken, it risked others discovering what I'd planned before the time of my choosing."

"They didn't have to die!" Caitriona sobbed, her face stricken with rage and pain. "You didn't have to take them!"

"Child, there was no personal insult in what I did," Lord Death said, his paternal tone sending a shiver up the back of my neck. "This isle was only ever a doorway to collect what Lady Morgan and the other sisters promised me. Not everyone can join me in the mortal world, not when they are so valuable to me dead. But I chose you to join me. My favorite of them all, my perfect, steadfast knight with a heart so fierce and loyal."

Cabell flinched at his words, his gaze fixed on the man with need.

"Tell me, Caitriona," Lord Death continued in his velvety voice, "can it beat for me still? Or must I collect your soul as well?"

His hand stroked along the pocket of his overcoat, where a small lump was hidden. A silvery glow radiated from it in response. Olwen let out a low sob, realization setting in. Lord Death now carried the souls of all of their loved ones with him.

Caitriona threw herself forward with another scream that was choked off as the man held up a hand. Neve sent me a terrified look, uncertain of what to do. I gave a sharp shake of the head. We didn't know what he was capable of.

"A shame," Lord Death said. "There was a place for you as my steward, and I am loath to see my work on you come to naught."

"I will kill you," Caitriona vowed.

"I am certain that you will try," he said with a mocking bow of the head.

A familiar sound, like the scurrying of rats, filled the air. Children, alive again, scaled the wall behind him. They perched there, watching us. Waiting.

"Farewell, maidens of Avalon," Lord Death sneered, his long overcoat billowing out behind him. "You have made your choice, and I have waited an age for my revenge on the ones who caged me."

As he turned, so did my brother, following like the loyal hound he'd become. My heart shredded against my ribs. This had to be a spell. I could save him from this, too.

"Please," I begged. "Don't do this. Don't let him turn you away from us. From me."

All those years ago, our guardian, a storyteller, had walked into a storm and vanished, becoming a story himself. We were what remained. The two of us, alone in the world except for each other.

The tether of our shared past strained as Cabell looked over his shoulder at me, pulling tighter and tighter with each heartbeat. Everything we had seen and done and lived together stretched between us, and all he had to do was hold on. All he had to do was take a step toward me and I would fight with everything I had in me to get him away from the monster at his side.

Don't.

Don't.

Don't.

"Cabell," I said. "I love you. Please."

This time, he didn't turn back. The wind carried his words to me. "Don't die."

And the tether snapped.

I didn't see him walk away. My legs seemed to disappear beneath me, and I dropped into a crouch, shaking. Neve's hands gripped my shoulders as Caitriona charged past us, trying to reach them before they vanished into the ageless dark of night.

The Children leapt down, barring the way with clicking fangs and rotting faces. Struggling with her wounded shoulder, Caitriona brandished a bent sword and split one of their skulls with a ferocious scream. The others fled after their master, scaling the ruined walls of the tower.

It was a moment more before I realized that their screeching had given way to a very different sort of wailing. One that had no place in Avalon.

Emergency sirens.

I ran forward, climbing onto a broken section of the courtyard's wall. My nails had torn, and my hands and knees were skinned raw, but I felt none of it. I was only vaguely aware of the others climbing behind me.

Together, we gazed out along the curve of a steep hill covered by dead trees and mist. Children rose from the forest floors and gathered, reborn, into a pack behind Arthur—Lord Death—and Cabell as they made their way toward the distant town drowning in black mire. A river of water gushed from the earth beneath us, turning crimson as it mixed with dirt and blood.

"Blessed Mother," Olwen whispered.

As if in response, the clouds parted, spilling moonlight onto the world below. The ruined groves, the watchtowers, and the homes that had once housed the people of Avalon punctured the land like cleats on grass. The Avalonian structures had crushed or partly buried the modern streets and buildings that had stood in their way.

With the wreckage, it took more than a moment to recognize where we were. I'd been here before countless times with Nash and . . . and with Cabell.

We were standing on Glastonbury Tor, long rumored to have been the location of Avalon in our world before it splintered off into its own. The hill and its lonely tower had stood over the land like a benevolent sentry for centuries, keeping watch of the surrounding meadows and nearby town of Glastonbury.

Now it served as the perfect vantage point to bear witness to the complete and utter devastation below.

The glow of fire emanated from what remained of the town, smoke pouring up to cover the stars. Ambulances and police cars, their blue lights flashing, gathered along a road to the north. With the flooding, it was as close to the town as they could get. The whirring of helicopter blades seemed to approach from every direction at once.

"We have to leave," I told the others. "Neve, can you open a Vein? It doesn't matter where. We need to get our things and leave—right now."

"What's happened?" Caitriona asked. "What is this place?"

Neve looked like she might be sick from shock as she hugged her wand to her chest. A cut on her cheekbone wept blood, and it mingled now with her tears.

"The ritual didn't restore the isle by purifying it," I said, the words aching down to my soul. "It restored Avalon to the human world."

49

I brought them to the only place I could. Home.

I hadn't actually thought about how it would feel to return to the apartment. I hadn't even thought about how much time had passed since I'd last been there, until I saw the Christmas decorations that merrily adorned our quiet street and felt the cold promise of coming snow.

We'd only had a moment to retrieve our things—including Griflet, who had napped through the collision of worlds—before searchlights had swept over the tower's smoldering courtyard. No time for thinking at all.

Now there was too much time.

Olwen and Caitriona had taken in their first glimpses of our world with outright horror. The cars, the architecture, the people milling around and gawking at the dire state of us—all of it was too much, too loud, too bright after the harsh gray world of Avalon, even for me.

"Are you sure about this?" Neve whispered as I jimmied the lock on our small kitchen window. The herbs in the planter gave me a wilted hello—one far warmer than the shocked look of one of our neighbors as she spied on us from the nearby sidewalk. Bloodstained and filthy, I waved and gave her my best sheepish smile.

"Lost my key!" I called to her as the window lock finally released.

I pulled myself up and squeezed through the tight opening, wriggling over the counter and the kitchen sink. Once inside, I froze, the familiar scent of lemon and dried herbs bringing a fresh sting of tears. The kitchen appliances and furniture looked strange to my eyes—too sharp, too perfect. A light layer of dust coated the dining table and countertops, but the space was otherwise clean and tidy. There was no dark mud to scrub from stones, no linens to wash. There were no stories to overhear, or secrets hidden in its shadows. No monsters, either.

I stared and stared, trying to accept the unnaturally bright colors of the books on the bookshelf, the zigzagging pattern of our rug. Though it was full of things I'd picked out myself, the space seemed almost . . . achingly hollow.

It had never been a home. It had only ever been a dream of one.

Stepping down off the counter, I knocked a few stray pieces of mail and the potted plants onto the linoleum floor, but didn't bother picking any of it up. Instead, I looked across the length of what had been our home. The place we'd carved for ourselves in a world that had done its best to be rid of us.

A sharp ache cut through my chest. That wasn't right, not really. This was the place *I* had wanted for us—in the city I'd kept us in for my own selfish reasons. I'd convinced Cabell we needed to stay in Boston, just like I'd convinced him we had to find a way to break his curse, rather than help him learn to live with it.

It made me feel like I had to be afraid of myself, too.

I unlocked the front door and barely registered the others entering and taking a tentative look around. Caitriona and Olwen sat at the small kitchen table's two chairs—two, because that was all we had ever needed. Both stared blankly into the air, as if waiting for instructions. I poured everyone water, but no one drank it.

Neve sat on the couch, shifting so I could sit beside her. We leaned our heads against each other as we watched Griflet explore the space.

A neighbor's TV came through the thin wall that connected our houses "—*reports are only just emerging out of Glastonbury, where, overnight, officials claim a massive seismic event has unearthed previously unknown ruins of an earlier settlement and forest. We're getting a live shot now*—"

"God's teeth," I choked out. "Are they going to be able to see everything in the tower? The books? The springs?"

"Anything still possessing magic will be hidden to those without the One Vision," Olwen said. "Anything made by hand will not."

She clutched the basket containing Viviane's vessel on her lap, her legs jumping with unspent adrenaline. The vessel inside had shattered with the blast of magic from the ritual, but she'd brought it anyway.

"I'm so sorry," Neve said, agonized. Something broke open in her then, and her words spilled out with her tears. "If I hadn't pushed you to perform the ritual, this—this never would have happened. I'm so sorry. So, so sorry—"

"No," I said. "None of this is your fault. I'm the one who went to get the athame."

"I'm the one who fought for the ritual," Olwen said, her face crumpling. "I never questioned Bedivere's identity, nor noticed he still possessed the hand he claimed to have lost—what sort of healer am I?"

"Why would we have questioned it?" Caitriona asked. "Only the High Priestess had ever laid eyes on the living Arthur and true Bedivere, and Lord Death ensured she was dead before coming to the tower."

She stood and began to pace, catching each of our eyes in turn. "Listen to me. We will not play this game. We will not bear the burden of blame for what that monster has done. We will only make right what he has wronged."

My brows drew together. "What do you mean?"

"We have unleashed Lord Death unto this world, along with the Children," she said. "Whatever he has planned for the sorceresses, for all of this realm, we will stop it. And we will bring Cabell back."

I closed my eyes, releasing a shaky breath. "I don't know if we can."

The brother I knew wouldn't have stood by and let the last survivors of Avalon be slaughtered.

"He could be under Lord Death's sway," Neve said, wiping her eyes against her torn sleeve. "The way the Children are."

I wanted to believe that, but . . . that look on his face. *You made me feel like I was a monster.*

"The body at King Arthur's tomb," Neve said quietly. "It must have been the real Bedivere."

"I think you're right," I said. "And the full story is probably etched into the missing piece of that vessel—the one Flea found."

Caitriona raked a hand through her tangled mass of hair. "But we have no way of echoing—not with the vessel in pieces."

The Bonecutter did love a challenge, though I wasn't sure what they would make of this one. "We'll start with finding the person I think can mend it, and then we'll warn the Council of Sistren."

"Oh, I'm sure they already know," Neve said. "The eruption of magic was telling enough, but even sorceresses get cable news."

"Are we all in agreement?" I asked, a strange, trembling feeling in my chest at that word. *We.* At the thought of us facing this together.

"And until then?" Caitriona asked, returning to her seat at the table. Olwen leaned forward, resting her head on her crossed arms.

"We rest," I said.

In the exhausted silence that followed, the news anchor's voice bled through the wall again. *"We go now to Downing Street for a live statement about the events at Glastonbury this morning—"*

Neve reached down into her fanny pack and pulled out the old, battered CD player inside. Flipping one of the earphones toward me, she pressed the other to her ear and turned the dreamy music's volume up and up and up, until the anchor's voice faded and there were only the delicate, cosmic waves of sound, the pearly dewdrops the woman sang about.

And, for a moment, even memory released me, and receded.

After charging my cell phone, I searched my bedroom for cash, then made my way to the alcove that housed our desks.

I slowed as I approached them, my eyes widening as I took in the acrylic drawers Cabell used to organize his crystals. With the One Vision, I saw what I hadn't before—several pulsed with absorbed magic, like flame trapped within stone.

I didn't want to look any more after that. Not at the crystals. Not at the crusted stain remover on the rug covering my dried blood—the last evidence of the fight with my brother I'd barely survived.

Digging around in my own disaster of a desk drawer, I found enough singles to order us a pizza. As I waited for my cell phone to turn on, I listened to Caitriona cursing and sputtering at the shower faucet on the other side of the wall.

Neve and Olwen had already scrubbed themselves clean and changed into some of my and Cabell's clothes. While they chatted quietly on the couch, I returned to the kitchen to clean up the mess I'd left.

I retrieved the broom and dustpan, sweeping up pot shards, soil, the shriveled remains of Florence, and what looked like a trail of dead ants. Nearly three months of mail had piled up by the door, but the stack from my last night here had also fallen as I'd come in, along with my purse and my tarot deck.

Griflet batted at my boots' laces as I gathered everything into my arms. I started to rise, only to spot a card I'd missed. It was partly hidden beneath the refrigerator. My breath caught as I turned it over.

The Moon card.

That feeling was back, churning in my stomach, turning my head light as air. I brushed a thumb over the image—the moon, the towers, the blue hills. The wolf, and the hound.

As I touched the card, a different image swept through my mind, thrumming with darkness. A different moon, a mere sliver of a thing, was swallowed by the growing black of a starless night. Beneath it, a pack of black dogs tore through a field of mist, howling to the shadowed figure that waited ahead.

Say my name.

The answer was the whisper of an unfamiliar woman's voice, a song that faded to silence.

Lord Death.

"Tamsin?"

I startled at the sound of my name, breaking the horrified reverie.

"Tamsin?" Neve said again, leaning around the doorframe. "I think someone's at the door . . . ?"

Another knock sounded.

"Oh—it must be the food," I said, shaking myself out of my daze. "That was fast."

I rose, brushing my hands against my already filthy jeans, wondering if Neve could hear the way my heart was still pounding as I passed her.

Sliding the cash out of my pocket, I unlocked the door. "Sorry about that—"

The bills slipped from my hand, fluttering to the floor.

The man standing there was dressed in a rumpled suit. He fiddled anxiously with the brim of the hat in his hands, but I couldn't tear my gaze away from his face.

"What . . . ," I whispered, unable to catch my breath. "What are you . . ."

He looked younger than I remembered. The lines on his forehead had smoothed out, and his many scars were gone. His skin had a healthy glow, rather than the red of too much sun or the pallor of someone who had locked himself away in a dark room with a bottle of rum. And his eyes—a silvery blue, sparkled with humor and emotion.

Neve and Olwen hovered protectively behind me as they eyed the stranger.

Not a stranger—Nash. Alive.

Nash.

"Tamsy," he said, his voice gruff with emotion. "My gods, you've grown."

If my shock had been any less palpable, if I'd been able to move even an inch, I would have slammed the door in his face.

"What are you doing here?" I asked faintly. "You're dead."

"Yes, about that—may I come inside?" he asked, casting a wary glance up and down the street. "I need to speak to you. It's important."

"The time to talk to me was seven years ago," I bit out. "Before you abandoned us."

His eyes shut as he drew in a breath. "I was trying to find the Ring of Dispel."

"I know," I cut in, my hand squeezing the door. "To break Cabell's curse."

When they opened again, the glitter in his pale eyes was gone. They were graver than I'd ever seen them.

"No, Tamsin," he said. "To break yours."

Acknowledgments

After this story took its time simmering on the back burner of my brain for years, letting me slowly season it with strange family history, dark folklore, and uncanny little ideas that sprouted up like mushrooms, I'm so grateful to have this book finally down on paper and out in the world.

First and foremost, I'd like to thank the readers who have come along on this publishing journey with me over the years, gamely venturing into one new world after the next. If this is the first book of mine you've read, hello! I can't begin to tell you how much I appreciate you, and that, when confronted with the choice of *so many* remarkable books out there, you selected this one to read next.

It only feels right to start by thanking Melanie Nolan, who took a chance on me and this story, and welcomed me back into the fold of Random House Children's Books. This has been such an incredible homecoming for me, and I truly can't believe my good fortune to be on the Knopf Books for Young Readers list.

Katherine Harrison, your editorial guidance has utterly transformed this book. Your feedback amazed me with its depth and thoughtfulness, and I knew from the start that my characters and I were in the best hands imaginable. I'm also indebted to Gianna Lakenauth for her truly priceless support through the publication pipeline, as well as the time and energy she spent reading various drafts and offering important—and dead-on!—insight. A huge thanks to my UK editors, Rachel Boden and Harriet Wilson, who gave fabulous notes and helped usher this book into the world.

There are so many incredible people at RHCB to thank. I hope you'll take a moment to turn to the full credits page to help me recognize everyone for all the passion and dedication they poured into *Silver in the Bone*! This credits page was inspired by one created by Kristin Cashore, and I'm excited to add them to my books moving forward. I'd also like to thank Barbara Marcus, Judith Haut, John Adamo, Dominique Cimina, Adrienne Waintraub, Elizabeth Ward, Kelly McGauley, Becky Green, Joe English, and Emily Bruce for their enthusiasm and incomparable leadership. You are truly an author's dream team!

Likewise, I'd like to thank Jasmine Walls for her willingness to delve deep into this world and the characters and offer authenticity notes.

I'm so lucky to have friends in my life like Anna Jarzab, Valia Lind, Susan Dennard, and Isabel Ibañez, who were kind enough to not only read this story at various stages of its life but also pick me up and dust me off when I was feeling low and unsure about it. Marissa Grossman, your feedback helped me bring this story back to what it needed to be before I went down the wrong road. Merci! Huge, huge thanks to Leigh Bardugo, Jennifer Lynn Barnes, J. Elle, Stephanie Garber, and Elizabeth Lim for reading and offering such kind words about the book. Queens, the lot of you!

I absolutely need to thank my wonderful agent, Merrilee Heifetz, for being such an unwavering support to me throughout the years and always being the much-needed voice of reason. Rebecca Eskildsen, I just genuinely do not know how you do it—thank you for always being so on top of things, and helping me, a child of chaos, keep my head on straight. Alessandra Birch, thank you for going above and beyond for me, even when some of that planning ultimately got derailed by my rogue eyeball. Cecilia de la Campa, it can't be said enough that you are a superstar.

Thank you to my incomparable film agent, Dana Spector at CAA, for working so hard to find the best Hollywood homes for my books. You are an utter joy to work with!

Last but never least, I'd like to thank my family and friends for all of the love and support you continue to send my way, especially as I was going through the real ups and downs of multiple eye surgeries and each subsequent recovery. The brightest moment of the year was the birth of my adorable nephew, aka the other LD, Little Dan. Welcome to the world! We all love you more than words can say.

I jokingly said I should dedicate the sequel to my right eyeball, which never failed me throughout 2022, but . . . it's really not a joke. Thank you as well, right eyeball, for allowing me to keep working on this book and its sequel, which kept me sane. *This* book, however, is dedicated to my sister, Stephanie, who is truly hilarious, fearless, and so giving. It was a joy to write a book so centered on sisterhood and be able to reflect on the way our relationship has grown over the years. Thank you for always going out of your way to look out for me. Here's to many more sister adventures in our future!

Dramatis Personae

SILVER IN THE BONE

HOLLOWERS

Emrys Dye—The latest scion of the Dye dynasty, whose ancestors founded the North American guild. Unimaginably wealthy, annoyingly charming, and a Cunningfolk Greenworker, he is Tamsin's main rival within the guild and enjoys provoking and flirting with her.

Endymion Dye—Emrys's cold and imperious father, who rules his family and the guild with an iron fist.

Cabell Lark—Tamsin's brother, who is suffering a curse that turns him into a monstrous hound. He is an Expeller, an extremely rare type of Cunningfolk with the ability to break or deflect most enchantments using only his mind.

Nashbury Lark—Tamsin and Cabell's guardian. A notorious figure among Hollowers and sorceresses alike, known for his roguish ways and elaborate storytelling. He disappeared from Tintagel seven years ago and is believed dead.

Tamsin Lark—Thrust into the world of Hollowers as a child, she possesses no innate magical ability, but does have a photographic memory and a keen business sense. Wants nothing to do with most of the guild after they turned their backs on her and Cabell as children.

Hector Leer—A crony of Septimus and Endymion.

Phineas Primm—An old, scarred Hollower who is tasked with watching Tamsin by Septimus Yarrow.

Woodrow—A Hollower found encased in ice in the Sorceress Edda's vault.

Septimus Yarrow—An infamous Hollower best known for recovering Herakles's club; in league with Endymion Dye for reasons unknown.

SORCERESSES

Ardith—An unremarkable sorceress who was slowly poisoned by her sister, who desired her venom collection. Her Immortality resides in the guild library.

Callwen—An early sorceress who created one of the oldest Immortalities, recovered by Endymion Dye.

Edda—A crone sorceress whose icy vault the Larks open to retrieve Arthur's dagger.

Grinda—A crone sorceress who hires Tamsin and Cabell to retrieve a locket.

Hesperia—A sorceress who received the rank of mother, who had many dark adventures and took yet more lovers. Her Immortality is popular with members of the guild.

Madrigal—A mysterious crone sorceress known for her deadly dinner parties. Hires Emrys and Tamsin to find the Ring of Dispel.

Morgan—Leader of the priestesses who rose against the Druids and were later exiled for it. Half sister to King Arthur, as well as Viviane's lover.

Myfanwy—A little-known sorceress of the maiden rank, whose Immortality unlocks the mystery of why the Larks were at Tintagel.

Neve Goode—A cheerful, caring self-taught sorceress who seeks the Ring of Dispel and joins forces with Tamsin and the others.

THE NINE OF AVALON

Arianwen—A member of the watch, responsible for setting up the necessary elements for rituals. Despises laundry duty.

Betrys—A quiet, no-nonsense figure among her sisters, she's level-headed and a skilled fighter, but is quick to ensure her sisters are taking care of themselves.

Caitriona—Chosen to be the new High Priestess by her sisters, Caitriona is the de facto leader of Avalon, both spiritually and in its defense.

Flea (Fayne)—The youngest of the Nine, who has yet to come into her magic. She has sly fingers and a bad attitude.

Lowri—A skilled smith of both weapons and smaller items like jewelry, she is now the eldest of the Nine and mostly keeps to herself in the forge. She, too, serves on the watch.

Mari—A shy elfin who is caretaker of the tower and is highly knowledgeable about the legends and history of Avalon.

Olwen—The half-naiad healer of Avalon, who believes there's a larger role for Tamsin and the others to play in the salvation of Avalon.

Rhona—Serves on the watch and frequently leads the ritual songs; she has taken it upon herself to cheer the others up by creating stories and rhymes.

Seren—Frequently inseparable from Rhona, she serves on the watch and is a skilled archer.

Viviane—High Priestess and the last living priestess of the Arthurian age, who lived for centuries as she waited for the new Nine to be chosen. A motherly figure and tutor for the priestesses, she was killed in the early days of darkness in Avalon.

AVALONIANS

Aled—Uncle to Mari and keeper of the stables. One of the few surviving elfins of Avalon.

Angharad—A tough-as-nails gnome who works in the forge with Lowri.

Bedivere—The last living Knight of the Round Table, he returned Excalibur to the Lady of the Lake and now protects Arthur's body.

Deri—The last hamadryad who is bonded to the Mother tree and tends to it.

Dilwyn—Aunt to Mari. An elfin who runs the kitchen and cooks for the survivors.

King Arthur—The once and perhaps future king of Great Britain. His body lies in Avalon, protected and sustained by magic until the day he is needed again. Per Flea, he has grown somewhat pruny.

Merlin—Once a Druid and mentor to a young King Arthur, he attached himself to the Mother tree to survive a duel with Morgan and now babbles nonsensical prophecy to the few who will listen.

OTHERS

The Bonecutter—A enigmatic figure who acts as a procurer of skeleton keys to open Veins, as well as other oddities, such as basilisk venom.

Dearie—The sorceress Madrigal's pooka companion, who acts as both her butler and enforcer.

Franklin—Tamsin's lovesick tarot customer, who would really benefit from actual therapy.

Griflet—A kitten given to Mari.

The Hag of the Mist (Or Gwrach-y-Rhibyn)—A primordial deity who occupies liminal spaces and has the ability to pass between the boundaries of worlds unimpeded.

Ignatius—The hand of glory Tamsin carries to tap into the One Vision, also capable of opening any locked door.

Librarian—An automaton that used to guard the vault of the sorceress the guild library now occupies. Now tends to the library and protects its many treasures. Has a passion for soft, fluffy things and vacuuming.

Linden Goode—Neve's adoptive aunt, who is a Cunningfolk Finder. She hides Neve's true ancestry from her for her beloved niece's protection.

Pumpkin—A rascal of a library cat, but otherwise a very clever, sweet boy.

KNOWN VARIETIES OF CUNNINGFOLK

Brewer—creates tonics with potent abilities

Coaxer—able to soothe and control animals

Expeller—breaks curses and other enchantments

Finder—able to locate things with accuracy

Grayspeaker—able to commune with the dead

Greenworker—able to commune with and influence the growth of plants

Healer—specializes in healing arts

Mindwalker—able to inhabit creatures or other people and see through their eyes without them knowing

Seer—experiences visions of the future

Greenwich, Connecticut

In all the time he'd been a member of the Hollower guild, Cabell had never been invited to the Dyes' Summerland Estate.

Curiosity may have once been enough to tempt him, especially if it came with some assurance of a big job—an expedition he'd never be able to fund himself for a relic he might otherwise never set eyes on. But on the whole, it had been easy to live without knowing what the inside of the palatial home looked like. He hadn't even tormented himself with wondering what treasures or resources the Dyes were jealously guarding from the rest of the guild behind tony walls.

Nothing good came of coveting things that were never going to be yours. It only made you feel bad, knowing what you lacked. Better to focus on what was meant for you, and to hell with the rest of it.

The gravel driveway crunched under his feet as he strode forward, matching the powerful strides of the dark figure a step ahead of him. They'd arrived in an icy whirlwind of shadowy magic that had bit at his senses. It wasn't necessary to travel by Veins—he couldn't believe he'd ever been excited to find and open them. His lord could transport them between locations with a fleeting crush of death magic.

Cabell had never been a stranger to magic, but this—Lord Death's magic held the vastness of a night sky. It was no misty, sweet song. It thundered, triumphant and unrelenting. It was inescapable, like death itself.

The elaborate iron gate at the base of the driveway had been left open, anticipating their arrival. Cabell shook his head. That was the way of it with the Dyes. They assumed everything would always go to plan, that others would come when they called, that nothing was beyond their reach, not even a god.

Their house reflected that confidence with its grim-faced determination to take up as much space as possible. He wasn't sure he'd ever seen such a grand structure, accented by turrets and sweeping stone arches, outside of actual castles.

The sharpness of the air promised snow. A chill rolled down his back, not from cold but the green scent of the holly adorning the impressive marble steps.

Black candles shuddered in their sconces on either side of the iron door, then went out, extinguished by some unseen wind.

Summerland Estate. A mirthless chuckle escaped him. It would be as good of a new home as any.

Cabell stood taller than his lord, and taller still, knowing that of everyone, of all the apprentices he had trained, it was Cabell who had been chosen. By his lord. By Fate itself.

In the past, Cabell had always been treated as an inferior. Barely tolerated, a source of amusement, maybe, but little better than dirt tracked in on Endymion Dye's boots. Now he knew his worth, and there was no greater power than that.

His lord had supplied him with a heavy coat of the deepest black, the sort that absorbed all light. The silken quality of his new clothes and the soft leather of his boots were unlike anything he had ever worn, and far too fine to be the product of mortal hands.

The door opened. Endymion Dye's pale face hovered in that slit of darkness. Lord Death moved into the light of the lanterns on either side of the door, lowering his hood. His face—the face of the man who had once been Arthur Pendragon—was cold as he took stock of the mortal man.

Cabell smirked at Endymion's groveling look of veneration and pride to find the King of Annwn standing on his threshold. Satisfaction curled in his chest when Endymion's eyes shifted over to him.

A flicker of shock passed over Endymion's sharp features as he recognized Cabell—a no one, a nothing in the hierarchy of his world—standing beside the god.

"You have summoned me here through ritual and smoke," Lord Death's baritone voice began. "And yet you do not invite me in. Tell me, Endymion Dye, are you so ungracious to all your guests?"

Endymion bowed, opening the door wider and backing into the shadows of the house with a nervous flourish.

Cabell almost laughed. How snakes turned to worms when a bigger predator arrived. Lord Death glanced over, arching a brow.

"I've never seen him so . . . agreeable," Cabell said. "Allow me, my Lord."

He stepped through the door first, knocking his shoulder into Endymion to push past him. In life, you were either the person who charged forward or the one who stepped aside. Cabell refused to step aside ever again.

Once inside, he surveyed the grand foyer, letting his gaze skim over the handsome oak staircase curving up either side in perfect symmetry. A dazzling chandelier sent candlelight sparkling down upon the marble floor.

He drew in a deep breath. The hair on his arm rose and stung, as if threatening a shift into his other form. There was something off about this place. Cold, yes, but that he'd expected. A kind of . . . stillness, then. The smell of must and something else lingered—rot.

He tilted his head toward another door to the left of him, this one looking like it had been ripped off an ancient fortress. The wood was inlaid with swirling patterns and symbols made from iron. Strange. He didn't recognize them, but he did recognize the scent that escaped from the room behind them.

Blood. Old blood.

Cabell turned sharply on his heel. He nodded to Lord Death, feeling that prickling of pride again that he had been entrusted with such a powerful god's safety.

Lord Death entered Summerland Estate as if he had done it thousands of times before. He stopped beside Cabell, assessing its fine offerings for himself.

"I hope it is to your liking, my Lord," Endymion said, with yet another bow.

Lord Death cast a cold eye on him. "It will suffice. For now."

"The others are eager to meet you," Endymion said. "I cannot tell you how long we have awaited your return. To bring you forth into this world."

To his credit, he knew not to show his back to Lord Death. That, as Cabell had witnessed, was an insult the god wouldn't tolerate.

Instead, Endymion Dye—the great, proud Endymion Dye—walked backward, his eyes lowered like the servant he was. Cabell was unsurprised to discover their destination was that imposing door with its strange symbols. He studied them again as they drew closer. Some looked vaguely like the sigils the sorceresses used for protective wards, but he couldn't be sure. Of the two of them, Tamsin—

A phantom hand seemed to close over his throat. Cabell rested a hand on the sword hanging from his side, gripping the hilt until his fingers ached with it. At the edge of his vision, pale blond hair flashed. He spun, searching for the source of it, but found only shadows.

The massive door swung open with a sound like a dying beast. Cabell felt his feet slowing as he entered, almost against his will. Sheets of silk had been draped to block off the rest of the room, dividing the ordinary from the sacred. Before them, a dozen men, some he recognized from the Hollower guild, stood in the shape of a crescent, wearing wreaths and crowns of holly. The table, or what might have been a desk, had been transformed into an altar. Beneath the stench of incense, greens, and nervous sweat was the faintest hint of old books.

Cabell's gaze drifted down. At his feet, a dark stain was just visible on the carpet. The muscles of his stomach tightened, and for the first time, he wondered what ritual had been powerful enough for Lord Death to feel the summons.

"Lord Death," Endymion began, taking his place in the assembly of men. All of them wore simple robes, and a silver pin that Cabell recognized from his old life. A hand holding a silver branch. "We welcome you once more to the mortal world, and offer you our service, to whatever end."

"You offer more than what I ask," Lord Death said, enjoying the way some of the men quailed under his scrutiny. Cabell took more than a little pleasure walking in slow, searching loops around them. It felt good, so good, to give into that need. It was in his blood to herd.

"My Lord?" Endymion prompted.

"No one summons death, unless they seek its power," the god continued. "Tell me, then, what you desire of me in exchange for your service. Will you be like the ancients, who merely wanted to smite their enemies? Will you walk in the steps of the Druids, grasping at knowledge and power forbidden to mortal man?"

Endymion seemed to regain some of his composure, though he still didn't dare look into Lord Death's pale eyes. "We seek to hunt those you hunt yourself. To serve as your sworn blades, your disciples in magic, and end the tyranny of those who hold power they do not deserve."

Of course, a voice whispered in Cabell's mind. *This has always been their objective.*

It was only a wonder he hadn't guessed it before. Some men hunted relics for the glory. These men, to steal power from the sorceresses.

Cabell sat at the edge of their pathetic altar, arms crossed over his chest, his pulse quickening. His breath came in light pants. He watched the god eagerly. No one would ever replace him. Lord Death had sworn it.

He would have a different role for these fools to play.

Lord Death paced in front of them, a king inspecting his soldiers. When he came to Endymion again, he stopped. A small smile slanted over his face as the man struggled to hold his head high. His bowels had probably turned to water by now.

"You wish to serve in my retinue?" Lord Death asked. "To join the Wild Hunt?"

"Yes," Endymion said, scarcely above a whisper. "More than anything, my Lord. Grant us your power, and we will not fail you."

Lord Death placed a gloved hand on the man's shoulder, leaning in closer, as if to embrace him. "I accept."

Endymion let out a shuddering breath, his eyes closing behind his thin-framed glasses.

"But, my dear child," Lord Death continued, his voice low and tender, like a true father. The room's shadows gathered to the fist at his side, wrapping it in writhing ribbons unseen to the others. "Do you not know my retinue is not comprised of the living?"

Endymion's eyes flashed wide, his breath choking off as Lord Death plunged his fist straight into his chest. Passing through skin and muscle and bone to reach the soul—and tear it out at the root.

Cabell closed his eyes and breathed in deeply, releasing the weakness that had held him captive for so long, welcoming in the darkness, and the terror, and the screams.

Credits

ALFRED A. KNOPF BOOKS FOR YOUNG READERS

Art and Design

Ray Shapell
Jen Valero
April Ward

Contracts

Amy Myer

Copyeditors and Proofreaders

Artie Bennett
Judy Kiviat
Alison Kolani
Barbara Perris
Amy Schroeder

Editor

Katherine Harrison

Editorial Support

Gianna Lakenauth

Managing Editor

Jake Eldred

Marketing

John Adamo
Michael Caiati
Natali Cavanagh
David Gilmore
Katie Halata
Jenn Inzetta
Kelly McGauley
Shannon Pender
Erica Stone
Stephania Villar
Meredith Wagner
Adrienne Waintraub
Elizabeth Ward

Production Manager

Tim Terhune

Publicity

Lili Feinberg
Noreen Herits
Josh Redlich

Publisher

Melanie Nolan

Sales

Raven Andrus
Suzanne Archer
Amanda Auch
Jill Bailey
Andrea Baird
Stacy Berenbaum
Maggie Brennan
Emily Bruce
Enid Chaban
Amanda Close
Vicki Congdon
Brenda Conway
Dandy Conway
Colleen Conway Ramos
Nichole Cousins
Sara Danver
Stephanie Davey
Nicole Davies
John Dennany
Stephanie Devita
Madalyn Dolan
Tyler Duke
Cletus Durkin
Joe English
Thomas Gengozian
Becky Green

Susan Hecht
Riley Hubby
Christina Jeffries
Todd Jones
Steve Kent
Kimberly Langus
Katie Lenox
Lauren Mackey
Cindy Mapp
Deanna Meyerhoff
Carol Monteiro
Mary Raymond
Amy Rockwell
Samantha Rodan
Devin Rutland
Michele Sadler
Judy Samuels
Mark Santella
Linda Sinisi
Kate Sullivan
Rachel Weisenthal
Nicole White

Subsidiary Rights

Keifer Ludwig
Kim Wrubel

Listening Library

Emily Parliman
Rebecca Waugh

WRITERS HOUSE

Alessandra Birch
Cecilia de la Campa

Rebecca Eskildsen
Merrilee Heifetz

About the Author

Alexandra Bracken is the #1 *New York Times* bestselling author of *Lore* and the Darkest Minds series. Born and raised in Arizona, she moved east to study history and English at the College of William & Mary in Virginia. After working in publishing for several years, she now writes full-time. Her work is available across the world in over twenty languages and has been adapted for the big screen.